I0763523

Awkward is just the beginning...

Books 1,2, &3

Girls

USA TODAY BESTSELLING AUTHOR

JB HELLER

AWKWARD GIRLS COMPLETE SERIES

Published by- Author JB Heller

Cover Design by- JeBDesigns

Editing by- Creating Ink

Proofreading by- Jenn Lockwood Editing

Formatted by – JeBDesigns

AUTHORS NOTE

Please note this series is based in Australia, written by an Australian author, in Australian English. As such you may think there are a few spelling errors, however that's just how we spell things Down Under.

Thank you and enjoy,

xo

JB

AWKWARD IS JUST THE BEGINNING...

JB HELLER

Chapter 1

Reagan

Did you know that swans are the only birds with an external penis? It's totally true—and fascinating, if you ask me. I mean, can you imagine a little hummingbird flying around with a penis? Disturbing, right? But a swan—I can get behind that.

This is the latest fact I've submitted into the Pink Bits database. I love my job so much. Spending my days searching out weird, wonderful, and completely random facts is a dream come true. It helps that Pink Bits Hygienics is my dad's company, and he created the position especially for me. Hell, he created the company *because* of me, and his sisters.

"Reagan, are you coming to dinner with your mother and me this evening?"

Shifting my gaze from the computer screen, I eye Dad's lean build propped against the doorway to my office. "My stepmother, you mean?"

He rolls his eyes. "Well, yes. Unless your biological mother has changed her mind about removing my testicles with her bare hands. Then she'd be welcome to join us as well."

I cringe at the imagery manifesting in my brain. "Thanks for the visual." I mime sticking my finger down my throat, and my dad chuckles. "Anyway, no, I will not be joining you and The Wicked Witch of the West for dinner tonight. I have plans."

"Plans?" he asks, completely ignoring the jab at my stepmother. He strides into my office and drops into the pink loveseat I have situated by the large floor-to-ceiling window, then props his feet up. "What kind of plans? Plans with a—dare I say it—man?" He waggles his eyebrows suggestively as he speaks, making it impossible for me to keep a straight face.

A snort escapes as I try to hold back my laughter. "No, sorry to disappoint, Daddy. I'm going to the movies with Charlotte."

His shoulders drop. "I want grandchildren, Reagan, and you're not being very proactive about it." He huffs, planting his feet on the floor and pushing off. Straightening his suit jacket then tie, he says, "Just go on one date a month. I'm not asking much. Even without grandbabies, I want to see you with someone. You're twenty-seven, and I've never met one of your boyfriends. It's time, honey."

"Pfft, don't hold your breath. Have you met the douchebags in the dating pool these days? Trust me,

Daddy, you'd rather I die an old cat lady than bring one of them home."

When he reaches the door, he pauses and looks back over his shoulder, his fingers flexing around the frame. "If anyone can find the needle in the haystack, it'll be you. But you've gotta be out there looking for it, baby."

Once he's gone, I drop my head into my hands. He's right. But I'm just too awkward for the dating scene. I'm fascinated by the fact that swans have penises, peni, peens, whatever. The point is, it's hardly a topic I can bring up on a dinner date. Any potential boyfriend would run out screaming or think I was into some really weird, kinky shit. And I'm not. I swear I'm only into a normal amount of kink.

Tucking my hair behind my ears, I strum my bright pink fingernails over my keyboard. My eyes drift to the time displayed in the corner of my computer screen: five-fifteen. I'm doused in an ice-cold bucket of self-pity as I acknowledge just how pathetic it is to be sitting in my office at five-fifteen on a Friday afternoon with no intention of leaving until I have to meet Char at seven.

I slump back in my gorgeous rose-print velvet armchair, kick my heels off, and prop my feet on the corner of my desk. This small act of unprofessionalism makes me feel a wee bit less pathetic. But my dad's words roll around my head, refusing to leave me be. *If anyone can find the needle in the haystack, it's you.* I sigh audibly with all the dramatics of a three-year-old beauty queen and flop my head back to stare at the ceiling.

It's not like I don't want to find someone. I'm just not

the kind of girl that has man-catching skills. I was never taught, and even if I had been, I doubt I would have been able to master it. I'm not equipped with the required talents. I have no filter, no sense of appropriate conversation, and small talk? Yeah, not my forte.

If only I could find someone as wildly inappropriate as myself.

My phone chirps with an incoming text, and I drop my feet from the desk, swivelling around to riffle through my bag and find my phone. Sliding my finger over the screen, I see a message from Charlotte. A grin tugs at the corner of my lips until the words register.

CHARLOTTE: Babe I'm SOOO sorry but I have to cancel tonight. I'm surfin' the crimson wave and Mother Nature is being an extra cruel bitch this month. I feel like a slasher film is being enacted inside my uterus.

Her description makes me cringe. Char has endometriosis, so she suffers from particularly bad periods—to say the least. It's given her the motivation to come up with extremely creative ways of describing her pain and discomfort.

ME: Thanks for that graphic depiction. It will haunt my dreams tonight. And good news, I'm no longer hungry, so that takes care of missing our dinner date before the movie.

CHARLOTTE: You're welcome, my friend. I know you

were looking forward to our Taron Egerton perv-fest, but alas, it must be postponed. Next Friday work for you?

My shoulders slump. I really was looking forward to spending some quality screen time with the dreamboat that is Mr. Egerton.

ME: I hate you and your moody reproductive organs. Until next week then. Kisses.

No longer having a reason to hang around at the office, I shut down my computer, slide my feet back into my heels, slip my bag over my shoulder, and stride out like a woman on a mission.

Let it be noted—there is no mission. And I have nowhere to go but home to my empty apartment to sulk about the lack of supersized man candy in my life this evening. I. Am. Pathetic.

I WINK AT THE BARTENDER AS SHE LEANS FARTHER FORWARD than necessary to slide my beer across the timber expanse separating us. "Thanks, sugar."

The tip of her pink tongue glides across her full bottom lip. "You're welcome, handsome."

A blonde stripper shakes her plentiful arse in front of

Simon's face. Laughter bubbles up my throat. Simon is pressing his torso back in his seat, trying to get as far away from her as possible; it's fucking hilarious. And I'm immediately pleased with myself for organising this buck's night for him.

A grin splits my face as I drop down into the seat beside him. "There is a gorgeous woman rubbing herself all over you, and you're cringing ... That's the wrong response, man."

Simon's head snaps to me. "You are a sick son of a bitch, Rhett. Jessie is going to go nuts if she finds out about this." His eyes bug out of his head. "Look at this, look." His eyes drop down to indicate the red smear on the collar of his white dress shirt. "There's lipstick on it!"

My grin transforms into a smirk. "I know, but it's my duty as your best friend and best man to get you in as much shit as possible."

"Well, you've certainly lived up to your obligations over the past fifteen years, you prick."

"And you've loved every minute of it. You would have died of boredom without me in your life, and you know it," I tell him with a nudge to his ribs.

He shakes his head, and finally, having had enough of the stripper's attention, he leans forward and whispers in her ear. She instantly straightens, moving away from him, and glares at me. *Me.* What the fuck did he just say to her? Before I can ask, she slaps me across the face and storms —as much as one can storm in stripper heels—away from the corner of the bar we've taken up.

I glare at Simon. "What did you say?"

The smug bastard shrugs. "I did what I had to do. Now, if you'll excuse me." He plants his feet then stands, dusting imaginary lint off his shirt. "I'm going to find some club soda to get this shit off my collar before I go home to my fiancée."

Three steps into the abandonment of his own buck's party, he looks back to me and calls out, "Thanks, dick-face. And I think that new cream should really help the rash on your balls. Just don't forget to apply it three times a day."

Conveniently, the cute bartender I was planning on taking home is standing close enough to hear my once best friend's implication that I have an STD. That asshole.

Eight or nine drinks later, I stumble into a cab—alone.

JESUS CHRIST. WHAT THE FUCK IS THAT?

CLUNK *THWACK* *THWACK* *THWACK*

For the love of GOD! My hand shoots to my throbbing skull. The sound on the other side of the wall continues, and with each thwack, my brain flinches.

I sit up and instantly regret the sudden movement as my stomach rolls. Another thwack vibrates through the wall behind my bed, and my eyes squeeze shut. What the hell is she doing over there?

I'm drowning in sweat—stupid bloody air con. Once the urge to throw up eases, I gingerly swing my legs over the side of my bed, pressing the soles of my feet to the floor. Only when I'm sure I'm not going to empty the contents of my stomach all over the carpet do I stand. My head spins, and I press my hand to the wall to steady myself, then make my way over to the air-conditioner unit above my drawers.

Glaring at it, I reach up and give it a little love tap. Nothing. I do it again, a little less lovingly. Still nothing. Frustration boils under my skin until another loud thwack fills the room, and an idea blossoms in the pits of my hungover brain.

Striding down the hall with purpose, I head straight to my front door. Wrapping my fingers around the handle, I yank it open and stalk towards my quirky little neighbour's apartment. I bang on it with a heavy hand to make sure she can hear me over the sound of whatever the hell she's doing in there.

I only cease when the door swings away from my pounding fist and I'm met with a dishevelled little psycho clutching a hammer. I blink at her. What the fuck—

"Rhett?" she squeaks. "Where are your pants?"

My gaze drops down to my cock, now half-erect due to the sexy little number in front of me. A vision of this gorgeous creature standing just like that at the foot of my bed while offering to play handywoman for me plays out in my mind. "Umm ..." I shake my head and wince at the movement. "It's not important," I mutter as I shove past her on my way inside the apartment.

The cool air inside sends a chill scattering over my skin. Spotting a plush grey couch, I smile and head over to my new hibernation zone. I grab a few of the throw pillows, toss them on the floor, then snatch a particularly cosy-looking one back out of the pile I just discarded. I squish it a few times to make sure it's a keeper, then wrap my arm under it as I lie down, snuggling into the surprisingly soft fabric of Neighbour Girl's couch.

Just as I've closed my eyes, she appears. "What are you doing? And where are your pants?"

I pop one annoyed eye open to glare at her. "What does it look like I'm doing? I'm going to sleep. And pants are overrated."

"Pants are overrated," she mumbles under her breath. And I think she's taken the hint to leave me alone, but I'm wrong. "No, I—this is weird. Even for me, this is weird. *I* wouldn't even do this. I barely know you. Do you even know my name? Why are you naked in my apartment at five in the morning? No, wait, the time doesn't matter. Why are you in my apartment? And why are you naked?"

Opening both my eyes to give her the full power of my sleep-deprived, hungover glare, I spell out what should be quite obvious. "I'm in your apartment because *you* woke me up, and my air conditioner is broken, and it's hot as fucking hell at my place. A fact that I was oblivious to when I was asleep but became very aware of after you started trying to knock out the wall that divides our apartments with that fucking hammer."

She blinks down at me several times. "I see."

I nod. "I knew you would. Now, if you'll kindly stop staring, I'd like to go back to sleep."

She does not stop staring. I can't sleep when someone is looking at me. It's creepy as fuck. So, I stare back at her, then slowly raise a brow when she makes no move to leave. "Did I miss something?" I ask.

She licks her lips and wrinkles her forehead. "Do you even know my name?" she asks tentatively.

Uh, shit. I rack my brain in a vain attempt to come up with it. The look on my face must give me away, because she draws her shoulders back and mutters, "That's what I thought."

When she doesn't say anything else, I release a heavy sigh and gingerly sit up. "Look, it's not like we've been officially introduced or anything, but I know who you are. You're Neighbour Girl; you've lived next door for the last four years. You have one friend you always hang out with who laughs like a hyena. I'm guessing no boyfriend because I've never seen a man here, and—"

Her hand flies out and covers my mouth. "Okay, I get it. You don't have to tell me how sad my life is."

I'm tempted to lick her palm just to see how she tastes, but that would be inappropriate.

After dropping her hand from my face, she holds it out in offering to me. "I'm Reagan."

I glance at her outstretched palm then take it, wrapping my much larger one around her delicate one. "Rhett."

She nods, seemingly pleased with herself. "I already knew your name. Girls scream it so loud it practically makes my bedroom wall quake in orgasm along with them."

The hell did she just say?

My jaw pops open, and I wait for her to attempt to take

back her words, to blush, to do anything but stare at me like she didn't just say that out loud. But she doesn't. I'm still clutching her hand in mine, and I notice how soft her skin is. The pad of my thumb strokes across the pulse point in her wrist, and she smiles.

That semi I was sporting when I arrived inflates to straight-up hard-on as dimples pop in her cheeks. Then her eyes flash downwards, and she drops the hammer she was still holding. Glass shatters. I release her hand to cradle my skull as my brain tries to burst through my eyeballs at the god-awful sound.

"Fuck," I moan.

"Shit, my coffee table!" she yells. Then she crouches down in front of me and asks, "Are you okay?" Her palm comes into contact with my forehead. "You're awfully warm."

Her position gives me a bird's-eye view straight down her loose top. And—sweet Jesus—she's not wearing a bra. If I didn't want to die this very second, I'd be hitting on her like there was no tomorrow. My throat thickens, and so does my cock.

All of a sudden, she's no longer touching my forehead because she's plastered to the wall on the far side of the room. Her hand rises and points—to. My. Dick. I drop my gaze to it, too. "Uh, sorry?"

She shakes her head back and forth slowly, then licks her pink lips. "Does it have a name?"

My brows pop. "What?"

Reagan blinks. Her big blue eyes slowly travel up my body until they come to meet mine. She repeats her question. "Does it have a name? Your penis," she clarifies —as if she had to.

I gape. "My dick." I tilt my head. "You— What—" I close my eyes. Am I still asleep? Surely that's what's happening here; I dreamt this whole situation up. I nod to myself then open my eyes again. Nope, she's still there. No hint of embarrassment on her pretty face at all. And she's still pointing.

My cock twitches as if waving to her, and I wrap my hand over him protectively. "He does, but it's personal."

She frowns and lowers her hand. "Oh, okay." She shrugs but stays stuck to the wall.

I've had a hell of a lot of different reactions to the size of my dick, but this is new. Not once has anyone asked if he had a name. Or run away from him that far and fast. I observe her curiously. I've always known Neighbour Girl was on the quirky side, but this?

It would appear she is observing me just as closely as I am her. Those big doe eyes of hers rove over me. Inquisitiveness glints in their depths as she continues to stare.

For the first time in my life, I feel self-conscious. I sneer. *Self-conscious?* Ugh, I don't fucking think so. I'm fucking glorious, and so is my dick.

Chapter 2

Reagan

I KNOW I'M BEING RUDE, BUT I CAN'T LOOK AWAY. IT'S impolite to stare. I'm vaguely aware that I've slipped into full-blown creeper territory, but holy shit, that thing is out of this world. I swallow hard as it bobs against Rhett's tight stomach.

How is this even my reality right now? Sexy men do not turn up at my apartment door at five a.m., naked, and throw themselves on my couch to settle in for a nap. This isn't normal behaviour. Nothing normal ever happens to me, but this feels next-level.

He's staring back at me, waiting for me to say something else. At least, I think he is. So, I bite down on the edge of my bottom lip, trying to think of something, anything, to say. "I'm not a creeper, it's just... well... you're very well-endowed. It's quite shocking, really. I'm a little stuck on it."

Rhett blinks back at me, then a tiny grin lifts the

corner of his mouth. "Um yeah, he's impressive. But I've never quite had a reaction like this before."

"Oh, I suffer from a debilitating case of awkwardness. I've gotten used to it, but other people find it kind of jarring." I shrug. It's the best explanation I can give.

His grin widens until it's covering his entire gorgeous face. "Debilitating awkwardness? That's a new one. Normally I get, *Oh that thing's huge. Fancy a blow job instead?*" He mimics the high-pitched tone of a pub bunny's voice, then covers his mouth and flutters his strangely long—for a man's—eyelashes.

I snort. "You're not serious."

That sexy grin morphs into an unimpressed scowl, all traces of humour gone. "I wish I weren't. But I am. Apparently there is such a thing as *too big*."

My nose and forehead crinkle. "Too big? Women think your penis is too big? I mean, yeah, it's big—like, really big—but I wouldn't say *too* big." Then I think on it for a moment. "Well, I guess it depends on what you're wanting to do with it as to whether it's too big. It's all about perspective, you know?" As I talk, a wide grin stretches across his gorgeous face.

Arching a brow, he asks, "Perspective? And what would you do with my dick, Reagan?"

I scratch my head. "I don't know. You'd have to give me time to ponder on it. I haven't come into contact with anything like that before, so it would require brainstorming, I think."

A rich belly laugh fills the room as Rhett throws

himself back into the couch cushions, laughing his arse off at my expense. Now this is something I'm used to.

Crossing my arms over my chest, I glare at him. "Are you done?"

It takes him a few minutes to pull himself together, and when he does, he smiles at me—a genuine, happy smile, making my defences drop just a little.

"You're one weird chick, but I like it," he says.

I have to consider if I want to take this as a compliment or an insult. Finally, I decide it's a compliment. "Normal is overrated," I tell him, repeating his line about pants.

He nods. "I dig it. Nice ink." He gestures to my shoulder piece with his chin as he speaks. "You like roses?"

"I like all flowers," I tell him, then realise I've unglued myself from the wall and somehow made my way back into the middle of the lounge room.

"Shit," I mutter when a sharp pain sears through my foot. Looking down, I see blood pooling under my left foot. Nausea rolls through me. My head spins rapidly, and sparks fly in my vision. *Oh no, here we go ...*

A fraction of a second before I hit the glass-covered floor, Rhett's big arms wrap around me, and he tugs me into his hard, defined, *naked* chest. Our bodies crash back into the couch, sending it screeching across the tiles from our combined weight.

I'm somewhat aware that I should be extracting myself from his hold, seeing as he isn't wearing any clothes, but I'm too dizzy to even try. I'm a limp noodle in this gorgeous man's arms, and he's anything but. Somehow, when Rhett rescued me from certain face mutilation, our bodies got so tangled that I'm splayed across his lap. And his penis is now lodged between my breasts, poking its head out as if to say, *Hello*.

My head sways a little, and I'm no longer sure if it's from seeing the blood or from being this close to *it*. I wish he'd told me its name; I feel rude just staring at it and not knowing.

"… lot of blood. I think you might need stitches," Rhett says.

I blink slowly then rotate my head so I can look up into his face. "What?"

He's holding my bloodied foot in the air, examining it closely. "It looks pretty deep. I think you're going to need stitches."

"Oh," I say, as if this is perfectly okay when it is anything but. I do not do hospitals. I do not do blood, or needles, or any of the other shit involved in what he just said. Turning my face forward again, I rest my now sweaty forehead against his firm thigh, close my eyes, and take several deep, calming breaths.

I've barely begun my internal calm-your-tits speech when his thigh goes rock solid. My eyes pop open. "Can you chill for like five minutes? I'm in the middle of a crisis here. I can feel your lack of chill, and it's making it hard for me to remain calm." Every damn inch of him is statue-like by the time I finish my request.

"Uh, yeah, that's not going to happen when my cock is nestled between your fun bags and you're blowing nice warm breaths over his head like you're about to show him some love."

My head rolls to the side, and I peer up at him with one eye. "Seriously? I'm about to bleed out on my couch and you think I want to give you a BJ?" What is wrong with him?

Rhett frowns. "Bleed out? That's a little dramatic. You're going to need stitches, not a funeral director."

With herculean effort, I move my arms to the outside of his thigh and push my torso up so I come eye to eye with him. "I am not dramatic."

It would have been a much bolder statement had my arms been stable beneath me and had I not just caught sight of the blood running down my ankle and pooling at the back of my bent knee. Lightness fills my head, and I feel it droop as my arms give out and the world around me goes black.

THERE COMES A TIME IN EVERY MAN'S LIFE WHEN HE MUST ask himself, *how did I end up here?* This is my moment: sitting naked on a practical stranger's couch with her sprawled over me, her face mashed against my fully erect cock as I hold one of her legs up in the air in an attempt to slow the blood flow from her foot. Oh yes, and let's not forget that she's currently unconscious.

Using my free hand, I slide the curtain of blonde hair that escaped from her bun-thing off her face. She's white as a sheet, and when I press my palm to her forehead, I feel how clammy she is. Shit. I need to get her to a hospital, but I'm naked.

How do I get myself into these situations? Given, this particular one is a first, but still, how?

As smoothly as possible, I slide out from underneath her, keeping her injured foot elevated. Then I notice the blood now soaked into the cushions of her nice couch. Double shit. I lower her ankle to lean it on the armrest, then survey the ground before stepping back. Last thing I need is to stand on a piece of glass, too.

Gripping my hips, I stare at her. Her face is squished into the cushion, and her mouth is open. It looks like a fucking crime scene in here. My hand slips off my hip, and it's because it's covered in blood. Great. It looks like I tried to kill her. Somehow, I don't think my reason for being here would help my case—*I swear, Officer, I was just coming over to take a nap.*

Fuck it, I have to fix this. Sleep will wait, but this headache needs to be dealt with now. It takes me less than a minute to get the layout of Reagan's apartment figured out. It's very similar to my own, only nicer.

I rummage through her bathroom cabinets and find some Advil, bandages, and sterile wipes. They'll do just nicely. Glancing at her shower on my way out, I decide it's probably a good idea to jump in real quick, seeing as I look like an axe murderer at rush hour.

Adjusting the temperature, I slide in and soap up with

her girly rosewood body wash and remove all traces of her blood from my skin. This stuff is actually pretty nice; it smells delicate and enticing. I quickly rinse off and grab the first towel I can find—it's sunshine yellow. I swiftly dry off then wrap it around my hips and pick up my medical supplies.

When I stride into the lounge room, Reagan is no longer horizontal. You'd think that would be a good thing, but the look on her face says it's really not. Tears shine in her baby blues, and I rush to her, mindful of the glass. "Hey, it's okay. You're okay," I tell her.

She shakes her head, and big fat tears roll down her cheeks, wrinkled from being smooshed into the couch. "I forgot I hurt my foot, and tried to stand up, and stood on another-piece-of-glass-and-now-it's-stuck-in-my-foot-and-I'm-going-to-die ..." she wails, folding herself into my body as I sit.

My arm automatically curls around the eccentric woman beside me, and I hold her, stroking her arm in comfort. "You're not going to die, Reagan. I won't let you."

Her big blue eyes connect with mine. "Promise?"

I don't even hesitate. "I promise."

Keeping our eyes locked, I reach down and wrap my free hand around her ankle. "Close your eyes, beautiful," I instruct. I don't want her to pass out again. Then, I lift her foot towards me while sliding my arm out from under her and guide her to lie back. "Just breathe, Reagan."

Her eyes screw shut, and she does as I say. Shifting my attention to her foot, I cringe. A large piece of glass sticks out of the side. Thick, sticky blood runs down her leg and drips onto the floor. It's so fucking gross. The metallic smell makes my stomach roll, and I have to look away for a second to get my shit together.

"I'm going to pull out the glass, Reagan, then I'm going to take you to the hospital." My fingers slip twice before I'm able to get a good grip on the shard. I don't wait for her to respond. Holding it firmly, I pull it out in one fluid motion, then press the towel that's around my waist to the area.

I expect a scream or something from her, but she stays silent. Peeking back at her face, I realise it's because she's out cold. It's probably better that way. Snatching up the bandages I found in the bathroom, I wrap one around her foot and secure it with some medical tape.

Sliding out from under her, I crouch by her side. "Reagan," I whisper as I stroke her cold cheek. She stirs. "I'm going back to my place real quick to get some clothes and my keys. I'll be right back. Don't go anywhere."

She mumbles something incoherent, and I don't think she'll be moving off this couch without my help anytime soon.

I take off back to my apartment, but not before putting a piece of the medical tape over the latch of Reagan's apartment door to make sure I can get back in. Once inside my place, I duck into my spare room and grab a pair of pants and the first tee I find. My keys, however, are not as easily found.

Then, I have a light bulb moment and check the pockets of the jeans I was wearing last night—success! Wrapping my fist around them, I snatch my phone off the kitchen counter and slide my feet into my shoes on the way out the door.

Reagan is where I left her, but she's awake now. When I walk in, she stares at me like I've grown a second head, then bursts out laughing. Shit, maybe she's lost so much blood she's delirious? The closer I get to her, the harder she laughs, until tears slide down the sides of her now rosy cheeks.

I raise my brows. "What's so funny?" She could at least let me in on the joke.

She raises a shaking finger. "Your shirt," she snorts.

Fuck. My. Life.

I grabbed the tee my sister gave me for my birthday last month. It says, *Sexy and I Mow It,* with a picture of a stick man pushing a lawnmower. I roll my eyes at Reagan. "It's not that funny. I mowed my sister's lawn for her once —just once—and it was really fucking hot, and I had to take my shirt off, and her friends were over. And yeah, I may have made the joke to one of them who was drooling a little." I shrug. "I didn't even look at what I was putting on. I was just trying to be quick."

"Thanks," she says, smiling brightly, "and I like the shirt."

"Come on. Let's get you some medical attention," I say with an outstretched hand. She takes it and I help her sit. "You want to change your clothes first, or want a bra or something?"

An adorable wrinkle forms between her brows. "A bra? No. I'm in pain; why would I want to inflict more discomfort on myself right now? Let's just get this over with."

I grin. "Suits me fine; I'm not complaining." In fact, I really like that she doesn't want to doll herself up, or some shit like that, before leaving the house.

"I'm sure you're not, you perv. Don't think I didn't see you lookin' earlier," she mumbles as I help her stand, then wrap my arm around her slim waist and take most of her weight.

I deliberately look down her top, which is easy since she's tiny next to my six foot two. "I wasn't trying to hide it. And it's only fair since you spent a solid ten minutes staring at my dick."

She playfully shoves my side as I escort her out the door and down to the basement garage, leading her to my truck. She leans on its side while I fish out my keys and unlock my baby, then I scoop her up and deposit her inside.

"I could have climbed up," she mutters.

"I know, but you would have hurt your foot. It's no big deal."

Fifteen minutes later, I slide into a park by the emergency entrance. "I'll help you out," I tell her and jog around the front of the truck before she tries to climb down on her own.

Her door is already open, and she's about to slide out when I wrap my arms around her little waist. "I told you I'd help you."

She stares into my eyes as I slowly lower her to the ground.

"I'm okay; you've done enough. Really, I can take it from here. You should go now." She says all this with a pleasant smile plastered on her face. And it's fake as fuck.

I scrutinise her for a minute longer. "What are you planning?"

Her eyes widen. "What? Nothing. I'm going to go in and get fixed up good as new, and then I'll call my dad to come get me. No hidden plans here."

"Really? 'Cause your eyes keep darting to that taxi rank over there, and I'm having flashbacks of you burying your face in my crotch to process the fact that you need stitches. So, I'm thinking you have a plan of escape and you're trying to get rid of me."

Her smile falters. "Damn it. I'm such a shitty liar. I really need to work on that."

I'm about to release my hold when her body tips to the side. I tighten my grip. "Whoa there, come on, drama queen. I'll hold your hand the whole time, okay?"

She swallows. "Uh no, you don't need to do that. Nobody wants to see what's about to go down in there."

I hook a finger under her chin and tilt her head up when she refuses to meet my gaze. "And what's going to go down?"

Reagan releases a deep breath. "A whole lot of crazy you are not prepared to handle. I should call my daddy," she says and gnaws on her bottom lip.

At this point, it's hard to keep a straight face. "More crazy than our morning so far, you mean?"

Finally, a fraction of a real smile quirks her full lips. "Yeah, probably."

Chapter 3

Rhett

What the actual fuck am I seeing right now?

I blink several times then wriggle my fingers. Well, I try to wriggle my fingers.

Reagan has my hand in a death grip as she shrieks, "WHY ME, GOD?"

My ears are actually ringing. "Calm down, woman. They haven't even touched you yet."

Her chest heaves as she pulls air into her lungs in sharp, harsh pants. "I am calm, you dick-hole! This is all your fault. You did this to me. You cut me!" Her rabid eyes bounce around the small sterile cubicle.

She already tried to do a runner but collapsed two feet in, presumably from the numerous cuts on her foot. I scooped her up, and I've been holding her like this for the last ten minutes. My arms lock around her middle a little tighter. "Jesus, you weren't lying about the crazy."

"You did not just call me crazy! You're crazy. You, you

made me come here. This is your fault." Her rambling would be cute if she hadn't been doing it since we walked through the doors.

Seriously, we crossed the threshold, and her mouth started moving and hasn't stopped since. She's even more pale than she was when we were back at her apartment, and sweat is gathering at her temples, across her nape, and down her slender neck. I'm struck with the urge to kiss her there, right in the curve where her neck meets her shoulder. Just rest my lips there to soothe her.

Jesus, her crazy is rubbing off on me. I shake my head and ask the doctor, "What's taking so long?"

He smiles, clearly way too amused by the rabid banshee in my lap. "Oh, just waiting on another set of hands. Won't be too long."

I nod. Right. Another set of hands can't hurt, even though there are already two nurses hovering in the corner. Can't we get this show on the road? The curtain parts and another doctor steps inside. His eyes land on Reagan and he smiles at her. "Hello, sweetheart. It's been a long time. What have you done to yourself?"

Her bottom lip trembles, and she points to her foot wrapped in the bloodied bandage. "He cut me," she sobs.

I roll my eyes. "I didn't cut her. She dropped a hammer on her glass coffee table, then stood on the shards when she was staring at my—" I cut myself off. They don't need all the details.

The guy nods, then extends a weathered hand to me. "Jim. I've been Reagan's doctor since she was a child."

"Rhett. I'm her neighbour."

After releasing my hand, he clasps his in front of him and crouches down in front of us. "Honey, you need to calm down. I'll get the nurse to bring you a Valium, then we'll take a look at the damage."

Reagan nods, finally fucking silent.

When Jim returns to standing, Reagan's eyes zero in on the blood-stained bandage. The longer she stares at it, the looser her stiff body becomes in my arms. "Reagan?" I question, cupping her jaw with my hand, swivelling it so I can look into her eyes. They're cloudy and her cheeks have a slightly green tinge to them.

"So much blood," she mumbles, then her head jerks out of my hold as she vomits all over both of us. And promptly passes out, again.

The nurses scurry to clean up the mess, and Doctor Jim jumps to action. "Right, let's have a look at this while she's out," he says to the first doctor. Glancing at one of the nurses, he instructs her to get something. I'm not sure what, as I'm too busy trying to hold my own vomit back. I've always been a sympathetic vomiter.

I clench my jaw as nausea grips my stomach. "Ah, Doc, I'm going to have to lay her on that there bed before I add to the—" I retch before I can finish my sentence.

Thirty minutes later, I've showered in the patients' bathrooms and am wearing a pair of blue scrubs. Reagan's been moved to another cubicle—a clean one, thank god. I'm grateful for the strong scent of hospital-grade cleaning products filling my nostrils as I walk past our previous one.

Reagan's still passed out when I enter the small area

we've been designated, the doctor hovering by her side. "Umm, Doc, is she supposed to be out still?"

"We gave her a little something to keep her under while we cleaned the wound and sutured it. We have administered local anaesthetic to the area, but with Reagan, it's best she not be conscious for such things."

I nod along as he explains. Makes sense to knock her crazy arse out. She'd probably kick the doctors in the face sooner than let them look at the cuts.

I'm told she can leave an hour after she comes back around if her hysteria has calmed down. I drag a chair up to the side of her bed and wait.

Reagan

My head lulls to the side, and I squint. My surroundings are weird. I look around fully and realise I'm in a hospital bed. Then, my eyes land on him.

I swallow hard as the memory of my morning comes crashing down on me. Holy-baked-not-fried-potato-chips. He saw my crazy. All my crazy. My hot-as-sin neighbour—who I may have fantasised about a few (hundred) times—saw me at my ultimate level of crazy. Kill. Me. Now.

An audible groan leaves my lips, and I smack my hand

over my mouth to hush the sound. Rhett's eyes fly open and lock on my face.

I am beyond mortified. Then, he smiles.

"Hey there, crazy girl," he says with a smirk. "How you feelin'?"

Is it wrong that I want to both slap and kiss that smirk off his face?

When I don't answer his question, he shuffles to the edge of the chair he's sitting on and rests his elbows on the side of my bed. His eyes rake over me, from the top of my head right down to my toes.

Wait, what the hell am I wearing? I pluck at the offending garment covering my upper body. Scrubs?

"You threw up on us, then I threw up on us," Rhett explains, cringing.

For the love of God. Can this day get any worse?

"I recall. But I don't remember putting this on." I pluck at the top I'm wearing again. "I would never—and I mean *never*—willingly wear scrubs."

Rhett's lips twitch. "You'd prefer to stay in your manky, puke-covered clothes?"

And that's when it dawns on my sluggish brain that Rhett, too, is wearing scrubs. But unlike me, he looks like a sexy doctor from *Grey's Anatomy*.

"I'd prefer to be naked than wear these." I sniff. Before he can comment, my brain chooses that moment to filter through his explanation of the scrubs. I narrow my eyes. "Did you say that *you* threw up on us?"

His smile falls. "Umm, yeah. I have a weak stomach when it comes to that kind of thing. I've been a sympathetic spewer since I was a kid when my baby sister would vomit up her milk; I'd be there, right beside her, chucking up my breakfast."

Right. Well, that's disgusting.

"You didn't answer me before. How are you feeling?"

Glancing down at my pristinely wrapped foot, I shrug. "I'm fine."

Rhett arches a brow. "Just like that? From crazy to cruisy with the flip of a coin?"

I shrug again. "I can't see the... you know... anymore. It's a visual thing."

"But you were fine on the car ride over here. You didn't turn into a nutcase until we walked in the doors."

Clearing my throat, I explain, "The bandages were clean when you drove me here. But by the time we got inside, the red stuff had seeped through, and bam—welcome to Crazytown."

"I think I get it. It's like me with the vomit, but you go crazy at the sight of blood."

I nod. "Yeppers. Now, can we go? I hate being in here."

"Gotta wait to see the doc first, then I'll take you home," he tells me.

I wonder why he hung around, especially after the cray-cray came out to play. I want to ask him, but at the same time, I'm content to just sit here in silence for a few minutes. This day has been one I'll never forget for the rest of my life, as much as I want to. And it's only ten a.m.

Hobbling into my apartment, I glance over my shoulder at Rhett who's standing in the doorway. "You coming in?"

He scratches his temple. "Do you want me to?"

I shrug. I had just assumed he would, seeing as he barged in here this morning like he owned the place. "Umm, I guess? I don't know. I mean ..." I'm stumped for what to say. Hell yes, I want him to come in, but this is all so strange. I'm not sure what the appropriate response is here.

He's so damn pretty I want to lick his face. But if I said that out loud, he definitely wouldn't come in. And he'd never try to sleep naked on my couch again. I gnaw on my bottom lip. I really want to call Char and ask her what I should say, but my phone is in the lounge room still, and I can't just make him wait in my doorway while I scurry off to phone a friend.

"Look, it's fine. I can go home. But maybe you should give me your number so I can check up on you, and you can call me if you need anything, yeah?"

My eyes shoot to his. "No, it's okay. You can come in. I'm just, well, I told you, I'm super awkward."

He takes a step inside, then closes the door behind him. "If you want me to go, that's totally fine, Reagan. Don't feel like you have to invite me in," he says while running his calloused hand through his messy hair. "You were right; this is my fault. If I hadn't forced my way in here this morning, none of this would have happened. I was just so tired and really fucking hungover—it seemed like a great plan." His shoulders rise in apology, and he drops his gaze to the floor.

I swing my body around to face him using the horrendous crutches the hospital supplied me with. "Don't apologise. If you didn't come over, I never would have had the nerve to introduce myself to you, and we'd still be strangers."

His eyes lift to meet mine. "That's true. But you'd still be in one piece."

With a roll of my eyes, I swivel back around and continue hobbling into my lounge room, only to freeze at the sight before me.

It's clean. No glass, no blood, nothing.

I can feel the heat of Rhett's body at my back.

"What happened? I don't understand." I crane my neck to look up at him as an impish grin spreads across his face.

He scratches the back of his neck as he says, "I rang my sister. I didn't want you to freak out all over again, trying to clean up the mess. So, yeah, I made a call to the most OCD woman I know, and she did her thing."

A lump of emotion forms in my throat; he's so thoughtful. I totally would have lost my shit again if I'd had to face the crime scene. Licking my parched lips, I wait for his eyes to meet mine. "Thank you," I whisper, unable to make my voice any louder for fear of it breaking.

Rhett shrugs his wide shoulders, his grin having morphed into a megawatt smile. "It's no problem. I'm just glad I could do something to make it better for you." His warm hands slide around my hips as he leans forward. "Is this okay?"

I'm stunned at the contact and how my body hums with delight at the small gesture. "More than okay," I breathe. I want him to kiss me so badly my lips tingle.

He tilts his head in a small nod, then applies pressure to my hips, urging me forward. I'm instantly confused. I thought he was making a move, not guiding me into the lounge room.

Once in front of my gloriously clean couch, he turns me around and pushes my hips back until I sit. Then, in one swift move, he lifts my legs and swings them up onto it. I stare at him—like really stare. He's so sweet and chivalrous. Such a contradiction to the naked man who barged in here at the arse-crack of dawn to take a nap on my couch.

Chapter 4

Reagan

RHETT DOESN'T LEAVE, INSTEAD TAKING UP RESIDENCE ON my floral velvet daybed opposite me. He is way too big for it, but he looks comfy enough with his arms tucked behind his head as he lounges.

I flick on the TV and pretend to watch it. I'm not even sure what channel it's on—it could be playing porn for all the attention I'm paying to it. I can't look away from him. This is all so surreal.

"You're staring again," he says.

"This whole day has been one bizarre event after another. I'm just processing."

"Can you process while not staring at me?" he asks, turning his head to eye me.

I shrug. "Maybe, but you're part of it. So I'm processing you, too."

He rolls onto his side, propping his head up with his arm, keeping eye contact as he speaks. "I think I'm the one who should be processing. This has been, by far, the strangest day on record for me. From your reaction to my dick, to the shitshow at the hospital ..." He shakes his head. "Mind fuck." He uses his free hand to mime an explosion coming from his brain.

Snorting, I turn the TV off, then correct him. "Uh no. You're the one who showed up at my place—naked, I might add—to take a nap. Who does that? We didn't even know each other six hours ago."

"Pfft, you woke me up! I was sleeping like a fucking baby until someone"—he raises his brows pointedly at me—"tried to take down the wall between our places. What were you doing with that hammer anyway?"

I shift a little and avert my gaze. "I don't know what you're talking about." His eyes bore into me, and I squirm, refusing to meet his inquisitive examination.

"Reagan, I can just go look for myself, you know. You'd be too slow to stop me, so you might as well just spit it out."

"Hmph, fine," I grumble but keep my focus on my pretty, pale purple toenails. "I couldn't sleep, so I thought I'd do some remodelling."

"Remodelling. I see."

I don't like his tone. I bet he thinks I'm incapable of doing it myself. Typical male. I slide my gaze towards him, but he's gone. I didn't even hear him get up. My eyes widen in panic as I swing my feet to the floor, and I wince in pain at the slight pressure on my injured foot.

"Don't bother coming after me; I've already found it. There's no sense in you hurting yourself trying to stop me." His voice comes from the short hallway that leads to my bedroom.

I drop my head back in defeat. Damn him. He has some serious ninja-like stealth abilities.

A few minutes later, Rhett emerges, an amused smirk in place. "Not happy with the layout of your closet, huh?"

Glaring at his stupidly gorgeous face, I cross my arms under my boobs. "No, I wasn't. I need more room for my shoes and more hanging space."

He nods as he approaches me. Crouching down at my feet, he lifts them, swings them back up onto the couch, then hands me a light pink tank top. I frown, and he smiles shyly. "You were bitching about the scrubs, and this was on the end of your bed." He shrugs and moves his right hand back to my ankle. "You should keep your foot up," he instructs. "It will help with the swelling."

"Okay." I swallow, the intensity of his gaze making my heart beat faster. I blink at him several times then shift my focus to the tank he handed me. He makes me feel so weird, all twisty inside. I yank my top off and throw it to the floor, then slip the tank over my head. He's so thoughtful.

"Sweet Jesus," Rhett breathes, and my eyes find his again, but they're locked on my breasts.

"Something wrong?" I ask.

He releases a slow, controlled breath. "You're not wearing a bra, Reagan." His eyes finally meet mine. "You just flashed me your amazing tits."

"Oh," is all I can say. Holy shit. He's going to think I'm a whore. "I haven't had sex in ages!" I blurt. His eyes widen, and I try to explain myself. “I’m not trying to get into your pants or anything, is what I mean. I... um... shit. I didn’t even think about it. You gave me the clean, non-nasty tank, and I really did hate that other top, so I just changed it.” I shrug pathetically. “Sorry,” I mumble.

“Don’t ever be sorry for who you are, Reagan. Besides, I didn’t think you were trying to seduce me or anything. After only half a day with you, I’m beginning to realise you just do and say whatever pops into your head.”

I nod. “I do. It’s an illness. Not everybody is as chill about it as you. Although, I wasn’t apologising for being me; I was apologising for flashing you.”

He frowns. “Oh, well, don’t be sorry for that either.” His thumb grazes over the ankle bone of my injured foot. “Doc said you should stay off it for at least a week before you try getting around again. Will that be a problem with your job?”

I shake my head. “No, I can work from home.”

“Good,” he murmurs, his thumb still lightly tracing the contours of my foot. “I can come check on you each morning, make sure you’ve got breakfast and supplies for the day, if you want.”

Hazel eyes bore into mine, and I’m caught in a daze. “Yeah, that’d be nice.” Truth be told, I could get Char to come stay with me and help, but she doesn’t look like Rhett. So, I push that thought away.

The answering smile he gives me says I definitely made the right choice. That and the butterflies swarming in my chest. I grin back.

Could Rhett be the one guy who doesn't find my awkward nature overbearing?

Rhett

THIS CHICK IS UNLIKE ANY I'VE EVER MET. I'M A *HIT IT AND quit it* kind of guy with no need for conversation or bonding. I only put in the time needed to secure myself a warm body for the night. But Reagan is different. I want to help her, feed her, hang out with her. And I'm not even thinking about banging her.

Okay, that's a lie. I'm totally thinking about having sex with her. It's really freaking hard not to stare at her tits. Especially when I'm this close to her and she just changed in front of me. And ... now I'm doing exactly what I was trying not to do: staring at them.

"They're pretty impressive, huh?"

My eyes snap to hers, expecting her to be pissed or something, but a genuine smile lights her features. I should have known she wouldn't care. "Umm, yeah, they're pretty fucking awesome."

"And they're real," she says, squeezing one in her hand.

Goddamn, *she's* unreal. Before I can say anything in response, her stomach growls. Loudly. "Hungry?"

She nods. "Yeah, I haven't eaten today. There's food in

the fridge. I got groceries on my way home last night." She tries to swing her legs around, but I stop her.

"No, I'll get it. Stay here."

Her apartment is the same layout as mine, so her kitchen is just beyond the lounge area. In her fridge, I find all the fixings I'll need to make us some sandwiches. While I throw them together, I check out her space. The benches are shiny hot pink laminate, the cupboard doors are deep plum purple, and the splash zone is like a chalkboard with notes and scribbles here and there.

My kitchen looks the same as it did the day I moved in: simple black benchtop with white cupboard doors. Reagan's is much cooler. *Maybe I should do something with mine?*

Sliding the two sandwiches onto a couple of plates, I carry them back into the lounge room and hand hers over. Taking a seat opposite her, I watch her from the corner of my eye as she takes a bite, grinning when she spots me watching her.

"It's good. Thank you."

I smirk. "I know."

We're eating in companionable silence when she speaks up. "Did you know flamingo tongues were a common delicacy in Roman feasts back in the day?"

I pause, the bite I just took falling from my mouth back to my plate as I gape at her. "What?"

"True fact; the Romans had some freakishly disgusting tastes."

Suddenly, my sandwich doesn't look so appealing. I glance at it, and back to Reagan, who is still munching away happily on hers, then put my plate with the remainder of my lunch on the floor beside me.

"Where did you pull that little gem of knowledge from?" I ask while crossing my arms behind my head as I lie back on the couch.

"It's what I do. I am the queen of random facts," Reagan says from the couch opposite me.

"Aha, so you just like collecting weird little bits of information for fun? Or to gross people out while they're trying to eat?" I joke.

Her blue eyes widen and shoot to my plate on the floor with the remains of my sandwich. "Shit, I'm sorry. I didn't mean to turn you off your food. I'm hopeless. Small talk is not my thing. I always say the wrong thing. I'm such a loser."

"Whoa, that's not what I meant. It's fine, Reagan, seriously. It was just a strange thing to say out of nowhere, that's all."

She doesn't look convinced, so I pick my plate up and shovel another bite of food into my mouth, all the while thinking about flamingo tongues in place of the ham on my sandwich.

When she smiles, God, it feels good. It's a weird thing to say about someone's smile. But when it's directed at me? Damn.

She finishes chewing the last of her sandwich, and I stand to take our plates to the kitchen. "Explain why you thought to bring up flamingo tongues while I make us a coffee. You have coffee in here, right?" I call over my shoulder as I go.

I hear her snort, and I grin. This chick.

"Of course I have coffee; I'm not a serial killer. There's a pod machine by the toaster and an array of pods to suit every mood in the stand beside it. Mugs are in the cabinet above," she calls back.

She's silent for a solid thirty seconds, probably trying to dodge my other question.

"Flamingo tongues, Reagan. Talk."

Her sigh is audible all the way from here, and I'm grinning like a fool again.

"Okay, so I'm not just some crazy who likes weird shit. It's literally what I do. It's my job. I'm the fact-checker at Pink Bits. I spend all day verifying random and quirky facts, and I freaking love it. But it leaves me a little ill-equipped when it comes to holding a normal conversation."

The job definitely suits her. But I have one question. I quickly make our coffees then stride back into the lounge carrying two steaming mugs of life-giving liquid. "What the fuck is Pink Bits? It sounds like a strip club, and I don't think the clientele go to those places for fun facts."

I sit on the edge of the seat she's on. In my rush to make the coffees, I hadn't noticed the mugs I'd pulled out for us to use… until now. Mine says, *The Muggle Struggle is Real,* and the one I grabbed for Reagan says, *She Believed She Could, So She Ate The Whole Pizza.*

"Nice cups," I say as I hand over hers. "Hope you like it with milk and sugar, 'cause I made it on autopilot and forgot to ask."

Her fingertips graze mine as she takes it from me, and

I swear I feel a spark shoot up my arm. *I'm turning into Simon.* A shudder crawls under my skin, and I have to shake my arm out to get rid of the feeling.

Reagan quirks a brow. "You okay?"

I look at her like she's the crazy one here. "Uh, yeah. So back to your job. Pink Bits—strip joint?"

She takes a sip of her coffee and hums as she swallows. My dick twitches. I close my eyes and think of my grandma in her underwear. Only when I'm sure my dick has gotten the message do I lift her feet and slide back farther on the couch, then place them in my lap, down near my knees.

I take a swig from my cup to distract myself from her reaction to it, and damn, it's good.

With a flick of her tongue, she removes a drop of coffee from the corner of her lip, then answers my question. "No, Pink Bits is not a strip joint. It's my father's female hygienics company. You've never heard of the Pink Bits brand before?"

I shake my head. "I don't have any reason to know anything about female hygiene products, so that's a no for me. But now that you say it, the name fits. It's actually kinda cool."

She smiles proudly. "It really is. My dad has done wonderful things in the industry."

But I'm struggling to understand why a company that makes that kind of shit needs a fact-checker. "And where do you come into the equation? I'm not seeing it."

Shuffling back slightly, she lifts her hand to gesticulate as she speaks with way more excitement than I think the topic requires, but I love how into it she is. "Right. So, pads and tampons are nobody's idea of a good time. They're ugly and boring. So, I came up with the idea of putting random little facts on the packaging for women to read while they're doing the mandatory change over."

Her eyes are shining like sapphires; I can't look away. They sparkle as she speaks, and I'm caught in a daze as she blabs on about something I really don't care to know about. But her excitement makes me want to hear every word she has to say.

I am so utterly screwed.

Reagan

I'M DOING IT AGAIN—TALKING INCESSANTLY. BUT I'M SO passionate about Pink Bits and my role in the company. "What woman wants to look at a bland sticky strip on the inside of her pad when she could be finding joy in the fact that you can create five new starfishes by cutting one single starfish into pieces? I mean, how cool is—" He's looking at me like he wants to kiss me, and I stumble over my words.

My train of thought has officially left the building.

Rhett's eyes fix on my face. He's listening so closely to every word I'm saying that I'm suddenly nervous. That never happens. My lack of filter is my weakness; I get the slightest bit nervy and I blurt inappropriate facts. But now I'm having trouble even finding my tongue.

A shiver I can't suppress runs from the tips of my toes up my leg, and I realise he's gently running his fingers over my tender foot. His gaze locks on mine. My skin prickles as his rough hand slides across my ankle and over my calf on its way up my body.

"Swans are the only birds with an external penis!" I blurt.

Oh my God.

Yes, ladies and gentlemen, I just said that out loud to my sexy-as-sin neighbour.

Kill me now.

Chapter 5

Rhett

I'm about to tell her just how stunning her eyes are when those words explode from her mouth. My hand freezes midway up her toned thigh. "What?"

She holds her breath for a moment before expelling it in a rush. "It's the most recent fact I entered into the database: swans are the only birds with an external penis. All other birds have internal ones that only come out to play when it's showtime."

A deep, rough laugh erupts from my belly. This chick is fucking crazy, and I'm loving every second of it. She's so random. I'm never sure what's going to come out of her mouth. I mean, I was in the process of making a move on her, but I'm not upset that she ruined the moment. Actually, I think she made it better.

When my laughter subsides, I can't help but smile at the blank expression on her gorgeous face. "What now? What's wrong?"

A deep crease forms between her perfectly shaped brows. “I thought for sure you would have been out the door by now, but you’re still here.”

“Yeah, and?”

The corner of her lip is trapped between her teeth as she gnaws on it. I can’t stand seeing her like that, unsure of herself. I reach forward, slide my palm around her jaw and free her lip with my thumb. “Don’t do that. I like your brand of crazy. You don’t have to try and hide it from me.”

Her grin is blinding. It lights up her entire face, widens her bright eyes, and takes my breath away.

With my hand still cupping her face, my thumb glides over her full, pouty bottom lip. “You have a beautiful mouth,” I tell her. It’s not a smooth compliment, but it’s an honest one.

“Yeah?” she exhales.

I nod. “Fuck yeah.”

I’m so close to her now I can feel her breath on my own lips, and I don’t even recall moving up the couch. She has me under some kind of spell.

I want to kiss her.

I want to feel her skin under my palms.

I want to hear her breathy moans as I slide inside of her.

I want. I want. I want.

Suddenly, her eyes widen in pain, and her breath hitches. “My foot,” she gasps.

I’d forgotten I was still nursing her injured foot in my hand, and my lust-driven thoughts must have caused my grip to tighten. Asshole!

Immediately, I release her, sliding back down the end of the couch to inspect the damage I've just inflicted. Blood has seeped through to the top of the fresh dressing. Shit.

I place my hand over the red smear to hide it from her. "It's all good down here. Sorry I hurt you; I didn't mean to. I was just looking at your lips and got carried away. I'm so fucking sorry, Reagan."

With a grimace, she tries to comfort me. "It's alright. It didn't hurt that bad ..."

I close my eyes against the obvious lie. "Reagan, it did. *I* did. Again." Seems like that's all I'm good at with this girl. Our first encounter and I've landed her in hospital, needing stitches, then squeezed the wound so tightly I made her bleed. I'm on a roll today.

"I should go and let you get some rest," I tell her, lifting her feet from my lap and gently depositing them back on the couch when I stand. My hand lingers on her ankle, though. I should cover the bloodied patch before I leave in case it sends her loopy when she spots it.

Holding up a finger, I instruct her to stay put, then retrieve one of the replacement dressings the doc gave us and place it directly on top of the current one.

Satisfied I've done a good thing, I know I need to leave before doing something else to cause her pain.

"I'll check in on you tomorrow?" I ask more than state as I turn to leave her.

Silence greets my back. Glancing over my shoulder, I see she's staring out the window. "Reagan?" I prompt. Her face is expressionless when she returns her gaze to me. I swallow. “I’ll see you tomorrow?”

She nods her head once, then goes back to looking out the window.

Reagan

And there you have it, folks: how to scare a man away in less than twenty-four hours.

I feel even more pathetic now than I did last night, coming home to my empty apartment on a Friday evening with no plans for the weekend.

It’s not like we were off to a good start anyway—what with the glass in the foot and all. But we could have been friends; I would have liked that. I don’t think he’ll be back tomorrow. He’s probably on the phone to the landlord now, abandoning his lease and searching for a new apartment building where he won’t ever have to run into the awkward girl again.

I need Char’s input on this. My eyes roam the room, searching for my phone, and I spot it on the TV cabinet. Roughly calculating the distance from my position on the couch to my goal, I figure I can make it no worries. It’s like ten feet, max.

Swinging my legs around, I gingerly place them on the

floor. I won't need the crutches for such a short jaunt. Licking my lips, I use my hands to push myself up and off the couch. I manage one, two, three steps—*shit!*

I cry out as I crumple in a heap in the middle of the room. My foot burns, and the stitches pull tight. I lie on the floor for a good five minutes, waiting for the pain to subside, before deciding to crawl the rest of the way to the TV cabinet. A wave of victory washes over me as my fingers curl around my phone. "SUCCESS!" I yell as I slide back to the floor and crawl my way to the couch.

Once I'm comfortably situated with my feet propped up by some throw pillows, I call Char. It rings for so long I think her voicemail is going to pick up, but it's Char's breathy voice that greets me.

"Hiya," I chirp.

"Hey, s'up?" she croaks.

I'm on high alert instantly. "What's wrong? You sound like death."

"I wish I was dead. There is no pain in death."

Oh shit. With everything that happened this morning, I forgot she had an endo flare-up last night. "Still hurting, babe?"

I hear Char swallow. "Yeah, you could say that. Or you could say Freddy Krueger has taken up residence in my uterus."

Dear God. I've never been more thankful for the mild cramps I experience during shark week. "Sorry, honey. I'd offer to come lounge around with you, but I'm out of action. Long story short, my naked hot neighbour barged into my apartment this morning, I dropped my hammer and smashed the coffee table, and then stood on not one, but two massive shards of glass. He saw *all* my crazy when he took me to the hospital, but he stayed and took care of me even when I puked on him. He's so sweet." I sigh at the loss of what could have been—at the very least—a beautiful friendship.

"I'm sorry, what? Back right up, sugar tits, 'cause it sounded like you said the sexy piece of man meat who lives next door to you appeared inside your apartment naked this morning," Char says, completely ignoring everything I've said except the naked neighbour bit.

"Yes, Char, but you missed the rest of it. And I'm not even done yet."

"The rest doesn't matter unless it ended in hot, sweaty sex," she retorts.

"I wish!" I snort.

"Oh babe," Char coos. "What happened?"

"I think he was going to kiss me, but my mouth got in the way again. I told him swans have external penises." I groan at my stupidity.

Char bursts out laughing. "Damn, girl, that is priceless. What'd he do?"

"He laughed. Said he liked my crazy and that he thinks I have a beautiful mouth. Then, he accidentally squeezed my ripped-up foot real hard, and he said he had to go." I'm still trying to work out exactly where I went wrong. It seemed like he liked me, like he wasn't put off by my quirks.

"Dude, he's totally into you," Char says.

I scoff. "Did you not just hear a word I said? This

disaster is my life, Char, and I'm tired of it. You should have seen it; it was brutal."

I just know she's rolling her eyes at me. "I didn't need to be there. From what you just told me, he's into you. Trust me, I know these things. My sexy-time senses are tingling. You're being dramatic."

My nose scrunches. I'm sceptical, at best, about Char's claim to have special sexual senses. "Your sexy-time senses can't pick up stuff that you're not even around to see unfold. That's not how those kinds of things work."

"Uh, yes they do. What would you know anyway? Your superpower is weirding people out with obscure facts. Mine is knowing when someone is attracted to another person."

It's my turn to roll my eyes. "They are not superpowers, Char. They're social handicaps, at best. You thought your gynaecologist was into you, but he was just doing his job. I think you're just as off the mark with this situation."

Char takes a sharp inhale of breath, and I know what it means: she's in a lot of pain.

"Babe, we can talk about this later. The doc gave me some good pain pills for my foot. I can try to figure out a way to get them to you if you need them," I offer. I hate not being able to help her when she's like this.

"Pfft, your pain pills have got nothing on mine." She breathes slow and deep. "I'll be fine. I was just trying to stretch out the time between doses. It was a stupid idea. I should have taken them a half hour ago. Now I have to wait for this lot to kick in."

“Okay,” I mumble, feeling shitty about not being there for her right now. “I’ll call you tomorrow to check on you.”

“I know you will. And, Reagan, he’s into you.” She makes kissy sounds, then hangs up.

Lying on my couch, I stare at the ceiling and contemplate my best friend’s words. Could he really be into me? Could Rhett be my unicorn?

It’s with these thoughts running through my mind that I fall asleep.

Chapter 6

Rhett

I'M SWEATING LIKE A PIG. LYING COMPLETELY STARKERS ON my couch isn't even helping with this oppressive heat. What I really need to do is buy a whole new air conditioner, but that requires more effort than I'm willing to put in right now.

After the events of yesterday, I just want to spend the day doing sweet F.A. But this heat is too much; I'm dying in here.

I jerk upright when I remember I told Reagan I would check on her this morning. Scanning the room, I search for my long-forgotten pants. Spotting them over the back of one of my dining chairs, I snatch them up on my way past.

A minute later, I'm knocking on Reagan's front door.

First silence, then a faint "hello" reaches my ears, and I call back, "It's me, Rhett. Checking on you, as promised."

I can hear her shuffling around inside, a few muted

curses, and then the door swings open. She's in the same tank I gave her yesterday and those sexy little shorts. My eyes eat her up; she's a hot mess.

"Hey," she greets and hobbles out of the way on her crutches, allowing me entry.

Sliding in past her, I don't miss the way her eyes track over my bare chest. It feels good—her eyes on my body, taking me in. Makes me feel like less of a creeper when I check her out—which is a lot.

I'm almost past her when my foot catches on one of her crutches, and I go down like a tonne of bricks.

"Oh my God, I'm sorry! Are you okay?" she asks from above me, her blue eyes wide and searching.

"I'm good," I assure her, shuffling out from under her and bouncing back to my feet. I don't even care that I face-planted; the temperature in here feels like heaven on my overheated flesh. Smirking at the miserable look on her gorgeous face, I ask, "What's wrong? You in pain?"

She shakes her head. "No, but I tripped you up. Not only am I awkward, I'm a klutz too," she says with a shrug. "I'm just a little over it all today."

I lead the way into her lounge. "You need anything? Have you eaten this morning?"

"Nah, I only woke up not long ago. I've been dozing in and out on the couch. The pain meds make me sleepy."

Well, that gives me something useful to do while I soak up the cool air coating my sweat-slicked skin. "Alright, you sit, and I'll feed you," I tell her while moving towards her kitchen. She doesn't argue.

I open her fridge and pull out the eggs and bacon I

saw in there yesterday, then check her drawers for a fry pan—bingo. It takes me ten minutes to whip up some fried eggs and bacon on toast for both of us since I haven't eaten either. And we can't forget the caffeine.

"Here you go, gorgeous," I say with a flourish as I pass her a plate and a steaming mug of coffee, then duck back into the kitchen to grab my own.

When I take the seat across from her, she looks up at me, eyes wide. "Wow, this looks great and smells amazing. I didn't even realise I was hungry."

I settle back in my seat and grin at her. "Can't go wrong with bacon."

She smiles back, then pops an extra crispy piece in her mouth. "Amen to that."

Just like yesterday, we eat in comfortable silence.

Until Reagan breaks it. "Did you know that coffee can be lethal in mass quantities?"

I quirk a brow and take a sip from my mug. This one says, *Sexy, Sassy and a Little Badassy*. I snort at it before answering her. "No, that's news to me. And exactly how much coffee does one have to ingest for it to kill them?"

Her answering chuckle warms my insides as much as the coffee I'm drinking. "Planning a murder, are we?" she asks.

"If I told you, I'd have to kill you," I tell her, my expression deadpan.

She shrugs. "Ten grams, or one hundred cups, in a four-hour period will do the trick, just for future reference. It might come in handy one day."

"Good to know. Got any other stealthy murder techniques for me? Purely for curiosity's sake, of course."

Grinning, she tilts her chin then purses her lips. "Nutmeg is extremely poisonous if injected intravenously."

"No shit?" I muse.

Her eyes light up. "Oh, and just one shot of the teeny tiny blue-ringed octopus's venom can kill twenty-six adult humans within minutes."

"Seriously? That's unsettling." I cringe at the thought of such a small creature being so deadly. My skin crawls, and I have to shake my arms out to be rid of the sensation.

Reagan's throaty laugh fills my ears, and I fix my gaze on her. "What?"

"You," she says between chuckles. "Your reaction—it makes me think you'd be afraid of spiders."

My eyes narrow. "And so what if I am?"

She beams. "You are, aren't you?"

Gritting my teeth, I mutter, "I didn't say that."

"You didn't have to." She laughs, her cheeks and eyes bright with mirth.

I roll my eyes. "Whatever, it's not a big deal. I just don't like the creepy little fuckers. I'm not afraid of them or anything. I just avoid them if I can."

"Aha, I'm sure you're not afraid. Not a big manly man like yourself." She snickers.

Finishing my food, I take my empty plate and mug to the kitchen. "I'm glad I amuse you." I huff on my way past her. Rinsing off my dirty dish, I slide it into the little single-drawer dishwasher, then rummage through Reagan's coffee pods. "You want a refill?"

"What kind of question is that?" she calls back.

"A polite one. I could just make myself another, and you can watch me drink it?"

She laughs again. The sound is quickly becoming one of my new favourites.

"Okay, fine. Although, I don't see you making such a dick move. Not when you've been so nice to me so far. I'll have a French vanilla latte please."

I poke my head around the corner to see her leaning over the back of the couch, facing the kitchen and me. "Don't doubt my ability to be a dick. I have skills you've never seen before."

Her grin is downright seductive. "I bet you do. I've seen enough to never doubt your particular skill set," she says with a waggle of her brows.

I burst out laughing and shake my head at her. "I think I'll keep you."

She stretches out her arm to me, her empty mug hanging from her fingers.

Closing the space, I snatch it from her. "You are somethin' else, Reagan."

"A good something or a bad something?" she asks my back as I return to the kitchen.

I consider her question. I've never come across a woman like her. She's a breath of fresh air. But I need to be careful; I can see myself becoming addicted to it. To her. Clearing my throat, I answer her as honestly as I can. "I'm not sure yet. I'll let you know."

Reagan

I SLEPT IN MY BED LAST NIGHT AND THOUGHT ABOUT RHETT on the other side of the wall that separates our apartments as I fell asleep. That's not creepy, right?

He stayed for most of the day yesterday. It was nice to have his company. We sat around watching movies and eating junk food. He even changed the dressing on my foot for me.

He'd said he would pop in before he left for work this morning, too, but I'm not sure when that will be. I'm kinda stressing about it. I like having him around, and I'm amazed I haven't scared him off yet.

I've been lying here, staring at the clock on my bedside table for the last twenty-three minutes, wondering what time he leaves for work. It's now six-fifteen, and I'm busting to pee. Should I hold it and go after he leaves or risk him coming while I'm peeing?

Stuff it, I'm about to pee my pants if I hold it any longer. Rolling off the side of my bed, I reach for my crutches and hobble to my adjoining bathroom. Leaning one crutch against the wall, I use my now free hand to roll my shorts and underwear down my legs.

My head drops back in pleasure as I pee, and pee, and

pee some more. I think this is the longest pee I've ever done. And it feels so good.

And, of course, that's the moment Rhett arrives.

The sound of his knocking echoes through my apartment, and I try to hurry up the waterworks, but it's not happening. It just keeps coming. "Give me a minute!" I call and hope he hears me.

Finally, I'm down to a trickle, and I snatch up the toilet paper to wipe, then grasp for my shorts, but they've fallen off my feet. I'm left with my undies sitting around my ankles. Grabbing them, I yank them up my legs as fast as I can one-handed. I can hear Rhett calling me—he sounds concerned.

"I'm coming!" I yell out as I quickly wash and dry my hands. Hygiene first, always.

I'm puffed by the time I reach my front door and swing it open. "Morning," I murmur on a particularly harsh exhale.

Rhett is standing in front of me in a dirty, grease-stained pair of jeans and navy button-down that's also covered in smudges. My eyes roam over him, and a little drool pools in my mouth. Wow. His biceps strain against the sleeves of his shirt, reminding me of what's under it.

Holy sexy mechanic. A dreamy little sigh escapes as I stare at him while catching my breath.

He frowns. "Ah, Reagan, are you okay?"

My eyes snap up to meet his. "Yeah, why?"

One of his thick eyebrows arches at my question. "You're wearing a pair of Batman panties, I can see your nipples through your tank, and you're panting ..."

I swallow hard at his description. "I wasn't flicking my bean if that's what you're thinking."

Both his brows lift, and his eyes widen. "Flicking your bean?"

"Yeah, you know: polishing the pearl, auditioning finger puppets, jilling off. I swear my hands were not in my pants. See?" I hold my right hand up to his nose to prove that there are no suspicious smells coming from me.

"Oh my God, woman." He buckles over laughing.

His head is now level with my bits. He might be down there laughing, but the visual is giving me other ideas. And they are not friend-zone ideas.

Snap out of it, Reagan! You're such a perv. Or just really hard up? Shaking my head at myself, I shuffle around him then hobble down the hallway to the lounge and plonk on the couch with a huff.

"Hey, where are you going?" Rhett calls after me.

I'm staring up at my ceiling one minute. The next, Rhett's head is hovering above me. I cover my face with my hands.

"Hey," he coos. His calloused palms wrap around my wrists and pry my hands away from my face. "I told you, you don't need to hide your crazy from me."

I frown. "I wasn't— Wait, you think I was being crazy?" *Was I?* I was just trying to get my head straight. That was why I walked away. Well, hobbled away.

Rhett smiles. "Well, you just held your fingers up to my nose to prove you weren't masturbating. That's a little crazy, babe."

Huh, okay. "I was just proving my point." I shrug.

"So, if you weren't embarrassed, why'd you do a runner?" he asks, still hovering over the back of the couch, staring down at me.

My jaw drops open, then snaps shut again. Nope. Not going there. I avert my gaze, avoiding his probing stare.

"Reagan," he says smoothly, "look at me."

I don't, choosing to ignore his request, until his hands wrap around my cheeks and he moves his head to the side. Right into my line of sight. Sighing, I stop acting like a child, letting our eyes lock and hold. "You don't want to know, so just let it go. Please?"

His eyes search my face for an uncomfortable moment, then he nods. "Okay, I'll let it go this time. Coffee?"

Relief has my lips lifting into a smile. "Please and thank you."

Rhett clatters around in my kitchen, already knowing where everything is. It feels good having him in my space. He fits in here. I think we were always supposed to be friends, just like Char and me. He seems to get me, and he can read me way too well for someone who only recently entered my life.

I'm lost in my thoughts when the couch dips beside me, and the smell of freshly brewed coffee fills my nostrils. I could get used to this.

Rhett

A PART OF ME IS DYING TO KNOW WHAT SHE REFUSES TO TELL me. But another part knows she's keeping it to herself for good reason. I know already that there's not much she won't say, so I can respect her wanting to keep this to herself.

Slinging my arm over the back of the couch behind her feels natural. Sitting here with her, drinking my morning coffee—which tastes better than the shitty coffee in my apartment—feels right. I've never felt so comfortable in a woman's home before.

Before I'm ready, my phone alarm goes off, letting me know I need to leave for work. I'm fully booked at the garage, otherwise I would have considered taking the morning off to chill with Reagan.

"That's me. I gotta roll," I tell her.

The smile that has been gracing her face for the last half hour drops slightly. "Oh, okay. Thanks for checking in."

I take her empty mug from her. "I'll make you another before I go," I say, taking our cups into the kitchen. After placing mine in her dishwasher, I snap a pod into her machine and make her a fresh cup.

"Here you go, beautiful." With a grin, I hand her the mug that says *Chaos Coordinator*. "This cup was made for you." I grin. "You need anything before I go?"

Looking up at me, she purses her lips. “Umm, my laptop? It’s on the kitchen bench.”

“You got it.” I retrieve her MacBook then, handing it to her, I press a kiss to the top of her head. “I’ll see you tomorrow,” I say over my shoulder as I head for the door.

Closing it behind me, I pause—why did I just kiss her head? That’s a boyfriend move, and I am not that kind of guy. I didn’t even think about it; I just did it.

It’s not a big deal though, right? I mean, it’s not like I kissed her on the mouth or anything.

Yeah, no big deal. I nod to myself. Right, no big deal.

Maybe if I tell myself that enough, I’ll start to believe it.

Chapter 7

Reagan

I SPEND THE DAY GOING THROUGH THE MOST RECENT LOT OF fact proposals from the Pink Bits website submission tool. Sometimes I get some good ones that come in, but it's mostly just crap people have made up or old wives' tales. I have to confirm every single one before I can then enter it into the database.

Before I know it, it's five in the afternoon and I've spent the whole day on my couch with my laptop. I made myself a coffee and a sandwich at some point and hobbled to the toilet a couple of times. But other than that, I haven't moved.

My foot is aching, and I need to get up and take more pain meds before it gets too bad. I'm shifting around, about to get up, when my phone chimes for the first time today.

It's my dad. I smile at his message.

DAD: Hey Pumpkin, I'll drop in with some takeout on my way home in an hour. Feel like anything in particular? You better be resting when I get there.

ME: Dim Sum, pretty please. Love you, Daddy.

Looking down at myself, I decide I should put on some clothes before he gets here. We're super close, but even we have boundaries. I don't ever want to see him in his underwear, so I'll give him the same courtesy.

I gingerly place my feet on the floor and slowly lift myself to standing. Putting most of my weight on my good foot, I slip my crutches under my arms and head towards the kitchen. My pain pills are sitting on the counter, and I pop two with a glass of water, then make my way to my bedroom.

Once I get there, I collapse on my bed. "Jesus," I pant. That was a mission. When I've caught my breath, I sit up. Pants. I need to find pants. And then I catch a whiff of myself. "Oh God." I gag. I realise I haven't had a shower in two days.

Yuck, yuck, yuck!

Shower. I need a shower. Wriggling until I'm at the edge of my bed, I get to my feet again. This time, I move towards my adjoining bathroom without my crutches. I make it two steps, then falter when I have to put weight on my bad foot. *Shit.*

Clutching the doorframe, I take a breath then hop into the room, each bounce making my boobs just about slap me in the face and my foot throb. Plonking down on the toilet, I realise I won't be able to get in the shower because I can't get my foot wet. The dressing isn't waterproof, and I probably wouldn't be able to stand under the spray unassisted anyway.

"Ugh," I groan in frustration. There is no freaking way I'm staying like this, though. So I slide to the floor, open the small cupboard door under my sink and grab a cloth, the extra bottle of body wash I have stashed away in there, and some feminine wipes.

Twenty gruelling minutes later, I'm as clean as I'm going to get without hopping in the actual shower. And I'm exhausted. Dear God, am I exhausted. You don't realise how much you use one bloody limb until you can't.

I grab the first pair of shorts I can find and slide them up my legs. And I do alright until I get to my arse, since I'm still on the floor. I'm wriggling around, hoisting my pants over my bubble butt, when I hear my front door swing open.

"Pumpkin, you in here?" my dad's voice echoes down the short hallway.

"Coming!" I call back, then roll onto my tummy and up to my knees. Snatching my crutches up, I hook them under my arms and trudge out to my lounge. "Hey, Daddy," I greet him and smile wide at the site of the big-arse bag of food he's bought me.

He sends me a nod as he makes his way to my kitchen. "Where's your coffee table?" he asks.

I can hear him pulling out plates and cutlery when I take my spot on the couch. "Umm, I broke it."

"You broke it? How?" he asks, coming in to sit by me

with two plates full of little buns and dumplings that smell incredible.

"Ah, well, if you must know, I dropped a hammer on it. I was thinking of changing things up in here anyway, so no biggy." I shrug.

He nods along before saying, "I see. And I'm assuming this is how you hurt yourself then? When you rang and said you wouldn't be coming to work this week because you'd hurt your foot, I thought maybe you'd tripped in those ridiculous high heels you insist on wearing and sprained it, or something like that."

I'd called HR on Monday morning to let them know I wouldn't be coming in and gave them very little explanation. I'm the boss's daughter; nobody questions me. Then I was super vague about it all when I spoke to Dad on Saturday night. I chose to avoid having the detailed conversation over the phone. He would have freaked and no doubt overreacted. I let him think what he wanted.

I shove a little ball of pork-and-chive heaven in my mouth and nod. "Uh-huh," I mumble through my mouthful of food.

Dad gives me the side-eye. "You going to tell me what happened?"

I finish chewing, then swallow. "You going to tell me why you're eating dinner with me and not Cruella de Vil this evening?"

He snorts. "Nice deflection. How about, I'll tell if you do?"

Popping another dumpling in my mouth, I consider

his offer. I chew slowly, assessing my father; he looks tired. The light that normally emanates from his steely blue eyes isn't there today. I don't like it. Narrowing my own, I finally say, "You go first."

With a tilt of his head, he concedes. "Okay, Susanna and I aren't getting along that well right now. I can't handle another conversation about flower arrangements for her daughter's wedding—that I'm paying for, mind you. Why is that, you ask? I asked it myself, and you know what she told me? She said it's because Marianna is as much my daughter as she is hers. Can you believe that shit? When I corrected her, she slapped me." He shakes his head. "Susanna's ex-husband makes more money than I do. So why isn't he paying for *his* daughter's goddamn wedding?"

I blink, and blink again. I was not expecting all that. My father's face is getting redder by the second, and I have zero clue what to say to him. I don't particularly like my stepsister, but I don't not like her either. I don't really know her. We were grown when our parents married, so it's not like we're a real family in that sense. I sure as hell don't think he should be paying for her wedding, but I don't think now is the time to agree with him. I need to calm him down, not rile him up more.

"So, Marianna is getting married?" That's the best I can come up with.

Dad sighs. "Apparently."

"Did she ask you to pay for it?" I wonder aloud.

"No. She's been at the house a lot, organising it with her mother, but I try to avoid them when they're in wedding mode." He sighs again, lifting one hand to cup his forehead and rub his temples with his pointer and thumb. "It's not that I don't like the girl. She's perfectly fine. And the money's not the issue either. It's just that I don't think it's my place to be paying for her wedding. Not when her own father is in a position to do it. I'd lose my shit if another man tried paying for yours," he says, looking directly into my eyes.

"Aww, thanks, Daddy. But don't hold your breath on that one. I may as well spray myself with man repellent for all the luck I have. Maybe you should just embrace this; it might be your only chance."

His eyes darken at my statement. "Don't start that shit with me again, Reagan. There is nothing wrong with you. You're fucking perfect. You hear me?"

My eyes prickle. He's always been my biggest supporter in everything that I do and especially in everything that I am. "Okay," I breathe, then straighten my spine. "There actually is someone I might be a little interested in. But I'm not sure. I think we'll just end up friends. And I'm okay with that, too."

The light that has been missing in his eyes since he arrived sparks to life. "Go on, who is he?"

I grin. "My neighbour, Rhett Jones. Don't get carried away, though. We only officially met over the weekend. He was here when I cut myself." I gesture down to the white dressing that covers half my foot. "He took real good care of me: drove me to the hospital, and even stayed when Psycho Reagan emerged."

"He stayed?" he asks, his shock reflected in his tone.

"He sounds like a keeper to me. If he can handle you when you're like *that*"—he cringes—"then he must be a good guy."

Rolling my eyes, I shove him. "Gee, thanks, Daddy."

Wrapping his arm around my shoulder, he pulls me into his side. "I'm glad he was here for you when you needed someone. I really do worry about you being alone so much, pumpkin." He squeezes me gently. "I promise not to get my hopes up if you promise to at least give this a try. Don't settle for friendship if you feel more for him."

I swallow hard, then nod. "Okay."

Chapter 8

Rhett

My fist raps against Reagan's front door all of three times before it swings open. A fresh-faced Reagan stands before me in a way-too-small Superman tee that—if I'm not mistaken—has a little cape attached to the back. My grin is instant.

"Morning, beautiful," I greet her.

She beams up at me. "Morning. I got up extra early to pee so you wouldn't catch me off guard again."

"You didn't have to do that. I don't mind waiting out here for you to do your girly shit."

She rolls her eyes. "That would just be rude. Besides, yesterday you clearly thought I'd been having some *me time*, and I didn't want you to think that again." She shrugs. "Anyway, I was awake. I just didn't lie there like a lush for the extra half hour like I did yesterday."

I reach out and scruff her hair up as I slide past her, then stride down the hallway. "Whatever. I prefer my version of events over yours." I continue through the lounge area to her kitchen and get to making our coffees and breakfast.

Instead of waiting for me on the couch, she hobbles in after me, sliding onto a high bar stool on the other side of the bench and resting her crutches beside her. She watches as I go straight to the cabinet that holds her mugs and examine them all before picking two for today.

"You like my collection?" she asks.

Looking over my shoulder, I grin at her. "It's impressive."

Her smile comes out and brightens the whole room. "Which ones did you decide on?"

I hold them up to show her. The one I got out for myself has a picture of a great white shark and says, *What doesn't kill you makes you stronger ... except sharks. Sharks will kill you.* And the one I chose for her has a little Yoda on it and the words, *Coffee I need or kill you I will.*

She grins at my choices. "Did you know you're more likely to be attacked by a cow than a shark?"

Her eyes sparkle as she speaks, and I fucking love how into all these random facts she is. "I did not know that. But I believe it, mostly because you couldn't pay me to set foot in the ocean. So that eliminates shark attacks completely for me."

Silence hits my back, and I turn around slowly to see why she's gone quiet. Her hand is covering her mouth, and I lean back against the bench behind me, then cross my arms and ankles. "What now?"

"Is it because you're afraid of the teeny tiny blue-ringed octopus?" She snorts, trying to hold back her laughter.

I roll my eyes. "No, it's all the other fucking huge shit in there that can—and would most definitely—eat me. I'm fucking delicious, don't you know?"

She erupts with laughter. Tears stream down her flushed cheeks as she attempts to calm herself and catch her breath, only for another round to take her under again. Then, I watch in slow motion as she tilts to the side and falls off her stool.

"Reagan!" I'm crouched at her side instantly. She's still laughing but rubbing her butt, too.

"I'm good!" she says quickly. "My arse took the brunt of it. Lucky I've got extra padding." She winks as I help her back up and onto the stool again.

"Jesus, woman, you need a crash helmet or something," I tell her, shaking my head and going back around the bench to start cooking our food. What I don't say is how sexy I think that extra padding is. Instead, I nudge her coffee over and eye her. "Try not to burn yourself."

"Funny," she mumbles and flips me the bird.

When I finish making our omelettes, I slide into the seat next to her. "*Bon appetit.*"

"You're quite the chef, aren't you? I wish we'd met a long time ago; I could have been using you for your culinary skills all this time." She sighs dramatically.

I shove a forkful of the cheesy eggs into my mouth, then watch her do the same, grinning at me as she chews.

"Sho goog," she says through a mouthful.

Shaking my head, I turn my attention to my plate and shovel in some more before I accidentally tell her just how cute I think she is.

My plate is empty before hers—not surprising, seeing as I fixated on my food to keep myself from doing or saying anything stupid. After rinsing off my plate, I drop it into the dishwasher along with a couple of cups and plates she has sitting on the side of the sink.

"You don't have to do that," she says, her eyes following my every movement.

"I don't mind. Keeps my hands busy."

She cocks her head to the side. Her loose hair falls over her shoulder, forming a blonde curtain. "Why do you need to keep your hands busy?"

Her plate is now empty, and I grab it, rinse it, and then place it in the dishwasher, too. "Dishwasher tablets?" I ask, glancing at her over my shoulder.

She licks her gorgeous lips, then points to the cupboard under the sink. "In there," she breathes and bites down on that full bottom lip.

Fuck me. *Is she trying to seduce me?* Because it's totally working. I want to walk over there, wrap my fingers in that mass of blonde, and tug her head back until she's staring up at me with those incredible eyes, then kiss the shit out of her.

I swallow hard and push my thoughts away. It's with superhuman strength that I keep myself in line and turn her dishwasher on. Leaning against the bench beside it, I slip my hands into my pockets. "Need me to change your dressing?"

She blinks a couple of times, then shifts her gaze to her foot. "Umm, yeah, if that's okay? You don't have to; I can ask—"

I hold my hand up, stopping her. "I'll do it. I don't mind." I smile reassuringly as I open another cabinet and retrieve the extra dressings the hospital gave her. I really just want to be able to touch her in a non-creepy way.

My attraction to her has grown exponentially over the last couple of days, and it's unnerving. What if I banged her and she wanted it to keep happening? That's not my thing. We live next door to each other; it would get awkward as fuck. I don't want that for us. So, I need to keep it in my pants and keep her as my friend.

The word *friend* feels strange—a chick as a friend. It's a foreign concept to me, but I'm willing to give it a shot. I like Reagan way too much to fuck things up between us.

Reagan

Rhett is an amazing cook. He made an omelette taste like a gourmet meal.

I can't stop smiling at him, even though he's currently changing the nasty dressing on my foot. Keeping my focus on him ensures that I don't look at my foot and risk seeing blood. Just thinking about what he's doing—touching that area voluntarily—makes me a little swoony. Not in a bad way, but in a "he's so amazing to be doing this for me" kind of way.

"There you go. All done. And you'll be pleased to know the skin has started knitting together, so you don't need to worry about seeing blood anymore."

I blink at him. "That was quick. Thank you."

He shrugs his wide, sculpted shoulders. "No problem. It's what I'm here for." He winks at me, and I swoon again.

This is ridiculous. I'm a puddle of goo and all he did was cook for me, make me coffee, and change my dressing. *Actually... having mushy feelings for him after doing all that is only natural, right?*

"You okay? There wasn't any blood; you shouldn't be feeling woozy ..." he says. The look in his eyes conveys his worry.

I shake my head in an attempt to clear it. "Yeah, no, I'm fine. I was just thinking, is all."

He raises a brow. "About what? You looked all spaced out."

My lips purse. Usually I have no issues sharing what's on my mind, but I think I'll freak him out if I tell him I'm having seriously swoony thoughts about him. I clear my throat. "Oh, you know, just normal stuff." I shrug. "I think I might be due to get my period in the next couple of days. I'm feeling hormonal."

His eyes widen. "Right, okay then. On that note, I've gotta be going." He glances at his watch. "I'll be late if I don't get on the road pretty soon."

At least I threw him off from my actual thought

process. "Okay, thanks for checking in. And feeding me, and the coffee, and company."

A lopsided grin tilts his lips, and I internally swoon again. He's so freaking sexy. And he's not even trying to be, which makes him even sexier.

"You are very welcome, Reagan. I'll see you tomorrow," he says as he stands. Then, he bends down and presses his lips to my forehead and walks away.

I sigh, watching his behind as he strolls out of my apartment.

He is beyond sexy. And that arse? I want to bite it. I'm an arse girl, always have been. And his is amazing.

I HEAR RHETT KNOCKING AND, UNLIKE YESTERDAY, I'M NOT waiting at the door for him to arrive. I'm still hobbling down the hallway on his tenth knock. "I'm coming. I'm coming!" I yell loud enough for him to hear me through the door.

Leaning on my now much prettier crutches, I swing the door open.

"Mornin', gorgeous," Rhett drawls, propped against the door frame.

I smile up at him. I love how much taller he is than me. "Morning. Like the modifications I made to my ugly crutches?" I ask, tilting them back and forth so he can get the whole effect of the pretty sparkles glinting in the light.

His eyes move down my body, inch by inch, then they

slide over to my crutches. "What the fuck?" he asks, a frown forming between his brows.

I grin. "I was bored last night. So, I bedazzled them!"

"I see," he says softly.

"Do you like them? I mean, I know they're still butt-ugly, but they look better, right?"

I can't describe the look on his face. It's not pained. Maybe it's indifferent? I'm not sure.

"Well, I don't *not* like them," he finally says.

Meh, I don't really care if he likes them or not. I think they look way better, and that's all that matters. I shrug, shuffle out of his way, and let him pass me.

"What I do like are those PJs," he says as he squeezes past me.

I look down and see the lightning bolt stretched across my chest. "Me too. You like The Flash?"

"I'm more of a Batman guy myself, but I can see the appeal of being Flash fast on occasion. I have always wondered, though, is he able to pace himself at times? Like when he gets excited?" He pauses and turns to eye me. "You know what I'm sayin'? Does he, like, lose control and fuck Flash fast? 'Cause that would suck."

In all honesty, it's something I've contemplated myself. "I've thought about that, too. I would hope not, but who can say?" I shrug. "Makes no difference to me; he's not my type."

Rhett tilts his chin. "He's not?"

I shake my head. "No. Speed isn't an attribute I'm looking for in a potential bedmate." I laugh at his perplexed expression.

His Adam's apple bobs as he swallows. "So, what are you looking for?"

That's a great question—one I'm not sure how to answer. My lips pinch as I consider it. What am I looking for? *Him!* my sex-deprived brain screams. Then my daddy's words echo in my head: "*Don't settle for friendship if you feel more for him.*"

I'm ninety-nine percent sure I want more from him. So, I mentally pull up my big girl panties and tell him the truth. "Well, if I'm being honest, you're my type. Physically, for sure. And from the little I know of you, you tick all the boxes in the personality department, too."

I watch him carefully. He doesn't say anything, and I worry I've overstepped. "I'm sorry, I didn't mean—"

"No, it's fine. I'm a sexy beast. I know it, and you have eyes, so you know it, too." He winks.

"Umm, okay. Well, that right there." I point at his mouth. "What just came out of there—not an attractive quality in any man. Even one as sexy as you."

He grins. "Noted. Now, I need caffeine."

And that's the end of the conversation.

He strides into the kitchen and is pulling things out of the fridge by the time I make it to the counter and take my seat to watch him weave his culinary magic. I could watch him move around my kitchen all day long. A grin tugs at my lips as I imagine him doing just that—but naked.

It's Thursday, and I've adjusted to this little routine Rhett and I have going. I wake up at six, pee, and then make my way to my front door right in time for him to start knocking. I swing it open the second his knuckles connect with the wood.

He's leaning on the actual door this morning and tips forward, losing his balance. He tries to grab at the doorframe to stop us from colliding, but it's no use. His heavy body falls into mine, and I topple backwards. Rhett curls his arms around me, one at my waist, one behind my head, and we hit the ground with a thud.

All the air leaves my lungs in a rush. I swallow and try desperately to take a breath, but it doesn't work. He's still pressed flat against my chest, making inhalation impossible. My eyes widen as I struggle, and I start slapping at his back to get him to move.

"Fuck, Reagan. I'm sorry," he rambles, pushing his upper body up with his arms braced on either side of my head.

Relieved, I relish the air rushing back into my oxygen-deprived lungs. He's staring down at me now, and I can only imagine what's going through his mind. His eyes hint to a million different thoughts—all of them tantalising. But he just stays there, frozen.

Slowly lifting my hand, I press it to his jaw. My fingers feather over his stubbled cheek, and he closes his eyes. When my thumb grazes his bottom lip, they flash open again—the heat in them just about burns me alive. I want him to kiss me so, so badly. "Rhett," I sigh his name, and he leans into my touch.

His hot breath skitters along my wrist, sending tingles up my arm. Our eyes remain connected as he lowers his head, closing the gap between our mouths. He pauses a whisper away from my aching lips. "Reagan," he groans my name, then finally his mouth crashes into mine.

The feel of his lips is intoxicating... and right. So, so right. But it's not enough. I need more, but he pulls his head back when I try to deepen the kiss.

"I don't do girlfriends. I don't date. I don't hang out. That's just not me, Reagan. But I want you so much," he confesses.

My stupid emotions rise to the surface. I am not a fuck-buddy kind of girl. It's just not who I am. But that's all he wants. I can see he's holding back; there's something he's not saying. He knows I want all the things he doesn't. My eyes sting, and I squeeze them shut. I don't want him to see that his words have hurt me.

He's been so amazingly sweet to me, and there's no reason we can't be friends. Keeping my eyes closed, I push my palms against his chest, letting him know I want him to move. He does so immediately, then takes one of my hands in his and helps me stand.

I lean against the wall as he scoops up my crutches and slides them under my arms. I'm thankful when he turns away from me, closes the door that's still wide open, and then makes his way down the short hallway.

But he pauses at the end. Keeping his back to me, he says, "You are the coolest chick I've ever met. If anyone could make me want to change my ways, Reagan, it's you.

Maybe one day, but I'm not there yet, and I refuse to give you less than you deserve."

Then he's gone.

Dropping my head back, I stare up at the ceiling. Of course I would find an amazing, sexy, funny, and sweet guy who can handle me at my worst, but he doesn't want me the way I want him. I take a few minutes to collect myself. *He didn't say never, right?* And we haven't known each other long. Maybe I just need to let things unfold on their own.

Nodding to myself, I push off the wall and go to find him.

I find him in the kitchen with two mugs of coffee already made and a perplexed expression on his handsome face as he leans back against the bench. His hands are shoved in his pockets, and his ankles are crossed.

He lifts his head when I enter. "I'm sorry," he murmurs. His eyes lock with mine.

I shake my head. "Don't be. You were honest with me. I can't fault you for that."

He snakes one big hand up around the back of his neck, rubbing it. "Yeah, but I just ..." He sighs and looks back down to his boots.

"Hey, it's all good. I promise. I know where you stand, and that's okay. As long as you know where I stand, too," I tell him.

His eyes lift to mine. "Where exactly do you stand? Just so there's no confusion going forward for either of us."

My lips lift in a shy smile, and I shrug. "I like you. I'm comfortable around you, and I don't feel so awkward and out of place when I'm with you. So, yeah, I would like to see if there's more there. But I'm not going to push you for something you're not willing to give. I'm fine with friendship if that's all you want."

Rhett watches me closely as I speak, nodding along. "Friendship is good. I've never really been friends with a chick, but I'd really like to try with you. I mean, we're friends already, aren't we?"

I can't contain my grin. "Yeah, I think so."

"Okay, good." A relieved smile tugs at his lips. "Now that that's out of the way, let's get some food into you."

Pulling out the stool I sat on yesterday, I hop onto it and rest my chin in my hand as I watch Rhett buzz around my kitchen, smiling to myself.

"What's that look about?" he asks over his shoulder, not stopping what he's doing.

"Just because you don't want me doesn't mean I can't still admire the view," I tell him, grinning when he drops the spatula he was holding.

Spinning around, he glares at me. "So this is how it's going to be, is it? You can check out the goods, but I can't?"

I roll my eyes. "Pfft, like you can keep your eyes to yourself, you perv. You couldn't help yourself if you tried—you're staring at my tits right now."

His eyes bounce back up to mine. "You're not wearing a bra! And what the fuck are you wearing? Are they Powerpuff Girls?"

Grinning, I nod. "Yeah, they are! Powerpuff Girls are

awesome. And you know how I feel about bras. This isn't a new development. I'm not going to start wearing one now just because you don't have any self-control."

He sighs and presses a hand to his heart. "Thank God. I was worried you'd start dressing like a nun."

I laugh. "Yeah, no. That's not going to happen… ever."

"Good." He smirks and turns back to the stove, preparing our breakfast.

Chapter 9

Rhett

I've been thinking about her all day. So much so that I almost stuffed up an oil change. And you have to be pretty fucking stupid to stuff that up. I've never been interested enough in a chick to care what she was doing through the day. Now, I'm kicking myself for not getting Reagan's number so I could text her to check in.

I almost went back home on my lunch break just to check up on her—almost. How fucking pathetic is that? What? I can't go a full day without seeing her? I can't be pussy whipped. To be that, we'd have to have had sex. And we haven't.

It feels like I've known her a hell of a lot longer than a couple of days. Besides my sister, she's the first chick I've actually spent time around. And the thought of spending more time with her makes my heart beat faster with anticipation.

What the fuck is wrong with me? I'm turning into

Simon. That pansy-arse bastard; he's gone and rubbed his lovesick-puppy shit all over me.

I scowl at my reflection in the steam-fogged mirror. *Snap out of it, dickhead. She's your friend.*

Drying myself off, my thoughts inevitably wander back to her and her reaction to my dick the day we met. My lips tug up in a smile. God, she is something else. And there I go again, thinking of her all fondly and shit.

I wasn't lying this morning when I told her if anyone could make me want to try for more, it would be her. She's smart, funny as shit, and so fucking sexy in that nerdy way that makes her not just sexy, but adorable, too. I've got half a chub just thinking about her.

Closing my eyes, I can almost smell the floral scent that coats her soft skin. I inhale deeply; I want her. And it's not just because she's hot. I knew she was before we actually met. We'd passed each other in the hallways before and shared the elevator a few times. I didn't start wanting her until I started getting to know her.

She's gotten under my skin in just a few short days, and I don't know if I want to shake her off or tie myself to her.

Scrubbing my hand through my hair, I glare at myself again. I've never been so confused. I throw my towel on the rack to dry and stalk into my bedroom. After collapsing on the bed, I lie there, thinking about her on the other side of the wall until I fall asleep.

I'm not a morning person. So the fact that I've gotten out of bed the second my alarm has sounded every morning this week says a lot. Especially since it's set an hour earlier than usual so I can spend time with Reagan —I mean, check in on her.

I snort at myself. I think it's time to admit I'm not doing this for her benefit but my own. She puts me in a good mood for the rest of the day. I haven't thrown a spanner at my worker, Jake, all week.

Leaning over the small sink in my bathroom, I fill my hands with warm water and scrub at my face, then reach for my toothbrush and paste. I give my teeth a good once-over, then go into my spare room to rummage through my clothes. Finding a set of work gear, I throw them on, then slip my feet into my boots before walking out the door.

At six a.m. on the dot, I'm knocking at Reagan's door.

She opens it slowly, cautiously poking her head around, before opening it fully for me.

I frown down at her. "What's wrong?"

"Nothing, was just making sure we didn't have a repeat of yesterday. You know, when you fell through the door and nearly killed me." She smiles at me.

I have to force my hands to stay at my sides. That damn smile—it gets me every time. Clearing my throat, I push past her. "That's not exactly how I remember it. It was more like you couldn't wait to see me and threw the door open, knowing I would fall right into you. It was all a ploy for your dirty little hands to rub up on me."

She scoffs as she closes the door and hobbles along after me. "I don't think so. You're the one who can't keep your eyes off my tits. I think you positioned yourself just right so that you would fall into me, thereby giving you the perfect excuse to cop a feel."

I throw back my head, laughing as I open her fridge. "Yeah, okay, whatever you need to tell yourself. Now, let's see what we have to work with today." I scan the contents of her fridge and frown. She needs groceries. "You need to go shopping; your stocks are seriously depleted."

"That's your fault. You eat like a horse," she says from her spot on the bar stool.

True. I should probably get her some stuff to replace what I've eaten. "I'll take you tomorrow and go you halves."

"Okay."

"You've still got cheese and bread; how do you feel about grilled cheese for breakfast?"

"I'm good with whatever you put in my mouth," she chirps.

I straighten and stare at her. Does she even realise what she just said? One of my brows raises. "Whatever I put in your mouth? You're so dirty!"

She rolls her eyes. "*You* have a dirty mind. You know what I meant."

"I'm beginning to think you do this shit on purpose," I tell her, and the look of mock innocence that blankets her face gives her away. "You're such a bad liar."

Unable to contain her laughter any longer, she erupts. "Yeah, okay. You got me. But I don't mean things to sound that way when I say them. I usually only realise it after the words have left my mouth." She shrugs. "I don't really care though; I crack myself up."

"I bet you do." I shake my head at her, turn back to the kitchen, and start making our breakfast.

"How'd you get to be so comfortable in all your naked glory?"

I stop buttering the bread and look at her over my shoulder. "I don't know. I've just never been a shy kind of guy. Where the hell did that question come from anyway?"

"I was just staring at your butt, and Saturday morning popped into my mind. I'm kicking myself for not paying attention to it when you weren't wearing any pants." She sighs, her regret evident.

I swallow, my mouth suddenly feeling way too dry. I snatch a glass out of the cabinet, fill it with water, and down it. She's being her playful self. Nothing has changed between us, and I'm both relieved by the fact and a little frustrated. I mean, I don't want her to change, but it's her chill, "anything goes" personality that I'm attracted to. She's not making this easy on me.

Snapping myself out of my thoughts, I reply, "Right, well you had your chance. It was a one-time show. Not my fault you were so preoccupied with my cock you forgot to check out the buns, too."

A devilish grin spreads across her mouth. "It was hard to look past." She shrugs. "What can I say? It was just right there, you know? And it's very impressive. I was a little afraid of it for a minute, but something that perfect can't be scary. I wish you'd tell me his name. I don't like thinking of him as an inanimate object."

Stupid me for thinking this conversation couldn't get worse. She thinks about my dick. And damn, if that doesn't make him happy. He's paying attention now, listening to every word out of her devious little mouth.

"I'll tell you his name, if you tell me *her* name. Fair is fair." I dip my head down and gesture to her promised land with my chin.

She shrugs. "Okay. Her name is Mary."

My brows pucker in a deep frown. "As in, the Virgin Mary?"

"Ugh, no," she says, shaking her head adamantly. "As in, Mary, Queen of Scots."

"I don't get it."

She clenches her jaw, puckers her lips, and averts her eyes.

"Reagan, what aren't you telling me?" I prod.

A guttural groan fills the space, and I laugh at her dramatics.

"Fine! I'll tell you. Okay, so my first was a guy named Scot. It was super awful and awkward—as is every important moment in my life. Anyway, prior to this exchange with Scot, her name was Mary. Just Mary. Afterwards, she became Mary, Queen of Scots. Then, as it happens, the next two men I slept with were also named Scott."

"Seriously? Was that by design? Or ... " I'm really fucking curious now.

Leaning her elbows on the bench, she rests her chin in

her hands. "Not really. Not *my* design, anyway. But Char thought it would be hilarious, and seeing as she's like my only friend, she made it her mission to set me up with guys called Scott after I told her about Mary's name evolution."

I'm laughing so hard I have to support myself against the bench. "That is fantastic. I think I need to meet this friend of yours."

Lifting both her shoulders, her face remains expressionless. "She's just as strange as me. No, actually, she's worse. Much worse. Just so you know."

I grin. "She sounds like a good time."

She grumbles something to herself, then suddenly perks up. "Your turn!"

"Alright, alright." I take a deep breath. "Prepare yourself. It's pretty epic."

Her eyes glitter, and she shuffles to the edge of her stool, leaning farther forward on her elbows. "I'm ready. Tell me."

"His name is Prince Everhard of the Netherlands," I announce proudly.

It takes a solid five seconds for her to react. She blinks once, then twice, then her forehead hits the counter, and her whole body quakes with laughter.

My chest deflates. "It's a good name, dammit. I don't know why you're laughing."

I get no response this time. She completely ignores me as she gasps for air through her fits of laughter. I roll my eyes, then move about the kitchen, making our coffees.

Ten minutes later, she's wiping tears from her cheeks

and grinning at me like the fucking Cheshire Cat. I glare back as I slide her mug of steaming coffee over to her. "I picked this mug just for you."

The cup I gave her has a picture of a cartoon uterus holding up a sign that reads, *Stay Nasty*. How fitting for the little creature sitting across from me.

She just shrugs and takes a sip of coffee. Dried tear streaks stick to her pink cheeks, and her eyes shine the brightest blue I've seen them yet. Why does she always have to look so damn appealing? It's frustrating as fuck. I run a hand through my hair, then snatch up the plates with our grilled cheese on them. "You're a killjoy, you know that?"

Her lips tug to the side. "Prince Everhard," she snorts, then composes her features by taking a deep breath. "That's the best name for a penis I've ever heard. Seriously, you were right, and I wasn't prepared."

I nod, satisfied. "Damn right it is."

Just as I'm about to leave for work, I remember to ask for Reagan's number. I enter her name as Queen of Scots in my phone, then put mine in hers as Prince Everhard.

Chapter 10

Reagan

It's been exactly one week since I had a real shower. The thought makes me cringe. I showered before bed last Friday night, and that was the last time. I can't begin to express how much that disturbs me. I think I should be able to handle one now since my foot is feeling a little better.

I strip off my clothes and hobble into my bathroom. Leaning in, I reach for the tap when the distinct sound of knocking reaches my ears. I drop my head back. *You have got to be kidding me.*

Twisting around, I wobble my way back out, pausing to snatch my silky bathrobe off the back of my bedroom door. I wrangle it into place while balancing precariously on my crutches.

The knocking continues.

"I'm coming!" I yell down the hall, frustrated by

whoever is standing between me and my first shower in seven days.

When I reach the door, I tug it open with more force than necessary, causing the flimsy knot I tied in my robe to unravel with my jerky movements. Before I can do anything about it, Rhett's big hands are tugging the two sides back together for me.

"Holy shit," he breathes.

I watch his Adam's apple bob as he swallows hard. Then, keeping one hand curled tightly around the two sides of my robe, he reaches blindly for the ties with his free hand. Once he has both pieces, he ties them together so tight I know it's going to take me forever to untie them.

Only when he's satisfied that I'm fully covered does he speak. "Jesus, Reagan, what the hell? You can't answer your door like that. What if I was an axe murderer looking for my next victim?"

My eyes narrow on him. "If you were an axe murderer, I'd take you down with a swift crutch to the crotch," I shoot back. "And I didn't mean to answer the door like that. My robe was tied; it just came undone when I pulled the door open. I wasn't expecting anyone, and I was about to take a shower."

"A crutch to the crotch, huh?" He smiles.

I nod. "Yes. I may be incapacitated right now, but I still know how to protect myself."

One of his hands rises to the back of his neck, rubbing it as he looks down at me. "Okay, well, sorry for interrupting you. I just... ah... I was just wondering if you wanted to eat with me tonight? We could get takeout?"

He's looking at his boots when he says, "It's cool if you're sick of me, though."

My grin is instant. "I'd like that."

His eyes rise, meeting mine. "Great, good."

I shift to let him in, then close the door behind him. I follow him back to the lounge but hover by the hallway to my room. "I'm just going to shower. I'm dying to feel the hot water against my skin. It's been too long. You go ahead and order whatever, and I'll be out in a bit."

He nods. "Okay, cool."

My shower is the best. I have a sunken bath with the most amazing shower head above. I turn the water on, then slip my robe off. Leaning my crutches against the sink, I hold onto the wall and stare into the tub.

How the hell am I going to get down there?

Using the wall to keep my balance, I slide down until I'm on my butt, then slip my legs into the tub. Putting most of my weight on my good foot, I edge towards the hot spray of the water, sighing when it hits my body.

It feels incredible. I stand, absorbing the warmth and letting the shower head work its magic on my sore muscles. Getting around on crutches all week has got me aching in places I hadn't expected.

Tipping my head back, I close my eyes and let the water run over my face and down my body. My hair feels so nasty after using nothing but dry-shampoo for the last few days. Reaching for my shampoo, I squirt a huge dollop into my palm and bring it to the top of my head. My fingers get to work spreading and massaging it in when a stray glop slides down my forehead and into my eyeball.

Dear God, it burns! I squeal and rub at my eye, forgetting my hands are covered in the stuff.

"Shiiiittttttt!" I scream. *Too much; I used too much.* Tears are streaming down my cheeks when I try to pry my eye open under the shower spray to wash it out.

The bathroom door flies open with a bang, startling me so much I jump. The tub floor is slippery as shit from all the shampoo, so down I go in a mass of flailing arms and legs.

"Fuck! Are you okay?" Rhett is saying from above me. His hair is wet and hanging in his eyes, droplets of water streaming over his head.

I blink up at him. "What?" I'm so confused. One minute I'm washing my hair, the next I'm horizontal with a fully clothed and very wet Rhett in the shower with me. "What happened?" I ask him, dazed. *Did I hit my head?* It hurts.

Lifting my hand to rub my forehead, my fingers meet suds. I close my eyes and shake my head slowly. Why do these things keep happening to me?

IF FULLY CLOTHED REAGAN IS HARD FOR ME TO RESIST, LET'S just say naked Reagan is almost impossible. It's the flash of pain in her eyes as she runs her fingers over her scalp that stops me from doing something stupid, like kissing her.

I swallow. Beautiful isn't a strong enough word to describe the woman splayed out before me. She is perfect. There is nothing I would change about her. Not one single thing.

Smiling down at her, I ask, "You think you can sit up now?" I'm careful not to let my eyes linger too long where they shouldn't.

She licks her wet lips. "Yeah, I think so."

Wrapping my hands around her bare shoulders, I help pull her into a sitting position. Her wet hair hangs around her, full of suds, and it dawns on me what must have happened. "You got shampoo in your eye?"

Biting down on her bottom lip, she nods then looks up at me. Her left eye is red and angry-looking. "Honey," I murmur, cupping her jaw in my palm. Her skin is slick and soapy, and I have to remind myself that she's hurt.

"Here," I say, "turn around." She brings her knees to her chest, and I take her shoulders in my hands again, then help spin her. "Close your eyes," I instruct as I gently tilt her chin back so her head is partially under the shower spray.

Moving so my legs are in the tub, I sit on the edge and run my hands through her hair, removing the shampoo. Once it's all out, I put some of her conditioner in my palm and spread it evenly through her long locks. Silky strands slide between my fingers and she sighs.

Her arms curl around her knees, and her head hangs

back, resting in my hands. It feels surreal sitting here, washing her hair. I've never done anything like this before. It strikes me that this moment feels more intimate than any other I've shared with a woman before.

Sex is about mutual satisfaction. But this... this is all about her. She's so vulnerable. Yet, here she is, giving me her trust. My chest constricts with emotions I don't know how to handle.

I clear my throat. "There you go. All done," I tell her, removing my hands from her head and getting out of the way. I find a stack of towels on a shelf in the corner, grab one for her, then help her out of the tub. When I'm sure she's stable, I release her and take a step away.

Turning my back, I tug my sopping shirt over my head and drop it on the floor, then I remove my wet jeans and kick them into the corner with my shirt. I hear her sharp intake of breath behind me, and my cock stiffens. I grit my teeth and yank a towel from the rack, wrap it around my waist, then stalk out of the room because, God, do I want to turn around and devour her.

Fifteen minutes later, I'm sitting on the couch, flicking through Reagan's Netflix list, when she emerges.

"Guess we're even now," she says as she sits next to me but doesn't get too close.

My eyes slide across to her, and my cheek ticks as I smirk. "You didn't need to go to all that trouble just to make us even, you know."

Her elbow shoots out and jabs me in the ribs. "You wish."

And just like that, we're back to normal.

Thank God, because I am not ready for whatever the fuck I was feeling in that bathroom.

Our dinner arrives a few minutes later, and we settle in on her couch, watching some ridiculous British TV series about a fictional royal family while stuffing our faces with pizza.

"Cyrus is a dodgy little prick," Reagan says, bringing me up to speed on who is who and what is going on.

I don't really care, but the animated look she gets on her face as she watches makes it all worth it. I nod along as she rattles on about a second son and a secretly good bodyguard pretending to be an arsehole.

I'm ashamed to say, by the third episode, I'm getting into it. It does help that Liz Hurley plays the queen. She is smokin'. But she's got nothing on the girl curled into my side right now. *Wait, when did that happen?*

At some point, Reagan ended up snuggled against me, her head resting against my chest, while my arm has found its way around her waist. My fingers trace up and down her side and she sighs, until I feel her body completely relax. Glancing down, I realise she's fallen asleep.

Hair falls across her face, and my fingers itch to touch it. So I do. I run the glossy blonde strands through my fingertips, then tuck some of it back behind her ear. Lifting her upper body, I try to slide out from beneath her, but she groans and locks her arms tightly around my chest and snuggles in deeper.

My eyes drift over the couch; it's wide enough for the both of us. *Fuck it.* I can't believe I'm doing it, even as my legs rise up to the cushions. I shuffle my body down to lie beside her. Through it all, she remains asleep and wrapped around me.

I close my eyes and inhale her scent; it's as sweet as she is. And that's my last thought as I drift off to sleep with Reagan in my arms.

Chapter 11

Reagan

SOMETHING IS POKING ME IN THE BUTT. SOMETHING HARD. I wriggle, trying to dislodge whatever it is, but it's no use.

My eyes pop open when I register the warm, solid chest pressed against my back. Turning my head, I come face-to-chest with Rhett. *Oh my God.* My gaze roves down our tangled bodies and widens when I see that the towel he was wearing while we were watching TV has fallen off through the night.

It's his penis poking my butt. His huge, beautiful penis. I wriggle again on instinct. I want to be closer to it. Then, his name pops into my mind—Prince Everhard of the Netherlands—and I nearly lose it. My hand flies up to cover my mouth in an attempt to stifle my laughter as my body shudders with it.

"Stop rubbing up on my cock, Reagan," Rhett grumbles in a deliciously husky tone.

It sends a shiver down my spine, and I squirm. "Sorry," I whisper.

"You will be if you don't stay fucking still," he says, all traces of sleep gone from his voice as his hands grip my hips. His fingertips dig into my flesh, and I love it.

I know he's telling me to stop, but I can't help it. The combination of his stern words, his hard grip on me, and his throbbing cock pressed so close to where I want it is too much. My hips wriggle against his hold all on their own.

"Reagan," he growls.

I'm so turned on right now it's unbearable. "I'm sorry," I say again, "I can't help it. You feel so good."

His breath comes out hot, hard, and fast against the back of my neck, and I swallow as his hands squeeze my hips harder.

"Fuck it," he says, then his lips press to my neck, sucking as he pulls my hips back into his hard-on with so much force I moan.

One of his hands snakes around to my centre, and he roughly shoves my underwear aside then slides his finger through my folds. My whole body shudders. "Oh God, yes."

"I tried, Reagan. I tried really fucking hard to keep my hands off you."

"I know," I pant as his finger presses inside me. "I'm sorry," I cry as my back arches into his touch.

"Stop me, Reagan. Stop me right now, and I'll go home and fuck my own fist until I come to thoughts of your sweet little pussy wrapped around my aching cock. Tell me to stop," he pleads against my throat.

But I can't. I want it too much. I want *him* too much.

His lips never leave my flesh for longer than a second. His finger pumps inside me in time with his hips pushing into me from behind, and my inner muscles tighten. One of my hands wraps around his wrist, keeping him in place, as my other glides up around his neck and locks in the hair at his nape.

He moans, "Fuck, honey, so tight and wet for me."

All I can do is nod as I'm overtaken by sensation. It starts deep inside—a sweet tingle that emanates outward until I'm shuddering and convulsing in his arms. "Rhett," I cry as my orgasm takes me away.

I'm floating down from the best climax I've ever had when his hand slides out of my pants and tugs them down my legs. He lifts my thigh, spreading me, then thrusts forward.

His knob touches my opening, and I shudder again. "Yes," I breathe, suddenly desperate to have all of him inside me. I push my hips back.

"Condom?" he asks.

"My room," I tell him.

Then, he's swooping me up in his strong arms and throwing me over his shoulder as he stalks towards my bedroom. I watch his gorgeous arse as he walks and grin like a fool with my knickers hanging around my ankles.

Rhett

I'm not thinking straight. I know I'm not, but how can I with her in my arms?

The second I'm close enough, I drop her to her bed. She bounces once, then shimmies her way up the mattress, losing her panties as she goes, her eyes never leaving mine.

"Top drawer," she says, using her chin to gesture to her bedside.

Yanking it open, I find a brand-new box and rip it apart. Her eyes sparkle as she watches me slide the condom down my shaft. She's practically glowing under my gaze. Climbing over her, I slide my hands under the hem of her top, pushing it up her perfect breasts then over her head.

My breath catches in my throat at the sight of the intricate vine tattooed around her torso. I hadn't seen it when she changed her top in front of me that first day, and I didn't take the time to examine it in the tub last night. But now, I'm mesmerised by it. Reaching out, I trace its path from her hip bone, up her ribs, around the underside of her breast, then to the point where it twists back and disappears at her side. Blue, purple, and yellow flowers sprout from the vine, some in bloom, some still just buds. It's delicate and beautiful.

"You like it?" she asks, drawing my attention back to her face.

"I fucking love it."

Her smile is blinding, and I have to kiss her. Not like the other day. No. I need to kiss her properly. Dropping down to my elbows, I hover a mere inch from her mouth. "I've wanted to do this since I first saw you standing in your doorway, clutching that hammer and wearing those frilly pink shorts."

"Really?" Her eyes shimmer with uncertainty.

I nod. "And the more time I spend with you, the harder it is to stop myself. But I can't stop this time, Reagan. I need to taste you like I need my next breath."

She swallows, then tips her chin up, offering me her mouth. I close the space, softly grazing my lips over hers once, twice, three times, then slide my tongue over her plump bottom lip. Her mouth parts on a breath, and I deepen the kiss.

Her fingers glide up my biceps, over my shoulders, up my neck, and over my scalp. I groan when her hands tighten into fists in my hair. She squirms beneath me, and our bodies align perfectly. Parting her legs further, she invites me in. And I don't hesitate, thrusting my hips forward until I'm buried balls deep in her warmth.

She whimpers, and I still.

"I'm sorry, honey. I should have gone slow," I murmur against her cheek, feeling like an arsehole for taking her so fast. I'm big and I know better than to ram in like that.

Surprising me, she shakes her head. "No, no, it's good. So good. Don't stop now."

I smile down at her. "You are somethin' else, Reagan."

She grins back. "A good something or a bad

something?" she asks, mimicking our conversation from earlier in the week.

"Definitely a good something," I assure her, then kiss the shit out of her.

She comes twice more before I can no longer hold my own orgasm in check. I throw my head back as I come harder than I have in all my life. Dropping to her side, I tug her over to me, wrapping my arm around her as we catch our breath.

"Did you know that coffee drinkers have sex more frequently than non-coffee drinkers?" she asks, her palm resting over my heart.

I kiss the top of her head, smiling. "And there she is—the chick who can find a random fact to complement any situation."

She laughs and snuggles in more closely. "It's a gift. Or a disability. I'm not sure which."

"A gift for sure, honey," I tell her, then slap her bare arse. "Come on. I'll help you shower, then we need to restock your fridge. There's nothing in there for breakfast."

An hour later, we've showered and had sex in the shower, then I ducked home to get fresh clothes, and Reagan is waiting for me in front of the elevator. I wrap my arm around her neck and kiss the top of her head. She smells so damn good. *Will I ever get sick of the way she smells?*

The elevator doors slide open, and I release her so she can hobble in on her crutches. "Where do you normally get your groceries?" she asks as we descend to the basement parking lot.

I shrug. "Wherever's closest when I realise I need them. Is there a particular store you want to go to?"

"No, I don't mind where we go. Seen one supermarket, seen them all." She smiles at me.

Nodding, I tell her, "I know of one a few blocks away; it'll do."

Pulling into a parking spot, I jump out of my ute and grin when my eyes land on a disability shopping cart. I go get it and bring it around to her side of the truck, looking at her expectantly.

She looks down at it and shakes her head. "Uh, no."

Frowning, I gesture to the padded seat in front of me. "Come on now, you don't really want to try getting through the whole shop on those crutches. You need a lot of stuff. We're going to be a while."

Her shoulders slump. "Fine," she grumbles, then holds her arms out for me to help her.

We're in the fresh produce section when she pipes up. "I can see the advantage of this contraption now."

Glancing down at her, I raise a brow at the cheeky glint in her eyes. "Oh yeah? What's that?"

"I'm at eye level with Prince Everhard. He and I can have a conversation while you do the groceries."

I choke on air. "Ah, what? You're insane, you know that?"

Now she raises a brow at me. "You're just figuring that out now? A little slow, aren't you?"

Rolling my eyes, I turn my attention back to the

vegetables, then grab some baby broccoli and asparagus to go with our breakfast when we get home. *Wait, home? Am I planning on going back to her place when we're done?*

Umm, fuck yes, I am. And that thought should produce fear in me. But for some bizarre reason, it doesn't. Having sex hasn't changed anything between us. Reagan's still her random self, and I don't have the urge to run as far away as possible.

Maybe we could work after all?

Reagan

"HELLO, EARTH TO REAGAN?" RHETT SNAPS HIS FINGERS IN front of my face, making me startle.

I glare at him. "What?"

He shakes his head, smirking at me. "I was asking what kind of ice cream you like? You were spaced out, staring at my dick."

Heat blooms in my cheeks. "Oh, umm, cookies and cream."

I was totally staring at his penis. Well, not like, directly at it. I'd have to open his pants to do that, and I'm pretty sure the other shoppers would not appreciate that. Not the male ones anyway; I've seen more than a few of my fellow female shoppers running their greedy little eyes over Rhett's magnificent assets.

I don't blame them. I used to look at him all the time when I'd pass him in the foyer of our building. Or when we'd share the elevator. I'm sure I looked like a total creeper, though, since discretion has never been my strong suit.

"You're doing it again," he says.

I roll my eyes. "So? What's your point?"

He snorts. "People are going to think you're a bit special—your eyes all glazed over, staring at my crotch. And I think there's a bit of drool just here," he says, running his thumb over my bottom lip. Using his pointer fingers, he tilts my head back then bends down and presses a kiss to my lips. "Lucky for you, I kinda like your brand of special," he whispers against my ear, then winks when he straightens and goes back to pushing the cart down the aisle.

My cheeks hurt from smiling so much. I'm a happy-go-lucky kind of person—I normally smile a lot—but this week I've broken a record. *Why didn't I just introduce myself to him when I moved into the building? Why?!*

After just one week, I'm already fully in like with him.

I bite my lip. *Slow down, Reagan. He made it clear where he stands on dating. You're setting yourself up for heartbreak.*

Rhett

Reagan has been unusually quiet since we got back in the truck. It's worrying me. "You okay? Your foot hurting?"

She shakes her head. "No, I'm okay. Tired, maybe. We stayed up pretty late, then we rose crazy early this morning. Plus, the exercise. I'm not used to that much physical activity," she says, smiling.

This smile lacks the punch that usually accompanies her true smiles. Something is bothering her. Should I push her to tell me or let it go?

Before I can decide, she says, "Did you know thirty thousand people are seriously injured from exercise equipment each year? True fact. Scary fact, if you ask me. That's the reason I have never set foot in a gym. No, sir. Not this little blonde duck."

I frown. "Blonde duck?"

She nods and shuffles around on the seat until her back's pressed to the door and she's facing me. "Yeah, you know the saying, '*not this little black duck*'? Well, I'm blonde, so duh."

"You're a crack-up. Have you ever considered a career in stand-up comedy?" I think she'd rock it. All she'd have to do is get up there and be herself. She'd be a hit.

Her nose scrunches adorably. "Umm, no. Have you seen the clothes those women wear? Not once have I seen a decently dressed stand-up act. Not once. If I even thought about wearing those kinds of clothes"—she pauses as a shudder runs over her—"Char would shoot me."

"That's a bit rough."

Reagan widens her eyes at me. "It's true. Think about it. Have you ever seen an attractive stand-up? It's like a job requirement to be dowdy. Or maybe it's what the job does to you? Like, they could have been perfectly good-looking, then they became comedians and boom."

I laugh at her antics. She's being completely serious right now, and that makes it even funnier. "And why would your friend want to shoot you for becoming average-looking?"

Her cheek lifts in a sneer. "That's if I didn't shoot myself first. I have standards, you know. And have you ever heard of Charlotte's Closet? It's the most popular fashion blog in the country. That's my Charlotte."

Now that I think about it, I do remember my sister going on about something like that. "Yeah, I think Piper follows it. But I'm not exactly a fashionista, in case you hadn't noticed."

Reagan's eyes roam over me. And just like that, the punch that was missing from her smile before is right back again. "You do just fine. You could wear a paper bag and you'd still be sex on a stick."

I burst out laughing. "What does that even mean?"

She grins. "I'll show you when we get back to the apartment."

My foot presses down a little harder on the accelerator.

Chapter 12

Reagan

The rest of Saturday was a blur of amazing sex, incredible orgasms, delicious food, and binge-watching Netflix. In other words, absolute perfection.

I squint as the sunlight peeks through my curtains. *It's morning already?* Lifting my hand, I rub the sleep from my eyes. It feels like we only just fell into bed. But as I focus on my alarm clock, I'm shocked that it's eleven a.m.

Reaching out, my hand slaps about on my bedside table until it comes into contact with my phone. Scooping it up, I swipe my finger across the screen when I see two missed calls from Char and a few texts from her and my dad, too.

I shoot Dad a quick reply, then open the first message from Char that reads:

CHARLOTTE: Bitch where are you? I called! I never call!

It's true; we aren't the phone call types unless it's an emergency—like my mini-meltdown earlier in the week. Her next message is a little more aggressive:

CHARLOTTE: Woman, you better be dead because I called TWICE!

And her third and most recent:

CHARLOTTE: Okay, I've had time to think it over, and I've decided you're dead to me. That's right. You just lost the best thing that ever happened to you. I hope you're happy.

Pfft, and she thinks I'm the dramatic one of the two of us. *Please.*

Rhett's arms squeeze my middle. "Why are you awake?"

My fingers are flying across the screen when I answer him. "Sun woke me up; it's after eleven. And Char is having a nervous breakdown because I haven't answered her calls."

He nuzzles his face in my neck and breathes deeply. "Okay, you deal with that. I'm going back to sleep. You wore me out, you little sex fiend." Then he presses his lips to my throat, and all of a sudden, I'm thinking about sex again.

I wriggle my arse against his morning wood. "Don't act like you don't like it."

"Never said I didn't." He chuckles, then moves his

head back up to rest on the pillow beside mine, keeping his arms wrapped securely around me.

Shaking my head, I drag my attention back to my phone.

ME: Settle down, psycho. I've been wrapped up in an orgasm-fest. I'll call you later.

Little dots appear immediately on my screen, signalling Char's imminent reply.

CHARLOTTE: You dirty little whore! I want details right damn now. You can't say orgasm-fest, then not share the deets.

ME: So your sexy-time sensors weren't as far off as I thought they were ...

CHARLOTTE: I KNEW IT! Tell me everything. Every filthy little detail. I need it all. You know how long it's been for me.

ME: Can't I just call you later? I'm in bed with him right now. He's sleeping next to me.

CHARLOTTE: I need photographic evidence.

Licking my lips, I lift my head to check if Rhett has fallen back to sleep or not yet. And yep, he's out. With sloth-like slowness, I lift my phone above us and snap a selfie, belatedly realising my phone isn't on silent. *Shit.*

"Did you just take a picture of me?" Rhett asks, his eyes still closed.

"Huh? Uh, no. What a weird thing to ask," I deflect.

"Then why did your phone just make the camera shutter sound?"

Shit! When in doubt, use half-truths to sound convincing. "I was taking a selfie... for Char."

"You just took a naked picture of yourself for your friend?" His eyes remain closed, and he doesn't sound phased by any of this.

"No. The sheet is covering all the important bits," I tell him.

"Can I see it?" he asks, then he's on top of me, pinning me beneath his big body, a wolfish grin covering his mouth, showing me his white teeth.

I squeal, "No! It's private!"

With everything I have, I fight him, trying to keep my phone out of his grasp. And with a pathetic amount of effort, he snatches it from me. Looking at the screen, he grins, taps it a few times, then hands it back to me. He rolls to the side, wraps his arm back around my waist, and makes himself comfortable again.

"What did you do?" I ask when I see there are no signs of vandalism on the picture staring back at me.

"I sent it to myself, then your friend, with the caption '*he has a huge cock*'."

I snort with laughter and check my sent messages.

Sure enough, the little dots in Char's message window are flashing away.

CHARLOTTE: You tease. You didn't need to be in it. And you could have moved the sheet down a few inches. I can tell he's hard under there, but an unobstructed view would be preferable.

Closing my eyes, I shake my head at my best friend. "She's as big a perv as you are. She's requesting a photo, sans sheet and me."

Rhett chuckles beside me. "Not happening; I don't do dick pics. And if I did, I wouldn't be sending them to your friend."

Rolling into his side, I kiss his cheek. "I'm glad to hear it. And just so you know, I wouldn't be opposed to receiving them," I whisper against his ear, then suck the lobe into my mouth.

His hands move down to my arse and drag me on top of him until I can feel him between my legs. I throw my phone over my shoulder and move my mouth back to his.

SHE IS INSATIABLE; IT'S FUCKING AWESOME.

We spent the whole weekend between her bed and the couch. Now, it's Monday morning, and the last thing I want to do is leave the warmth of her small body tucked into mine. But it's time to return to real life.

She's sleeping soundly, and I do my best not to disturb her as I slide out from behind her and collect my clothes off the floor. Tugging my jeans up, I head for the door.

"You going already?" Her husky sleep-filled voice hits my back.

Glancing at her over my shoulder, I'm struck by just how perfect she is. I can't go without kissing her one last time. Striding to her, I kneel on the side of the bed, brush her hair out of her face, and press my lips to hers. She's so sweet, so pliant under my touch, so perfect.

Her hands snake up into my hair, holding me to her. "Stay a little longer," she whispers.

God, do I want to.

Using her grip on my head, she lifts her upper body to mine, pressing her bare tits into my chest. Her nipples pebble, and my hand slides between us, plucking one between my fingertips. My decision is made; I can't leave without one more taste. I'm the fucking boss—if I want to come in late, I will.

Reagan's hands leave my hair. Digging her nails in, she scrapes them down my back, then slides them into my pants, squeezing my arse. She really does love my arse. I grin into her mouth. Then, she's tugging on my zipper and shoving my jeans down my thighs.

"You've turned me into a sex-crazed maniac." She chuckles when she can't get my pants off quick enough. She hooks her good foot into the fabric gathered at my knees and pushes, trying to force it down.

I lose my balance over her and topple off the side of the bed. She's on top of me in seconds, eyes alight with need. Her hand slaps around blindly on the bedside table, her gaze never leaving mine. She grins wickedly and produces a condom, holding it in two fingers between us.

Snatching it from her, I rip it open with my teeth, then slide it down my shaft. I'm so fucking hard; I'm aching to be inside her.

As soon as the condom is in place, she positions herself above me and lowers her sweet pussy onto my cock. My muscles clench as she takes her time sliding down until she's fully seated, then she rocks her hips back and forth.

My fingers sink into her flesh, and I jack knife up, sucking one of her nipples into my mouth. Her hands are back in my hair, gripping it in her tiny fists as she rides me. Nothing has ever felt better.

I move my mouth to her other nipple, and she moans. I suck harder, then let it pop from my mouth and bite down on her lush tit. It's going to mark her, and I love knowing she will be carrying the imprint of my teeth with her when we're apart.

Her movements lose their rhythm, she clenches around me, and I have to grit my teeth, holding back. I help her get there, moving her hips for her as I suck on her throat. Seconds later, she's shuddering, whimpering, and coming all over my cock, and I come with her.

We stay like that on her bedroom floor for I don't know how long, until Reagan tugs my head back by my hair. Her eyes sparkle like sapphires. She lightly runs her nose over mine, then her lips whisper over my cheeks.

"Are we okay?" she breathes across my parted lips.

I swallow. I knew this was coming. The talk. I have no fucking clue what to say. I can't remember ever being this happy, this comfortable with a chick, this content. "I think so," I tell her honestly. That's the best I can give her right now.

Resting her forehead against mine, she breathes, "Okay."

She doesn't seem angry or annoyed with my less-than-confident reply. I'm not sure if that's a good thing or a bad thing.

Striding into the shop an hour after opening, I ignore Jake and Taj's stares and go straight into the break room. I need more caffeine.

Jake follows me—the prick. "Where were you this morning, big man?"

I flip him off. "None of your fucking business."

The arrogant bastard grabs a chair, swings it around, and sits on it backwards, arms crossed over the top as he stares at me. "You've been in a good mood recently," he says, then raises a brow. "Who is she?"

I turn my back to him and go about making my coffee. "Don't know what you're talking about."

To make matters worse, the door swings open with a bang against the wall. "Where the fuck have you been?

Jessie had a meltdown yesterday because you weren't at the fucking rehearsal dinner." Simon is in my face, shoving at my chest.

I frown. *Rehearsal dinner?* "What are you talking about? The wedding isn't for two weeks."

His eyes are feral. "I told you we had to do the rehearsal dinner early because Jess was freaking out about the catering. Don't you listen to anything I say? You're supposed to be my best man, and where were you? Off fucking some bimbo?"

My fist launches into his jaw before I even know what I'm doing. *Shit!* "Simon! Fuck. I'm sorry, man. I didn't mean—"

"You son of a bitch," he yells, wrapping his hands around my throat.

I swing my arms up from below and break his apart, loosening his grip, then shove him away. "I said I was sorry."

He paces back and forth but says nothing, his fists clenching and unclenching at his sides.

Jake just sits there watching, not bothering to get in between us. Smart man. This isn't the first scuffle Simon and I have had in here, and no doubt, it won't be the last. He's my best friend. Who's going to pull us into line, if not each other?

Once Simon's calmed down, he straightens his shirt and runs his hands through his hair. "So, where were you? What was more important than being there for me?"

Rubbing the back of my neck, I look at my boots. "I

forgot. I'm sorry, man. I ah ..." I swallow. "I was with someone."

Simon balks. "Someone? That's it? That's all I get? You missed my rehearsal dinner, Rhett. I'm going to need more than that."

I don't know what this thing with Reagan is yet. I don't want to tell Simon about her. Hell, I have no idea what I would even say. *Oh, hey man, I completely forgot about your rehearsal dinner because I was screwing my trippy little neighbour girl all weekend. She's awesome, and funny, and fucking perfect.*

I'm not prepared to answer the inevitable questions that would come after that little confession. So, I lie to my best friend. "I fucked up. I'm sorry. It won't happen again. Whatever you need, man, I'll be there."

He narrows his eyes. "I don't believe you."

I shrug. "What do you want me to say?"

"I want you to tell me the truth. This isn't like you missing my mum's birthday party. This shit's important."

Cracking my neck, I fix my gaze on him. "Fine. Fuck. Okay, I was with my neighbour, Reagan. She hurt herself last weekend, and I've been helping her out."

Simon's brows raise. "You were ... helping her out?"

I nod. "Yeah." Dropping my eyes, I rub the back of my neck again. "It was kinda my fault she got hurt. So, I've been checking in on her, making sure she's getting on alright. And we ended up spending the weekend together."

Tilting his head, he sizes me up. "You've been checking in on her and spent the weekend with her?"

Then his face splits with a grin. "You like her. After all these years, you've finally found a woman."

My head is shaking, and I can't stop it. "She's just a cool chick, is all. It's not a big deal."

He smirks. "It's a huge fucking deal. So, are you bringing her to the wedding?"

What the fuck? Where did that even come from? I stare at him like he's lost his damn mind.

"What? You think I'm going to let you screw this up? Oh no, my friend. I'm going to make sure this chick hangs around. You've already put in more time with her than any other woman you've ever met. You checked in on her all week and spent the weekend with her; you've got it bad." He claps me on the shoulder and heads for the door.

He's gone before I can get my thoughts in order, and Jake is grinning like a fool. "Don't you have a job to do?" I snap at him, then snatch my coffee off the sink, spilling it over my hand as I storm out to the work bays.

Chapter 13

Reagan

I GOT A FEW CURIOUS STARES AS I HOBBLED AROUND THE Pink Bits offices on my bedazzled crutches. But I had way too much on my plate to worry about funny looks. An issue had come up over the weekend with the submission tool on the website, so I was busy dealing with that all day.

By the time I get home, I just want to curl up and sleep for a week. Rhett and I didn't sleep nearly enough over the weekend, and now I'm really feeling it.

Sinking onto the couch, I drop my crutches and bag on the floor then snuggle into one of my many throw pillows. It doesn't take long for sleep to take me.

I wake with a start. My phone is ringing loudly in my bag, and I reach for it, rolling off the couch in the process. My face breaks my fall with a thud. *Ow.* I rub my sore cheek and pull my phone out. "Hello."

"Hi. Listen, you don't know me. My name is Simon. I'm Rhett's best friend."

The mention of Rhett has me jerking upright, and my head spins from the rapid movement. "Is he okay?"

"Oh, yeah, no, he's fine, he's fine. Look, I'm just calling to invite you to my wedding. It's next Saturday. I know what Rhett's like at remembering shit and figured I'd just call and ask you myself."

Holding my smarting cheek, I pull my phone away from my ear to stare at the screen. Am I awake right now, or is this a weird dream? Placing it back against my face, I ask, "How did you get my number?"

The man on the other end chuckles. "I had to be resourceful. When Rhett mentioned you this morning, I went back to his apartment building and checked the name registry. I knew you were his neighbour, and that your name is Reagan, so I just needed your last name, Miss Moore, then I was able to Google your number."

I scrunch my face up. *That's a lot of effort to get my number.* "Okay, that's kinda creepy, but I guess it sort of makes sense. I still don't understand why you're inviting me to your wedding, though."

He sighs. "Rhett is going to do something to screw things up with you. I've known him my whole life. And not since we were seniors in high school has he spent more than a single night with a woman. But he said he was with you all weekend. You have to realise what a big deal that is."

Rhett's words from Thursday morning run through my head: *I don't do girlfriends. I don't date. I don't hang out.*

That's just not me, Reagan. My eyes sting because I can't help but hope our time together means as much to him as it does to me. But I have to be realistic. "I'm not trying to make him something he's not," I tell his friend. "If he wants me to come to your wedding, he can ask me himself."

"I guess I can respect that," Simon mutters. "Just ... can you do something for me, please?"

I lick my dry lips. "Maybe. Depends what it is."

"Whatever he does next, don't take it to heart. He has hang-ups that he needs to work through. Can you just—I don't know—keep that in mind for me?"

I'm nodding, then I realise he can't see me. "Yeah, I can do that."

"Thanks. I'm really looking forward to meeting you, Reagan," Simon says, and he sounds genuine.

"Umm, thanks?"

He chuckles. "Okay, well, I'll be seeing you. Hopefully." Then he hangs up.

Well, that was strange and unexpected. Getting off the floor, I make my way to my bedroom, too tired and confused by that phone call to even bother having a shower. I strip off and crawl into bed.

The next time I wake, it's to sunlight streaming through my curtains. I roll out of bed and shuffle to the shower.

I half expect Rhett to show up for breakfast, but he doesn't. I wait an extra half hour before finally making my morning coffee. He isn't coming.

We didn't make any plans yesterday morning after we

parted ways. Maybe that was his way of ending things. But why get my number if he was just going to drop out of my life two days later?

My traitorous emotions get the better of me, and my eyes prickle right before a few tears escape. I sniffle and scrub them away—I refuse to cry about this. We had a really good time together. I won't regret it. I won't. Even if I wish it wasn't over.

I WANTED TO GO TO HER LAST NIGHT. BUT I DIDN'T.

Instead, I went to the pub and ended up nursing the same beer for two hours before I slid it back across the bar and left. I didn't go home, though. I couldn't.

My sister's couch is nowhere near as comfortable as Reagan's. And her coffee mugs are boring as shit. I scowl down at the plain purple mug in my hands, wishing it had some smart-arse quote on it.

"Okay, I let you sleep on my couch, and I didn't ask any questions. But now I want answers. You're even more grumpy than you usually are in the mornings. What's going on?" Piper asks, standing on the other side of her kitchen table, hands on her hips, presumably waiting for me to spill my guts.

Averting my gaze from her expectant glare, I look out the kitchen window. "Nothing. My air conditioner is broken. I just needed somewhere to crash that wasn't a sauna. I'll get it fixed this week."

She says nothing, but I hear the distinct sound of her tapping her foot against the floorboards. Glancing back at her, I know she's not buying my story, even though it's partially true.

I sigh. "Okay, I'm avoiding my neighbour. Don't worry, it'll blow over in a day or two, and I'll be out of your hair."

She cocks a brow. Her electric-blue-streaked hair falls around her shoulders as she leans over the table, bracing her hands on it. "You're a shit liar. That's why you always got busted when you pulled stupid pranks as a kid, and I got away with murder."

Jesus Christ. Why can't I just figure this shit out on my own without everyone trying to make me talk it out?

I scrub the back of my neck and stare into my coffee. "We might have hooked up over the weekend, and now I just need a bit of space. It's not a big deal, Piper. Let it go."

Piper's jaw drops. "Since when do you actively avoid hook-ups? You've never had a problem telling women it was a one-time deal. What's different about this one?" she asks, dragging the chair opposite me out from under the table and taking a seat.

"She's different. It didn't start as a hook-up. We hung out a few times, and it progressed." I shrug. "Now I don't know what to fucking do."

My little sister blinks at me dumbly. "You go with it, you moron. I haven't seen you interested in anyone since Meghan cheated on you in high school. That was ten years ago, Rhett. That's a long time to let one person dictate your life."

I know she's right. What happened with Meghan really screwed me up. I thought I loved her. I saw it all in my head: we'd get married, I'd finish my apprenticeship and open my own garage, then we'd have a couple of kids.

Yeah, I was that guy. I was Simon. All full of hope and big dreams for the future. Then, I walked in on Meghan blowing my fellow teammate, and it all went up in flames. I haven't pictured a future involving another woman since.

After that, I ploughed through women like I was born to do it, making up for the two years I had been faithful to Meghan. Well, I went through as many as would take me, that is. The amount who saw the size of my junk and offered me a handy or blowjob instead is ridiculous.

"Rhett." Piper's quiet voice pulls my attention back to her.

"What?"

"Meghan was a mole. End of story. But you've been letting her determine the outcome of your life for far too long. She's in your past, but you've been carrying her around all this time. What's this new girl like? Tell me about her."

The shadow that creeps in when I think of what Meghan put me through is superseded by the light I feel whenever I'm around Reagan.

"She's funny, even though she doesn't always mean to be. She's really accident-prone. In just a few days, she stepped on two shards of glass, tripped on her own feet, and fell off a bar stool." I shake my head thinking of her.

"She's easy-going and super chill, has a vendetta against bras, and lacks a filter."

Piper smiles. "She sounds pretty awesome to me. What's her name?"

"Reagan." Just saying her name out loud makes me miss her even more. It's a foreign feeling for me. Actually, everything I feel about her is foreign to me. I really don't like it.

After Meghan, I promised myself I would never allow my happiness to be reliant on another person. And look at me now; I'm miserable, and it's only been twenty-four hours since I was with Reagan.

My head throbs. I don't want to think about this anymore. I simply want to go back to the way things have always been. It's safe, satisfying, and headache free.

Piper's warm hand curls around my wrist. "Why are you fighting it? You obviously like her, and the look in your eyes when you talk about her tells me everything I need to know. I think you should see where this goes, Rhett. Give her a chance."

I swallow past the lump in the base of my throat. "I'll think about it." Catching sight of the time on the wall clock, I push my chair back. "I gotta go, big day at the shop today."

"Okay, I'll call you later," Piper says, going up on her tippy-toes to kiss my cheek before I leave.

When I walk into my garage, Jake and Taj stay out of my way. Jesus, I must look as bad as I feel if those two aren't giving me shit for being late two days in a row. I make myself another coffee, then get to work. I've got a vintage Cadi waiting for me today, and I plan on losing myself in her all day long.

Reagan

Another day of radio silence from Rhett, and I'm driving myself mad with worry. Is he okay? Did something happen to him? Is that why he hasn't checked in the last two days?

Chewing on my bottom lip, I decide it's time to call in Char. She will know what to do. Hitting her name on my phone screen, I wait for her to answer.

"S'up, sugar tits?" she greets in a super chipper tone.

My shoulders slump before I even start talking. "Char, he's dropped off the face of the Earth. I haven't seen or heard from him since Monday morning. Everything was fine—no, it was great. We went our separate ways when we left for work, and that was the last time I saw him. Is this him ghosting me, or was he murdered by psychotic dwarfs?"

"Whoa, slow down, babe," she says, and I take a breath, trying to calm myself.

"Okay, so it's Wednesday night, and you're panicking because it's been crickets since Monday. Correct?"

"Yeah," I breathe. "I mean, he told me he didn't do

girlfriends or anything. Then the weekend happened, and I don't know, I thought ..." I can't finish my sentence because I'm not sure what I thought.

"Oh, babe," Char coos. "I'll be over in half an hour with wine and chocolate."

"Thank you," I whisper and end the call.

My work clothes feel too tight, so I start tugging them off on my way to my room. I'm able to get around without my crutches now if I'm careful. I'm naked when I reach my closet, and I grab the first pair of jammies I see, yanking them on. Then, I flop back on my bed and wait for Char to arrive.

Almost exactly thirty minutes later, my apartment door bangs open, and Char's voice sings out, "Honey, I'm home!"

I don't bother getting up. "I'm in here," I call out.

A couple of seconds later, she leans against the doorframe. She's got two bottles of wine tucked under her arm and a bag that I'm sure is full of chocolate swinging from her wrist.

I smile at her. "Lifesaver."

She throws the bag of chocolate to me, then drops her purse on the floor and kicks off her shoes. "I'll get us some glasses. Be right back," she says with a wink, then she disappears.

We're sitting side by side in my bed, leaning against the headboard with a bottle of wine each. *This is what best friends are for.*

Char ended up going home and packing a bag so she could stay with my sorry arse for the rest of the week. It's not like me to mope, but Rhett is worth moping over.

We're in my bed, where we've spent every night after finishing work with wine, chocolate and pretzels. I'm staring at the ceiling, wishing my phone would ring. Hell, at this point I'd even be happy with a text. But nada. I haven't so much as seen a glimpse of him since Monday morning.

Char smacks her forehead with her palm, and I give her the side eye. "I can't believe I haven't already asked this, but when did you first text him?"

I look at her, confused. "I haven't."

Her red lips pop open in a perfect *O*. "Not even just a 'Hey, thanks for the great sex' or a 'You're an arsehole with a tiny penis' text?"

Shaking my head, I tell her, "Firstly, nothing on that man is tiny, especially his epic penis. And secondly, I didn't know I was supposed to."

She scoffs. "Give me your phone. We're fixing this right now."

Before I can stop her, she snatches my phone off the quilt, and she's tapping away on my screen.

"Hey! What are you going to say?" I screech, my arms helicoptering, trying to reclaim my phone.

Char rolls her eyes and stands up on the bed, then holds it above her head. She's almost a foot taller than me, the cow.

"I can't find his name in your contacts," she complains.

I grin, victorious. "And you won't. It's not in there

under his real name."

A minute later, she busts out laughing. She buckles in half, then drops to her knees as tears stream down her cheeks. Yep, she found his contact info. My lips quirk. It really is a good name—and very accurate.

"Prince Everhard of the Netherlands ... Oh God, Reagan, why didn't you warn me?" Char pants.

I shrug. "It would've ruined the effect."

"It's fitting that a queen would end up with a prince." She giggles.

Taking several deep breaths, she shuffles back to sitting against the headboard. "Babe, you need to text him. Doesn't matter what you say; just keep it light and easy. You can do that. Give him a chance to explain himself before you start having nightmares about midgets again."

"Okay, I can do that."

Char hands my phone back, and I stare at it, praying for inspiration. Then it hits me like a freight train, and my fingers fly over the screen.

ME: More than ten people a year are killed by vending machines.

I sit back, satisfied I've done a good thing. Until Char grabs my phone to read it and starts staring at me funnily. "What?"

Her brows pinch together. "This is what you sent to the man you want to be having sex with? Babe, I'm going to be honest. I'm not sure how he's going to respond to this, if at all."

Oh. My chest deflates. "He likes it when I tell him random facts."

Char chews her lip for a moment, then her eyes widen. "Look, he's typing!" she squeals and hands me back the phone.

His response takes forever, but my eyes never leave the screen.

PRINCE EVERHARD OF THE NETHERLANDS: Are you planning on dropping a vending machine on me in the near future?

ME: I wasn't. Should I be?

PRINCE EVERHARD OF THE NETHERLANDS: Maybe.

I frown. I don't like that response. My chest squeezes, then my heart takes off at a gallop.

ME: Why?

PRINCE EVERHARD OF THE NETHERLANDS: Because I've been avoiding you.

ME: Oh. You don't have to. I understand. You don't do girlfriends.

PRINCE EVERHARD OF THE NETHERLANDS: No, you don't understand.

Chapter 14

Reagan

My head whips up at the banging coming from the front of my apartment. I look at Char, who seems to be just as startled by it as me. Crawling off my bed, I go to the front door and open it cautiously.

I jump back when Rhett pushes the door open. Stalking towards me, he forces me backwards until I'm pressed against the wall. His fingers glide over my cheeks, then up into my messy hair. He tips my head back, and then he's kissing me like a man starved.

Sighing, I relax into his hold, returning his kiss with as much passion as he gives me. My arms curl around his shoulders, and he moves his hands to my butt, hoisting me up to his hips. I lock my ankles behind his back.

"I'm sorry, honey. I got buried in my past, but I'm here now," he breathes against my kiss-swollen lips.

If I wasn't tethered to him, I swear I would soar into the sky with happiness.

He's actually here. I blink back tears as my emotions rage for control. Problem is, I'm not sure which I'm feeling more: relieved that he's here, or pissed that he could have been a body in the morgue and I wouldn't even have known.

I push my hands against his solid chest. He takes the hint and lowers me to the floor, keeping his hands on my hips.

"Where have you been?" I ask, then change my mind. "No. Scratch that. What the hell took you so long?"

His answering grin is everything.

Lightly gliding his rough fingertips over my cheek, he looks deep into my eyes and says, "I had to get my head straight. I'm sorry, honey. It won't happen again; I swear. This has been the worst week of my life. I'm miserable without you."

Swallowing becomes really freaking hard, and my unshed tears spill over. It takes me a minute to gain control of my vocal cords. "Well good, because I reverted to an overly angsty teenager who eats her feelings this week, so at least we were both suffering."

"It's true. She's been moody as hell. She bit me last night when I tried to take her fifth chocolate bar from her."

Rhett's head swivels to Char, who's leaning against my bedroom doorframe, her arms crossed under her boobs and a smug expression on her face.

"Uh, hi there. Sorry, I didn't realise there was anyone else here."

Char snorts. "That's because you were too busy

sucking face with my girl. But I'll forgive you this time. That's the first smile I've seen out of her all week."

Rhett grins back at me, then kisses my nose and presses his forehead to mine. "You bit her?"

I shrug. "She knows better than to touch my chocolate. Especially when I'm in the throes of an emotional breakdown."

His expression sobers with my last statement. "Baby, I'm so sorry. I didn't mean to hurt you. My head was so far up my own arse I didn't stop to think how my silence would affect you."

"I should have called or messaged you sooner. At first, I thought you might just need some space, but then after a few days, I knew it was more than that. I thought my crazy was too much for you to handle for more than a weekend," I admit.

Running the pads of his thumbs under my eyes, he wipes away my tears. "Reagan," he says, then stops until I meet his intense gaze. "I fucking love your brand of crazy. I had more fun with you in one weekend than I've had in years. You are so much more than you give yourself credit for.

"You're crazy smart." He presses a kiss to my forehead. "Crazy beautiful." A kiss to my left cheek. "Crazy clumsy." A kiss to my right. "Crazy fun." A kiss to my nose. "And I'm fucking crazy about you." His soft lips meet mine, and I wrap my arms around his neck, never wanting this to end.

"Ahem." Char interrupts us before we can get carried away.

"Shit, sorry," I mumble. It takes me a moment to catch my breath.

Char rolls her eyes. "Well, it looks like my work here is done. I'll get my stuff and leave you two horndogs to it." She turns back to my room and gathers her things quickly.

She strides down the hall and pauses when she reaches us. Holding her hand out to Rhett, she says, "By the way, I'm Charlotte. Otherwise known as the best bitch or friend, depending what day it is. I'd say it was nice to meet you, but we haven't really had a chance to do that yet, so we'll put a pin in it and take care of the formalities some other time."

Rhett takes Char's outstretched hand. "I'm good with that."

Char's eyes roam over his body with obvious approval, then her gaze stops at his crotch. On his boner, to be precise. She swallows and blinks slowly. Finally looking back to me, she smirks. "You weren't kidding about the goods. Have fun with that." She blows me a kiss then leaves, the apartment door slamming shut behind her.

Epilogue

SIMON'S WEDDING...

Reagan

WEDDINGS MAKE ME NERVOUS. THEY ARE THE PERFECT place for embarrassing things to happen. And if it's going to happen, it's going to happen to me.

At least I don't really know anyone here. I met Simon and Jessie last weekend. But other than them, I only know Rhett, and he's on best man duty most of the day.

Jessie was super-lovely, though, and said I could tag along to the photo shoot and even sit with Rhett at the reception. She'd been terrified Rhett was going to bring some whore he'd picked up the night before to the wedding, and since he brought me instead, I get special privileges.

Rhett and I have been an official couple for two weeks, and I've never been happier. I can't stop staring at him. He's so damn sexy, and he knows it. His tux is fitted to perfection. The way it moulds around his biceps is giving me all kinds of spank-bank material. Not that I need it; Rhett is just as ravenous in bed as I am.

And oh my God, those pants. I've been resisting the urge to sink my teeth into his arse since he put them on this morning. Watching him walk away wasn't the hardship I was expecting it to be when he left me at my seat ten minutes ago to join the other groomsmen.

He catches my eye from his place beside Simon on the podium, while everyone waits for Jessie to arrive, and blows me a kiss. I pretend to catch it, glance around to make sure nobody is looking, then tug up the hem of my dress and release it up my skirt.

He chokes on a laugh, and Simon elbows him. I smirk, then wink. He just shakes his head and smiles wider.

I'm sitting in the fourth row, all by myself. I don't know if it's because I'm the only visibly tattooed person at this wedding or just because nobody knows me. I don't really mind, though. Saves me making a fool of myself trying to make small talk. I keep my eyes on Rhett when the music starts, signalling Jessie's arrival.

I only look away when she strides down the aisle, and I see her stunning dress. It's beautiful. I've never seen anything like it. When I met Jessie, I thought for sure she would be the kind of woman to wear a super-traditional, white dress. But she looks like Cinder-freaking-ella in a light blue gown that puffs out at her small hips in layer upon layer of tulle encrusted with sparkly gems.

When Rhett finally looks at her, his eyes widen, and he shoves Simon's shoulder. Simon glares at him for a split second before going back to staring at Jessie in wonder. It's so cute, the way he looks at her like she's the light of his life.

Then, my eyes meet Rhett's again, and that's exactly how he's looking at me.

"I love you," he mouths to me, and I swear my heart stops beating in my chest.

Clutching my throat, I blink back tears. *"I love you too,"* I mouth back.

Rhett

I DID IT. I TOLD HER I LOVE HER. I COULDN'T HOLD IT BACK a second longer when I saw the look in her eyes.

She is everything.

As soon as the ceremony's done, and the minister says, *You may now kiss the bride*, I bound down the stairs, not caring that I was supposed to stay there for a bunch of photos.

I've got Reagan wrapped in my arms a moment later, my fingers intertwined in her silky locks, probably messing up her hairdo, but fuck it. I press my mouth to hers and take in all her sweetness, releasing a moan I can't contain.

Gliding my tongue over her pouty bottom lip, I suck it and groan when she digs her fingers into my back beneath my suit coat. "I fucking love you," I breathe into her parted lips. "So much, Reagan. So fucking much."

Her smiling is blinding, and I feel it like a punch to the chest.

"I love you too," she murmurs before pushing up on her tiptoes to take my mouth again.

So fucking perfect.

The End

LLAMAS, FARMERS & SWEET TREATS OH MY...

JB HELLER

Dedication

To Endo Warriors all over the world,
I see you.
I feel you.
I am one of you.
Stay strong sisters.
X

Chapter One

Charlotte

I LIKE TO THINK OF MY REPRODUCTIVE SYSTEM AS AN ABYSS where happiness goes to die a slow, excruciating, bloody, and torturous death.

My lack of a fulfilled sex life is all her fault. She has deprived me of the ability to have sex whenever I want. And I *love* sex. I'm not unattractive, and I don't lack confidence. No, I have the uterine tissue from hell. She and her friends are possessed by the demon known as *Endometriosis.*

It's because of her that I grab life by the balls and live it as fully as I can when I am able.

Having a debilitating yet invisible disease is the worst. For one, people think I'm making up the constant horrendous pain I live with. Why would anyone do that? Yes, I'm a creative person. I have a flare for the dramatic, it's true, but not even *I* could conjure the crippling pain that grabs me by the vagina each and every month.

It's also hard to maintain friendships when you bail on plans all the time due to the unforeseen flare-ups that bring you to your knees.

Reagan is the only real friend I have these days. She is the sweetest person I know, and she'd never let my disease ruin our friendship.

When I'm in the throes of a *Uteruses Gone Rogue* episode, I don't want to see or speak to anyone. Give me a handful of painkillers, a heat pack or two, paired with Netflix or a romance audiobook, and I'm set.

But Reagan always shows up armed with wine, chocolate, and stories of her sexcapades with her new boyfriend, Rhett. Her hilarious antics distract me from the discomfort that persists even after consuming Endone by the bucket load. Reagan is a true friend in every sense of the word. She's always there for me, no matter what is going on with her.

She scrutinises me from her place on the purple beanbag next to my sofa. "Do you want me to warm up your heat packs again?"

I grimace as I shift forward to pull one out from behind my back and hand it to her, then grab the one that's covering my bloated stomach all the way down to my stabby vagina. "Thanks. Two minutes on high should do it."

She takes them from me, concern etched in her features. "The painkillers should have kicked in by now, shouldn't they?"

Wrapping my arms around my middle, I nod. "Yeah, but I'm becoming resistant again. I think it's time to switch it up. I'll go see my doctor next week, and we'll find a new one to try."

That's the thing about chronic pain; you build up a resistance to the pills after a while. Ones that worked like magic only six months ago now don't have any effect unless I take a double dose. And that's just playing with fire.

I can feel Reagan's eyes on me from the kitchen as she waits for the heat packs to warm. She strums her manicured purple nails on the benchtop as she watches me. "Maybe it's time we find you a new doctor. This one seems to be more interested in covering up your pain than actually treating the disease."

She's right. But I've seen so many doctors that I've lost hope of finding one that will actually help me. There is no cure for endo, only management. And I do everything I can to help my situation. I haven't eaten a bite of gluten in more than two years, and my sugar intake is minimal and strictly reserved for days when the pain is so bad I need a pick-me-up.

I've learnt more from other women with the same condition than I have from a list of quacks as long as my leg. I've managed to bring my pain levels down to mere discomfort during the weeks surrounding *the shedding*. But once it begins, it's no longer in my hands.

Reagan runs to me, juggling the heat packs in her hands as she goes. "These things are scalding; you'll burn yourself if you put them on straight away."

I snatch them from her. "I'm used to it. The hotter the better."

She pulls a face—one that says I've lost my damn mind—and hands them to me. I arrange them quickly—one at my lower back, the other at my front. My eyelids flutter as sweet relief seeps into my muscles as the heat penetrates my skin.

When I open my eyes again, Reagan is pulling yet another face. "That looks like your come face."

I snort. "How would you know what my come face looks like?"

Placing her hands on her narrow hips, she arches a perfectly shaped brow. "Remember that one time I walked in on you polishing your pearl after school in the twelfth grade? Or when I let myself in here when you had a backpacker all up in your business?" She pauses. "I could continue, but the point is, you just did that eye-flutter thing, and that's your *O* face."

I grin. "Oh yeah. My bad. The heat feels so amazing. I'd say almost as good as an orgasm."

Reagan scrunches up her nose. "No, just, no. You're clearly not getting quality *O*'s if you think a heat pack can deliver that kind of satisfaction. I'd lend you Rhett, but I don't like sharing."

Now it's my nose that scrunches. "Rhett is hot and all, but he's a grease monkey. No way I'd let him touch me. He'd ruin my clothes."

A devilish glint twinkles in Reagan's blue eyes. "That's why I don't wear any clothes when he's around." She waggles her brows and thrusts her hips, making me choke on the sip of water I just took, spraying it all over her.

"You've turned into a nympho, Reags."

"It's all the quality O's I'm getting."

I roll my eyes. "Pour a little salt in the wound and rub it in, why don't you."

Her shoulders drop, and she sits on the edge of the sofa I'm curled up on. "How long's it been?"

"Three months," I tell her.

Her eyes widen. "That's a freaking long time for you, Char. Why so long? What happened? Something happened, didn't it? I know you pull in the guys when you're not"—she gestures up and down my prone body—"like this."

I release a deep sigh and brace myself to tell my best friend about the most awkward sexual experience I've ever had. "Okay. So I met this guy from a hook-up app. He was smokin' hot and packing a python in his pants. I was so freaking excited to get that thing inside of me. The foreplay was phenomenal. He went down on me for like fifteen minutes and didn't stop until I'd come three times.

"Everything was super slippery around there because of all the coming, and when he flipped me over to go in from behind, he kinda ... slipped ..."

Reagan is blinking at me. Long, slow, drawn-out blinks. "Are you saying what I think you're saying?"

I nod. "Yeah. He breached the one-way canal, and I screeched, '*Wrong hole, wrong hole!*' He pulled out immediately and was super apologetic, but the moment was over. Soiled. Ruined. And my butt hurt. I've been too scared to hook up again since."

Sympathy fills my bestie's eyes as she takes one of my hands and cradles it between hers. "I am *so* sorry that happened to you, babe. I completely understand and support your temporary celibacy."

This is just one of the many reasons I love this girl so much. "Thank you. It was time I put Betty on a leash. The break has been good for her. She's not happy about it, but she's dealing. No more sex for us until I'm no longer suffering from untimely flashbacks."

Even if Betty turns blue, we will prevail.

Elijah

YOU'D THINK AFTER GETTING UP AT FOUR-THIRTY EVERY morning for the last ten years, I'd be used to it. But no. I am still not a morning person.

Delilah snuggles deeper into my side, and I shove her over a little. I don't like to be touched when I'm sleeping, but she won't take the damn hint. We do this push-pull thing every morning.

"Goddammit, Delilah, stop smothering me! I swear if you didn't need the warmth, I'd kick your little arse into the barn," I grumble at her when she burrows against me again.

Don't get me wrong, I do love her. She's the cutest damn thing I've ever seen. But a man needs his space. Especially when he's forced to get up before the bloody sun every day.

Throwing the covers back, I roll out of bed and out of

Delilah's reach, then trudge to the bathroom across the hall. The one good thing about getting up this early is I don't have to fight anyone for the shower. After slamming the door shut behind me, I slip out of my flannel pyjama bottoms and turn on the hot water.

Five minutes later, I'm running a towel through my hair when I hear Delilah knocking on the door. I sigh and swing it open. She looks up at me with her big, adorable, brown eyes, and I can't stay mad at her for being a bed hog. "Hey, baby, sorry I'm such a grumpy fucker."

I crouch down and rub behind her ears as she nuzzles into my throat. Running my hands over her long neck, I give her a good scratch, and she mewls in delight. "Come on, let's go get some breakfast," I tell her, and she prances along the hallway after me.

Delilah does laps around the kitchen counter as I prepare our breakfasts. Her spindly little legs move too fast for her, and she ends up sliding into the cabinet beside me. She looks up at me and shakes her head, then wobbles back to her feet and stands by my side. I smile at her. She's got so much personality it's hard not to love her.

"Oh my god, Eli, would you stop looking at that llama like that? That's how you're supposed to look at a woman, not a bloody animal."

I roll my eyes at my baby brother, Juda, as he enters the kitchen. "Don't listen to him, baby. You're the only woman I need in my life," I tell Delilah as I drop a kiss on her silky little head.

"That's fucked up, E. You need to get laid," he says, snatching a rasher of bacon off my plate.

Using the spatula, I smack the back of his hand when he tries to steal another. "No, what's fucked up is the train of women you parade through this house. Mum would beat your arse. She didn't raise us to be man-whores."

It's his turn to roll his eyes at me. "Definitely need to get laid," he mutters as he starts making us coffees.

This is our morning ritual. I get up first and start cooking breakfast. Half an hour later, Juda generally emerges and gets the coffees going, then Asher rolls out of bed when it's chow time, which means his lazy arse has to do the dishes before he starts his chores for the day.

When Delilah's bottle is at the right temperature, I remove it from the pot of hot water then take the eggs out of the pan. She nudges my thigh and mewls at me again, wanting her bottle, but I've got to finish buttering the toast first.

Juda shoves me away from the toaster. "I'll do it. Go feed your woman."

"Thanks," I mumble then snatch Dilly's bottle from the counter and make my way to the dining table. She trots after me with so much enthusiasm she can't stop in time when I take my seat. She skids past me then falls as she tries to turn around too quickly on the slippery timber floors.

Juda bursts out laughing. "I think she's hangry."

I chuckle. "She's always hangry."

Dilly is back in an instant, eyeing my hands for the bottle I just hid behind my back. Her beady little eyes narrow, and she butts her head against my empty palms, demanding I produce the goods. I snicker.

"You tormenting my baby again?" Asher's deep, sleep-filled voice comes from behind me.

I scoff. "Your baby? Whose bed does she sleep in every night? Mine, that's whose. Get your own damn woman."

Juda cringes as he places the plates of food on the table. "You both have issues. You know there's such a thing as real-life women. Ones with boobs and puss—"

My hand shoots out, slapping him in the back of the head before he can finish his statement. "Language! We don't talk like that in front of ladies."

He glares at me while rubbing his head. "She's a fucking llama. Not a lady. You need to get off this farm more, experience what the world has to offer once in a while."

"And why would I want to do that? I have everything I need right here," I say, smiling down at Delilah as she discovers the bottle.

This farm is my life. Has been since our parents died ten years ago and I had to step up to keep things running or risk losing everything they'd built.

Even though Juda might have a slight point, I'll never admit to him that I'd more than enjoy the company of a woman. I just don't have time for it. When my day is done, I've got nothing left.

At thirty-one, I've started questioning if I'll ever find a partner to share my life with. If I can't make the time to even try meeting someone, what chance do I have? There's also the fact that I'm currently sharing my bed with a llama. And I'm pretty sure balls bluer than the sky on a midsummer's day are not exactly a turn-on.

Chapter Two

Elijah

THIS DAY HAS GONE TO SHIT AND IT'S BARELY EVEN STARTED.

The battery on the truck is flat because Juda left the light on inside the cab last night. *Dipshit.* After jump-starting it, I wipe my hands on my jeans and put the cables back in the toolbox on the side of the truck. *Just fucking great.* Now I'm running thirty minutes late for this morning's egg deliveries.

Pulling up by the back entrance to Buck's Big Burgers, I round the tray and grab Buck's daily order. I grit my teeth when I notice him stomping his fat arse up to the truck. I hated this guy in high school, and I still do, but I try everything I can to keep things between us professional. While he does everything he can to be a dick.

"Mornin', Buck," I say politely.

He curls his hands around his wide hips. "So nice of you to show up. I'm running a business here."

I tune him out as he continues to berate me for the next three minutes straight.

Maybe it's because Juda is right and I am severely sexually frustrated, or maybe I'm done with Buck's superiority complex, but when he mentions how unprofessional this is *for the fifth time*, I lose my shit. "For fuck's sake, Buck, I've got other stops to make. As you've pointed out, I'm already behind schedule, so would you just take your fucking eggs and let me get on with it?"

His upper lip curls in an ugly sneer. "How dare you talk to me like that? I'm a paying customer. Don't you know anything about customer service, you moron? The *customer* is always right! And you're fucking late. So what are you going to do to make it up to me?"

Over his shit, I pick up his crate of eggs and drop them at his feet. "I'm going to let you find a new supplier. That's what I'm going to do, Buck."

I can see his blood boiling in his veins. His face reddens so much I'm sure he's on the verge of busting a vessel. Before he can get another word out, I stroll back around the truck, hoist myself into the cab, then send him a one-fingered salute out the window as I pull away.

That felt fucking amazing. I grin to myself as I make my way to my next stop.

DELILAH TRUNDLES ALONG AT MY SIDE AS I HEAD OUT TO the birthing paddocks to check on a couple of llamas that should be dropping a bundle any day now. She likes doing the rounds with me, and it's good for her to get out and about with her own kind.

Some days, I'm sure she thinks she's a human. That girl is going to get a rude awakening when she's strong enough to be out in the paddocks full-time. I ruffle her soft coat as she trots along at my side.

"Yo, I'm goin' into town. You need anything?" Juda calls out to me, leaning on the timber railings around the paddock.

I shake my head. "Nah, I'm good. What are you going in for?"

His mouth kicks up in a smirk. "To let off a little steam." He winks. "Then I'll drop 'round to Aunty K's and pick up this week's treats."

Nodding, I shift my attention back to the llama I currently have my entire arm inserted in.

Juda calls out again. "I was serious this morning. You spend too much time with animals and not enough with females of the human variety. Mona has a sister."

"Fuck off," I grumble. I hear his laughter as he makes his way to his car. Then he tears down the dirt drive, flicking rocks and dust all over the side of the damn house and pissing me the hell off.

Genie must sense the tension in my body and stiffens up. I stroke her back with my free hand. "It's okay, honey, shhh." I soothe her as best I can. It can't be comfortable having someone's arm up your arse end, but it had to be done. She had issues with her last cria, so I'm keeping an extra close eye on her this time around. "Baby's doing fine, girl. I think you'll be able to meet her tomorrow," I say as my arm slides out of her.

After removing the lubed-up shoulder-length glove, I throw it in the bin on my way out of the barn. Juda's taunts roll around inside my head as I stomp up to the house. I run a hand through my hair, and I let the back door slam shut behind me.

Asher arches a brow. "Juda?"

"Is it ever anything else?"

Asher shrugs and goes back to whatever he's doing on his laptop.

For the most part, we all get along pretty well. But recently, Juda has really been pushing the whole "*you need a woman*" bullshit. He doesn't understand that being in a relationship takes time and effort, and I don't have the energy required for that. I'm not like him; I can't do one-night stands. It was never my thing, not even when I was younger. I mean, yeah, I've resorted to it over the years, but it never felt right.

Pouring myself a scotch, I knock it down in one hit, drawing Asher's eyes to me yet again. He closes his laptop, places it on the coffee table in front of him, and turns his torso towards me.

"What?" I snap. Asher has always been the quiet, contemplative one of us. And it's clear he has something to say now.

He throws an arm over the back of the couch and tilts his head to the side. "Maybe Juda has a point. You spend all your time here. You don't go out. You don't socialise. You're just going through the motions every single day."

"And your point is?"

"There should be more to life." He says this like it's the most obvious thing in the world.

I shake my head. "Life isn't a party. It's hard work and sacrifice."

"That's where you're wrong, brother. Yeah, some of it is about working your arse off and sacrificing things occasionally, but that's not *all* it's about. If you have no joy in your life, what's the point of living it?"

A lump forms in my throat, and I look away from him, unable to maintain eye contact. I gave up my own dreams and aspirations to take over the farm after Mum and Dad died. It was so long ago I don't even remember what I wanted to do with my life back then. Raising Juda and making sure the farm brought in enough money to pay for Asher to go to college was all that mattered.

Keeping my gaze fixed on the empty scotch glass in my hand, I mutter, "I'm going for a shower."

Asher speaks to my retreating form. "You should be a little selfish for the first time in your life and pass some of your workload on to me and Juda for a while. We can handle it, you know. Just think about it, Eli."

Could they handle it? Probably. Would it really be that simple?

Once under the hot spray, I allow myself to imagine what it would be like to come in from working in the yards to a beautiful woman waiting for me. My chest constricts with longing. I want it so much.

When I get out of the shower, I need to go for a drive. I

don't know where I'm going, but between Juda and Asher's words, I have a lot of thinking to do.

Charlotte

DAY SEVEN OF BATTLING THE RED RIVER, AND I'M CRAVING sweets big time. And not just any old sweets—I *need* McKenna's Heavenly Treats. It's just over an hour's drive away but *so* worth the trip.

I pop a couple of my lower-grade painkillers since today is only a level six on the pain scale, then throw my heat packs in to warm. The second the microwave dings, I pull them out, drop them straight into my oversized handbag, and make my way to my car. Once inside, I secure the heat packs in place, hook up my Bluetooth to play Krista and Becca Ritchie's latest book, *Tangled Like Us*, then reverse out of my drive.

In preparation for eating all the things, I'm wearing my favourite stretchy black leggings, a chunky black cable-knit sweater dress that stops just above my knees, and a pair of brown suede booties. It's understated yet stylish, and most importantly, baggy, thus somewhat hiding my bloated endo belly that I plan on extending with all the bingeing I'm about to do.

I swoon along to the story as I drive. These girls can write some seriously amazing stuff. Part of the reason I haven't bothered finding a bakery with gluten-free awesomeness closer to home is because the drive gives me an opportunity to get my audio romance fix.

Pulling into a parking spot three stores up from McKenna's Heavenly Treats, I just about squeal in excitement. This is what life without sex has come to: excessively over-the-top levels of enthusiasm for baked goods.

After throwing my heat packs into the back, I snatch my bag from the passenger seat, swing my door open, and step out of my car. I gasp in terror. Air pushes into my body. A vehicle careens past me. I plaster myself to the side of my car. My heart thunders in my ears. *Christ.* In my eagerness to get my sugar fix, I didn't even look.

I press my shaking palm to my torso, swallow hard, and count back from ten under my breath to calm myself. That was too close. I didn't even have time to see who or what almost hit me. Smoothing a hand down my ponytail, I swing my head from side to side, checking the traffic this time before rounding the hood of my car and stepping up onto the footpath.

"Hey, you!" A pair of seriously pissed off, blazing blue eyes scan over my body, causing my throat to constrict as a man storms towards me.

"Umm, yes?" I squeak.

His eyes narrow to slits. "You just stepped out in front of me. I could have killed you! What were you thinking?" He comes to a halt a mere foot from me.

He thinks I did that on purpose? Straightening my spine, I glare up at him. "Excuse me?"

"You heard me. Next time you get out of your car, maybe check for traffic first." His eyes sear through me.

My top lip lifts in a snarl. "You're the one driving like a lunatic down a busy street—filled with people, I might add. Maybe you should drive a little slower and be aware of your surroundings."

Lifting a large hand, he scrubs it through his dishevelled sandy brown hair and shakes his head at me. "You're saying that was *my* fault? Lady, you're insane."

Strangely enough, this is not the first time the opposite sex has questioned my sanity. Sliding my tongue across my top lip, I brace myself for battle. If this guy thinks he can call me insane before he even knows me, he's deluded. I'm about to let fly with a litany of insults, when I realise the annoyance that filled his blue eyes moments ago has been replaced by heat.

I swallow, my anger faltering. "Uh," I mumble. *Shit, get it together, Charlotte! He's a redneck country bumkin, and he just called you insane.* In an attempt to get my head right, I take a deep breath, but it backfires. He's so close I'm overwhelmed by his intoxicating scent: a mixture of soap, earth, and leather.

Leather? Where the hell did that come from? Does he work with leather? My head spins a little at the possibilities as my eyes leave his to travel over his muscle-clad body. Firm biceps strain the fabric of his red chequered button-down, followed by defined tan forearms protruding from his rolled-up sleeves. I just about swallow my tongue. I love arms.

Continuing my perusal, I'm met with thick denim-encased thighs. I follow them down to the cowboy boots they're tucked into and sigh. He's so fine. If I hadn't recently taken a vow of celibacy, and there wasn't a murder-scene-type situation in my pants, I'd be climbing him like a tree already.

When my eyes finally return to his, I'm in more of a *make-love-not-war* kind of mood. And he's looking at me like I'm his next meal. The longer we stare at each other, the thicker the air around us becomes. Need pulses through me as he slowly lifts his hand towards my cheek.

His warm palm cups my jaw, his thumb tugging my bottom lip free from between my teeth. My tongue snakes out to wet my lips and grazes over the tip of his thumb, still pressed against my flesh. A deep but quiet groan escapes him, traveling right through me to my very core.

But while it served to turn me on even further, it seems to have pulled him back to reality. He drops his hand as though he was just touching a leper and takes a step away from me. Confusion at this whole encounter fills me, and I rub at my forehead, trying to remember how I came to be standing here with this delicious stranger.

Elijah

What the ever-loving fuck?

I got out of my truck, intent on ripping this broad a

new one. How did I end up touching her and imagining those full red lips wrapped around my dick?

Swallowing hard, I force my incredibly inappropriate thoughts down, then grip the back of my neck and rack my brain for something to say.

Nothing comes to mind. Great. Just fucking brilliant.

Her lips purse, and her hazel eyes stare straight through me, shining with lust just as powerful as my own.

"Fuck," I growl. An image of shoving her up against the red brick wall just three feet from us and filling her mouth with my tongue swirls behind my tightly closed eyes. I clamp my jaw shut, grinding my teeth together.

I'm jolted from the fantasy by cool fingers sliding over my exposed forearm. My eyes pop open. She's stepped closer and is looking up into my eyes with confusion. I take another step away from her, breaking our contact. It's hard enough to think without her touching me.

"Look," I say. "Just be more careful in future." Then I turn around and stalk back to my truck parked haphazardly a few spaces up.

"Seriously? That's it? You eye-fuck the shit out of me then just walk away?" she demands, storming after me.

I turn, looking at her over my shoulder as she follows my retreat. She's not going to let it go, so I pause at my truck—hand on the handle, ready for a quick escape. Clearing my throat, I gear up to apologise for my behaviour, but she cuts me off.

"Don't you dare say the word sorry right now."

Raising a brow, I'm stumped. *What does she want then?* "Uh, what would you like me to say?"

She tilts her head, her bright-red ponytail swishing over her shoulder as she places a hand on her hip. "How about introducing yourself, then buying me a coffee?"

Clearly, I heard her wrong. Furrowing my brows, I lean towards her slightly. "I'm sorry, what?"

Her eyes flash with annoyance. "So that's how it's going to be. You're going to bitch out and leave me hanging. What a gentleman." She shakes her head, then turns on her heeled boots and walks back towards McKenna's Heavenly Treats.

Chapter Three

Charlotte

WALKING INTO MY FAVOURITE PLACE EVER, I'M WRAPPED UP in the comforting aroma of the best bakery in the whole freaking world. I inhale deeply, filling my senses with the heavenly scent of freshly made breads, cakes, pastries, and an assortment of other delicious, enticing goodies.

I shake off my encounter with the scrumptious stranger. I'm closed for business anyway, so nothing could have come of it. Closing my eyes, I relax my stance, then smile. This is my happy place. A bakery in a small, hick town in the middle of nowhere. I thank God every day that I stumbled onto it a few years back when I came out here to interview an up-and-coming designer for my fashion blog. This is where she chose for us to meet, and I've been coming back here ever since.

"Charlotte, honey, how are you?" McKenna's voice calls from the counter along the back wall. She comes around to greet me and wraps me in her signature bear hug. McKenna is not a small woman. No, she stands almost six feet tall with broad shoulders and a massive smile.

"Hey, Kenna. I'm doing okay."

But she knows me better than to let my white lie slip past her. "Uh-huh. And since when do you come to visit me when you're feeling okay? You go sit your butt down, and I'll bring you out some of your favourites," she says with a wink as she shoos me towards a corner booth I'm rather partial to.

A couple of minutes later, she places two hazelnut lattes and a plate full of awesome down in front of me, then slides into the booth seat opposite me. "So, how's the blog going?" she asks and pops a bite-size square of vanilla slice into her mouth.

Picking up a brownie, I take a bite and chew. My eyelids flutter and a deep, gratifying sigh hums from the back of my throat. Contentment fills me, and I settle farther back into my seat, smiling. "It's great. I've seen a steady incline in sales over the last three months. Hiring Myrtle was a good move."

McKenna nods. A knowing glint shines in her eyes. "I just knew she was a good fit for you. She's the only one in this town—aside from myself, of course—who has any dress sense at all."

I wouldn't say that McKenna has *good* dress sense. I just let her think she does. I give her the occasional pointer here and there, but I can't seem to get through to her that flannel is not an acceptable fabric choice in any wardrobe.

Myrtle Mayer, however, does have a certain something when it comes to style. What she has is quite unique. She's quirky yet practical. I guess being a single mother has something to do with the practical side of things. It was McKenna's idea to bring Myrtle onboard, and I'm glad I listened to her. Myrtle's become quite the asset.

Licking brownie crumbs from my fingers, I catch McKenna staring at me. "What? Is it stuck on my teeth?"

She shakes her head. "No, love. You just look tired. I worry about you, you know. Someone as wonderful as you should have somebody to take care of you when you're unwell. A person who will come get these treats for you so you can get the rest you need."

I smile at her. She has only ever shown me kindness. Placing my hand over hers, I give it a gentle squeeze. "Thank you for the thought. I appreciate it, Kenna, I do. But I don't need anyone to take care of me. I take care of myself just fine. Besides, I listen to raunchy books while I'm driving," I say with a wink.

McKenna rolls her grey-blue eyes at me. "I bet you do," she says with a grin, but it drops quickly. "I know you're quite capable of looking after yourself, but wouldn't it be nice if someone else did it for you?"

Shrugging, I take another tasty treat from the plate and pop it in my mouth. *So damn good.*

The bell over the door chimes, and she peers over her shoulder, then shuffles out of the booth. "Juda, how are you, baby?" she greets a tall guy with shaggy blond hair falling in his eyes. I watch their exchange, curiosity building as he bends down to wrap his muscular arms around her.

"Hey, Aunty K. I'm good. You got anything out back for me?" he asks with a butter-wouldn't-melt-in-his-mouth grin.

McKenna swats his shoulder. "You save that smoulder for someone like my pretty friend over there. It's wasted on me. You know I bake extra for you and your brothers every Friday."

My gaze drops away from them the second she throws her thumb over her shoulder, gesturing to me. She knew he was coming in. That's what all the questions were about. I should have known she had an angle.

I'm busy deciding what I want to eat next when a large, tan hand approaches *my* plate. I slap it away without thinking, then my eyes shoot up, coming into contact with his. Holy-swoony-deliciousness. He looks tastier than these treats.

Damn, there must be something in the water around here. First the guy on the street, now this specimen ... *God must be testing the strength of my vow.*

I blink and shake my head. "Don't you know it's rude to touch a girl's treats without asking?"

He smirks. "Can I touch *your* treats?"

I scoff. I do not share my sugar fixes with anyone but Reagan. "Uh, no. I drove more than an hour for these babies. I'm not sharing."

His smirk transforms into a genuine smile, and its brilliance catches me off guard. It transforms his face, making him look almost boyish. While he's still beyond attractive, I have rules, and one of them is not sleeping with anyone younger than myself.

"Mind if I sit?" he asks.

There's nothing in my rule book about looking. In fact, I'm quite partial to the view in front of me right now. But there's a very obvious glint of interest in his eyes, so I give it to him straight. "You may, but don't get any ideas. You won't be touching any of my *goodies*." I pause for effect, then add, "Ever."

He nods. The strain of keeping his facial expression neutral is evident by the way the corner of his mouth keeps twitching. He clears his throat and straightens his shoulders, making him look even taller, then says, "I would never dream of touching a lady's goodies. Not until she *begged* me to." Heat fills his light-blue eyes as he stares down at me.

He's serious ... I burst out laughing. I laugh so hard it hurts—like seriously, my insides do not appreciate the hilarity of this moment. A sharp pain shoots through me. I suck in a harsh breath and hold it, willing the stabbing in my abdomen to cease.

Next thing I know, McKenna is at my side, rubbing my back and glaring daggers at the would-be Mr. Grey. "What did you do?"

His hands raise in immediate surrender. "Nothing."

I pat her leg. "It's fine, Kenna. He was just being funny and, well, you know what happens when I laugh too hard on devil days."

Understanding dawns, and embarrassment fills her cheeks. "Oh," she says softly, then turns her focus back to the man-child across from me. "Sorry, sweetheart. I'm a little overprotective of Miss Charlotte here."

He shrugs, then eyes me. "Do I even want to know what *devil days* are?"

I shake my head. "You really don't."

"Well, alright then. You ladies have a lovely day, and I'll see you 'round, Aunty K," he says as he gets to his feet, taking a large white box from the table that I hadn't even noticed.

"Okay, baby. You be good now."

He grins at her, then drops a kiss atop her head. He turns to leave and throws a small wave over his shoulder as he exits the store.

Once he's out of view, I turn to her, rest an elbow on the tabletop, place my chin in my palm, and then stare at her. She looks everywhere but at me. I clear my throat. "Are you trying to set me up, Kenna?"

Pressing a hand to her breastbone, she gasps, "I would never." Then she shuffles out of the booth. "I'll just go box you up your usual."

I snort to myself as she hoofs it back to the service counter and starts picking out some of my favourite treats.

Elijah

I NEEDED A STIFF DRINK AFTER THAT RUN-IN WITH THE redhead. I'd hoped it would help deflate my stiff dick.

So here I am, taking up space against the bar at Hank's Tavern. I can't remember the last time I set foot in this place. My eyes roam over the dark-stained wooden shelves filled with booze and backed by mirrors. The place has a classy feel to it now that I definitely don't recall it having back in the day.

My forehead wrinkles as I take in my reflection behind the bar. *When did I get so old?* Glancing around, I notice the crowd is mostly early twenty-somethings bumping and grinding on the dancefloor. There are only a few couples around my age sitting in the booths that line the left wall.

"Need another?" Hank asks me, pulling me from my perusal.

Facing him, I grin. He looks the same as he ever did: grey hair shaved close to his scalp on the sides and styled to perfection on top. The guy's a silver fox, and the ladies love it. I reach out and shake his offered hand.

"What the hell are you doing in my neck of the woods, Eli? I haven't seen you in here since, well, I don't even know." He shakes his head, an easy smile on his face as he says, "Elijah Marshall. Now that's a name I haven't said in years."

"How you doin', old man?"

"Who you callin' old?" he grunts.

The truth is, Hank is only a couple of years older than me, putting him in his mid-thirties. Poor guy started going grey before he even left high school. But he went with it. I couldn't imagine him any other way now.

I roll my eyes at him, knowing he's not offended. "Looks like some things never change," I say, flicking my gaze to the end of the bar where half a dozen chicks take turns sending him *come hither* glances. Super grey, but super fit—that's Hank.

He smirks. "You know it, brother." He winks then hands me a fresh beer. "You hanging around for a bit? We should catch up. I'll take a break in a few."

I shrug. "I ain't got nowhere else to be."

Settling into my stool, I take a swig from the bottle clutched in my hand. Asher's words play on a loop in my head. I guess I could hand a little more of the load over to them, but Asher's got his graphic design shit going on, and Juda's still a kid. I want him to decide what he wants for himself, not be stuck on the farm out of a misplaced sense of duty or obligation to me.

"You look older than me, mate. What's on your mind?" Hank asks, sliding onto the stool beside me.

I sigh. "The boys think I need to get laid."

Hank snorts. "Amen to that. When was the last time you were with a woman? By the look of you, I'd say it's been at least a year."

Frowning, I scrub my palm over the scruff on my cheek. *Is it really that obvious?* "It's been a while." There's no way I'm telling him exactly how long. That shit's embarrassing. "I'm busy, man."

"Aha, let me give you some solid advice." Hank rests an elbow on the bar and leans closer to me, his expression serious. "If you don't take care of your man"—his eyes drop to my crotch for a fraction of a second—"he's going to stop working altogether. You know the saying, 'If you don't use it, you lose it'? It's true. So, get your head out of your arse and go get some."

"That's it. That's your solid advice?" I ask, feeling dejected. "I was hoping for something insightful."

He shrugs. "I own a bar; what do you want from me? I'm not Doctor Phil."

I tip back the rest of my beer and place the empty bottle on the bar. Slapping Hank on the back, I tell him, "Thanks for the chat." My stool scrapes against the floorboards as I stand. "I'll see you around."

Trudging out to the parking lot, I have no more clarity than I did when I left the house.

Chapter Four

Charlotte

This is not happening. I groan, dropping my head to the steering wheel as smoke pours from under the hood of my car. *Maybe it has something to do with that stupid little red light on the dash I've been ignoring for the last two weeks?*

I should have had Rhett check it out when he and Reagan were over the other day. But I was too busy drinking all the wine.

Pulling my shoulders back, I hit the *hood release* button and get out to inspect the damage. I cough and splutter as I attach the little latch to keep the hood up, then step back. Smoke continues to billow. I swipe my hand around my face, trying to get a clear look at what's going on in there.

I bite my lip as I peer at the setting sun. Darkness is encroaching. This is not an ideal situation. I'm stranded on the side of the road in the middle of nowhere. *Shit.* Climbing over the driver's seat, I rummage for my phone in my big bag. Relief sweeps through me when my fingers curl around the smooth rectangle, only for my heart to sink when I see that my battery is dead. I pace back and forth a few feet away from the smoky mess that is my vehicle. *It's okay. No need to panic. Someone will drive past and offer you assistance any minute now, and everything will be fine.*

Country folk aren't usually serial killers, are they?

Oh God, I'm going to die. A psycho, plaid-wearing redneck is going to abduct me and lock me in their sex dungeon.

I'm hyperventilating. I need to calm down, but I can't. Pressing my hand to my chest, I bend at the waist and try my best to take deep breaths into my lungs. Then, the sound of tyres crunching on the loose gravel at the side of the road steals my attention, and panic really sinks in.

My fight-or-flight instinct kicks into action. When a tall guy approaches me through the fog of smoke, I send my booted foot in the direction of his crotch as hard as I can. My boot meets his jeans, and he sinks to his knees instantly. I take the opportunity to run to the open door of his truck, praying I'll find a phone.

Before I know it, big hands wrap around my waist and tug me backwards into a hard chest. I scream and thrash with all my might.

"Jesus, lady, what the hell?" a deep voice grumbles as strong arms curl around my body, pinning my flailing limbs to my sides as I continue to kick and squirm.

"Let me go! I will not be your sex slave!" I scream into the night air.

He freezes.

Then drops my arse to the ground.

I catch my breath before I turn to face my attacker.

You have got to be shitting me.

Elijah

SWEET BABY JESUS.

I look down at the woman crumpled at my feet only to be met with the same hazel eyes that were taunting me earlier this afternoon. But this time, they're filled with fear.

Then, her fear morphs into annoyance, I think. Reaching down through the smoke that's pouring from her engine, I blindly offer my hand with what I hope is a friendly smile. "I'm not going to hurt you," I assure her. The "sex slave" comment ricochets around inside my brain. *What has she been watching?*

She blinks up at me, then gingerly places her palm flush against mine, wrapping her fingers around my hand. The contact feels good. The press of her soft skin against my rough skin—although completely innocent—has the hairs on my arm standing at attention.

As soon as she's back on her feet, she yanks her hand free of my grasp. Her eyes narrow to slits as she glares at me. "Are you following me?"

I snort, shocked at her accusation. "Not likely."

Her glare only intensifies. "So how do you explain this then?" She gestures wildly between us with a pointed finger.

Strands of rich red hair hang in her eyes. I itch to move them, tuck them behind her ear, but she'd probably kick me in the balls again. "Explain what? That I saw a car broken down on the side of the road and pulled over to help?" I shove my hands into my pockets, pushing down the urge to touch her.

She swallows, and her tense facial features relax ever so slightly. Then she goes and licks her top lip like she did earlier, and my dick twitches in my jeans.

After what seems like a lifetime of silence, she stretches her hand out towards me. "I'm Charlotte. Thank you for stopping. There seems to be something wrong with my car."

I glance at her offered hand, taking it with caution just in case she freaks and tries to karate chop my arm off. Her delicate hand fits right inside mine. *So perfectly*. I hold onto it for a beat too long before releasing it. "Elijah. I'll, uh, take a look for you, but I can't make any promises."

The smoke that surrounded us moments ago has dissipated somewhat, and I poke around under the hood until I find the problem. "I think you've got a busted head gasket."

"What exactly does that mean?" she asks.

Gripping the back of my neck, I try to explain it to her. "Basically, you shouldn't be driving it anywhere. You're going to need a tow truck to pick it up and take it to a garage."

She licks her lip again. *Jesus, she's trying to kill me.* My heart thuds as she stands there staring at me with a blank expression on her gorgeous face. "I can take you back to my place so you can call someone?"

She raises a brow. "Can't I just use your phone here?"

I shake my head. "We're in a dead zone. There's no service, but we've got a landline back at the house." I point towards the porch lights shining in the distance. "That's my place there. It's only about a K or so up the road."

Charlotte glances in the direction I'm indicating, then squints. Releasing a deep sigh, she runs her hands down her sides, straightening her dress. "Okay. But I swear, if you try to shove me in a dungeon or attempt to turn me into a skinsuit, you will regret ever meeting me."

My lips curve despite my efforts not to smile. "Understood," I tell her, then open the passenger door and help her climb into the cab.

The drive is short, and Charlotte mumbles to herself the whole way about country folk giving her the creeps. I don't take offence. It's clear she's a city girl, through and through. Pulling into my parking spot, I notice Juda is home from his exploits. *This ought to be interesting.*

Charlotte meets me in front of my truck, and I offer her my arm. Tentatively, she curls her fingers around the crook of my elbow, and I lead us up the path to the house.

"I should warn you. My brothers are home, and the youngest one can be a bit ..." I try to think of a way to accurately describe Juda. "... over the top."

Lifting her chin, she frowns up at me. "Okay ..."

I can see the question in her eyes. "Sometimes, he's a

bit much. I just wanted to warn you, because he's probably going to make inappropriate sexual remarks when we walk in the door. He's been on my back about my lack of a sex life ..." *Christ, I can't believe I just said that out loud.* My mouth slams shut, stopping any other embarrassing facts from pouring out.

A wicked grin twists her full lips, then she winks. "I think I can handle him." Her eyes make a slow run down my body then come back to meet mine.

I swallow. *Yep, definitely trying to kill me.*

The second we're through the door, she shocks the shit out of me by spinning on her heels and pressing her body into my chest, then backing me up until my body hits the hard wood. I blink down at her. "What are you doing?" I whisper as she pushes up on her toes, bringing her mouth closer to mine.

She glances over her shoulder at my brothers sitting on the couch, their jaws unhinged. Charlotte smirks at them, then wraps her hands around the back of my neck, tugging my face down to meet hers. Her eyes fix on mine, then her tongue caresses my bottom lip in a long, smooth stroke. My eyes close—it feels so damn good. She tilts her head to the side, then her sweet tongue is inside my mouth.

My dick hardens as I taste her. I dig my fingers into her full hips and squeeze, lifting her and urging her legs around my waist. She complies, hooking her ankles at my lower back.

I switch out positions, pinning her to the door and taking over the kiss. She moans softly and wriggles her hips against me. Fuck, I want inside her so bad my balls throb with every slide she makes against my denim-covered dick.

Breaking the kiss, I press my forehead to hers, staring into her eyes as I pant for air. It's been a long fucking time since I kissed a woman like that. And it's got me wanting more. My heart hammers behind my ribs, and my cock pulses with need.

"Charlotte," I breathe, "what are we doing?"

She swallows, her eyes glazed with lust. "I ..." She releases a heavy sigh, then shakes her head. "Shit, I'm sorry. Please put me down."

Charlotte

What am I doing?

I didn't mean for it to go that far. When he mentioned his brother giving him shit about his sex life, I thought it would be funny to screw with him. And then I saw it was the cocky kid from the bakery on the couch, and next thing I knew, I was kissing Elijah like my life depended on it.

Elijah's forehead is still resting against mine. "Okay. Sorry, I got carried away," he says softly.

I feel every word against my damp lips and wish like hell I could keep kissing him. He tastes so good: like beer and man. I sigh as he gradually lowers me to my feet, letting me feel every part of his hard, sculpted body on my way down.

I squeeze my eyes shut. Stupid hormones, sending me on an emotional rollercoaster just for the hell of it. I've felt too many varying emotions in such a minimal timeframe: frustration at my car, anxiety because I couldn't fix it, annoyance at the battery life of my phone, terror at the possibility of becoming a skinsuit, then all-consuming lust.

Exhaustion takes over, leaving me feeling tired and heavy on my feet. Tonight has been… I don't even know what to call it. Overwhelming? Yes, that's definitely the word.

I slump against the door.

Elijah's calloused palm cups my cheek. "You okay?"

Nodding, I gaze up into his concerned eyes and plaster on a fake smile. "Yeah, I'm fine." I wink. "Put on a good show for your brothers, huh?" Shifting my gaze for a moment, I see they're still watching us closely, their eyes wide.

Elijah straightens, dropping his hand from my cheek and taking a step away from me. "If it was all for them…" he shakes his head, "…you shouldn't have."

I bite down on the corner of my lip, drop my gaze from his, and shrug. "It was nothing. I just thought you might like a little payback on your brother. Sounded like he was getting under your skin." I will absolutely not tell him that it may have started out that way, but he's the reason it escalated. I only planned to flirt my arse off and maybe kiss him. Just a peck or two.

His jaw clenches and he turns his back to me. "The phone's this way," he says over his shoulder as he walks towards a hallway, and I follow.

He leads me to an office with a large timber desk backed by larger glass windows and bookshelves lining the walls on either side of it. Elijah shuffles some papers around, locates the phone, and hands it to me. "I'll give you some privacy," he says. Then he's gone, and I'm left alone.

I round the desk and take a seat in the high-back leather chair before spinning it to face the window. All I see is black. Glancing back to the phone in my hands, I press the green *Talk* button and dial Reagan. It's the only number I know by heart. Nobody memorises phone numbers anymore—that's what mobile phones are for.

It rings and rings, then rings some more before connecting with her voicemail. I wait out her recorded message, then leave one for her. "Hey, Reags, it's me. I'm stuck in Bumfuck Nowhere, and my car broke down. Please call me back. I need you to come get me. Some guy stopped to help me and said it's a… umm…"

"Elijah?" I call out, hoping he's nearby so I can ask him what's wrong with my car.

A moment later, his head pops around the doorway. "Yeah?"

"What's the thing that's busted on my car called?"

He props himself against the frame, his ankles crossed. "The head gasket."

"Right," I mutter, then go back to leaving my message for Reagan. But I'm met with a dial tone. Crap, it cut out. I punch in her number again, then start my new message where the last one left off. "So, Elijah says the head gasket is blown or busted or something. The point is, I can't drive it, and I'm stuck in a house full of strange men. My phone is dead, so call me back on this number. Love you." Satisfied with the information I've provided, I blow a bunch of air kisses into the receiver then hang up.

I can feel Elijah's eyes on me. I swallow, then lift my eyes to meet his.

Ever so slowly, one of his thick, dark brows arches at me.

"What?"

Crossing those damn sexy arms over his broad chest, he says, "Stuck in Bumfuck Nowhere, in a house full of strange men?"

My focus is still stuck on his defined forearms when I answer him. "Well, what would you call it?"

His deep chuckle has my eyes darting back up to his face. "Now what?"

A sexy grin curves his lips, and dear God, the man has dimples. This isn't fair. The arms, the dimples, the thighs ... God is definitely testing me.

Chapter Five

Elijah

It's been an hour, and Charlotte's friend still hasn't called her back. She's sitting on the couch watching a movie with my brothers, and I'm sitting at the dining table, staring at her.

She seems relaxed, comfortable even. And I can't make myself look away. She's a breath of fresh—albeit crazy—air. She already told Asher and Juda about mistaking me for a serial killer and kicking me in the nuts, which they, of course, found hilarious.

Juda keeps looking at her like he wants to eat her, and Asher has his arm draped over the back of the couch behind her. Both those little fuckers are trying to steal her from me.

No, wait. She's not mine.

But tell that to my pounding heart.

I grit my teeth, the direction of my thoughts darkening my mood.

Delilah trots down the hall, spots me at the table, and breaks into an excited gallop-bounce-run-type thing that looks comical. "Hey, baby, you been napping?" I ask, giving her a scratch behind her big, banana-shaped ears. She nuzzles into my chest, her front legs propped on my lap.

My attention is snatched away by the sound of something crashing in the lounge area, then a high-pitched screech. Charlotte is plastered against the far wall, her eyes wide as she stutters, "G-giant r-rat!"

I look around the room, searching for the rodent, but come up empty. Juda and Asher do the same, shifting the coffee table and looking under the couch until Charlotte speaks up again.

She points at me. "Wh-what is that?"

Delilah doesn't respond well to loud noises, so she's fully in my lap now, shaking like a leaf. I stroke her long neck and coo, "Shh, it's okay, baby. Don't mind the crazy lady."

"Crazy?" she shrieks, pressing her palm to her chest. "I'm not the one cuddling an oversized rat!"

I narrow my stare at her. "Delilah is not vermin. I'll have you know she's a pedigree llama." Delilah snuggles into my neck, hiding her face from the banshee screaming at her. I don't blame the poor little thing.

Charlotte tilts her head to the side, examining me as my hand continues to run long, soothing strokes down Delilah's neck. Asher and Juda gave up the rat search and are now sitting back on the couch, their eyes flicking back and forth between Charlotte and me.

Neither of us is willing to break the stare-down we've got going on. Then she goes and licks her damn lip, and I drop my eyes. Grumbling obscenities under my breath, I gently place Delilah on the floor, then go about making her a bedtime bottle.

The whole time, my mind is on Charlotte's lips. How can one simple action turn me on so damn much? My dick presses so firmly against my zipper it's painful. Reaching down, I rearrange my junk but freeze when Charlotte steps into the kitchen, her eyes going to my hand. I look down, seeing what she's seeing, then release my dick like it's on fire.

Charlotte purses her lips for a brief moment, then curls them up into a flirtatious grin. "Llamas really do it for you, huh?"

My jaw slackens, then I glare at her as I stalk towards her, backing her against the pantry door. I stop mere inches from her, bracing my forearms on either side of her head. "No, Charlotte, I'm not into bestiality. What I am into, apparently, *is you*."

Her big hazel eyes widen impossibly as she stares back up at me. They roam over my face, then flick down to my crotch where I'm now sporting full wood. Her tongue slips out to wet those perfect lips that I haven't stopped thinking about since she kissed me. *Goddamn.*

I am usually a gentleman in every sense of the word. But right now, this very second, I want nothing more than to throw her over my shoulder and take her to my bedroom.

It's a struggle keeping my arms pressed to the pantry

door, not touching her. She asked me to stop before, and I won't touch her again until she asks me to. *Fuck, I want her to ask me. I want her to beg me.*

Breathing through my nose, I pick up her deliciously enticing scent. It's just as enticing as everything else about her. Keeping my gaze on hers, I wait for her to say something—anything—in response to my statement. But for once, she's completely silent.

Her hands shift from their place at her sides to clutch her stomach.

I frown. "What's wrong?" I ask as pain flits across her features. She inhales deeply through her nose, then releases her breath slowly through her mouth. I tilt my head. "Charlotte, what's happening right now?"

She swallows. "I need my painkillers. And a heat pack, if you've got one."

The crease between my brows deepens. "Why? What's wrong?" I cup her jaw as her face crumples in pain.

"I have endometriosis. It's a girl thing," she mutters through clenched teeth. "I need to sit down."

I move immediately, following behind her as she shuffles to a chair at the dining table. Collapsing into it, she folds herself in half, and I watch all the colour leech from her face. *Fuck me, what the hell is endometriosis?*

"Asher," I snap. "Where are your heat packs?"

He turns to face me and jumps to his feet the second his eyes land on Charlotte. He's sprinting to his room a second later, no questions asked.

I crouch at Charlotte's side. "Asher's getting you a heat pack. What else do you need? What can I do?"

Unshed tears pool in her eyes. It's a punch to the gut. I'm winded by the look of sheer anguish in her gaze. "Jesus, sweetheart, tell me what to do."

"My bag," she whispers. "I have some pills in there."

I shoot to my feet, but Juda is already making his way over to us with her huge handbag in tow. He hands it to me, then goes to the kitchen, grabs a glass, and fills it from the tap.

Her bag has so much shit in it, and I have no idea what I'm actually looking for. It's like Mary freaking Poppins' bag of tricks. Finally, my fingers curl around a bottle at the bottom, and I pull it out. "Is this it?" I ask, holding it up in front of her.

She nods and snatches it from my hand, twisting off the cap and throwing a few pills in her mouth before Juda can even give her the glass of water. He passes it to her after she's already swallowed them dry. I cringe. I've never been able to do that.

Asher returns with the huge heat pack he usually uses for his back and throws it in the microwave. Is there something else I should be doing right now? She asked for heat and pills, but there must be more I can do to help her. She looks so uncomfortable. Then it hits me.

"Charlotte, I'm going to pick you up, okay?"

She nods but stays silent. I slide one arm under her knees. The other curls around her waist, and I stand. "I'm taking you to my bed. You'll be more comfortable there," I tell her as I close the distance to my bedroom at the end of the hall. Juda sprints ahead of us to open the door.

Her body twists into me, and I tighten my hold on her.

I can feel every one of her deep inhales and her shuddering releases. Juda pulls back my covers, and I gently place her on the mattress. She curls into herself as I tug the covers back up and over her.

Running my hand over my head, I grip a fistful of hair and stare down at her as her small body rocks in my bed. Asher bursts in a second later with his heat pack.

"Charlotte," he says as he approaches. "Where do you want it, honey?"

I frown at his term of endearment but don't dwell on it. I'm too worried about the woman who stormed into my world just hours ago.

She doesn't reply, just reaches a hand out for the offered heat pack and snatches it from Asher. The three of us stand around the bed, watching her.

"Stop staring. I'll be fine," she mumbles. When none of us respond, she sighs heavily. "Creepers," she whispers under her breath, and I crack a smile.

That sounds more like the woman I met this afternoon.

JUST FREAKING GREAT.

This had to happen right now? I grit my teeth to keep

from gasping as another stabbing pain shoots through my pelvis.

Half an hour ago, I was horny. Now, I'm curled up in the object of my desire's bed ... in excruciating pain. The varying expressions of horror covering the faces of the three men surrounding me are the very reason I don't do relationships—well, part of the reason.

The heat pack is helping already, and I can take a deep breath. I meet Elijah's eyes. He's worried. "I'm okay, really," I say, but his frown deepens.

"I think we have different definitions of the word *okay*."

I grin. "Yeah, we might. But seriously, I'm used to this. I'll be fine."

His eyes bug. "What do you mean you're used to this? This is not fucking normal."

Shrugging, I tell him the truth. "It is for me. I've lived with this for years."

"Years? Jesus, what's wrong with you?" Juda bursts out.

"Endo-something," Elijah answers his brother.

Juda looks confused. "And what the fuck is that?"

I give him the blanket answer I give most people who find out I have it. "Lady problems. Thank the gods you're a dude," I say with a wink.

Asher, who has remained quiet throughout this conversation, suddenly shoves a notepad and pen in my face. "Write it down."

Scribbling the word *endometriosis* on a piece of paper, I hand it back to him. He pulls his phone out of his back pocket and immediately begins tapping away, referencing the notepad then focusing back on his phone. Both Juda and Elijah move closer to him and look over his shoulder as he does this.

It's strange. I've never had anyone look it up to see what I'm talking about before. I watch them for a few minutes until I can't fight the drowsiness that comes from the painkillers I had to take. I give in to the weight of my lids and close my eyes.

I GROAN, GROGGY FROM MY PAINKILLER-INDUCED SLEEP, AND shift to get more comfortable.

My eyes flash open—someone is spooning me.

I roll to face said someone only to scream my lungs out at the sight before me.

There is a llama in the bed.

A fucking *llama*.

The creature startles awake and screeches back at me. Its long limbs kick out, and it lands a solid hoof to the vagina. Tears prickle my eyes as I coil into myself, clutching my throbbing beaver.

Two seconds pass, then the bedroom door is flung open so hard it bounces off the wall behind it and slams shut again. Muttered curses filter through as it's opened with more care the second time.

Elijah stands in the open doorway in nothing but a pair of long flannel sleep pants. If I wasn't in the middle of nursing a broken vagina, I'd take time to appreciate the view.

"What happened?" he asks, eyes wild, searching the dimly lit room.

I watch him take two long strides to the side of the bed and flick on a lamp. The overgrown rodent flings itself at him like I'm the bad guy in this scenario. I glare at it. Manipulative little—

"Shh, it's okay, Dilly. It's okay, baby." He soothes the furry beast.

"I'm not!" I blurt. "That thing was spooning me, then it kicked me in the vaj so hard Betty was seeing stars."

He pauses, his hand in mid-air, about to stroke the llama's freakishly long neck, and stares at me. "Wha—who's Betty?"

I know I'm giving him crazy eyes right now. But it can't be helped. I'm in the midst of an emotional breakdown. "Betty is my vagina!" I cry. And that's when I notice two more shirtless men standing in the room with us. *Great. This is just freaking peachy.*

Juda is clearly trying not to laugh. I say *trying* because the ginormous grin on his stupid face and the shuddering of his torso is giving him away. *Asshole.* At least Asher has the decency to turn and face the wall to hide his mirth.

Meanwhile, Elijah is still staring at me, slack-jawed.

Chapter Six

Charlotte

You know how sometimes you just know you're going to have a shit-tastic day before it's even really started? Well, today is one of those days.

I'm sitting on the couch, nursing a steaming mug of tea that Elijah just made me, replaying the last twelve hours in my head, going over every detail that brought me to this point.

"You look like you're thinking pretty hard there," Asher says as he takes a seat beside me.

I nod. "I'm just trying to figure out where I went wrong."

Leaning over, he rests his thick forearms on his knees and faces me. *What is it with this family and the sexy forearms?*

His brows furrow in concern. "What do you mean?"

I lick my lips and shuffle around, leaning my side into the back of the couch so I can look at him properly. "Well, yesterday I was going about my business like normal, and today, I woke up with a llama who assaulted my womanhood."

Asher snorts. "Assaulted your womanhood? You're a hoot, Charlotte. I'm so glad your car broke down. I haven't laughed this much in ages."

Raising an unimpressed brow, I stare at his smirking face. "So glad I could be of service," I deadpan.

He reaches a big hand over and musses my hair. "Me too."

My eyes pop. "First, don't ever touch my hair. And second, you should look up the term sarcasm. You clearly don't understand what it is."

"Oh, I do. I just chose to ignore it," he says with a wink, stands, then joins Elijah and Juda.

I have to admit, I could get used to this. Kicking my legs up on the cushions, I lean back against the armrest and watch the three brothers move around the kitchen, preparing breakfast. It sure is a sight to behold.

I'm about to take another sip of my tea when the flea bag trots into the lounge and jumps up on the end of the couch near my feet. I scowl at it. The nerve! After what she did to me, she thinks she can just waltz in here and share a seat with me? I don't think so.

"Shoo, shoo, you little beast," I whisper harshly at it while doing the classic shooing motion with my free hand.

She ignores me.

No surprises there. I'm about to get up and move to the single-seater when the shrill ringing of a phone pierces the air. *Reagan!* I run down the hall to the office I made my call in last night and snatch the phone up, hitting the answer button.

"Reagan? Please be Reagan."

"Char, I'm so sorry, I only just got your messages! Are you okay? Where are you?" Reagan's sweet voice fills my ears, and I sigh in relief.

I fill her in on my whereabouts, and she tells me she's on her way with Rhett in tow. My shoulders slump in relief. My rescue party is coming for me.

Elijah

I SLEPT ON THE COUCH LAST NIGHT AND LET CHARLOTTE have my bed. She looked so beautiful curled up in my sheets, her red hair splayed over my white pillowcases. I'd be lying if I said I didn't stare at her for a good half-hour before finally leaving her alone and crashing out on the couch.

For the first time in a long time, I woke up with pep in my step, even though I'm too big to comfortably sleep on the couch. It was her. Everything about her makes my heart beat faster. She makes me feel alive. I never know what she's going to do or say next, and it's exhilarating.

The boys and I read up on endometriosis a little bit last night, and it sounds like a shitshow of epic proportions. I've never been so thankful to have a dick.

I'm cracking eggs into the pan when Charlotte enters the kitchen.

"I assume that was your friend?"

She smiles so bright it lights up her whole face. "Yeah, she and her boyfriend are on their way to get me. He's a mechanic, so he'll work his voodoo car magic and get me on the road again."

I nod, turning my focus back to the eggs as I try not to let my disappointment show. My chest squeezes with the knowledge that I'll probably never see Charlotte again. That this was all just a random, one-in-a-hundred-thousand-chance meeting.

A sense of urgency bubbles up in my gut, telling me I have to do something, anything, to ensure I see her again. *But what?* We have nothing in common. There is no logical reason for us to reconnect.

Fuuuck ... I grip the back of my neck. There has to be something.

Delilah sidles up to me, nudging my hip with her nose. She's hungry, and I've been so distracted with Charlotte this morning I haven't even started preparing her bottle. I scratch between her big ears as I remove the last of the eggs from the pan. "I'll make it now, baby."

"I already did," Asher says, waving Delilah's bottle in front of my face. "I'll feed her; you finish up in here."

I'm not used to him being up this early. It's weird, but not surprising since Charlotte's panicked shrieks woke us all this morning. Delilah scurries off after Asher, and I watch as Charlotte's face scrunches up in what I think is distaste.

"You feed that thing a bottle? Doesn't it eat grass and stuff?" she asks, looking between Asher and myself.

I shrug. "Yes, through the day when she goes out to the yards with me. But she's too young to go without the bottle yet. Her mother ... she, uh ... she didn't make it. I've raised her from a newborn cria to the little rascal you see now."

Charlotte pauses, her gaze fixed on me. Then she sighs dramatically and rolls her eyes towards the ceiling. "Well, I can't hate on her now, can I? What kind of bitch would that make me, hating on an orphan?"

My lips purse. "Ah, yeah, I guess so."

She shakes her head and rounds the kitchen island separating us. "You need a hand with any of this?"

"No, it's all done now. Time to eat." I wink at her, pick up the plates loaded with eggs, bacon, and toast, and take them to the table.

She follows along behind me, muttering, "I could have carried a plate or something."

Once we're all seated and digging into our food, Charlotte announces, "Reagan and Rhett will be here in about an hour to pick me up. I just want to thank you ..." her eyes meet each of ours, "... *all* of you, for everything you did for me last night. And apologise for being a burden on you."

My knife and fork clatter to the table. "Excuse me? What do you mean, a burden? You weren't a burden, Charlotte. You're probably the most exciting thing to happen around here in a long fucking time."

Shit. I said fuck.

"Uh, I mean, in a long damn time."

She bites down on her bottom lip and grins. "It's okay; you can say fuck. I say it all the time."

I close my eyes. The sight of her is just too much. And hearing her say fuck? Well, it makes me think about fucking. And that's the last thing that should be on my mind right now, especially when surrounded by my brothers. But knowing them, they're probably thinking about it now, too ... *perverts.*

"Hell, you sure you have to go?" Juda says. "You're kind of awesome. I wouldn't mind keeping you around for a little while." He says this with a wicked grin, and I kick him under the table. He glares at me, and I glare right back at the little shit.

Charlotte just snorts and rolls her eyes at his attempt at seduction—which makes me really fucking happy.

She pats his arm. "Oh, honey, if I stuck around, it wouldn't be for you." Then her eyes land on ... me.

I choke on the toast halfway down my throat. Coughing and hacking, I thump my chest and take a swig of my coffee, washing the lump down. Jesus, that was embarrassing. I sneak a peek at Charlotte, and she's grinning at me.

Closing my eyes, I drop my head and shake it. *You're so smooth, Eli.* Running my hand through my hair, I shovel another bite of food into my mouth.

We finish eating in surprisingly comfortable silence.

After breakfast, Asher clears off the table and sets about cleaning the kitchen and dishes. I watch Charlotte as she watches him. Frowning, she leans over the table and whispers, "Is he doing that because I'm here? Or is this some parallel universe where men clean up after themselves?"

I smile and give up the struggle to not touch her. Reaching out, I tuck her unruly hair behind her ear and reply, "It's not for your benefit. It's one of his chores around here. We all have a role to play."

Her eyes brighten. "So he does this every day? Can I take him home with me? I'll pay you for the inconvenience."

With a chuckle, I scrape my chair back from the table and stand. "The things that come out of your mouth," I murmur, shaking my head.

Charlotte snorts again. "Oh, you haven't heard anything yet. Just wait until you meet Reagan. You should hear the stuff that comes out of her mouth; I've got nothing in comparison."

I raise a questioning brow. "You sure about that? 'Cause you just asked to buy my brother ..."

She shrugs. "He cleans. I was being perfectly serious, Elijah. A man that looks like he does and cleans without being asked is a hot commodity. You could start a bidding war for him on eBay. You'd get top dollar."

I glance at Asher as he moves around the kitchen, placing scraps into the bin, loading plates in the dishwasher, and wiping down the benchtop as he goes. She's probably onto something, but I'll lose my man card if I admit it. That and I'm a tiny bit pissed off she wants to take him home and not me.

A subject change is definitely in order. Checking my

watch, I figure I've got about twenty or so minutes before her friends arrive. I extend my hand to her. "You want to have a look around? See the place in the daylight?"

She nods and takes my hand. "Sure."

The second our skin makes contact, I feel it, just like yesterday and every other time we've touched—this undeniable pull towards her.

Charlotte

Elijah tugs me towards a huge, red barn, and I freeze.

He looks back at me over his shoulder, and I widen my eyes, pointing at the barn. "That is exactly the kind of place where one would attempt to make a skinsuit out of another human being."

His answering chuckle eases my irrational fears enough for me to continue trudging along behind him. Well, that and the fact that my rescue party is already on its way to retrieve me.

In one smooth motion, he swings the barn doors open wide, pausing in the threshold. "See any skinning equipment?" he asks, sweeping his arm out in front of us.

I elbow him. He lets out a puff of air and glares down at me. "What was that for?"

Rolling my eyes, I take a step forward. "For being a smartarse."

Our fingers find each other again as he leads me through the large structure to a side access. Gesturing with his chin to the door, he tells me, "This is the birthing paddock. If you're lucky, there'll be a brand new cria in here."

I scrunch my nose. "I don't know what that is. You said it before about the little hellion in the house, but I thought you meant it cried a lot."

With a shake of his head, he opens the door and steps through, tugging me with him. When we're standing in ankle-high grass, he points to the far side of the paddock. A massive smile splits his handsome face. "See? That's a cria. It's what baby llamas and alpacas are called."

"Oh." Well, don't I feel like an idiot.

"Come on," he urges and walks towards the mama llama and its baby.

I dig my heels in. "No, I'm good. I can see it from here. One llama encounter a day is plenty enough for me, thanks."

Just as the words are out of my mouth, the critter I was referring to scampers past me, startling me so badly I leap onto Elijah's back. My arms and legs wrap around him like a boa constrictor squeezing the life out of its prey. "That thing will be the death of me!"

Elijah chuckles, then curls his arms around my thighs. "Why are you so bothered by her?" he asks, closing the space between us and the mama llama again.

My limbs lock around him. "I'm not bothered. I just—I'm not an animal person."

"You came to the wrong place then."

I roll my eyes. “I didn’t come here by choice, remember? You kidnapped me off the side of the road!”

His head tips back, resting against my shoulder as he laughs, and I glare at his stupidly gorgeous face and those damn dimples.

Chapter Seven

Charlotte

I relax my hold around Elijah's neck. I don't want to suffocate him. He'd drop me, and then I'd be alone in this paddock, surrounded by furry demons.

He comes to a stop a few feet from the new mother and glances at me over his shoulder. "You want to get down? She won't hurt you."

A loud snort rips from my nose. "Yeah, no. I'm good here. Thanks."

His smirk is downright delicious. "Okay then. Well, this is Genie." He gestures with his chin to the tall, black-and-white llama standing in front of us. Then, he drops down into a squat, and I squeal, wrapping myself more securely around him. He chuckles at me and moves his attention to the little ball of fur curled up in the grass.

I peek over his shoulder. It's a little bit cute. All black except for its little white head. I smile as it flutters its long lashes, peering up at us. "She's kinda cute," I whisper, afraid to startle it. Then I frown. "It is a girl, right?"

"If you'd let me put you down, I could check."

Licking my lips, I ponder his words. My eyes take in our surroundings. There are three other big fatties in the paddock, but they're far enough away that I'd have enough time to scale Elijah again if they came at me. Taking a deep, calming breath, I lower my feet to the ground then release him as I stand and take a step back.

Elijah glances at me over his shoulder, a satisfied smile curving his lips. I cross my arms and shift my attention back to the big mama. She's eyeballing me, and I take another cautious step away from her.

"It's a boy," Elijah says. "What should we call him?"

My eyes widen. "How should I know? He's your llama."

One side of his mouth kicks up in a grin. "Humour me. What would you call him if you could name him anything at all?"

I draw my bottom lip between my teeth as I think it over. Tilting my head, I look down at the little guy. His lashes are so thick and long I'm actually jealous. *Good Lord, what is happening to me? I'm jealous of a llama ...* I blink away the thought and scrunch my brows in concentration.

The pressure is real, I tell you. Dishing out names is not for the faint-hearted. A name can make or break you. It's important. Super important. I don't want to ruin his little llama life by giving him the wrong one!

"Whoa, there," Elijah says, coming to stand in front of me. He cups my jaw before plucking my lip out from between my teeth with his thumbs. "You're thinking way too hard. You'll end up chewing right through your lips. And I can't have that. I like them too much."

A big fat lump of surprise clogs my throat. *He likes my lips?* I'm not usually self-conscious around men. I'm comfortable in my skin, even if my body is a dud. But the way he's looking down at me makes butterflies swarm in my chest. That's never happened before.

"Rue," I blurt out.

Elijah frowns. Both his big, rough palms are cupping either side of my face. "What?"

I blink furiously up at him. "Rue. I'd call him Rue. You know, like RuPaul, the drag queen? Because he's just so pretty. He could easily pass as a girl." The words just tumble out of my mouth before I even have time to process them. But now that they're out there, I know it's the perfect name for him.

One of Elijah's hands moves to scratch at his eyebrow. "You want me to name him after a drag queen?"

Nodding, I lick my lips, and his gaze tracks the movement of my tongue.

My heartbeat triples. His blue eyes darken like storm clouds as he stares down at my parted mouth.

"I'm going to kiss you now, Charlotte."

He doesn't wait for a response. Lowering his head, he closes the distance between our mouths and crashes his lips against mine. Keeping one hand on my jaw, he moves the other to the small of my back, tucking me in closer to his big, broad body.

Holy shit, he's a good kisser.

My arms circle his neck as I tilt my head and let him take the lead. The hand on my back splays wide until two of his fingers are on my butt, then he slides it all the way down to cup a full cheek in his palm. When he squeezes the flesh on an upward pull, I feel his erection grind into my belly, and I moan.

Digging my hands in the hair at the nape of his neck, I tug him closer, relishing the feel of his large body surrounding me so fully. I feel warm and safe in his strong arms.

"What the fuck?" I screech. My feet disappear from beneath me. I'm falling.

Landing flat on my back in the grass, my eyes widen as Elijah tumbles on top of me. He manages to keep from crushing me by catching himself on his hands on either side of my head.

The furry, crotch-kicking demon scuttles over, nudging Elijah with her head and making a weird sound. I glare at her.

Elijah's eyes search my face. "You okay?"

I meet his eyes and nod, one curt tip of my chin, then I go back to murdering the moment-ruining beast at our side with my eyes. "She's got the devil in her. You should knock her off before she kills someone."

Deep, masculine laughter is the only response I get.

My eyes scan our surroundings, making sure the other llamas haven't come any closer. "I'm serious. She's a menace."

He rolls to his side, propping himself on his elbow and

staring down at me. I catch my breath. The look in his eyes stops my heart in its tracks.

"Can I call you?" he asks.

I blink. Then blink again.

He raises a questioning brow.

I raise both of mine. "You want to ... call me?" I sputter.

His smile is bright. "I do."

"But I don't do phone calls. Talking on the phone is an absolute last resort—reserved for emergency use only."

Elijah scratches at his brow again. "I would message you, but like I already told you, we're in a dead zone. It'd really be easier for me to call."

My shoulders lift in a shrug. "Sorry to break it to you, but nothing about me is easy. Also, I feel I should inform you that I recently made a vow of celibacy. That may affect your reasons for wanting to stay in touch."

Shock widens his eyes. "Wha—I mean, I didn't—shit." He sighs and scrubs a hand over his face. "I'm sorry if I'm coming on too strong. I just ... I've never met a woman like you before, and I don't want you to walk out of my life as fast as you walked into it."

I can't stop my smile. His words settle in my chest, and those butterflies go crazy again. "Okay." How could I possibly say no after that?

He leans over me, using his free hand to support his weight. "I promise I'll text as much as I can and only call if I'm desperate," he says with a wink, then presses a kiss to my swollen lips.

Just as I wrap my fingers around his neck, a voice that

can only belong to my best friend yells, "Did you know llama poo has special powers?!"

Elijah's lips leave mine instantly, and he stands, then offers me a hand up. I silently fume. What is it with bitches ruining my moments today?

Once on my feet, I peer around Elijah's wide frame to see Reagan perched on top of the timber fence railings.

She smiles wide and waves. Her vigorous wave tilts her off balance, but Rhett steps up behind her, steadying her just before she face-plants.

After reaching back, Elijah takes my hand and strolls over to my friends. Coming to a stop in front of them, he offers up his free hand. "Hi, you must be Reagan. I'm Elijah."

Reags takes his hand. "I figured. Char mentioned you on the phone this morning." Then, her bright blue eyes meet mine, and she waggles her brows. "He's a bit of a sexy one. Bet you're regretting that celibacy thing now, huh?"

My eyes bug. "Reagan!"

She rears back. "What?"

I huff. "Maybe a little. But it's for the greater good. At least that's what I've been telling myself," I mumble.

Rhett props his elbows on the top rung of the fence beside Reagan's rear. He gives Elijah a once-over, then the universal *'sup* chin-lift thing that guys do. "Thanks for lookin' out for this one. She's a bit of a handful. But you're still in one piece, so she must have kept her crazy in the closet."

Elijah chuckles and tugs me into his side, slinging an

arm around my shoulders. "She did kick me in the balls and accuse me of being a sexual predator attempting to turn her into a skinsuit."

My friends are not surprised. Not one little bit. They both simply nod as if that's normal behaviour.

I cross my arms over my chest and scowl.

"So, what was that you were saying about llama powers?" Elijah asks Reagan.

Her face lights up. She's found another person to wow with her knowledge bank of random facts. "In Bolivia, they use llama poop to clean polluted water from the mines. It reduces the acid and removes the diluted metals in the water."

"Huh, that's pretty cool. I know a fair bit about my babies, but that one's news to me. How do you even know that? Do you have llamas?"

"Pffft, I wish. Actually, no, I want an alpaca. But Rhett says they're not apartment-appropriate pets," she declares with an exaggerated eye roll.

Rhett shakes his head at his girlfriend, but he's smiling.

Their love makes me want something like that for myself. Then Elijah squeezes my hip. When I look up to meet his gaze, he's looking down at me with something I can't name. But I really like it.

Reagan and Rhett's soft bickering pulls my attention away from Elijah. Her hands are on her hips as she tells him alpacas are smaller than llamas, therefore they don't need as much space and would be fine with daily walks around the block.

I snort at the look on Rhett's face, because he knows Reagan is one hundred percent serious.

Elijah interrupts their debate. "I'd have to agree with your man here on that one. I've got alpacas in the next paddock over. I can assure you none of them would make good flatmates."

"You have alpacas? Show me!" Reagan excitedly squeals as she scrambles off the fence into the paddock with us. She slips on the last rung and lands hard on her butt. Getting to her feet, she rubs her rear. "That hurt," she mutters.

And that's when Delilah, the demon spawn, sidles up to our little group. I glare at her. "Watch out for that one, Reags. She's vicious."

Reagan frowns, angles her chin, then crouches down, coming to eye level with the nasty little wench. "She doesn't seem vicious to me," she says, reaching out to stroke Delilah's long, skinny neck.

Instead of spitting on Reagan or head butting her like I expect, Delilah closes the space between them and cuddles up to her.

My jaw drops in shock. That little ...

Chapter Eight

Charlotte

A FEELING I'M NOT ACCUSTOMED TO SETTLES OVER ME AS Rhett pulls out of Elijah's drive. He brought a car trailer with him, and we're going to tow my car back to his garage.

I sit in the back seat, staring at the landscape out the window. It is kind of nice out here. Quiet. I've always been a city girl. Small towns make me twitchy, as do the majority of people who live in them.

But my obvious wrong assessment of Elijah has me thinking that maybe I judged this place too quickly. I mean, I love McKenna and Myrtle. *I wonder if she still speaks to her mother after naming her that?* Myrtle, I mean. What an awful name. I shudder.

See? That's what people in small towns do: they give their children godawful names like Myrtle. I've been trying to think up a cute nickname for her since she started working for me on the blog. No luck yet, but I'm sure I'll come up with something eventually.

Reagan turns in her seat next to Rhett in the front. Wrapping her arms around the headrest, she stares at me expectantly.

I pretend not to notice.

She clears her throat.

I look at my nails like they're the most interesting thing ever.

That makes her huff. "So, what's the go with that Elijah guy? He's so into you. Even I could tell. Now that's saying something."

Rhett snorts. "What gave it away, honey? The way he didn't take his eyes off her the whole time we were there, or them sucking face when we arrived?"

My shoulder lifts in a small shrug. It's an attempt to play it off. But nothing about the last twenty-four hours was normal. Not for me, at least. "He's just a guy who helped a stranded stranger out. I didn't know that kind of hospitality even existed anymore. He and his brothers took me in like it was no big deal. They let me use their phone, watch their TV, eat their food. Then, when I had an endo episode, they took care of me. Who does that? It's weird, right?"

Reagan blinks at me, dumbfounded. "You had a flare-up and they didn't freak out? I freaked out the first few times, remember? Hell, even now, I just want to bundle you up and take you to the nearest hospital."

Rhett pulls the truck off the road then backs it up to

my car. Reagan and I don't offer to help him; we'd just get in the way.

I nod at her. "I know, right? I'm on day eight today, so things have settled right down and it's almost over. But the stress of my car dying, then thinking I was going to be mugged by a dirty farmer and kept in his crusty sex dungeon—it just set everything off."

"I get that. But what'd they do when you went all pale and glassy-eyed?"

Shuffling around, I make myself more comfortable on the hard bench seat. "It's a little fuzzy. I'm pretty sure Elijah carried me to his bed. His brother, Asher, has heat packs that he got for me, and then they gave me my pills. I remember trying to tell them it was no big deal and them not believing me. Next thing I knew, I was waking up next to the devil's mistress and copping a hoof to the vulva."

The look of complete and utter horror on Reagan's face reflects my feelings on the matter perfectly.

"No," she gasps. "Not that gorgeous little one that was following us around on the farm tour? She wouldn't. She was so sweet."

My snort is involuntary and loud. "You have no idea. I felt sorry for her for, like, twenty minutes because she's an orphan and Elijah has been bottle-feeding her since she was born. But then she knocked me on my arse in the paddock. She's got it out for me, I tell you."

Rhett climbs back in the cab with us and starts laughing, his shoulders shaking violently as he loses his shit. "A llama has it out for you? A baby one, at that. Do you even hear yourself?"

I cross my arms over my chest defensively. "When you've taken a hoof to your favourite body part, then we can talk."

My phone chimes with an incoming text, and I reach for my bag, rummaging around until I find it. Juda lent me a power-bank thing to charge it up on the drive home. I agreed to drop it in to McKenna for him next time I'm in town.

When the screen comes to life, I see it's a text from Elijah. My smile is instant. I can't swipe my finger across the screen fast enough.

ELIJAH: Travel safe. Let me know how you go with your car.

I deflate. How underwhelming. I don't know what I was expecting, but it was more than I got. My reply is concise.

CHARLOTTE: I will. Thank you for your hospitality.

A moment later, my phone chirps again. I didn't think he would reply.

ELIJAH: Is it bad of me to be thankful for your car breaking down?

I grin and punch out a response.

CHARLOTTE: Maybe a little. But I'm glad it happened too.

Elijah

I CAN'T STOP THINKING ABOUT HER.

When I close my eyes, it's her I see. Red hair splayed over my pillows as she sleeps. Her beautiful hazel eyes and the kaleidoscope of colours within them. Her brilliant smile when I kissed her in the paddock. The glare she wore whenever Delilah got too close.

She is under my skin, and I don't know if it's because of all the shit Juda's been putting in my head or ... No, I know it's not that. It's all her.

I want Charlotte. I just have to figure out how to get her.

Chapter Nine

Charlotte

Now that my lady problems are over for the month, I can get some work done. I've spent the morning writing an article I've titled "*No, I'm Not Pregnant.*" This is a common statement for women with endometriosis when the bloat hits. We can stand next to a woman who is actually expecting a small human being to erupt from her vagina and have the same size mid-region.

My fashion blog, Charlotte's Closet, focuses not just on clothing but the issues that women face that, in turn, affect their wardrobe choices. For instance, the clothes I wear during hell week are very different from my general wardrobe. I'm a big fan of simple bottoms and loud tops.

However, when I'm fighting the red sea, I stick to dark tones. They hide most unexpected leaks, helping lower the mortification levels when such a situation does occur. I also stick to stretchy fabrics on the bottom half, even when it's not a devil day. You never know when the bloat will strike, and it's best to be prepared and comfortable.

Then, we have the issue of what to match them with. Tunics are always a winner in my book, but they don't suit everyone. Basically, anything that is longer than your classic T-shirt is going to be a good idea. I have a whole segment of the blog dedicated to this very subject.

Just because our bodies are faulty doesn't mean we shouldn't get to look fabulous when we feel up to it. Every day that I'm not crippled by pain, I celebrate by dressing up. I accessorise and do my makeup, hair, and nails to match.

Don't get me wrong, I like lounging around in yoga pants as much as any other woman. But I've spent too much of my life in my PJs already.

Right now, I'm wearing a pair of dark-blue skinny jeans, strappy caramel wedges, and a cream peasant top that drapes off one shoulder. My long, crimson hair is in a fishtail braid hanging down my spine, and I've applied extra mascara to really make my eyes pop.

I feel strong and in control of my life.

Scanning over the article I've just finished, I pause. Here I am trying to empower women, telling them not to let one thing get in the way of them going out and living their lives to the fullest, yet I'm not taking my own advice.

I may still be presenting myself as a queen, but I've cut out one of my favourite activities—one of the few things that truly makes me feel *good*—all because of one sexual disaster.

It's time to get back on the horse. After saving the

article, I shut down my computer then grab my phone, opening my favourite hook-up app. It's settled. I can have sex with whoever I want, and it will be absolutely fine.

I'm scrolling through the list of potential bed mates when my phone chimes, a text notification popping up at the top of the screen.

Elijah's name is staring me in the face. I've been actively trying *not* to think about him.

Yes, he's attractive—okay, that's an understatement, but moving on. He's all the physical things I look for in a bed buddy, but he's also so much more. He is also all the things I avoid like the plague.

He's the triple C threat—considerate, charming, and confident. Then, on top of that, he has this wholesome vibe I never knew I was into until I met him.

Swallowing back my apprehension, I open the message.

ELIJAH: I've been thinking, and I decided we should go for dinner this weekend.

I blink at the screen several times, not sure how to react or respond. He wants to take me out for dinner. Why? I live in the city; he lives in a little podunk town in the middle of nowhere with llamas. Dinner is something you take a date to—someone you plan on having a relationship with.

I need to quash this right now. I know what I have to say, despite the little voice inside my head telling me I should at least give this a chance. *He's not like— No.* I cut that thought short. I refuse to think about *him*. I'll just be dragged into a pit of regret and self-loathing.

CHARLOTTE: Thanks, but no thanks.

There. Directness is the best way to handle such situations.

My phone rings in my palm, startling me. I jump. The phone flips and slips between my fingers until I get a good grip on it again. It's Elijah. And I accidentally answered while fumbling with it.

"He—hello," I sputter.

"Charlotte," he drawls.

I swallow. I'd blocked out how much I like the deep timbre of his voice.

"Why don't you want to go to dinner with me?"

Taking a deep breath, I ground myself then straighten my shoulders. "It's not a good idea."

"Because?"

"Because I said so." *Duh …*

"I think it's a very good idea. In fact, I think it's an excellent idea."

I can't help it; I smile. "Do you now? And what makes you think that?"

He doesn't even hesitate. "Because I haven't stopped thinking about you since you left my house. I want to see you; it's that simple. What's stopping you?"

I chew my bottom lip. *Should I tell him?*

"I bet you're biting that plump bottom lip of yours right now …"

I catch my breath. "Yes."

"I knew it. Just come to dinner, Charlotte. Put me out of my misery," he says, his deep voice gruff.

My heart is beating a million miles a minute. I want to see him, no doubt. But he's the kind of guy I could fall for. And that just can't happen. "No, I can't. I don't do dinner dates or relationships. I shouldn't have given you my number, Elijah."

"The hell you shouldn't have," he bursts out. He sounds angry. *Oops.* "You felt what I felt. I know you did, Charlotte, so don't even try to deny it. You don't do dinner or relationships? Well, I haven't for the past ten years either, so it'll be new for both of us."

I drop my head back and stare at the ceiling. He's not giving up as easily as I'd hoped he would. Focusing on a small cobweb near the cornice, I tell him, "I just can't. I'm sorry," then end the call before he can respond.

Elijah makes me want things I haven't wanted in a long time—things that don't work out when you're me. My emotions are high and all over the place. He does this to me—messes with my perfectly planned life and makes me question my reasons for choosing to be perpetually single. I have a damn good reason for avoiding relationships. I don't need a man in my life. I might occasionally want one, but I don't need one.

What I do need is chocolate. Stat.

Elijah

She hung up on me. *Son of a bitch!* I throw my phone across the cab of the truck. It hits the passenger window then clatters to the floor.

The door swings open, and Asher climbs in then raises his brows. "Wanna talk about it?"

"No," I huff. Turning the key in the ignition, I pull the truck out of the lot of our last delivery of the morning. I can feel Ash's eyes boring into the side of my head. "What?" I snap.

"You're *literally* grinding gears ..." he points out as I change up from second to third less than gracefully. "What's up, big brother?"

My jaw locks, then the words are pouring out of my mouth. "I called Charlotte and asked her to dinner. She said no. But she won't tell me why. I know she's into me. I kissed her and she responded. She liked it. I know she did. So, what the fuck?"

Asher erupts with laughter, slapping his thigh.

I glare at him. *Little bastard.*

He eventually gathers his control. Taking a deep breath, his entire demeanour changes to serious.

The way he can flip his mood like a coin trips me out. He's always done that. Makes me think of Two-Face from the *Batman* comics I used to love. Creeps me the hell out too. "You know I hate it when you do that," I mutter.

"Whatever." He rolls his eyes. "You like her and she shut you down. What are you going to do about it?"

My fingers curl around the steering wheel so tight my knuckles go white. "Fuck if I know. It's been forever since I was interested in someone."

He nods, his gaze far away. He's formulating a plan. Silence engulfs the cab as we drive.

Out of nowhere, Asher clicks his fingers and points at me. "I've got it. I overheard her when you guys were talking while I was cleaning the kitchen. She likes a man who cooks and cleans, right? So, we'll take photos of you doing that shit and drip feed them to her. It'll drive her crazy. We already know she's into you physically; this will keep you on her mind."

"I think you might be onto something. But I need more. That's not going to be enough to convince her to go out with me. I don't just want to bone down with this chick, Asher."

He nods. "Maybe you should do some research on that disease she has. Learn a bit about it, then wow her with your awareness of her situation?"

"Okay, I can do that."

I feel much better about everything by the time we get home. Having a solid plan of attack has reinforced my determination. I've got this.

"Jesus Christ, why do I have to take my shirt off?" I bitch at Asher.

He stands on the other side of the kitchen counter with my phone aimed at me while I cook breakfast. "Because I said. Just do it."

I grind my teeth but follow his coaching. I'm halfway down the buttons when he stops me.

"Wait, new plan. Leave it just like that. A tease is better than the whole package."

Juda is laughing his arse off. *Little prick.* I glare at him and the coffee he just spilt all over the kitchen floor—a result of his amusement. I can tell he's about to say something.

"Don't you fucking dare."

He clamps his mouth shut, but his smirk remains in place as he cleans the mess he made.

"Just act natural," Ash instructs, angling the phone and clicking away.

"I feel like a fucking moron," I grit out. I can't believe I'm even doing this. It sounded like a good idea at the time, but now that I'm actually standing here ... not so much.

Slapping my phone on the counter, Asher grins. "But you look hot."

I frown, eyeing my brother. "Say what?"

He rolls his eyes. "You don't have to be gay to recognise attractive traits in other men, Eli."

"I know that," I spit, defensive. "It's just weird to hear my brother say I'm hot."

With a shrug, he collects Delilah's warm bottle from the hot water and takes a seat at the dining table to feed her. "I got a few good shots. You can send her one when you get into town."

I finish up buttering the toast and head to the table with all the plates of food. I hope this works, because I've never felt so stupid in my life.

When I've made all the deliveries for the morning, I pull the truck into the parking lot of the supermarket and grab my phone. Opening the pictures Ash took this morning, I'm pleasantly surprised to find I don't look as stupid as I felt while he was snapping away.

I pick the best one and send it to Charlotte. No caption, because I have no idea what to say. I'll let the picture speak for itself.

Chapter Ten

Charlotte

HOLY-MOTHER-OF-HIGH-FASHION.

The picture that just landed on my phone is … I'm speechless.

And there you have it, folks: a sure-fire way to shut me up. While I may be lacking words, I am producing a ridiculous amount of drool.

Elijah is standing at the cooktop in his kitchen, his red flannel shirt open to his belly button, exposing a tantalising sliver of his rippled chest and stomach to my greedy eyes. I just about swallow my tongue when I finally make it to his face. His square jaw is locked, pronouncing his high cheekbones and those full lips.

Just kill me now. I'd die a happy woman.

I wipe my chin, just in case the drool pooling in my mouth has overflowed.

He didn't say anything—just sent the photo. I can't

help but wonder why. I shut him down yesterday, told him it's not going to happen between us.

A light bulb flickers to life in my head. He's tempting me, showing me what I'm missing. That sneaky bastard.

It takes all my willpower to exit the messages app, put my phone on the desk (face down), and get back to work on next week's feature outfit page on the blog. My eyes drift back to my phone no less than a dozen times over the next hour.

Somehow, I find the strength to resist staring at that picture for hours on end and get some actual work done. Who knew I had that kind of self-control? Not me.

Knocking at my front door startles me. Glancing at the clock, I'm happy to see it's after five. Reagan has arrived. "It's open!" I call out. I don't know why she even bothers knocking half the time; she has a key.

"Heeeey," she sings as she sweeps into my home office.

I shut down my laptop and swivel my chair around to face her, my eyes instantly finding the bottles of white wine clutched in her hands. "Yes, girl! You have no idea how much I need this." I tug her into a hug, then we make our way to my kitchen.

Sliding into a bar stool at my floating island, Reagan unscrews both bottles of wine, sliding one across to my side while I rummage through the fridge for snacks. We drink from the bottles because we're classy like that, and she's already taking a swig from hers by the time I reappear with a couple of dips, kabana, and a block of cheese.

"Hey, wait for me!" I snap.

She puts her bottle down, and I slide her a cutting board with the cheese. Selecting a knife from the block on the bench beside her, she gets to chopping while I do the same with the kabana. It only takes us five minutes to make a big platter of goodies to complement our wine.

Relaxing into my black suede couch, I prop my feet up on the dark-purple ottoman that serves as a footrest slash coffee table. A stack of fashion magazines is spread across the middle, and I kick them aside to make more room for my feet.

"So, I did some research on llamas this week," Reagan says.

I raise a brow. "Why?"

She shrugs. "After meeting your llama farmer, I wanted to know more. Anyway, Freddie Mercury and Michael Jackson were recording a duet back in the eighties, right, and Freddie cancelled it because Michael insisted on bringing his llama, Louie, to the recording studio every day."

I snort. "What? No way. That's not even true."

"It is. You know I always do my research."

"Yeah, but seriously? That's crazy." I chuckle. "Okay, hit me with another llama fact."

My bestie's grin is huge. Reagan is in her element when talking about random shit. "Okay, so scientists have made a crossbreed between a male camel and a female llama. They call it a cama. They're pretty damn cute too. Not as cute as an alpaca though. Especially after seeing those gorgeous little things at your sexy farmer's."

I choke on my wine, almost spraying it all over her.

Once I've regained control of my throat muscles, I correct her. "He's not my anything."

She chuckles. "Who are you trying to kid? He's totally yours. He's your sexy llama farmer. Charlotte the fashionista has the hots for a plaid-wearing llama farmer." She snorts at her own joke.

I want to wipe that satisfied smirk off her face. Rolling my eyes, I pop a cracker with a chunk of cheese and kabana in my mouth, then chase it with more wine. I have a feeling one bottle isn't going to be enough for me tonight if this is the tone of the conversation.

"You can't deny it. You want his hot farmer body," she states.

My mind conjures the picture he sent me earlier today. Hell yes, I want that. But I just can't have it. It's a bad idea. Guys can't handle me on my bad days. They don't know what to do with me. That night at Elijah's was just a fluke, a one off.

"Hello, Char, you in there?" Reagan clicks her fingers in front of my face.

I shake my head and focus on her. She tilts her chin, clearly waiting for me to say something to confirm her assessment. I swallow, then hold up my hand. "Hold that thought," I tell her, then go to retrieve my phone.

Returning, I hand it to her, the picture already open. Her jaw drops.

"Right?!"

Her eyes eat up the image on the screen. "He's got a six-pack."

I snatch my phone back. "He has actual pecs too—not just nipples."

Now that I'm looking at it again, I can't stop. He's so delicious. I wonder if he would be okay with a one-and-done arrangement. But no, he's not the type. That's pretty obvious. *That* and I'm, like, ninety-nine percent sure it wouldn't be enough for me. His kisses proved that. His amazing kisses ... I sigh.

Reagan raises a brow. "See? You want him. And if he sent you that picture, he wants you too. Even I can figure that much out. Why not go for it?"

I look at her like she's lost her damn mind. "You know exactly why. I won't do that again. I can't. I'm only good for two weeks at a time. Outside of that and they freak the fuck out because I'm a completely different person when Lilith shows her ugly face."

My bestie's brows furrow in confusion. "You've lost me. Who's Lilith?"

"Lilith is the demon who inhabits my nether regions every month. That's what I'm calling her now. I thought I told you."

Reags shakes her head. "I don't remember. You might have, but I've got sex brain these days. Not much sticks."

I close my eyes and shake my head. "Reagan, I don't think sex brain is a thing."

She whacks my shoulder. "It totally is. It's all I think about, even at work. And you know how much I love my job. Yesterday, I was verifying if the velociraptor screech in the *Jurassic Park* movies was really a recording of tortoises having sex, then *bam*, I'm thinking about the sounds Rhett makes when we're having sex."

This time, I do spray her with wine. I cough and sputter. "What the fuck?"

"It is, by the way, the velociraptor screech ..."

I burst out laughing. I love this woman so much. She always knows how to pull me out of a funk.

An hour later, I'm happily buzzed and my belly is full. Reagan and I are lazing on the couch, our wine long gone, when Rhett waltzes into my lounge room.

"Ladies," he greets us, then strides over to Reags, dropping a kiss on her forehead. "You ready, honey?"

She smiles up at him and cups his scruff-covered jaw. "Yeah," she breathes.

They're so disgustingly cute. I divert my gaze when he leans down for a real kiss, only looking back when I catch movement from the corner of my eye. Rhett has swept her up in his arms, bride style. Reagan rests her head on his shoulder, staring at him all dreamy like, her hands wrapped around the back of his neck.

Her head pops up just before he exits the room. "Char, I think you should give Elijah a chance. He didn't freak out on you when you had your flare-up out there—not in a bad way, anyway. I think he can handle Lilith." She winks then lays her head back down.

"Later, Char," Rhett says over his shoulder as they leave.

I grab my phone and open the picture of him cooking again. Maybe ...

Elijah

The second I pass through the dead zone on my way into town on the egg run, my phone starts going crazy with incoming texts. It goes off for thirty solid seconds. I pull over to see what it is. It has to be something important for that many texts to be sent, right?

My eyes widen when I see that *every single one* is from Charlotte, sent late last night.

The first is a picture. I click on the small, unintelligible thumbnail to see it better and about swallow my damn tongue. Boobs. It's her boobs. At least, I'm assuming they're hers, because I can't see her face. The size is right, but there are tattoos stretching across her collarbones. I tilt my head, examining the picture closer.

She was wearing a long-sleeve dress thing that came up close to her throat when we met. Therefore, these could most definitely be her boobs. They're encased in see-through black lace. My dick perks up at the sight.

The next message confirms that they are, indeed, Charlotte's breasts I'm drooling over.

CHARLOTTE: You're not the only one who can send provocative pictures.

I swallow. Hard.

CHARLOTTE: I spent some quality time this evening with that photo you sent me. ;)
CHARLOTTE: Is that a six- or eight-pack you're packing? I can't quite tell. Too many clothes in the way.
CHARLOTTE: Who took that picture anyway?
CHARLOTTE: I want a money shot next time. If you're going to tease me, do it right.

Jesus. I read, then reread all her messages. *A money shot? She doesn't mean a ... does she?* I have never sent a dick pic in my entire life. I've never even taken a picture of my dick, let alone sent it to somebody.

My tongue feels thick in my mouth. She wants a dick pic. It's the only way *that* can be translated. My jeans suddenly feel too tight, constricting blood flow to my cock. Or maybe it's my thought process doing that.

I run my palm over the surface of my jeans, over my dick. It feels so good. I want to stroke it, palm on flesh, but I'm sitting in a truck on the side of the road. This is not the time or place to rub one out. Damn if I don't really fucking want to, though. I grit my teeth and throw the stick shift into gear.

I get the deliveries finished in record time. After the last drop-off, I go straight home with one thing on my mind.

Giving Charlotte what she asked for.

Chapter Eleven

Charlotte

I WAKE WITH FOGGY WINE BRAIN. I FOUND ANOTHER BOTTLE in the bottom of the pantry after Reags left me last night, and I drank it.

I'm tangled in my white sheets, blanket nowhere to be found. Peering over the side of the bed, I spot it crumpled on the floor. Makes sense. I'm a restless sleeper. It's a miracle the sheet stayed on the bed, but that's probably only because it's twisted around my limbs.

Fighting my way out, I stumble to my adjoining bathroom. I turn on the shower, then do a quick pee while it heats up. When I step under the spray, my mind instantly begins to clear, the fog dissipating with each passing second. I wash my hair then shave all the important parts.

What to wear today ... I stand in my wardrobe with one towel wrapped around my body and one around my hair, tapping my bottom lip as I peruse my options. Finally, I decide on a pair of light-wash skinny jeans with artful tearing at the knees. I match them with an off-white camisole with spaghetti straps and lace trim.

I grab an army-green sweater off the shelf on my way out and slide my arms in it as I make my way to the kitchen for my morning coffee.

I've been working for an hour or so when I hear my phone go off in the distance. Unsure where I left it, I go in search, finding it in the snarled mess of my sheets. A text from Reagan is waiting for me, asking me to lunch today. I shoot off a quick reply, telling her I'll meet her at the café down the block from her office.

As I'm standing there, another incoming text beeps at me. It's Elijah again.

Thank God for my bed catching my fall or I would have collapsed to the floor. It's a dick. His dick, I'm assuming. Fully erect, veins pulsing, the head thick and purple. *Holy-Prada-midseason-sale.* This is so out of left field. I thought it might be another cooking shot, not his glorious spunk cannon.

This time he has attached a caption.

ELIJAH: This what you wanted?

My eyes widen. What is he talking about? I mean, yeah, it's a pretty great shot. But did I want an unsolicited dick pic? Not really. It's just rubbing in that he has an amazing package and I won't be unwrapping it.

CHARLOTTE: Yep, that's a dick. While that is an

impressive weapon you have at your disposal, I'm not sure why you're showing me.

ELIJAH: You asked me to! Oh God. Is that not what you meant by a money shot?

My heart rate has officially left the building. I quickly scroll through all our previous texts. *Please, please, please* ... I chant on repeat. But there it is, right in front of my eyes.

CHARLOTTE: Umm, about that ...
CHARLOTTE: I may have had a few wines last night and ... well ...

ELIJAH: You drunk-texted me? So, you didn't want to see my junk ... I am SO sorry. I'm so fucking embarrassed. I swear I do not send random pictures of my dick to women. Ever.

CHARLOTTE: Yeah, I did. You have nothing to be sorry for. And you certainly have NOTHING to be embarrassed about. As far as dick pics go, that is a really good one. Trust me, I've seen some shockers.

ELIJAH: I'm just going to go dig a hole, climb inside it and die now.

I laugh. He is genuinely embarrassed. How cute is that? And it's kind of endearing too. Dick pics are a dime a dozen these days, yet here he is, feeling like a douche for it. *So sweet.*

CHARLOTTE: Seriously, don't feel bad. It's all good. But in the interest of full disclosure ... I'm adding that photo to my jill till.

ELIJAH: Jill till?

CHARLOTTE: You know. Rub hub, flick files, bean dreams, pole vault ...

ELIJAH: So lost right now. What the hell are you talking about?

CHARLOTTE: You really don't know? How long has it been since you got laid, dude? These are common terms. It's the female equivalent of your spank bank.

ELIJAH: Jesus. Is it that obvious? I have never heard any of those. Also, in the spirit of full disclosure, that was my first dick pic. You popped my dick pic cherry. I'm pleased you find it jill till worthy.

My smile is so big it's hurting my cheeks. I haven't talked to a guy in forever. It feels good, this playful, no-pressure banter. The guys on the hook-up app I use are all business, and that's the way I like it. But I'm really enjoying this casual flirting.

CHARLOTTE: Was it as good for you as it was for me? Lol

ELIJAH: Considering I used the picture you sent me as my inspiration, I'm going to say yes, yes it was.

I burst out laughing. And then his next message comes through.

ELIJAH: You ready to go out with me yet? I mean, you have seen my money shot … I'm a catch, damn it.

Elijah

As mortifying as that whole conversation was, I can't stop smiling. That could have been a lot worse. I swear my heart stopped beating for a solid ten seconds when I hit send on that picture of my junk. It took ages to get a decent shot, too. Who knew there was an art to taking cock shots?

I'm sitting in my car, parked on the side of the road just outside the dead zone, grinning like a fool. This is the most I've texted a chick in my life, and I'm finding I actually like it. If this is all she's willing to give me right now, I'll take it. I only sent that last message to mess with her. I know she's not ready.

Over the next couple of weeks, I send her a picture each morning—not of my junk, but of me doing various things around the farm. Sometimes she responds; sometimes she doesn't. This morning I sent her a picture of me with Uma Furman. She has a beautiful face and a fabulous hairdo—for a llama, that is.

Charlotte's response comes through almost immediately.

CHARLOTTE: Oh my God, look at her hair! She's beautiful! Not like that overgrown rat you share your bed with. Did you put it in rollers just to take this picture for me?

I chuckle. I may have suddenly become a selfie king these last few weeks, but I'd never stoop to doing a llama's hair.

ELIJAH: Uh, no. I'd lose my man card for that. She just has amazing natural curls. When the town throws its annual fair, Uma is one of the girls I take with me. Everyone loves her luscious locks.

The fair is coming up in the next couple of weeks. I'd love for Charlotte to come with me. But seeing as she doesn't want to actually date me—*yet*—I'll hold off on asking her for now.

CHARLOTTE: You take your llama to the fair? Also, I think you lost your man card the second you started sleeping with Satan's mistress ...

I roll my eyes. She really doesn't like Delilah. But Delilah clearly doesn't like her either. I've never seen her react to someone the way she did with Charlotte. So weird.

ELIJAH: Stop hating on my baby. She's no fan of yours either. I think she might be a little possessive of me ...

CHARLOTTE: I bet she has that berserk llama syndrome thing that Reags told me about. They think they're a person and get aggressive and shit.

ELIJAH: It's entirely possible that Delilah thinks she's a person. She's been inside with us since she was born. She's not aggressive though.

CHARLOTTE: HA! Not to you! I'm the one with a hoof-shaped bruise on my beaver. Now tell me again she's not aggressive.

I burst out laughing. No way. There's no way Delilah kicked her that hard ... *is there?*

ELIJAH: I'm not sure if you're serious or not. You don't really have a bruise, do you?

Her reply takes longer this time. I tap my fingers on the steering wheel as I wait. Two minutes later, a photo pops up in our chat.

A photo of the bruise on Charlotte's ... I swallow. Right above her slit.

Jesus Christ. Calm down, man. It's not like she's flashed you her whole pussy.

She's unzipped her pants. Her thumb is hooked in the fabric of her panties, holding them down just enough to see the offending mark my llama left on her.

I'm torn between being turned on and horrified, because technically, that bruise is my fault.

ELIJAH: I am soooo fucking sorry!
ELIJAH: What can I do to make it up to you?
ELIJAH: I can't believe she kicked you that hard!

I'm typing another message when her response comes through.

CHARLOTTE: Chill. It's fine. It's not like YOU kicked me in the crotch. In fact, I kicked you ... Maybe your psycho llama was just getting one back at me?

How is she being so cool about this? Why isn't she pissed off? Wouldn't righteous indignation be a more realistic response?

ELIJAH: I still feel responsible. I should have closed the

bedroom door so she couldn't get in the bed. I wasn't thinking.

CHARLOTTE: Seriously, it's okay. Don't stress. It gave me an excuse to send you another sexy pic ... minus the bruise—that kind of ruined it. Stupid llama. Anyway, I've got work to do, and you're distracting me. Ciao.

I send one last message.

ELIJAH: You wouldn't have to send me sexy pictures if you just let me see your pretty face in person ... on a date.

She ignores me, as she always does when I bring it up. But that's okay because we carry on messaging like this for the next two weeks. Texting like a pair of teenagers. Maybe she was right to reject me when I first asked her out. This has been fun. I like that, with us, there is no pressure, no expectations.

I am getting antsy to see her, though. I'm just not sure what to do to show her how serious I am about her. She's made it clear that she doesn't want to go on a date. I'm going to have to get creative, because there is no way I'm letting this woman slip through my fingers.

It's my turn to pick up our box of goodies from Aunt Kenna this week. After my last delivery, I park the truck out the back of her bakery. “Mornin’, Kenna,” I call as I come in through the staff entrance.

“Hey, honey,” she calls out from the front of the shop. “Just give me a minute.”

I spy our box of treats on one of the stainless countertops and make my way over to it. After lifting the lid, I take one of the apple pies and start eating it. It’s so good, still warm. *Mmm.*

“Couldn’t wait until you got home?” Kenna says, wiping her hands on the apron tied around her waist.

Shaking my head, I grin. “Uh, no. They always taste better when they’re fresh out of the oven. Plus, I’ve gotta get my cut while I can.” I stride over and wrap my arms around my favourite aunt, giving her a big hug—the kind she’s given us since we were kids.

She chuckles and pats my back. “Your brothers tell me you’ve been talking to a young lady,” she says, waggling her brows.

I roll my eyes. “Of course they did.”

“Someone has to keep me in the loop. You boys are so secretive about your love lives.”

“That’s ’cause there’s nothing to tell.” Sliding my hand under the box, I realise there’s another one beside it. “Do we get two boxes this week?”

Kenna’s eyes land on the second box. She shakes her head. “That’s for one of my regulars. She usually drives out here to get it herself, but she’s not in a good way, so she called and asked me to have the courier deliver it for her.”

This piques my curiosity. A regular from out of town

... I did almost run over Charlotte out the front of McKenna's Heavenly Treats. And this is where she went after telling me off. I glance down at the box, then back to Kenna. "Do you mean Charlotte?"

My aunt's eyes widen. "Yes. You know her?"

"Uh, yeah. We met last time she was in town. Hey, I can take these to her instead of you having to organise the courier. It's no problem; I was heading into the city today anyway." *Big fat fucking lie.*

"Really? That would be fantastic. You know I hate dealing with the courier service out here. They're hopeless. I think the sneaky bastards take samples from the boxes before they deliver them. I was actually considering taking these to Charlotte myself. But if you're already headed that way ..."

I nod. "I'll drop them off. No sense in both of us making the trip. Just pop her address on the box, and I'll take them to her this afternoon."

Kenna grabs a pen and scribbles Charlotte's address on the lid. Then, as if it just occurred to her, she lifts her gaze to me, scrutinising me.

"What?"

"Is Charlotte the woman you've been talking to?" she asks, watching me closely.

I clear my throat. "Yes."

Kenna throws her arms around me with so much force I almost drop my box of goodies. "Whoa, Kenna!"

When she releases me, she's smiling so damn wide you'd think I told her Charlotte and I were engaged.

"I'm just so happy. That girl needs a good man. She shouldn't have to go through what she does all alone."

My eyes narrow to slits. "Go through what?"

"She has endometriosis. She suffers terribly every month. I've been telling her she needs a man, but no, she's a stubborn little thing. Says she can look after herself," Kenna says, rolling her eyes. "I know she can, but that's not the point."

I nod in complete agreement. "Is that why she couldn't come to get her box of treats?"

Kenna nods. "I'd say so, honey. She left a message on the shop's machine. She didn't sound great, but I know how much she loves a sugar hit when she's like this."

"I'll take care of it." I drop a kiss to Kenna's head, then pick up Charlotte's box of goodies that, suspiciously, weighs more than mine, then head out to the truck. The boys can handle the rest of my chores for today. I've got somewhere I need to be.

Chapter Twelve

Charlotte

JESUS, LILITH IS IN FINE FORM THIS MONTH. AFTER INHALING a deep breath through my nose, I release it slowly from my mouth. I've been doing this for the last five minutes, hoping the painkillers kick in soon.

The actual blood bath hasn't even started yet, but it's on its way. This is just Lilith's warm-up. Lying on my couch with a heat pack on my lower back, another across my pelvis, and one tucked between my legs, I continue my deep breathing.

I'm so thankful that nobody sees me like this. I'm in so much pain I can't move. I'm stuck like this: my jaw locked tight, curled in the foetal position, wearing my most comfortable leggings and an oversized T-shirt. My hair is everywhere, sweat covers my brow, I haven't brushed my teeth, and tears slide down my crumpled face from my tightly closed eyes.

I'm so deep inside my head that I don't hear the

knocking at my front door until it turns to pounding. Swallowing hard, I attempt to sit up. Red-hot, searing pain shoots from my pelvis down my thighs, and I crumple back to my side.

Shattering glass is the next thing I hear, and I can't even bring myself to try and get up this time. If someone has come to rob me, so be it. Just don't touch my painkillers or I'll have to cut a bitch. Everything else, they can have.

"Charlotte!" A masculine voice penetrates my pain-addled thoughts.

Prying my eyes open, I'm shocked to see Elijah leaning over me. His face is ashen, his eyes searching mine.

"What are you doing here?" I manage to ask on a whisper.

"Tell me what you need. What can I do to help?" he says.

I shake my head. "Nothing. Pills will work soon," I mutter.

He runs a hand through his hair, staring down at me as he nods. "Okay, I'll be right back. I left my stuff outside. Hang tight." His eyes look tortured. I can tell he wants to make this better for me, but he just can't. After a moment, he drops a kiss to my forehead, then disappears from my line of sight.

Finally, finally, finally, the painkillers start to work. I feel their effects slowly blanket my senses, not taking the pain away, but masking it. I relish this feeling the way an addict soaks up the euphoria of a hit. My spent body relaxes into the cushions, and I release a deep sigh.

Elijah reappears in front of me, and I frown. I half-thought he was a figment of my imagination. It wouldn't be the first time I'd imagined someone coming to my rescue. But he's really here, standing above me, holding a white box with a big pink bow tied on top, and with a red backpack hanging off his shoulder.

"What are you doing here?"

Instead of answering me, he goes about placing the box on my purple ottoman, then drops his backpack to the ground and unpacks it, placing things on the ottoman beside the box, his back to me.

"Elijah?" I ask.

When he's finished whatever the hell he's doing, he turns to face me. The anguish I see there hits me like a tidal wave. I gasp and bite down on my bottom lip.

His face crinkles as he comes to his knees at the side of the couch, tugging my lip from between my teeth. A sad smile lifts his perfect lips. "You should have called me."

I frown. "Why?"

Frustration pulses off him in waves. "Because you're in fucking agony and you shouldn't be by yourself."

The force behind his words makes me angry. "I can take care of myself, Elijah. I don't need you or anyone else to do it for me."

He runs his hand through his tussled hair again. "I know that! But you shouldn't have to, Charlotte. I backed off because it's what you wanted, but you know *I care*. You know I would have come if you'd asked."

I swallow. Yeah, I do know that. But calling would have meant he would see me like this, and that's the last thing I want. "I don't want you to see me this way." I wave a hand down my body. "This isn't fun. It isn't light-hearted and exciting. And that's what I want you to feel when you're with me, not this!" My eyes burn and my heart pounds. I need him to understand.

"I don't want your sympathy. I don't want you to feel obligated to hang around. I've been in that position before, and I'll never let it happen again." Great, now I'm crying. *Goddamn it!* I squeeze my eyes shut and grit my teeth.

His big, calloused hand cups my jaw. "Charlotte, don't shut me out now, baby. Keep going. This is the most you've ever said about why you keep me at a distance. But I'm here, I'm listening, and I'm not going anywhere."

Cracking one eye open, I peek at him. He's so damn beautiful. Being this close, I get a clear view of his ocean-blue eyes and see nothing but sincerity staring back at me.

I take a deep breath and tell him about my shithouse relationship with Sunny. "Sunny and I started dating in our early twenties. The first year was great; everything was sunshine and cupcakes. The second year wasn't as wonderful, but we were past that honeymoon phase, you know? Then, I found him in bed with his best friend's sister.

"Apparently, they'd been seeing each other for six months, and he didn't break it off with me, because he didn't want me to be alone during ..." I sweep my hand down my body again, "... this."

Elijah's jaw is set, showcasing his sculpted cheekbones. His eyes practically scream how much he wants to beat the crap out of Sunny—which makes me a little too happy.

Then, Elijah's thumb glides over the curve of my cheek, his eyes watching the motion with intensity. "Charlotte, that guy was a dickwad. But he clearly cared about you. I kind of understand him not wanting to leave you when you were like this. However, he should have talked to you about it, told you what was going on with him."

"But being with me ... it's hard, Elijah." My voice breaks on his name. Damnit. This is what endometriosis does; it ruins everything.

Elijah shakes his head. "The way he handled the situation is not on you. That's all him. You hear me?" His eyes lock with mine. "It's *all* on him. It wasn't your fault."

I blink back tears. Emotion clogs my throat, and I wrap my arms around Elijah's shoulders, pulling him into me. I can't talk; I have nothing to say. He just said everything I needed to hear.

Elijah

It all makes sense now—why she doesn't date, why she's been keeping me at arm's length.

I want to hunt down the fuck-knuckle that made her think she needs to brave this godawful disease on her own. My fingers slide up into her messy hair as she sobs into my neck. "Let me look after you. I'm not asking, Charlotte. I'm telling you. Just so we're clear."

She sniffles and nods.

Holding her shoulders, I tug her away from me, pressing her back into the pillow she has propped on the couch. I hold out a finger, signalling for her to wait a moment. Spinning around, I show her the box of camomile, vanilla, and honey tea I grabbed with the few other supplies I picked up for her on my way here.

"I'm going to go make you a tea. You need those heat packs to be done again?"

She blinks up at me, a shy smile tugging her lush lips. "Please," she says, handing them to me.

Then I remember the front window and pause. "Uh, I should tell you ... I, uh, I smashed the window by the front door to get in. I knew you were in here, and I was knocking for ages and you didn't respond ... I kind of freaked myself out, thinking the worst, and yeah. I threw a rock through it. I'll pay to get it fixed, though."

Her smile is blinding. "That's the sweetest thing anyone has ever done for me."

My chest swells and I throw her a wink. "I'll break as many windows as it takes to show you I'm not going anywhere, babe. You're stuck with me."

With that, I go in search of her kitchen, which isn't hard to find.

The layout of her house is very simple with an open kitchen-dining area directly behind the lounge room wall. Her kitchen is huge. White granite bench tops with black cupboard doors and shiny silver handles glint in the overhead lighting. Silver appliances top it all off.

I take in the heavy white-and-grey marble table with six black high-back chairs surrounding it in the dining space, and the silver candleholders evenly spaced down the centre. This whole place is so damn fancy. Nothing at all like my old country-style farmhouse. This place might be high-end, but it doesn't have that warm, welcoming embrace a home should have.

This feels more like a display house.

I throw the heat pack in the microwave and set it to run for two minutes while I flick on the kettle and go in search of Charlotte's teacups. I find them in the cabinet below the kettle. My mother drilled into us boys the difference between a teacup and a mug at a very young age, and all Charlotte has in here are mugs—not one single teacup. I'll have to rectify that.

Grabbing the most delicate one I can find, I set it on the bench. It will have to do. And then I see the writing on the side and burst out laughing. It says, "I'm a pacifist. I'm about to pass my fist through your face." It suits my little firecracker.

I return to her, tea and heat packs in hand. Placing the tea on the big purple ottoman, I pass her the heat packs so she can arrange them the way she likes. She looks much better than she did when I arrived, which is a huge relief. I was about ready to call an ambulance.

She taps the edge of the couch. "Sit."

Assessing the position of her body, curled close to the

edge, I figure I can squeeze in behind and hold her. Kicking off my shoes, I snatch up my iPod and mini speaker that Juda got me for my last birthday. Then I climb over her, tuck one arm under her pillow, and tug her body back into my chest with the other as I settle into the cushions.

She glances at me over her shoulder, a small smile playing on the corner of her lips.

"What?" I ask.

To my complete shock, a faint blush tints her cheeks. "This is nice. I wasn't expecting it, is all."

I shrug. "Get used to it. I'm done keeping my distance. Now, are you ready for this? I have prepared a period mix for you." I waggle my brows, and hers furrow.

"A what?"

"Just relax and listen," I instruct.

With a cute frown, she does as I say, resting her head on the fluffy pillow and snuggling back into me. I find the list I made especially for her and the torment she's going through. Music always soothes me when I'm in a right shit of a mood or I'm sick.

I compiled a list of songs that relate to her current condition in one way or another. I hit play on the first song. Leona Lewis's melodic voice fills the room, and I smile, proud of myself.

Charlotte's back vibrates against my chest, and I prop myself up on the arm under her pillow. She's laughing. It's a good look on her.

"'Bleeding Love.' You made me a bloody playlist? Is that what this is?" she asks between chuckles.

I nod. "Sure did. Every song on this list has the word blood in the title."

She laughs harder. And I smile wider.

Making her feel even a fraction better fills me with a sense of rightness I've never felt before.

Chapter Thirteen

Charlotte

He made me a bloody playlist. Does it get any better than that? I think not.

I thought Elijah breaking into my house was sweet, but this? *This*. This is next level.

My heart is so full right now. I don't know what to do with all these intense emotions vying for my attention. His big arms squeeze me tight against his warm chest, and I melt into him.

"Thank you," I whisper.

He presses his lips to my temple in a soft kiss. "Brace yourself. I have very eclectic taste in music. Just because I'm country doesn't mean that's all I listen to."

"I think I can handle whatever you have to throw at me."

"We'll see," he murmurs into my hair as he, too, rests his head against the pillow beside mine.

We lie there listening to his insanely random playlist

for the next half hour, neither of us speaking. Amongst the collection, there is Good Charlotte's *My Bloody Valentine*, U2's *Sunday Bloody Sunday*, Shawn Mendes's *In My Blood*, and Taylor Swift's *Bad Blood*. He even has a few on here that I've never heard before. Eventually, I ask him, "What's this one?"

"5 Seconds of Summer, *Youngblood*," he says softly against my neck.

Being held in his strong arms feels amazing. I could stay here forever. I don't remember the last time someone held me like this. A tear slides down my temple at the realisation it's literally been years since I felt this kind of genuine affection from and connection to another person.

"You okay, baby? Need me to reheat your packs?" Elijah asks.

I shake my head. "No, your arms are all I need." The truth of that sentiment settles within me, and I drift off to sleep.

When I wake, I'm alone on the couch, and the pain has subsided. *Thank the Gucci gods!* But I know better than to think that means it won't return. I check my watch, surprised to see it's after five already. I slept for, like, three hours. Stretching my arms above my head, I let out a massive yawn.

"Hey, sleepy head." Elijah's voice comes from behind me.

Sitting up, I put my feet on the ground, testing my legs. No shooting pain. That's a good sign, so I stand and approach him. He leans against the archway that separates my kitchen and dining area from the lounge.

"Hey," I mumble into his chest as he curls his big, muscly arms around me.

He drops a kiss to the crown of my head and inhales. "You smell so good."

I roll my eyes at him. "I do not. I haven't had a shower or brushed my teeth all day. I'm gross."

"You're right; you are so gross," he says, chuckling. "Maybe that's my kink?"

The godawful snort that erupts from me is anything but attractive, but I can't help it. "So, you really are just a dirty farmer ..." I laugh.

Shaking his head, he looks down at me. "You have a bathtub?"

"Yeah, why?"

"Show me where it is. I'll run you one while the soup's simmering."

I gawk at him. "Soup? You made soup?"

"Yep, it was my mother's recipe. Best chicken soup you've ever had. Now show me where this bath is."

Damnit, he's going to make me cry again. Stupid hormones making me super-sensitive. But he is being pretty freaking amazing. Before I start blubbering like a baby, I take his hand and lead him to my bedroom, and my bathroom within.

He approaches the tub before turning it on and checking the temperature. "Okay, you go get some fresh PJs, but don't get in yet. I'll be right back."

I blink after his retreating back, then do as he said. I've just grabbed a pair of soft yoga pants and another big T-shirt when he reappears. Following him into the bathroom, I watch as he leans over the tub, sprinkling something into the water. "What's that?"

"Lavender bath salts. I've done some reading, and a lot of women say hot baths with Epsom salts are really helpful when they have a flare-up. That's what it's called, isn't it? A flare-up?"

The lump in my throat is now the size of a baseball. Holy shit. He's been reading up on endo? All I can do is nod in response because my vocal cords have left the building.

Elijah smiles proudly. "Okay, so yeah, I picked these up when Kenna said you weren't doing well. I, uh ..." he rubs the back of his neck and shifts his gaze to the floor, "... I told her I was coming into the city anyway and I could drop off your goody box instead of getting a courier. That's how I found out where you live ..."

My lips tug up despite my efforts to keep a straight face as he confesses his crime. Well, you'd think it was a crime, the way he's refusing to meet my eyes. "I see."

"I'm sorry. I would have asked you where you lived eventually, but this opportunity was too perfect to let go. I acted without really thinking it through, and now I'm realising how creepy this could all look."

Closing the distance between us, I slide my hands over his broad shoulders, up his neck, and into the hair at his nape. He sighs and closes his eyes as I rake my nails through the short strands there. "I don't think you're creepy, Elijah. I think you are the kindest, most considerate man I have ever met. Creepy doesn't even cross my mind when I think about you. At least, not anymore ..."

"Thank God," he says, his eyes popping open to stare down at me. "Because I don't think I'd take it very well if you kicked me out right now."

I grin. "Not going to happen."

AFTER MY BATH, I FEEL A MILLION TIMES BETTER. LILITH HAS crawled back into her cave for the time being.

We're eating chicken soup side by side on the couch while watching a British TV series that's a take-off of Jane Austen's *Pride and Prejudice*. It's absolutely brilliant. I've snort-laughed no less than a dozen times already.

"What is this called again?" I ask Elijah, who seems to be enjoying it as much as me.

Wiping a dribble of soup off his chin, he smiles. "Umm, *Lost in Austen*. My mum was an Austen fan, and she had quite the collection by the time she passed." Pausing, he takes a deep breath, the mention of his mother's death clearly still upsetting him. With a small shake of his head, he brings his focus back to me. "It's one of the things I couldn't get rid of. Just like her bone china teacups and the hundred or so silver spoons she collected over the years."

My eyes light up. "I'd love to see them all someday. Jane *is* the original independent woman; she's always been an idol of mine. Although I don't have a collection or anything."

"Of course," he replies. "Mum used to put these movies on when we stayed home sick from school. I think it was her way of making sure we were actually sick, not just dicking around to get out of handing in math homework or something. Because what twelve-year-old boy wants to watch *Sense and Sensibility* followed by *Emma* when they could be faking sick and playing with their *Star Wars* figurines instead?"

His eyes cast down as he finishes speaking, but I want to hear more. I hit pause on the remote then turn to face him. "Sounds like she had some pretty solid logic behind that theory."

He nods. "Yeah, but it backfired. We never admitted it to her, but after a while, we kind of liked those movies." He laughs, then takes my empty bowl. "You want seconds?"

"No, thanks. It was really good—and filling, too. But I want to leave room for dessert." My eyes land on the unopened box of sugary sweets from McKenna.

Elijah follows my line of sight. "Ah, good thinking. I'll just go put these up. You can keep watching; I've seen this before. It's about to get to the part where she tells Mr. Bennet she's into girls."

My eyes widen. "No!"

He nods. "*Yes!*" He grins, then takes our dirty dishes to the kitchen.

I'm leaning forward to grab the remote off the ottoman when I notice a piece of cardboard sticking out from under my box of goodies. My curiosity is piqued by the words written in a speech bubble in the corner: *You shall not pass!*

Sliding it out, a full comic-style drawing comes into view. I tilt my head, trying to decipher what exactly I'm seeing, when it's snatched from my grasp.

Elijah is standing in front of me, holding the drawing behind his back, hiding it from me. I frown.

"Hey, I was looking at that!" I growl, trying to peer around him.

"It's nothing." He looks slightly alarmed, which makes me even more interested.

"Show me."

"No," he snaps.

I get to my feet and attempt to take it from him, but he holds it above his head. I climb onto the couch, steady myself with one hand on his super-firm shoulder, and go for it. But he outmanoeuvres me, throwing the drawing to the other side of the room, then wrapping his arms around my thighs like thick metal bands.

He steps up to the couch, bringing our bodies flush. With me standing on the edge, it brings him chin level with my boobs. My unrestrained boobs. I swallow as his eyes scan my face, lingering on my parted lips.

"Elijah," I murmur.

"It's okay, Charlotte. I don't expect anything. Especially when you're not feeling well, baby. Just let me hold you. I'll be more than content with that."

His words are spoken softly and with sincerity. His breath warms the column of my throat, and I desperately want him to touch me.

I used to wonder how I could go from battling demons from hell intent on making a massacre of my nether region, to wanting a man in just hours ... but I stopped questioning it a long time ago.

Truth is, every woman is different. Some women can't ever have sex without being in excruciating pain. Some are good to go sometimes, but not others. There is no method to the madness that inhabits our bodies. It affects us all differently.

I've always had a strong sex drive. And while the act itself isn't painful for me, there are times afterwards when I wish I'd abstained. Times when, as soon as the glorious afterglow of an epic orgasm fades away, I curl in a ball, about ready to throw up I'm in so much pain.

But that's not how it always goes. It's about a seventy-thirty split in my favour. So, I take the risk.

Keeping my eyes on Elijah's, I push up on my tippy-toes. "You might be content with that, but I won't be."

A storm rages in his beautiful blue eyes. "Not like this. Not when you're hurting."

"Shut up and kiss me, Eli."

His mouth crashes down on mine, and I moan as his tongue sweeps inside my mouth. His arms unbind from my thighs so his hands can roam over my body, stopping to squeeze my butt, then continuing their upward journey. The second he reaches the collar of my T, he tugs it down, exposing my bare breast.

I shudder as he sucks my peaked nipple into his hot, wet mouth. So good. It feels so freaking good. His free hand slides up the back of my shirt, and he runs his calloused palm over my sensitive skin.

Digging my fingers into his hair, I groan as he releases my nipple with a pop, then claims my mouth again. His tongue teases mine with little flicks and licks, driving me crazy. I can feel the press of his erection on my thigh, and I reach down to cup him through his jeans.

Jesus, he's so hard. I give him a gentle squeeze, and he pulls away from my mouth, leaving both of us panting. "Don't take this the wrong way, but I won't take you tonight, Charlotte."

I swallow, disappointed, and maybe even a little hurt, by his rejection. "Wh-why not?"

"Because I want you so fucking bad I don't think I'll be able to take my time the way I *really* want to with you. And you haven't been well, baby. I'm not an animal. Even though you say you're good to go, I can't do that to you. You need to rest. Let me take care of you."

"Oh." That's all I've got, all I can say, as he runs his hand up and down my arms, comforting me. I drop my gaze, looking at the couch beneath my feet.

One of Elijah's big hands slides up over my shoulder, glides across my collarbone, then gently clasps my chin. "Look at me," he coaxes, his voice smooth and confident.

I bring my eyes to his.

"I said I'm not taking you. I didn't say anything about fooling around. You weren't wrong when you guessed it's been a while for me. I'm more than happy to spend some quality time polishing up on some old skills that have been out of action for far too long." His smirk is salacious, and naughty, and so freaking hot. I want to lick his face.

"Yes, please," I practically wheeze. I'm so turned on. Wrapping my legs around his waist, I grin. "You know where my bedroom is. What are you waiting for?"

Chapter Fourteen

Elijah

"Yes, ma'am," I say, tightening my hold under Charlotte's fine arse and stalking off towards her bedroom.

Her fingers run through my hair as I walk, and it feels a-fucking-mazing. A quiver skates down my spine. Approaching her bed, I lay her down gently, following after her until she's caged beneath me. I've imagined this view of her for weeks, but the reality is so much better.

"You're crazy beautiful," I tell her. I can't not tell her.

She smiles shyly. "You're not so bad yourself, Eli."

It's the second time she's called me Eli, and I really fucking like it. I want to be Eli to her. Eli is the fun, easy-going guy I slip into being so easily when I'm talking to Charlotte. Elijah is always serious, always responsible, always thinking of others' needs before his own.

But when I'm with her, it's easy to focus on me and what I want. Because what I want is right in front of me.

I can't keep my hands off her any longer. Gliding my fingers into her hair, I let the silky tresses slide between them as I lean down to kiss her. The soft press of her plump lips against mine is intoxicating, and I lose myself in the sweetness of her tongue caressing my own.

Kissing my way down her neck, I graze my teeth over her collarbone through her loose, white T-shirt. She squirms as I go lower, making my way down between the valley of her breasts. Bunching her shirt in my fists, I tug it up and over her head so I can run my nose down her bare, smooth stomach.

She smells like the lavender from her bath earlier, and I close my eyes, pausing to inhale her fresh, clean scent. Kissing my way to the band of her pants, I lift my gaze to her, making sure she's all right with this. Lust glazes her hazel eyes, and that perfect bottom lip is caught between her teeth.

I tug her pants and underwear down her legs until she's free of them. A faint yellow bruise still mars her flesh, and I bend down, kissing the spot tenderly.

Charlotte's back bows off the bed as my mouth glides down farther and my tongue parts her folds. She moans when I graze her clit but pass by it quickly.

"Eli," she whines, digging her small hands into my hair, holding me in place then spreading her legs wider for me.

I run my hands up and down her inner thighs, loving the feel of her skin against my palms. I work her with my tongue, muscle memory kicking in, reminding me just what to do to make this good for her.

She squirms and pants, making my dick throb harder in my jeans. But this isn't about me; this is all about her. I want nothing more than to make her feel good.

"Eli, I'm close, so close ..."

"I know, baby, I know. But you taste so good. I'm going to be here for a while," I murmur against her mound.

"Oh fuck," she breathes as I insert one finger inside her opening and graze my teeth over her swollen little clit.

I plant open-mouthed kisses all over her pretty pussy. I bring her to the brink, sucking on her lips, sliding my finger in and out of her warmth in long, slow strokes. Her body trembles and quakes as she comes for me, and it's spectacular.

Flattening my tongue, I lave at her sweet juices, drinking her up. "You taste so good, baby, so fucking good," I hum against her sensitive flesh as tremors wrack her body.

When she finally stills, I kiss my way up her belly again, pausing to suckle on her tight pink nipples, one at a time. Her shoulders draw back, pushing her breasts higher, and I bury my face in them. I tweak her left nipple hard while sucking gently on her right.

Her head thrashes from side to side. "Eli," she mewls.

Can I make her come like this? Just playing with her tits? My question is answered a moment later when Charlotte cries out, her body twitching and jerking in pleasure. And damn, if that doesn't make me feel like a fucking superstar.

Pressing light kisses over her tattooed collarbone, I then nuzzle my nose into her neck. She sighs softly, her fingernails skating over my back as her body goes lax beneath me.

"Sleep now, baby," I whisper in her ear as her eyelids flutter.

She gives the slightest nod, then her head lolls to the side, sleep taking her.

I tuck her in and go into her bathroom to take care of my raging hard-on before returning to her bed. After climbing in next to her, I roll on my side and tug her body into mine, and we spoon like we did on the couch this afternoon.

It doesn't take long for sleep to drag me under. I've had a hell of a long day, a good pull, and now I've got a beautiful woman in my arms. *Perfection.*

THE NEXT MORNING, I MAKE US BREAKFAST IN CHARLOTTE'S fancy kitchen. I prefer mine; everything is right where it should be. This kitchen is a disaster. Nothing makes sense. Cups and bowls are in the same cabinet, but plates and glasses are in another. *Who organised this place?*

I'm rummaging around for a spatula when Charlotte's arms wrap around me from behind.

"Morning," she murmurs into my back.

Turning to face her, I rest my forearms on her shoulders. "It would be if I could find anything in this place," I tell her with a teasing grin.

She drops her head to my chest and chuckles. "I don't cook. I'm surprised you even found a frying pan in here."

"Right, well I'll just have to get you some of the basics then. How are you supposed to cook for me without the proper utensils?"

Slowly, she raises her head, then arches a brow at me. "You are with the wrong woman if you think I'm going to cook for you, buddy."

I smile and shrug. "Don't worry, baby, I'll train you up real good." Then I wink, slap her arse, and untangle myself from her so I can find something to stir the eggs currently scrambling on the stove.

"Train me?" she yelps. "You're out of your goddamn mind if you think—"

I cut off her rant with a kiss. When I pull back, she's glaring at me, and I roll my eyes. "I'm just messing with you, cranky pants. Jeez, anyone would think you didn't have two earth-shattering orgasms last night."

Her mouth pops open in a perfect O, then slams shut again. "I never thought I'd say it, but there it is ... you're an arsehole," she quips.

Waggling my brows, I bend down and kiss her again. "But I'm an arsehole who cooks and cleans and gives really good head."

I smirk and she grins.

"You've got me there. I guess I can put up with your arsehole-ish tendencies if I get to reap all the other benefits," she says with a dramatic sigh, then presses up on her tiptoes and offers me her lips for another kiss.

Charlotte

WATCHING ELI STRUT AROUND MY KITCHEN IN NOTHING BUT a pair of low-slung jeans while he cooks me breakfast is the best porn I have ever seen.

My gaze fixates on the dimples on either side of his spine just above the waistband of his pants. I want to lick them. Then, my eyes travel higher, to his muscular shoulders and his thick biceps, down to his amazing forearms. I swallow down the lust clawing at my insides.

Unfortunately, lust isn't the only thing I'm feeling this morning. Lilith is going to make an appearance; I can feel the slight twinges deep in my pelvis, letting me know she's awake. There will be no sexy times for me today.

Flashes of last night flicker behind my eyelids, and I sigh happily. I'm so glad Eli didn't take me up on my offer to have sex. I'd be in a world of hurt already if we'd done the deed. That, and what he gave me instead was incredible. He was so attentive. Every little touch meant something.

I feel kind of bad that I didn't return the favour, though. Clearing my throat to get his attention, I say, "About last night—"

"You don't have to say anything. I know you still don't want to date me. That's not what last night was about. I just wanted to make you feel good for a little while. You don't owe me anything in return. I don't expect you to suddenly be all for a relationship with me. But I will be around, Charlotte. I'm not going anywhere."

I blink at him dumbly. "Oh," is all I manage to say in response.

"If you want me to keep my hands to myself for a while, I'll try. Can't make any promises, but I will try. I can wait until you're ready for more. Your disease doesn't scare me. Not having your smiling face and smart mouth in my life does."

He says that last part with his brilliant blue eyes locked on mine, leaving no room for misinterpretation. I can't stop the smile that takes over my face as his words, his promise, settle in my heart.

I'M LOUNGING ON THE COUCH, DEVOURING THE BEST chocolate croissant I've ever eaten when the paper from last night catches my eyes. I listen to make sure Eli is still in the shower then scuttle off the couch and snatch it up.

A loud snort rips from my nose as I take in exactly what it is I'm looking at.

It's a cartoon—a cartoon of a uterus, a little stick-figure maiden inside, wielding a sword at the exit. The words in the speech bubble above have my stomach clenching in anticipation of the laugh about to erupt.

"You shall not pass!" the little warrior declares.

Riotous endometrial tissue sneers at her. A text box below states "They did indeed pass, infecting and embedding themselves in the brave warrior princess's body. But fear not, her Prince Charming is on his way to nurse her back to health.

Tears of laughter streak down my cheeks, dripping off my chin.

Eli appears at my side, wearing nothing but a towel and pink-stained cheeks.

"Did you draw this?" I ask.

His eyes dart to the cartoon clutched in my hands, then back to my face. He sighs as his blush coats his whole throat. "Yes," he mutters.

I throw my arms around his neck and squeeze him tightly. "I love it. And I'm framing it. Don't even try to stop me."

Epilogue

Elijah

THREE MONTHS LATER …

"You want me to take off my shirt and stand next to my tractor?"

Charlotte nods enthusiastically. She's been spending more and more time out at the farm with me the last couple of weeks, and she just discovered the tractor.

"Uh, hell yes, I do. Now get that disgrace to fashion off your sexy body and strike a pose," she says.

I shake my head, grinning. "You think my tractor's sexy."

She sighs. She does that a lot. "Not on its own, but you all bare-chested and manly next to it? Now that's sexy."

"Whatever. You think my tractor's sexy." Then I start singing the Kenny Chesney song as I remove my shirt.

Charlotte's lips part, and her eyes eat me up. "Oh my

God. He cooks, he cleans, he eats me like a champ, *and* he can sing." She puts her phone down on the work bench behind her without taking her eyes off me, then struts across the space separating us.

The second she's close enough, I tug her into me. Her hands slide down my shoulders, and she squeezes my biceps. She has a thing for my arms. "Hey, baby," I breathe against her open mouth.

She licks her lips then presses up on her tiptoes. "Shut up and kiss me, Eli."

"Yes, ma'am." I take her mouth in a searing kiss. She's so into it she's moaning already. My hands cup her arse cheeks, and I push my hips into hers, showing her how ready I am for her.

Ripping her mouth away from me, her glassy eyes flick from mine to the large cab of the tractor. "We can do dirty things in there," she whispers.

My cock jumps at the thought of taking her inside my tractor. *Fuck. Yes!*

I spin us around so her back is against the tyre and yank open the glass door, then guide her up the three steps to enter the cab. Once inside, I sit, flip the armrests up, and tug her into my lap.

She grinds down on my aching dick, and my head tips back. *If this isn't every man's dream right here, I don't know what is.*

Charlotte runs her greedy little hands over my chest, scraping her nails over my nipples, making me shudder. I yank the top of her sundress down and suck her through her thin bra. She squirms in my lap, then she's unfastening my belt and lowering my zipper.

She slides her warm palm down my stomach, then slips it inside my underwear and wraps her fingers around my girth. I grab her face and kiss her senseless as she frees my cock and begins stroking.

One of her hands leaves my dick and she lifts herself a little, tugs her panties to the side, then slides down my shaft. When she's fully seated, we both moan in pleasure.

"Fuuuck," I gasp at the sensation of her wet heat engulfing me. It gets better every fucking time.

Just like that, she rides me. The air suspension in the seat rolls with our rhythm, making for a smooth ride. My fingers dig into her hips, lifting her then slamming her back down on my dick, over and over again.

I dip my head, suck her nipple into my mouth, and she explodes around me, clenching and squeezing my dick so tightly that I follow her over the edge.

NEVER IN ALL MY LIFE DID I THINK I WOULD EVER HAVE SEX in a tractor. But there it is. I just did, and it was fucking marvellous. "We're doing this again," I breathe into Elijah's neck as we both come down from the high we always seem to hit together.

"Definitely," he agrees, pressing a kiss to my sweaty temple.

It's been three months since he broke into my house. Three of the happiest months of my life. We haven't put any official labels on our relationship status, but we're definitely in one.

We've had a smooth run so far, except for that little psycho Delilah. That bitch really has it out for me. Last weekend, she stole my last coconut and jam slice from the goody box I got from McKenna. I know it was her; I saw the jam on her furry little mouth. Elijah thinks it's all in my head. She never does shit to me in front of him, but I'll catch her out one day.

Elijah tugs the top of my dress into place, and I lift up and off of him. He tucks himself back in his pants and refastens them while I climb down the steps. I'm on the last one when—*ow!* Pain shoots through my ankle. Something *bit me!*

I squeal, lose my balance, and fall the last two feet to the ground.

Splayed out flat on my back, I blink up at the barn roof. Then the devil's bride's head pops into my view. That little ...

I'm about to wrap my hands around her scrawny little throat when Eli jumps down from the cab. "Jesus, what happened? Are you okay?"

"No! Your side piece just bit me!"

Offering me a hand up, Eli rolls his eyes. "This again? She's a llama. If anything, she's going to spit on you, not bite you, baby. And you're more than enough for me. I don't need a side piece."

I am seething as she sidles up to Eli like an angel who can do no wrong.

Oh, you don't know who you're messing with, lady. I glare at her, and she glares right back. It is on like *Donkey Kong*.

That night, while Eli's passed out in a sexcoma, I sneak out of his bed and retrieve the electric clippers I got off eBay the last time Delilah and I had a run-in. I tiptoe out to the lounge where she is sleeping, since Eli kicks her out when I come to stay.

Without making a sound, I pounce. I pin her down with my body so she can't escape as I shave one long stripe from the top of her curly head to the tip of her tiny tail.

SECOND EPILOGUE
NINE MONTHS LATER ...

Elijah

"THANKS KENNA, YOU'RE THE BEST," I TELL MY AUNT AS I drop a kiss on her cheek then take the box with my special order from the counter.

Kenna beams at me. "You're welcome sweetheart. I wish I could be a fly on the wall when you give it to her."

I grin and shake my head, if all goes to plan, there is no way in hell I want anyone around for it.

Shaking my head, I chuckle on my way out the door. "Uh no. This is a strictly private occasion. But I'm sure Charlotte will tell you everything you need to know when she sees you next."

When I get to my truck I place the box on the passenger seat then crank it over. Charlotte is at home with Ash and Juda at the moment. I gave them firm instructions not to let her leave the house and to beat it the second I get back.

I'm as ready as I'll ever be for this moment, I just hope my woman is too. We've come a long way together in the past year, although a part of me is sure I should hold off for a little longer, give her more time.

We've talked about our future and vaguely discussed starting a family at some stage. But knowing how difficult that might be for us with her condition, I don't want to wait any more.

I know all I need to know about her and us, I'm ready for the next step.

As my tires crunch over the gravel down our long drive, nerves appear out of nowhere.

Am I pushing her for too much too fast?

But then a flash of red catches my eye, her hair is down and blowing around her as she stands in my parking spot, hands on her hips and suspicion in her brilliant hazel gaze. I pull up a few feet from her and get out, she waits for me, tapping her booted foot.

"Hey babe, what's up?" I ask as I approach.

She raises a brow. "Why wouldn't the boys let me go into town to see Tilly?"

Oh shit.

I run my hand over the scruff on my jaw, hoping to butter her up by bringing her attention to my arms. She has a thing for my arms. In the past they've been a great tool in distracting her... But not today apparently.

"Spit it out Eli. Reagan came to pick me up and Juda literally threw himself in front of the passenger door so I couldn't get in the car then he whispered something to her and she sped out of here like her life depended on it.

"*And then* Ash made up some bogus story about needing my help with a website he's designing for some up and coming designer I've never even heard of. And you and both know I would have heard of any new talent coming on the scene."

She finally pauses, taking a breath, then steps into my space and pokes me in the chest. "So, what the hell is going on?"

Well then, this isn't how I wanted to do this, but she's not giving me much of a choice.

I step into her, eating up the last bit of space between us then bend my knees, press my shoulder into her stomach, wrap my arms around her thighs, then stand, tossing her over my shoulder.

"Eli!" she squeals. "What are you doing?"

Ignoring her I call out to my brother, leaning against the porch, "Juda, grab that package off my passenger seat, and be careful with it!"

He nods and does as I asked while I stride into the barn with a pissy Charlotte slapping at my arse.

Luckily, I had the foresight to set this up earlier this morning, so when I lower my woman to her feet in the middle of the barn she finally stops grumbling about causing me bodily harm and shuts her mouth.

Her gaze widens as it travels around the space. I covered every work bench with native flowers and battery-operated candles.

Juda scurries in, hands me the white box I picked up from McKenna's then high tails it out again without a word.

I take Charlotte's shaking hand in mine and lead her over to a small cluster of hay bales I laid blankets over, and guide her to sit. She goes easily, for once.

She eyes shine with unshed tears as she watches me low to a knee in front of her.

All I have to do is stare into her eyes and the words fall from my lips. "Charlotte, you are the strongest, most incredible woman I have ever known. You battled alone for so long, and that kills me baby ... I want to be at your side, through the good, the bad, and the ugly for the rest of my days."

I take a breath, then open the box offering it up to her.

Charlotte

Air seizes in my lungs and for a moment, I can't breathe.

Tears fill my eyes, blurring my vision. I swipe them away as Eli holds a small cake box up to me and I peer inside.

Pure, unadulterated happiness floods my entire system as I take in my favourite glazed doughnut and the two words written in pink icing—Marry Me. I choke on a sob, covering my mouth with both hands I try to hold it in.

Eli's beautiful blue eyes never leave my face as he reaches inside and removes a stunning ring from a small round box placed in the centre of the doughnut. I extend my left hand, still unable to form words as he slides the ring onto my finger.

His smile is the most beautiful thing I have ever seen as he gently places the doughnut box on the hay bale next to me but before he can do anything else I launch myself at him. My arms wrap around his neck and I press my lips to his, showing him how perfect this all is, how perfect *he* is, with my kiss.

He rolls me to my back and hovers over me, his strong forearms braced on either side of my head as he peers down at me. "So, I take it that's a yes?" he murmurs.

"That's a hell yes," I breath into the space between us then tangle my fingers in the front of his flannel shirt and yank his mouth back down to mine so I can keep kissing him.

I slide my hand over his chest, taking time to appreciate every curve and dip of muscle on my way to his belt buckle. When I reach it he lifts his hips for me, giving me room to unfasten it and his jeans. I push them down just enough to free his length then stroke it, once, twice, three times.

With a moan Eli breaks our kiss, sitting back on his haunches. He stares down at me with so much heat, desire and passion I feel it in every ounce of my being. He loves me. And I love him.

He takes the hem of my sun dress and tugs it, I sit up and help him pull it over my head, leaving me in a blue lace bra and matching thong. My insides clench when he licks his lips and I know exactly what he's about to do.

Hooking his fingers into the sides of my underwear he drags them down my thighs, tosses them over his shoulder then drops to his elbows at my hips. Eli's gaze locks with mine as he runs his tongue through my folds and cry out. He does it over and over, licking, sucking, and nibbling, until I can't take it anymore and I explode on his tongue.

The moment I come back to myself I glare at his chest. "Why aren't you naked yet?" I demand.

He smirks and unbuttons his flannel and discards it before moving to his jeans. I enjoy the show as he lowers them over his hips and amazing arse then kicks them to the side. I curl my finger and he comes back to me, hovering just out of my reach.

I curl my legs around his hips and pull him down at the same time I thread my fingers in his hair and tug his mouth back to me. We kiss, long, slow, and deep. When his cock finally sides inside I'm already so close to coming again I can't think straight. "I love you," I murmur against his soft lips.

"I love you too," he groans with a deep thrust of his hips.

Over and over again he pulls out and slides back in. Drawing another orgasm from me, but this time, Eli comes with me.

He strokes my cheek as we stare at each other smiling. Until a rustling sound comes from behind us. We turn our heads at the same time and catch the dirty little scamp that is Delilah, in the act of trying to get into the proposal doughnut box Eli had left on the hay bale.

"I told you she steals my treats!" I say as Eli reaches a long arm out and saves it before the little wench can get to the doughnut inside.

Eli grins as he hands me his shirt and I wrap it around myself then cross my legs. His eyes glitter with humour as he gives me the box now missing half the lid.

"Okay, okay. Maybe Delilah really does have something against you," he freaking finally admits. Then adds, "But what do you expect? You totally stole me from her."

I shoot the fur ball a smug smirk, then lean over and kiss my man. "Hell yes I did. And I'd do it all over again."

The End

FROM FRIENDS TO LOVERS TO ... OH HELL NO

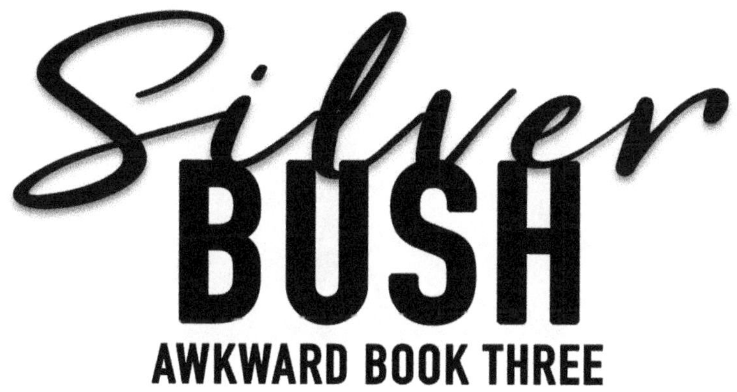

AWKWARD BOOK THREE

JB HELLER

Chapter One

Tilly

THERE'S NOTHING WORSE THAN GROCERY SHOPPING—EXCEPT grocery shopping with kids.

Running my gaze over the shelf on my right, I compare the prices of the peanut butter. I pick up one that's on sale and peruse the ingredients list on the back before placing it back on the shelf. *Too many preservatives.*

I'm reaching for the one I usually buy when a figure at the end of the aisle snags my attention.

Adjusting my three-year-old, Arabella, I lift my gaze but turn away just as fast. My heart lurches into my throat. *It couldn't be ...*

I chance another quick glance, and yep, it's definitely him. *What is he doing here?* Intent on fleeing before he notices me, I execute a rapid U-turn in the middle of the aisle and duck my head. I grab the first jar of peanut butter my fingers land on and throw it in the trolley without looking.

"Ouch!" Sailor cries.

Shit!

Sailor rubs the side of his little head. Great, I just assaulted my four-year-old with a jar of peanut butter.

"Sorry, baby, Mummy wasn't looking. You okay?" I ask, running my fingers over his velvet-soft cheek.

"Yeah," he huffs. "Lucky I'm tough."

I grin. "Yeah, you are." I would coddle him some more, but I need to get as far away from *him* as possible. Glancing over my shoulder, I check to make sure he didn't see me.

Crap. That was a bad idea. A very bad idea. He's staring right at me—those crystal-blue eyes are bearing into my soul, and now I can't breathe.

I'm like a deer caught in headlights, frozen against my will. Then, he moves one foot in front of the other, coming straight at me, and I snap out of the trance. Jerking my head forward again, I grip the handle of my cart and scurry around the corner so fast Sailor teeters to the side, almost falling out.

My hold around Arabella, perched on my hip, tightens, and I reach for Sailor with the hand that was steering the trolley, hooking my finger into the back of his little T-shirt and tugging him back down.

His eyes glow with excitement. "That was fun, Mummy. Do it again!"

Shit. Shit-shit-shit. I have to get out of here. Screw the groceries. I'll order them online and pick them up tomorrow.

"Come here, buddy. Mummy forgot something. We

need to go home—now," I tell Sailor with my hand extended to help him out of the trolley. He frowns at me.

No, not at me. *Behind* me.

The hairs on the back of my neck stand to attention, and my skin prickles in awareness of *his* proximity, just like it always does whenever he is close by.

"Now, Sailor," I say as strong as I can, but my voice betrays me, coming out soft and scratchy.

"Going somewhere?" His deep baritone washes over me, and I shiver.

"Sailor ..." I plead, but my son just stares at me.

"You're being rude, Mummy. That man is talking to you."

"Hi!" Arabella chirps over my shoulder, and I curl in on myself.

"Hey there, pretty girl," Lee drawls, and I swear my ovaries swell at the affection in his tone.

That's what he used to call me, once upon a time ...

It's been more than six years since I laid eyes on her. Dad and Trudie send me a Christmas card every year, and she's always in the family photo. But she's so much more in person.

The little blonde-haired angel wrapped around her

torso like a spider monkey grins at me, and her little boy stands in the cart, wearing an unimpressed frown.

"Till," I murmur. My hand reaches for her but stills before making contact. I shouldn't touch her.

When she finally turns to face me, it's like a punch to the gut. She hasn't changed a bit. Her big brown eyes slowly lift to meet mine, and it's like the last six years without her never even happened.

My lips lift in a smile. "It's good to see you." It's Gods honest truth.

She blinks at me but says nothing. Her full lips part as if she's going to speak, but instead, she shakes her head and remains silent.

Right, well, this is awkward. I slide my hands into my pockets and rock back on my heels. "These your kids?" I ask like a dumb-arse. Of course they're her kids. I've watched them grow over the years on the Christmas cards too.

She swallows then gives me a jerky nod. Okay, so she's not going to speak to me. *Awesome.*

Her little boy rolls his eyes at her then sticks his tiny hand out to me. I step forward and take it, giving him a firm but gentle shake. "I'm Sailor. This is my baby, Ari, and my mummy. Who are you?"

Tilly silently watches our exchange.

"Nice to meet you, Sailor. I'm Lee. Your mummy and me are ... we're umm ..." Well, shit. How do you tell a kid you're kind of his uncle, but had things been different, you might have been his daddy?

I shouldn't have come over here. I clear my throat and

desperately wrack my brain for something to say, but Sailor saves me.

"I know lots of cool stuff. Did you know swans have a sticky-outie peen—"

Tilly's hand shoots out, covering her sons mouth before he can finish his little factoid. "Sailor!" she chastises, her eyes widening at him.

But now I really want to know what he was going to say, because that sounded a lot like he was about to say penis. I smirk. "No, go on. I like learning cool new things."

Sailor yanks Till's hand away and glares at her. "It's okay, Mummy. I only tell people true stuff."

"I know, buddy, but why don't you pick another fact to share? One that doesn't involve body parts? I really wish Aunty Reags hadn't told you that one."

"But it's so cool. Aunty Weags says that swans are the only birds that have them," he huffs.

Clearing my throat, I hunch and crouch to Sailor's level. "So, you're telling me that swans are the only bird that has a penis?"

He nods enthusiastically. "Other birds just have a little one on the inside. But swans have a big one on the outside, like me."

I can't contain it; I bust out laughing. My hand curls around the side of their shopping cart for support. Ruffling his neatly combed hair, I tell him, "I like you, kid. I think you and I could be good friends."

I straighten at the strange gurgle that comes from Tilly and meet her eyes—they're shining. She bites her bottom lip and looks away.

Shifting into her line of sight, I tell her, "You look good, Till. How've you been?"

She swallows then clears her throat. "What are you doing here, Lee?"

Her voice is soft, anxious. I don't like it, but I understand it. We didn't exactly leave things on good terms all those years ago. And I didn't make it any better by staying away all this time.

Sliding my left hand back into my pocket, I rub the back of my neck with the other. "Mum's getting remarried. She wanted me to come home for it. I couldn't exactly say no." I'm not lying, but it's only part of the reason I'm back in town.

"Oh, right. I forgot about the wedding. But I thought it wasn't for another couple of weeks?"

I nod. "It's not. She was dead-set on me arriving early to spend some time with her and get to know all Denny's family before the big day."

"Makes sense," she mumbles, averting her gaze. She can barely look at me, and damn if it doesn't hurt like a son of a bitch. My chest aches as thoughts of what could have—no, *should* have—been roll through me.

I imagined the day I would see her in the flesh again a thousand times over, and not once did it go down like this. She was the centre of my universe, then our parents went and fell in love and made a baby together.

One day we were making plans for our shared future—the next we were coming to terms with our parents' upcoming nuptials and preparing for the arrival of a baby sister we would share.

At seventeen, we weren't capable of weathering that particular storm with our love intact. We broke up two days later, deciding it was just too weird for either of us to handle.

Tilly was my best friend. Then my lover. Until the day I became her stepbrother.

But I still want to be her baby-daddy.

Chapter Two

Tilly

I HAVEN'T SEEN LEE IN SO DAMN LONG. A BIG PART OF ME wants to reach out and touch him, just to be sure it's really him and I haven't actually lost my damn mind and started hallucinating. But my sense of self-preservation won't let me do that.

So, I keep my arms wrapped securely around Arabella's little body, and my eyes focus anywhere but on him. He's always been able to read me like no other. If I maintain eye contact for too long, he'll know exactly how much this small interaction is affecting me.

My nerves are going into overdrive beneath my skin just from his proximity. And he's not even standing that close to me. Simply knowing he's in town is enough to send them skittering like a kitten hopped up on catnip.

I bite my bottom lip and glance down, and oh, dear God—I'm wearing mismatched shoes. They aren't even in the same shoe family. *How did this happen?* The one on my right foot is a blue Converse and the left is a strappy tan sandal.

My teeth sink deeper into my lip. *What must I look like to him ...* My face crumples.

"If I knew approaching you would bother you so much, Till, I would have stayed away," Lee says.

"What?" My head jerks up. "Why would you think that?"

He arches a brow at me. "You're about to chew through your lip. That, and you haven't said a word in a solid two minutes. It's pretty clear I'm making you uncomfortable. I should go."

Shit.

Before I can brace myself for what it will inevitably do to me, I reach out and curl my hand around his forearm, stopping him from walking away. The second our skin connects, a current of electricity shoots through my fingertips.

We're both struck silent for a moment.

I'm thrown back to the last time I saw him. The day I told him I was pregnant with another boy's baby. The day he turned away from me, just like he was about to do now. I didn't stop him then, even though I wanted to more than anything in the world. But I couldn't.

Without removing my hand, I say the two words I desperately wanted to say back then. "Don't go."

Lee's Adam's apple bobs as he swallows hard. His eyes bore into mine, searching for God knows what, but I hope he finds whatever it is, because I can't let him go a second time.

A lot has happened since we went our separate ways, and I want to share it all with him. He was my best friend before we became more, that's the part I've missed the most. I want him back in my life—in any way I can have him.

And then he smiles at me. I feel it all the way down to the tips of my toes.

Happiness blooms in my chest, but did I really have to be wearing mismatched shoes? And as my eyes drift over my body, I cringe. Of all the things I could have thrown on this morning, it had to be one of *his* old T-shirts.

I slide Ari around in a front piggyback, attempting to hide the band logo that Lee will most certainly recognise. Unfortunately, my three-year-old is not down with my plan.

She squirms in my arms. "Down, Mummy. I wanna get down."

My arms tighten around her tiny body. "No, baby, you refused to put on your shoes this morning, remember? And the floor is yucky." Her eyes narrow on me, and I narrow mine right back. The sass is strong in this one.

Ari resumes squirming, so much so that my grip on her slips. Lee moves fast, catching her before she reaches the ground. He swoops her up in his arms and settles her on his hip. The little flirt throws her arms around his neck, burrows her face in close, and declares, "You saved me!"

Lee strokes her hair. "Shh, you're okay, pretty girl. I got you."

A coy smile tips her lips and she glances at me from

under her lashes. I roll my eyes. Yep, *total flirt*. She's playing him so hard and he has no idea. But I'm not going to say jack about it since it's distracting him from my shirt situation.

Or so I thought.

Lee's eyes home in on me, or more specifically, my chest. His big palm continues stroking Ari's hair, but those crystal-blue eyes sparkle with interest. "Is that my old Blink 182 shirt?"

I scoff. "No."

His brow arches and his lips quirk. "I think it is."

"You're not the only one who likes Blink, you know."

He chuckles then steps closer to me. My breath catches in my throat—he smells so good, like summer rain and man. His eyes lock on mine, and before I know what he's doing, his head tips and he peers over my shoulder.

Crap balls, the stain. I shove his chest. "What are you doing?"

When his attention moves back to my face, I know I'm busted. His gorgeous lips kick up in a killer smirk. I swallow at the memories that *that look* brings to the forefront of my thoughts.

"That is most definitely my shirt," he states. "I spilt bleach on the back, right in the middle, the one and only time Mum got me to do the washing."

Well, shit. I had forgotten about that stupid stain. I decide playing it cool is the way to go. Shrugging, I say, "That proves nothing. I could have spilt bleach on *my* shirt too, you know. I'm awfully clumsy sometimes."

Lee snorts. "Right." He shakes his head and smiles at me again. His teeth are so freaking white I bet they glow in the dark.

While I'm distracted by his pearly whites, he reaches for my hair before twirling a loose strand around his finger. "I like the pink," he murmurs.

"Thanks," I whisper, not sure what else to say.

"Mummy, I gotta pee!" Sailor calls, tugging on the back of my tee.

Lee releases my hair. Taking a step back, he nods to Sailor, "It was good to meet you, little man. I'll let you go take care of business." He hands Ari over to me then strokes her cheek once she's back in my arms. "I'll see you around, pretty girl."

"Bye, Lee," Ari says, smiling her biggest, brightest smile at him.

When his gaze moves to mine, I bite my lip.

"It was good to see you, Till," he says quietly. "I've missed you."

My eyes sting with tears I refuse to let fall. "I've missed you too." Those four words don't come close to how I really feel. But for now, they'll do. "I better go."

He nods. "I'll be seeing you real soon," he says with a wink then strides away.

Chapter Three

Tilly

"IN CONCLUSION, IT WAS A COMPLETE DISASTER AND UTTERLY mortifying." I sigh then shove a bite-size piece of passionfruit cheesecake in my mouth. But not even the creamy deliciousness is pulling me out of the funk I've been in since my run-in with Lee at the grocery store yesterday.

Charlotte and Reagan sip their coffees and listen with rapt attention to the horror story that was my past with Lee and yesterday's events. They're smiling like a pair of loons when none other than the man himself strides through the doors at McKenna's Heavenly Treats. I slink low in the booth, cup my hand around my mouth, and whisper-hiss, "That's him," while throwing crazy eyes towards the entryway.

Charlotte's eyes light with interest, and she grins at Reagan who returns the look.

Oh, shit. That's not good—I know what that look means.

Char's hand lifts in the air, and she waves it around until she's successfully snagged Lee's attention. A mischievous smile lifts her perfectly painted red lips as she calls out to him. "Lee? Won't you join us?"

My eyes bug out at her. "Char!" I grit from between my clenched teeth.

She ignores me completely, keeping her focus on a confused-looking Lee.

He approaches our booth cautiously, eyeing the gorgeous blonde and redheaded bombshell sitting across from me. Then, his gaze finds me, and he smiles. "Oh, hey, Till. I didn't see you there."

I shimmy until I'm sitting up in my seat again. "Uh, yeah, I umm, I dropped my napkin." I snatch a clean napkin from the tabletop beside my slice of cake and wave it around like a total spaz.

A knowing grin takes over his expression. "I see." The longer his eyes stay locked on mine, the thicker the air between us grows and everyone around us slowly disappears. I just want to stare at him and absorb his presence. God, I sound like a psycho—even to myself.

The delicate clearing of a throat snaps me out of my Lee-induced daze, and my head snaps in Charlotte's direction. Right, introductions. "Lee, this is Charlotte," I say, gesturing across the table with a sweep of my hand. "And Reagan. They're in town for the weekend; Char is dating Eli Marshall."

Lee tips his head to them politely. “Nice to meet you, ladies.”

Reagan extends a hand to him. “Nice to finally meet you, *Lee*.”

His brows bunch slightly. “Finally?” he asks.

Charlotte’s grin is blinding. “We were actually just talking about you,” she explains. “It’s so lovely to put a face to the name.”

Lee’s eyes track back and forth between Charlotte and Reagan, then they skirt over to me. A smirk tugs at the corner of his lips, and I swear my cheeks redden.

“Would you like to join us?” Charlotte offers.

“Sure, just let me put in my order. I’ll be right back.” He winks at me then returns to the short line at the counter.

I drop my head to the tabletop with a soft thunk.

“Don’t be so dramatic. We’re doing you a solid,” Charlotte says.

I lift my head and glare at her. “How do you figure that?”

She rolls her eyes. “Your kids are with their dad this weekend, and your past flame is in town … It’s time to reconnect, honey.” She makes a lude gesture with her hands when she says reconnect, and Reagan giggles.

I bolt upright. “Are you insane? I just told you the whole freaking story of how I broke both our hearts when I got pregnant with another guy’s baby right after we broke up. How do you jump to us reconnecting from that?”

“The longing in your pretty eyes told me more than

your words, sweets." Char rests her hand over mine on the table and smiles gently. "I didn't say you have to jump his bones tonight, but you two have a lot to catch up on. Now is as good a time as any."

"Agreed," Reagan chimes in. "Plus, the dude's H.O.T. Like, smokin'. He's got that whole Tom Welling in *Smallville* vibe going for him—you know, like in the later seasons—and I'm totally digging it."

"But ..." I blink at them, trying to come up with an excuse. I am so totally not ready for this.

Char shakes her head. "It's time. And you look gorgeous today—no mismatched shoes or nasty band tees." She cringes at the mention of a band tee then gathers her box of goodies and slides her handbag over her shoulder.

Reagan follows suit by slipping her cross-body bag over her head before she waggles her brows at me. "Get on it, girly." Then she trails Char out of the booth.

My heart rate skyrockets. "Where are you going?"

"Eli and the boys will be waiting for these." Char gestures to the goodie box. "Call us later with the goss." She drops air kisses on each of my cheeks, as does Reagan, then they walk away. They pause by Lee, say something to him I can't hear—*damnit*—and then they're gone.

I turn back around and stare at the empty seat across from me then take a deep, steadying breath. My pulse is frantic and erratic. I rest a slightly shaking palm over my chest and close my eyes.

I know they're right, but it doesn't mean I'm ready for

it. I'm nervous, excited, and terrified. *Great.* Not what I'd call a winning combination.

LEE

I HAD INTENDED TO GRAB A COFFEE TO GO, BUT I CAN'T turn down an opportunity to spend some time with Till, especially after her friends made a point of telling me they were leaving so I could have her all to myself. I place my order and stride over to Till's booth. Her eyes are squeezed shut, and she has a hand pressed over her heart, and my breath catches in my throat. I stand there just taking her in for a few more moments—she's still the most beautiful thing I've ever seen.

Her eyes snap open, landing right on me.

"Hey," I murmur.

A soft smile tugs at her full lips. "Hey," she breathes back.

I slide into the booth opposite her, my long legs tangling with hers under the table. Neither of us speak. We just look at each other, and I take in every new little detail about her. We're so focused on each other that I don't even notice McKenna placing my coffee and vanilla slice on the timber tabletop by my elbow.

"Just like old times," McKenna says.

We look up at her in unison. Her smile is sweet and sad.

"I've missed you two coming in here," she says. "It's good to see you together again."

I don't get a chance to reply before she leaves us. I'm not sure what I would have said anyway.

My hands curl around my coffee mug to keep them from reaching for Till, and I ask the first thing that comes to my mind. "No kids today?"

She shakes her head, her pretty, light-pink hair grazing the tops of her shoulders with the movement. "They're with Curt. He or his parents take them every second weekend."

I nod. I knew they had split—Dad mentioned it at the time. And I'd be lying if I said I wasn't happy about it. That guy is a douche.

Tilly chuckles. "I can see your mind working over there. I know you don't like Curt, but he's a good dad."

"Hmmm ..." It's all I give her.

She shakes her head, but she's still smiling softly. "I don't blame you for not liking him. But seriously, he's not a bad guy."

I take a sip of my coffee. *May as well get right to the heart of it.* "So, what made you two decide to end it?"

"We don't love each other. I mean, we do, but that's because of the kids. They were the only thing that connected us. We got along fine; we still do. But it was more like we were good roommates. We were never a love match, which you know.

"Anyway, he got a job offer in the city, and I didn't want to go. I've got friends and family here, support. I'd have nobody if I went to the city. So, we decided it was time. We gave it a good try, we really did." She shrugs and picks up her own coffee and takes a drink, leaving a small foam moustache when she's done.

I can't stop myself. I reach out and slide my thumb over her top lip, wiping it away. My fingertips graze her cheek, and she closes her eyes, leaning into my touch. God, I've missed this.

Reluctantly, I release her but not before I twirl a strand of her hair around my finger, loving the softness against my skin. Sitting back, I pick up my vanilla slice and take a bite.

Tilly rubs the back of her neck, her gaze fixed on her coffee. "So, what about you? Do you have a girlfriend waiting for you back home?"

My brows furrow. "No," I scoff. How does she not know this? "I would have thought you'd be aware of my relationship status. I assumed Trudie kept you as up to date as Dad keeps me about everything going on back here."

She swallows, still not meeting my eyes. "I, umm ... I asked her not to. It was ..." She chews her bottom lip for a moment. "... it was too hard."

I reach for her again. This time, I take her hand from the table and squeeze it. "Look at me, Till." She closes her eyes briefly before bringing them to mine. "I get it. It was hard for me to hear about you too."

Her eyes shine with unshed tears, and a lump the size of a baseball settles in my throat. *Why did I stay away so damn long?* I should have come back sooner.

"I thought about telling Dad to keep news of you to

himself. But I couldn't. And after a while, I looked forward to those little glimpses into your life. Knowing you were happy ... it's what kept me sane. Make no mistake, Till, I've thought about you every single day since I left. But I couldn't stay and watch you with Curt. I just couldn't."

She nods, a single tear escaping. "I know," she whispers then swipes at her cheek with the hand I'm not holding. She takes a deep breath, shakes her head, and blinks a few times.

My thumb strokes back and forth over the hammering pulse point in her wrist. "Can I see you while I'm here?"

"What do you mean?" she asks, an adorable frown creasing her brows.

"Go out with me, on a date, or five ..."

Her brows shoot up. "What?"

I shrug in a lame attempt to look casual when I feel anything but. My stomach is in knots; my heart beats so fast I feel it throughout my entire body. "You know how I feel about you, Till—always have and always will. Six years changed nothing for me. Go out with me."

She chews on her lip again, then—thanks to all that is holy—she nods. "Okay."

Chapter Four

Tilly

The next evening, I'm pacing my bedroom. *Why did I agree to this?*

The reasons Lee and I broke up are still relevant. His dad, Al, and my mum, Trudie, are married, making him my stepbrother, which is just eww. And if that wasn't bad enough, we share a sibling. Our baby sister, Dixie, is only four months older than my oldest daughter, Astrid. It's weird. Super freaking weird.

Dropping my head back, I stare at the ceiling, then "T-shirt" by Thomas Rhett starts blaring from my phone, and I scoop it up from my comforter. Charlotte's name flashes on the screen. "Hey," I answer.

"What are you wearing? Tell me!" she demands.

I can't help my laughter. "A towel ..."

Her huff fills the line, and I laugh again. "Very funny," she retorts.

She's rolling her eyes at me right now, I just know it,

and it makes me smile.

"What are you wearing on your date tonight, you cow."

I sigh. "I don't know. I'm actually having second thoughts about all of this. He's my stepbrother, Char."

"Heck yeah he is. It's like a steamy romance novel come to life, girl. Jump on it." She says this like I'm the luckiest woman in the world.

My head drops, and I rub my temples with my free hand. "Seriously, what the hell kind of books are you reading?"

She scoffs. "Honey, if you've never read one, you're missing out. You need to get on that—and your incidentally sexy-as-shit stepbrother, too, while you're at it."

"I don't know why I even talk to you about this stuff," I groan.

"Because you need someone to spell it out for you. It's not that big of a deal, babe. You're making it an issue when it doesn't need to be. You're a grown-arse woman. You can be with whomever you want."

I run my hand through my damp hair. "But I'm not the girl he fell in love with anymore. I'm a mother. I've given birth three times, Char. That changes a woman, like, down there." I whisper the last part.

"I'm sure he can handle all the changes, babe. But you'll never know if you don't give him that chance."

I nod, then snort, because dah, she can't see me. "Okay." I take a deep breath. "Okay, you're right."

"Dah," she says. "Now, what are you going to wear?"

Finally, a spark of excitement ripples through me, and I approach my closet.

An hour later, I'm dressed in a pair of cream, high-waisted linen shorts with huge pockets because pockets are life. My boobs look amazing in the best bra I own underneath a soft, loose-fitting cami, and I'm wearing heels for the first time in a long time.

I check my reflection in the mirror, making sure my makeup is just right.

I smile. *I tidy up okay.*

A knock sounds from the front door, and I check the clock on my bedside table. He's early. I snatch my bag off the end of my bed and race out of my room. I'm so intent on reaching the front door I don't even see Ari's fake pearl necklace hanging out of the toybox across the floor … I go down—hard.

I SLIDE MY HAND INTO MY POCKET AFTER KNOCKING ON Tilly's front door and wait. I know I'm early, but I figure I can sit on her couch and get a feel for her space if she's not ready. Then, a high-pitched squeal pierces the air.

I'm turning the handle on the front door and throwing it open in seconds. I don't know what I expected to find, but it was not the scene I'm greeted with.

Tilly is on her hands and knees in front of me, and I've

got a clear view right down the front of her top. I can't tear my eyes away from her beautiful breasts that are somewhat larger than I remember.

"A little help ..." she says.

"Shit, Till. What happened?" I ask as I help her to her feet.

She keeps her hands wrapped around my wrists when we're standing then glances at her feet. "I tripped on Ari's necklace." She lifts one foot, winces, then mutters, "Crap."

"What?"

"I broke my shoe and possibly my knees." Her forehead creases as she squeezes her eyes shut and sucks in a harsh breath.

I move, sliding one arm behind her knees, the other around her waist, pick her up, and take her to the couch where I sit, cradling her in my arms. She hooks her elbow around my neck. God it feels good.

She has curves now that she didn't have when we were teens. And I like them a lot. My arm curled around her back tightens, tugging her in closer to my body. It's been too long since I had her this close.

"I'm okay, Lee, really. I'll be fine. We can go," she says.

I have zero interest in ending this moment—besides the fact that I'm pretty sure she really did hurt her knees. I shake my head. "We don't have to go anywhere. How about you put your feet up and I'll get you an ice pack? We can order a pizza instead of going out."

Her gaze lingers on my lips as I speak, and my blood rushes south. *Fuck*. I need to get her out of my lap before she feels what she's doing to me. I slide her to the side, lowering her butt to the cushion beside me as I swing out from under her.

My eyes trace down her long bare legs, and I swallow. *Jesus.* I always did love those legs. Especially when they were wrapped around me.

My dirty trip down Memory Lane is pulled to a screeching halt at the sight of the swelling and bruising that's already started on both her knees.

Hovering over her, I sweep a few strands of hair from her eyes, tucking them behind her ear, then kiss her temple because I just can't help myself. "You got an ice pack or bag of peas in your freezer?"

She nods. "I've got three kids; I have ice packs."

Right, of course. I straighten and go in search of her kitchen. It's not hard to find. Her house has a pretty open plan, putting the kitchen just around the corner from the lounge we're in. I grab a Disney Princess ice pack and a Buzz Lightyear one from the freezer, then take a couple of cloths that hang from the oven door and wrap them.

When I return, Till's removed her strappy heels and is chewing her bottom lip. I place the ice packs on her tender knees, and if I wasn't watching her so closely, I would have missed the wince. "You okay?"

"Just dandy," she mutters, glaring at something.

I follow the path of her glare to a little fake-pearl necklace laying on the floor. She may hate that thing right now, but I'm not complaining. Because of it, I got her in my arms a hell of a lot sooner than I was anticipating. I grin and cup her jaw, turning it to face me. "Pizza sound good?"

"I can't believe I ruined our date before it even started."

"You didn't. I actually prefer this," I tell her honestly. "I get you all to myself."

She finally gifts me with a smile. "Okay. Pizza sounds good." She slides her phone from her pocket. "You still like Meatlovers?"

I nod and she makes the call to place the order while I gently lift her legs and slide in under them. I place them in my lap and throw my arm over the back of the couch as I turn to face her. She is absolutely breathtaking. Her pink hair hangs in soft curls around her face as she stares at me in return.

When she ends the call, I tell her what's on my mind. "I should have come home sooner."

"I get why you didn't," she says. "I hurt you. If I could have run, I would have."

A lump forms in my throat. I did run away. After our parents shocked the shit out of us by secretly dating and accidently making a baby together, Tilly broke up with me. I could handle that as long as I still had her in my life. But then, in an attempt to drown her sorrows, she hit the party scene and ended up pregnant. That had been my breaking point.

Her eyes search mine, and I let her see the pain in them. "You didn't hurt me intentionally. I know that. I just couldn't hang around to watch you making a go of it with Curt. It was too much. When I heard you two split up, I almost came back."

She gasps. "What?"

I take a deep breath and let it all out. I've done a lot of thinking since I saw her in the grocery store, and I need her to know where my head's at.

I take her hand, lacing our fingers, and squeeze. "You were my best friend, and I thought that was what I missed the most when I first left. But after three failed attempts at moving on, I realised I missed more than our friendship. I measured every girl I met against you. And none of them came close."

"Lee," she breathes.

"Just let me talk for a minute, Till. I need to say this."

She nods. "Okay," she whispers then squeezes my hand back.

"It's always been you for me. I understand why you didn't feel like we could be together back then. But, Till, babe, it's still you. I didn't come home straight away because I knew you wouldn't be ready to hear all this—you needed time." I pause, letting everything I feel for her come to the surface, hoping she sees it. "I want to give this—us—a real chance."

"You do?" she asks so softly I only just catch it.

"I do. So damn much. I know things are different now, but I can't imagine the way I feel about you ever changing."

She looks away, staring at seemingly nothing. "I have three kids, Lee. It wouldn't just be me you're dating. And Curt will always be a part of my life. I can't regret being with him. He treated me like a princess, and he's an amazing father. If you really want to do this, you need to accept that."

"I can do that," I reply immediately. I don't want her to doubt me for even a second.

Her eyes return to mine. "Astrid is a handful. She and Dixie are besties, which still weirds me out sometimes, especially when Dixie tells people Astrid is her niece. Sailor is constantly blurting out inappropriate things at the very best times. And Ari? Well, she's a typical three-year-old. My life isn't even a little bit simple, and that's a lot for anyone to take on."

I smile. "I'm not just anyone, Tilly. You and I both know that. I've thought this out. I get that Curt is part of the deal—I'm okay with it. And the kids?" I grin. "I won't pretend I know what I'm doing with them, but I'm willing to learn. They're tiny pieces of you. How could I not love them?"

Before she can respond, a knock comes from the front door. "That'll be the pizza," I say, sliding out from under her legs.

I pay for the pizza and return to the couch. "You want a plate or should we just eat it out of the box?"

"The box is fine, but we might need napkins," she says, starting to swing her legs off to the side.

Dropping the box on the far end of the couch, I grab her legs. "Tell me where they are—I'll get them."

She licks her lips. "There should be a roll of paper towels on the bench beside the microwave."

"I'm on it," I say with a wink.

Curt may have treated her like a princess, but I'm going to treat her like a damn queen.

My queen.

Chapter Five

Tilly

"It was perfect," I tell my girls on our three-way video chat. "Except for my buster at the start of the night, but I completely forgot about the pain in my knees after a while. We talked for hours. It's like we were never apart."

Reagan's eyes shine with delight. "I'm so happy for you, Till. I've been doing some research. Seventy-two percent of lost-love relationships that were rekindled after five or more years apart end up staying together for the long haul."

"You and your damn statistics. Love is not an equation, Reags," Charlotte points out.

Reagan shrugs. "It's my thing. I thought it was interesting and would be reassuring."

"Thanks," I say. "Those aren't bad odds."

"Odds schmodds," Charlotte interjects. "Now get to the good stuff. Did he kiss you?"

I sigh. "No. I wanted him to—so badly. Unfortunately,

he was a perfect gentleman. He kissed my temple earlier in the night when he was looking after me, and again when he left. But that's it."

Both my girls frown.

"Maybe he didn't know you wanted it? I'm terrible with reading subtle signals—that's why Rhett's perfect for me. Ain't nothing subtle about my man." Reagan beams.

I chuckle. "There's nothing subtle about you either, babe. You two are the biggest pair of horndogs I've ever seen."

"And proud of it," she chirps. "Damn straight," comes from the background before Rhett pokes his head into the video window and shoots a wink our way then plats a wet one on Reagan.

"Eww, get a room," I tease.

Charlotte rolls her eyes when the kiss goes on a little too long to be appropriate for an audience. "Are you two into exhibitionism now?"

Reagan giggles, and Rhett takes the phone from her. "Not particularly. So, on that note, I'm taking my girl to bed. Later, ladies!"

Charlotte and I stare at each other and burst out laughing at the same time. She shakes her head, a fond smile on her lips. "If I didn't have an amazing man of my own, I'd be seriously jealous right now."

"Lucky bitches," I mumble. "I haven't had sex in, like, two years."

Char's eyes widen with horror. "Say that again."

I shrug. "Curt and I split almost two years ago. We

hadn't had sex for a couple of months before that, so, yeah."

Her jaw drops. "Oh, honey, I—I don't know what to say. You poor thing. I had no idea it had been *that* long."

"It's okay. Truth be told, I was too terrified of falling pregnant again for it to bother me," I explain. "Obviously Astrid was a surprise. We planned for Sailor because we didn't want Astrid to be an only child, but then bam, three months later I was pregnant with Ari."

A look of longing flits over Charlotte's expression so briefly I barely catch it. "I'm sorry, babe. I didn't mean to—"

She shakes her head. "Don't you dare. You don't need to censor yourself around me just because I'm having difficulties in that department. I've always known it wouldn't be easy for me because of the demon that resides in my nether regions."

"All the same, I should be more sensitive about it," I argue.

"Don't be ridiculous. Now, back to the good stuff. When are you seeing your stepbrother dearest again?"

I shudder. "Could you not call him that? It weirds me out."

A devious smirk tips her lips. "No, and speaking of, you should really read that book. It's brilliant."

"Dude, no."

Her laughter fills my ears, and I shake my head. *Why are my friends such randy tarts?*

A knock sounds at the front door, and Ari calls out,

"Morning, Mummy!" as the door opens and she waltzes in, Curt's mother behind her.

"I've gotta go. My mother-in-law just brought Ari home. Talk later," I say then end the call and turn my attention to my little lady. "Hey, baby. How was your weekend?"

Ari climbs into my lap at the dining table and snuggles in for a big squishy hug like she always does after a weekend away. "Dood. Granma made cake!"

My mother-in-law, Gia, goes about making herself a coffee while I cuddle my baby girl. I'm lucky to have Curt's parents in my life. They're so good with the kids and to me.

"And who ate all the cake before everyone woke up yesterday morning?" Gia utters to Ari.

Ari's cheeks go pink, and she tries desperately to hide her cheeky little smile. "I did," she whispers.

My eyes widen. "You ate a whole cake?"

She nods then shrugs her tiny shoulders. "It was yummy."

I shake my head at her. She grins back at me then gives me a big kiss on the cheek and another snuggle.

"How about you go play with your dollies, Ari, while Mummy and Granma have our coffee?" Gia suggests.

"Okee!" Ari replies then scrambles off my lap.

Uh-oh. I turn my gaze to a smiling Gia. "What's up?"

"I had an interesting phone call from Mrs. Wintergreen that lives two doors up this morning. Her grandson, William, is the pizza delivery boy at Mario's." She pauses, raises an eyebrow at me, then grins.

Oh boy ...

"Apparently, he delivered a pizza here last night, and a strapping young man answered the door and paid for said pizza."

I say nothing, but I'm pretty sure my reddening cheeks are speaking for me. This is the price of living in a small town. Everyone knows everyone's business.

Gia smiles brightly, takes a sip of her coffee, and waits me out.

My teeth sink into my bottom lip as I ponder an appropriate response for my ex's mother. "So yeah," I start. "Umm, Lee is in town for a little while, and we were catching up."

"I know." Gia's eyes sparkle. "I saw him down Main Street through the week. I swear, I nearly crashed my car. That boy has grown into a fine specimen."

I spray coffee over the table. "Gia!" I snap at the same time as I get up to retrieve the dishcloth to clean the mess I've made.

She shrugs. "What? I have eyes, Tilly. Just because I could be his mother doesn't mean I can't appreciate the view."

My nose wrinkles. This conversation is not going how I expected it to.

"So, what was he doing here? Did you two *catch up*, if you get my meaning ... " She winks.

Oh God, I'm going to pass out. My ex's mother is asking if I had sex with my high-school boyfriend. *What is happening right now?*

She widens her eyes at me. "Well, out with it. I'm not getting any younger."

I shake my head. "No, we did not *catch up* like that. We haven't spoken in a really long time. We were catching up in the literal sense of the term."

Her shoulders slump. "Tilly, darling, you've been on your own for a long while. I wouldn't begrudge you for moving on. And besides, everyone knows you and that boy were made for each other. I would have liked for things to have worked out between you and my Curt, but they didn't. You've given me three beautiful grandbabies who I treasure with all my heart. But you need to start living for yourself a little too, sweetheart."

My eyes prickle, and I have to hold my breath to stop myself from crying. Her saying that means a lot to me. I didn't even know just how much until this very moment. "Thank you, Gia," I whisper, still trying to control my emotions.

"Phil and I just want you to be happy, honey. As does Curt," she assures me.

I nod. "Okay," I breathe.

She waves me off and moves right along with the conversation. "Now, when are you seeing Lee again?"

I grin and shake my head. "I don't know. Maybe through the week."

"Well, if you need a sitter, you just let me know."

Later that afternoon, Ari and I are waiting outside Sailor's kindy to pick him up when my phone chimes with a text from an unknown number.

~Hey, Till. It's me, Lee. Forgot to get your number the

other night, so got it off Dad. Hope that's okay.~

My smile is so wide it hurts my cheeks as I type out my reply.

ME ~Of course.~

I slide my phone back into my pocket, and Sailor runs out the door with his Doctor Strange backpack hanging off his tiny body. I crouch and catch him in my arms. "Hey, big boy. How was your day?"

He beams at me. "Great! I told the class that birds, sloths, and octopuses don't fart."

I snort. "I bet they liked that," I say as I scruff up his perfectly combed hair.

"Mummm," he whines, and I drop a kiss on his head.

A few minutes later, we pull up at the school where Astrid and Dixie are waiting at the gate with their teacher. They run out to the van when they see it and jump in with a joined, "Hey!"

"Hey, girls," I call as I wait for them to do their seat belts then pull out. "How was your day?"

"Good," they chime.

"I picked a booger as big as my thumbnail today!" Dixie announces.

I cringe. "Please tell me you didn't eat it, Dix."

Her toothy smile reflects in my rearview mirror, and she nods. "Yep, and it was slimy."

Bile rises in my throat, and Sailor is right there with me.

"That's disgusting. Do you know how many germs are up your nose?" he says, his little face scrunched in distaste.

Chapter Six

Tilly

There's a black Lexus parked in my usual spot out the front of Mum and Al's. "Who's here, Mummy?" Astrid asks.

I shrug. "Don't know, baby. Let's go in and see."

The kids and I pile out of the car. Dixie throws the door open before I get to the front porch and runs inside screeching, "Lee!"

Well, that explains the fancy-arse car out front. I trail behind the kids, and my heart melts at the sight of Lee swinging Dixie up in his arms. She smooshes her face in his neck and squeezes him tight. He squeezes right back.

"Hey, princess, how was school?" he asks when he places her carefully on her feet.

"Good. Me and Astrid are in the same class. Do you know Astrid?" Dixie asks, pointing at my daughter who is now hiding behind me.

Lee smiles at me then shifts his focus to the little

blonde head poking around my side. He crouches and extends a hand to her. "Hi, Astrid. I'm Lee."

She eyes him for a few moments, and I curl my hand around her shoulder. "It's okay, baby girl. Lee's a friend."

Astrid rolls her big blue eyes at me. "I'm not a baby," she huffs then stomps over to Lee, accepts his offered hand, and gives it a solid shake. "Hello, Mr. Lee."

He grins at her. "Just Lee is fine."

She shrugs. "Okay, Just Lee. I'm Astrid, and I'm a big girl. I'm six. Ari is a baby—she's only three."

"I see. Definitely not a baby then," he agrees.

Astrid turns to face me, a satisfied smile on her face. "See, Mummy? Just Lee knows."

I chuckle. So much sass. "My bad, honey."

She nods then turns back to Lee. "So, who are you, Just Lee? Why are you at my nanny's?"

Oh goodness. How to explain this in a non-confusing way to a six-year-old ...

Before either Lee or I can answer, Dixie does. "Lee is my big brother."

Astrid's little eyes bug out while Sailor frowns.

I add, "Lee is Poppa Al's son from before he married Nanny."

"So Lee is your brother?" Astrid asks me.

"Kinda," I hedge. I don't want to say yes since it seems like Lee is going to be around the kids a bit more from now on and they're already going to be confused by all of this. "He's not really my brother. But he is Dixie's big brother just like I'm her big sister."

"But Poppa Al married Nanny, so now Lee is your

brother too. That's what Jenny's mum told her when she married Josh's daddy. They are brother and sister now," Dixie adds helpfully.

Well, shit. I glance at Lee, then my mum enters the room holding a tray of cut fruit and veggies for the kids to snack on. This successfully distracts most of them from the conversation. But not Sailor. He saunters over, a carrot stick in hand and a confused little frown on his face.

"What's up, buddy?" I ask.

He takes a chomp from the carrot and chews slowly. All the while, his inquisitive eyes bounce from Lee to me then back again. When he's finished chewing, he narrows his gaze on Lee and says, "You didn't tell me you're my uncle at the grocery store."

Lee shoves his hands in his pockets and rocks back on his heels. "That's because I'm not, not really."

Sailor raises an eyebrow, and it's the cutest damn thing in the world—my wee man grilling Lee. "But you're Aunty Dixie's brother, so that makes you my uncle."

Sailor's not the average four-year-old. He's excessively smart—scary smart, if I'm being honest. He can already read and does so frequently, devouring information like it's candy.

Lee swallows, spins his baseball cap backwards, then crouches to Sailor's level, who in turn takes another bite from his carrot stick.

"You see, me and your mum? We've been friends for a really long time. We were already grown up when my dad and her mum got married and made Dixie. So, we're just friends. Good friends—no, best friends," Lee tries to explain.

Sailor mulls this over then nods slowly. "Okay," he says then turns his back on us before returning to the snack tray.

Lee's eyes meet mine as he stands to his full height. "I thought you said Astrid was the full-on one?" he asks with a quirked brow.

"She is, but Sailor is crazy smart. He's full-on in a whole different way to Astrid. She's a girly-girl down to the core and high-maintenance to boot."

He nods. "I see."

I snort softly. He has no idea. "A high-maintenance princess on her own wouldn't be so hard, but add in a borderline genius and a toddler? Absolute mayhem."

His brows crease as his eyes move back to the kids bickering over who gets the last apple slice. "Hmmm," he murmurs. "I'm sure I can handle them." He nods to himself as he says this. When he returns his gaze to me, he smiles. "What are you doing tomorrow night?"

"The usual: early dinner, bath time, bedtime, then collapsing on the couch with a glass of wine until the kids are actually asleep. Then, I finally get to take a shower and crawl in my own bed."

"Want some help with all that?" he asks.

I blink at him. "What?"

A serious air takes over, and his eyes bore into mine. "When I lost you, Till, I lost my best friend, my soulmate, my smile, my laugh—my everything. I'm not backing down or walking away this time, babe. So, tomorrow, I'm going to come over, give you a hand, and get to know the kids while spending some time with you."

My heart pounds. I draw my bottom lip between my teeth as tears prick the back of my eyes, and I nod. "I'd like that."

Lee's smile is everything. The dimples I've always loved pop in his cheeks, and his eyes shine with promise. I can't help but match his level of enthusiasm, even though I know he's in for an evening of hell.

LEE

SHE SAID YES. I WANT TO FIST PUMP THE AIR, BUT THAT would be corny as shit, and I'm a fucking grown-up.

I wasn't sure if it would be too much, too fast, asking to spend time with the kids so soon. But she needs to know how serious I am about this.

There is nothing I want more than her. And the kids are part of her. All three of them resemble her in different ways, and I love it. They also resemble their dad, and ain't that a hard pill to swallow.

I never liked Curt. He always had a thing for Tilly back in the day. The second she and I broke up, he was there. Arsehole.

A gentle touch yanks me from my thoughts. "You okay? You're clenching your jaw," Tilly says softly.

She must have moved closer while I was stuck in my

head, because she's pressed into my side now, her full breasts pressed snugly against my bicep. I shake my head. "I'm fine, babe. Just thinking."

Her eyes search mine, and I have to physically hold myself in check or I'll kiss her right here in front of all the kids. And I do not want an audience the first time I kiss my girl in more than six years.

She licks her lips, and goddamn it, blood rushes south, and I have to take a step away from her. I twist my cap back around, shading her view of my lust-fuelled gaze. Now is not the time. Besides, I'm pretty sure once I cross that line, I'm not going to want to stop for a long-arse time.

I'm trying to get a hold on my burgeoning hard-on when a little body wraps around my legs. A set of pale-blue eyes framed by white-blonde curls peer up at me. And just like that, the boner situation is a non-issue. I smile at Ari and run a hand through her soft hair. "Hey, pretty girl."

"Hey," she chirps. "Up!"

I bend, hook her under the arms, and lift her into mine. "And what did you do today, little miss?"

Ari giggles, and it wraps around me like a fist clenching around my heart. I want to be the one responsible for her making that adorable sound every damn day.

"I played dollies and trucks and pincesses," she exclaims excitedly.

"That sounds fun. Did Mummy play too?"

Her little face scrunches up. "No. Mummy worked."

This is news to me. I thought Tilly was a stay-at-home mum. My eyes move to her, and she shrugs. “I blog for my friend Charlotte. You met her the other day at McKenna’s.”

“You blog? About what?”

Her cheeks pink beautifully, and she glances away as she answers me. “Fashion, from a mum’s perspective. I have a couple of columns I do each week. Mumming Mondays, and Tips from Tilly, and Thrifty Thursdays.”

“That’s great, Till.”

She finally brings her eyes back to mine. “Yeah?”

I nod. “Hell yeah, babe. You’ve always had your own style. Except when you’re stealing other people’s T-shirts,” I tease then wink.

She blushes again. “I swear that’s my shirt.”

“Sure it is.” I chuckle.

Chapter Seven

Tilly

By the time four-thirty rolls around the following day, I'm full of nerves. Lee will be here any minute to do the evening routine with me. I don't want to scare him off, and Astrid can be extraordinarily painful some days. I'm praying today is not one of those.

Maybe I should have suggested a different activity for him to get to know the kids. This time of day is definitely their worst. *Crappity—crap—crap.*

Astrid struts out of her room in a floor-length princess gown and a tiara, holding a sparkly clutch and teetering in matching dress-up heels. She examines the pasta I've prepared for their dinner and turns her nose up. "I'm not eating that," she decrees.

And here we go. "Yes, sweetheart, you are. You like pesto pasta. All princesses do."

She sniffs at it and cringes. "Not this princess. I'll have a cheese toasty tonight."

I scoff. "Uh, nope. You'll have this yummy pesto pasta I made just for you and your brother and sister."

Astrid narrows her eyes on me. "No, I won't."

"Yes, you will."

A nasty little smirk twists her face. "No, I won't. And you can't make me."

I take a deep, calming breath. Her stubbornness will serve her well later in life. But right now, it's pissing me the hell off. Placing my hands on my hips, I glare right back at her. "Astrid Brielle Collins, you will eat this pasta if I have to force-feed it to you."

She scowls and mirrors my stance.

I'm saved from her rebuttal by a knock at the door. I walk away, leaving her stewing in the kitchen while I open the front door to a too-good-looking-for-this-time-of-day Lee. My face crumples when he extends a bunch of sunflowers towards me.

"Hey, what's wrong?" he asks, stepping in and wrapping his arms around me.

I don't even lift my arms to hug him back. I'm tired and frustrated, and he's being so sweet and lovely. I suck in a deep breath and close my eyes, just enjoying the feel of his warm, solid body against mine.

He takes a small step back, keeping one arm curled around my waist. "What's up?"

"Astrid is in fine form. You should probably go; you don't want to deal with this."

"I'm not leaving, Till. I'm here for the good, the bad, and the ugly." He winks and grins.

I shake my head and warn him, "You have no idea just how ugly it's going to get."

"I can take it. Bring it on, baby." He presses a kiss to my temple, and I relax into his side.

"Lee!" Sailor calls as he runs into the lounge room, a book in his hands and his miniature piglet, Pickles, hot on his heels.

Lee releases me and approaches Sailor. "Hey, buddy. Can you help me find something to put these flowers in?" Then he sees Pickles; his eyes widen. "Is that a pig?"

Sailor chuckles, drops his book on the coffee table, and scoops his piggy up in his arms. "Yep, this is Mr. Pickles, or Pickles for short. He's super smart, just like me," he tells Lee then offers Pickles to him. "You take Mr. Pickles, and I'll show you where to put the flowers."

Lee glances at me, and I give him a subtle nod before he takes the offered piglet. He cradles him in one hand, positioning him under his arm like a football. Sailor wraps his fingers between Lee's pinkie and the bunch of flowers Lee is still holding. My little man leads Lee into the kitchen.

I follow, my heart melting a little at the sight. Astrid is still standing by the dining table, hands on her hips, waiting for my return, no doubt, so we can continue our argument. When her gaze takes in Lee, her eyes narrow further. "What's Just Lee doing here?" she demands of me.

"Lee has come for dinner, Astrid. Now, would you please get Ari and tell her dinner is ready?" I ask, hoping like hell she'll do this one thing without fighting me.

She doesn't answer me, just turns on her little heels

and clip-clops down the hall to retrieve her sister. *Thank God.*

I set bowls out and dish up their pasta while Sailor and Lee sort out the vase for my beautiful flowers. A warm hand presses into my lower back, and I turn to find Lee at my side. "Where do you want me?"

"Ari might need a little help. Sailor can handle himself, and I'll handle the madam."

Lee nods. "Good game plan."

Sailor climbs into his seat then taps the table beside him, looking at Lee expectantly. "You can sit here, between me and Ari."

"Thanks, bud," Lee says. "Where should I put Mr. Pickles?"

"Just pop him on the floor," I tell him. "Sailor, you need to give him his dinner before you have yours, then go wash your hands."

A bashful little blush coats his cheeks. "Oops. Sorry, Mummy. I forgot."

I drop a kiss on top of his head as he passes me to retrieve Pickles' food. My skin prickles with awareness, and I turn to find Lee's eyes on me. He's at the sink, washing his own hands.

"What?" I ask.

He grins and shakes his head. "A piglet? You couldn't just get a dog, could you?"

"Sailor's allergic to dogs. Mr. Pickles is very clean, just as smart as any dog, if not smarter, and he's already potty trained." I shrug. "Besides, Sailor isn't a normal little boy. A dog wouldn't suit him."

Rounding the kitchen bench, Lee steps into me, rests his lips against my temple, and says, "God, I've missed you." Then, he strides away and takes his seat at the table. Butterflies swarm in my stomach, and my heart squeezes as emotion sweeps over me. I dip my head to hide the crazy-big smile brought on by his small gesture.

Astrid stomps back in, Ari skipping behind her. I scoop Ari up and plop her in her booster seat next to Lee. She beams at him, and he winks back.

When I turn to Astrid, she's got her hands braced on her hips again. *Dear God.* I heave a sigh. "Astrid, please sit down and eat your dinner."

"I want a cheese toasty."

"And I want an all-expenses-paid trip around the world, but we don't always get what we want, Astrid. Now sit your little toosh in that seat and eat." I drag her chair out from the table for her and gesture to it with one hand.

She rolls her eyes at me like I'm the one being a pain in the arse right now. "Fine," she huffs and slides into her seat, picks up her fork, and starts eating.

Lee stifles a chuckle, and I turn my flustered gaze on him, throw my hands in the air, and stalk to the fridge. I need my wine a little earlier tonight. I pour myself a glass then lift the bottle to him. "You want some?"

He shakes his head. "Maybe later."

The rest of mealtime goes smoothly, and I'm beyond relieved. One task down, two to go.

When the kids are all finished, I announce, "Bath time! Who's first?"

"Me!" Sailor shouts, taking his empty bowl to the sink and rinsing it. "The girls take forever," he mutters.

I pick up the other dirty dishes, but Lee takes them from me. "I'll do the kitchen; you do the bath thing."

"Okay," I breathe then follow Sailor down the hall to the bathroom. He's stripped off, leaning against the wall with his ankles crossed, waiting for me.

I get the water temperature right and put the plug in the bottom of the tub. "Lavender or Apple Fresh body wash tonight?" I ask him.

He purses his lips and taps his chin as he considers his options. "Lavender, please. I think Astrid needs it," he says, his eyes widening theatrically. "You know, 'cause lavender is relaxing."

I burst out laughing and scruff up his perfect hair. "Good choice, buddy." I pour a generous amount of wash into the water then put a little extra on a cloth.

Sailor climbs in and takes the cloth from me. I sit on the closed toilet lid and settle in for our nightly bathtub chat.

"Judy Turner is in love with me," he announces.

"I thought she was in love with Jackson?"

He rolls his eyes. "She was last week, but she loves me now. Why do all the girls have to love me? They annoy me when I'm trying to read and want to sit with me at lunch and talk, talk, talk. I just want some quiet time, Mum."

I have to curl my lips in and bite down on them to stop my laughter. *This kid*. I shake my head and give it to him straight. "Well, baby, you're a catch. You better get used to it now. It's only going to get worse."

His eyes widen in dismay. "What? Why?"

"Because you're awesome." I shrug.

Sailor's shoulders slump in defeat. "Fine. But I don't like it."

"I know, sweet pea. I know. Now, let's wash this hair so it's nice and fresh in the morning, yeah?"

"Okay," he agrees then reaches for the cup I use to wet his hair down.

When Sailor is done, he climbs out of the tub, dries himself off, then drops his towel and takes off running. I chuckle at his cute little butt disappearing around the corner on his nightly nudie run.

As soon as Pickles hears the familiar sound of Sailor's run, he comes skidding out of his room to do a lap of the house with my wee man.

"Whoa there, big guy!" Lee yells from the lounge room, and I laugh harder.

Sailor squeals and runs back down the hall, poking his head in to me. "I forgot Lee was here." He giggles. "He saw my penis!" His little hand flies to cover his mouth as he continues giggling.

"Oh no!" I mock gasp, placing my palm over my heart.

Pickles' little trotters can't bring him to a halt as fast as Sailor, so he goes sliding past the bathroom, his legs splaying from under him. He rights himself and scuttles over to sit at Sailor's feet, his curly tail wiggling.

Sailor's eyes shine bright blue as he cups his little hand around his mouth and whispers, but not quietly, "I bet mine's bigger than Lee's."

"Hey, I heard that!" Lee speaks from outside the

bathroom then pokes his head around the door frame above Sailor's head and mouths, "And you know that's not true," to me.

I throw my head back and laugh. Sailor grins at Lee, turns around, and shakes his bare butt at him, then takes off for his room.

"Eww, put some clothes on, Sailor!" Astrid complains on her way in to me.

Ari is wrapped around Lee's leg like a baby koala, looking up at him with love in her eyes.

Maybe tonight isn't a complete write-off. He hasn't run out screaming ... yet.

LEE

I'M GOING TO GO AHEAD AND CALL TONIGHT A SUCCESS. THE kids are all in their beds, and I'm sitting on the couch, nursing a beer with Till as she sips the same glass of wine from earlier. "That wasn't so bad," I remark.

She twists her head to me and smiles softly. "It could have gone better. But it's not over yet. Give it a few minutes, and it will all start again."

My brows draw in. "What do you mean? They're in bed. We're sitting pretty, right?"

"Pffft, not even close. We've got at least another half hour yet."

"Of what?" No sooner has the question left my lips

than Astrid appears at the end of the hallway, glaring at us.

"I'm thirsty," she states.

"That's nice, sweetheart. You know how to get yourself a drink of water," Till retorts.

Astrid shakes her head. "I want juice."

Till sighs. "And just like every other night, my love, juice is not an option."

My eyes volley between the two strong-willed women staring each other down until Astrid stomps her foot, turns around, and goes back to her bedroom. Interesting. She's so combative with Tilly, but she caves pretty quickly.

I throw my arm over the back of the couch and tug Tilly into my side. She relaxes against the cushions and snuggles into me, then sips her wine again. I could get used to this. My fingertips trail up and down her bare arm, just enjoying the feel of her in my space again after so long apart.

She tips her head back to rest on my shoulder, and I stare into her big brown eyes. They suck me in just like they always have. I drop my forehead to rest against hers, bringing our mouths so close together we're breathing the same air.

"I've missed you," I murmur.

Her mouth curves in a small, sad smile. "I've missed you too."

I drop my empty beer bottle on the couch beside me then curve my hand around her jaw before trailing my fingers around the side of her neck. She closes her eyes at the contact and leans into my touch. "Till," I whisper. "I need to kiss you, baby. It's been too long since I've felt your lips on mine."

"Okay," she murmurs and arches her neck, bringing her mouth closer.

My breathing becomes ragged, my pulse thunders in my ears, and I finally, fucking finally, brush my lips against hers.

Chapter Eight

Tilly

My senses are overwhelmed by the feel of him—his fingers entwined in my hair, his hard body pressed into me, and thank God above, his lips caressing mine.

I'm home.

His arm at my side tugs me impossibly closer, and his lips never leave mine. He tastes me, nibbling my bottom lip before his tongue snakes over it. I gasp at the sensation, and he takes the opportunity to delve inside. Slow, deliberate strokes make my brain short-circuit.

I grab his bicep, holding on for dear life. This kiss is everything; he is everything.

"I'll never get enough of your lips," he groans against my mouth, causing a jolt of electricity to shoot through my entire body.

"Yes," I whisper, my hand clutching his bicep and sliding up his arm, over his shoulder, and into his hair.

"Eww!" Sailor cries.

We fly apart, landing at opposite ends of the couch.

Lee's eyes lock on my son, and to my complete and utter shock, he laughs.

Sailor looks between us—my face is beet red, I just know it—then he approaches. He climbs up onto the couch, positioning himself in the middle. He laces his fingers in his lap, glances at Lee, then at me. "Want to tell me something?" he queries, arching a little brow.

I lick my lips and run my hands through my hair, pushing it away from my face, then clear my throat. "I suppose I do," I tell him. "Lee and I, we're very good friends. And sometimes very good friends, well, they umm—"

Sailor cuts me off with a raised hand. "Mummy, I know all about adults having the sex to make babies. But why are you having the sex with Lee? If you make a baby with him, it will be my cousin and my brother."

Horror. That is what I'm feeling in this very moment—pure unadulterated horror. "What? What do you mean you know all about sex?" I demand, only able to deal with one part of what he said at a time.

He rolls his eyes. "I read about it."

"What the hell kind of books have you been reading, Sailor? You haven't been taking books from Charlotte, have you?" God, I hope not. What the shit am I going to do if he's been reading her kinky books? My poor innocent baby's eyes have been tainted.

"No, her books have nakey men on the front." He giggles, pressing a hand to his forehead.

I close my eyes, inhale a deep breath through my nose,

hold it for a few seconds, then release. Sailor may be genius-level smart, but he's still a little boy who finds nudity hilarious.

When I open my eyes again, Sailor and Lee are exchanging looks. I rest my hand on Sailor's leg, getting his attention. "First of all, honey, you shouldn't be going through Charlotte's books; that's rude. Second, Lee and I were absolutely not having sex."

Sailor scrunches his little brows in a cute-as-hell frown. "It looked like you were."

"That was just a kiss, sweet pea."

"But kisses like *that* turn into the sex," he explains.

Oh, Lordy. I am not ready for this conversation—he's four!

I glance at Lee helplessly. He's trying and failing to hold his amusement at bay. His eyes are shining with mirth, and he seems to fight a smile. I narrow my eyes at him, and he clears his throat then scrubs a hand over his face. "You're right, buddy," Lee says.

What the shit? I bug my eyes out at him, but he ignores me.

"I know," Sailor replies, completely oblivious to my distress.

"But that's not what we were going to do. I just really, really wanted to kiss your mum. It's been a real long time since I've kissed her, and I missed it. I swear, bud, me and your mum? We're not going to have *the sex* on the couch." He looks so pleased with himself for delivering this explanation to my way-too-smart-for-his-own-good son.

Sailor scratches his temple, appearing to be mulling over Lee's words. He purses his lips then narrows his eyes.

"But you were going to have the sex. Just not on the couch."

"No!" I blurt. "No sex. None. Not even a little bit. Like you said, sex makes babies, and Mummy has enough babies. No more babies happening here, ever. Mummy is closed for business, Sailor. You understand?"

"So, I'm not going to have a cousin-brother?" he asks.

"No, sweet pea. No cousin-brothers for you," I assure him.

That seems to be enough for my boy. He nods, climbs up on his knees, and shuffles over to me before dropping a kiss on my cheek. Then, he trundles over to Lee and looks him dead in the eye. "I like kissing Mummy too. But not in the sexing way—just the *I love my mummy* way." Then, he wraps his arms around Lee's neck and gives him a quick squeeze before he gets off the couch and returns to his bedroom.

My shoulders slump. What a night.

Lee scoots back up to my end of the couch and wraps me in his arms again. "I'm still calling tonight a success," he murmurs in my ear, sending a shiver down my spine.

I place a hand on his chest, pushing him away just enough to be able to look him in the face. He's smiling, and I slowly mirror it. "Seriously? Tonight was"—I shake my head—"not great."

Again, he drops his forehead to mine, stares into my eyes, and lets me see everything he's feeling. "It was perfect."

LEE

I WOULD LIKE TO STAY LONGER AND JUST HOLD TILLY, BUT she looks exhausted, so I do the gentlemanly thing. I bow out for the night. "I'm going to go so you can hit the hay. But I want to do this again—soon."

"Okay," she agrees.

She walks me to the door where I stop her. "You don't need to see me out, babe. I'm a big boy. Just like Sailor." I wink and she chuckles. "I'll call you tomorrow." I press a light kiss to her temple and stroll down the paved pathway to my car, admiring the garden beds that line the path as I go.

I turn back when I reach the car; she's standing in the doorway, watching me. I lift a hand, wave, then press two fingers to my lips and throw her the kiss. She smiles then closes the door.

Driving back to my mother's house, I make the decision I've been mulling over since I saw Till in the grocery store last week. I'm moving back. It's our time. I feel it in my bones—and not just the one in my pants.

I want forever with her. And I can't expect her to believe that until my place here is permanent.

As soon as I'm back in my childhood bedroom, I pull out my laptop and draft a letter, laying it out to my current employer. I'm an architect, and a damn good one. I can do my job from anywhere. The firm I contract to can employ me from afar, or I'll go out on my own. Either way is fine with me.

I email the letter then close down my laptop with a sense of rightness I haven't felt since Tilly and I were planning our future together six years ago.

She said she doesn't regret being with Curt, and I get that. She wouldn't have those amazing kids if not for him, even if he is an asshat. And if I'm being completely honest with myself, the time apart was probably good for us.

But now it's time to pick back up where we left off and build our future together.

Chapter Nine

Tilly

It's been more than a week since the first night Lee came to have dinner with us. He's come every night since, and it's been amazing. I had forgotten how much just having another adult in the house eases the pressure.

Each night has ended with one of his mind-blowing kisses. But nothing more. It's driving me a little crazy. I've never been this sexually frustrated. I went without sex for two years—it didn't faze me at all. Now, it's all I can think about. I swear he's doing it on purpose. Like right now ...

He stands at my kitchen sink in a pair of low-slung jeans, a fitted black tee, and a backwards baseball cap, peeling potatoes with Ari sitting on the bench, acting as his little assistant. She adores him, and the warmth that fills his gaze every time his eyes are on her shows me the feeling is mutual.

My ovaries practically dance at the sight before me. *Down, girls!*

"I can feel your eyes on me, babe," Lee says, glancing at me over his shoulder.

I shrug and sip my wine. "Guilty as charged. And I'm not ashamed."

He chuckles and turns back to his peeling as Ari hands him a new potato.

A dreamy sigh escapes me; I could get used to this.

Sailor saunters in, hands in his pockets and Pickles on his heels. "What's for dinner, Mummy?"

"I don't know, sweet pea. Chef Lee is making dinner tonight."

His little nose scrunches. "Lee's a chef?"

"Tonight, he is." I grin at Sailor's adorable frown.

"Can he even cook?"

Lee smiles at Sailor and winks. "How about you help me? That way you can make sure I'm doing it all right?"

"Okay!" Sailor agrees quickly. "Mummy, I need my apron. Lee's going to need my help."

I stifle my chuckle and get a little apron out of the drawer by my hip and slip it over Sailor's head.

"Hey, watch the hair," he chastises, lifting his hand to fix the bit I just messed up.

Lee steps in to distract him from his hair disaster. "I need a pot for the potatoes to go in. Can you organise that for me, bud?"

Sailor nods. "I'm on it."

Lee scoops Ari off the bench and onto his hip, turns to the fridge, and gets out the bottle of wine. "Right, time for you to go have some girl-time with Astrid. She's got a movie lined up and her nail polishes at the ready," Lee instructs me, refilling my wine.

"What?" I ask. "When did you have time to sort that out?"

He smirks. "I am a man of many talents," he says as he slides a hand around my lower back and leads me out of the kitchen. "Now, sit and enjoy being pampered."

"Yeah, Mummy, I'm going to pamper you. I'm going to paint your nails and do your hair all pretty and your makeup while we watch *Frozen*," Astrid says, excitedly clapping her hands and bouncing on her toes.

I glance at Lee with panic in my eyes. He doesn't know what he's just unleashed. A six-year-old with makeup is never a good thing. Lee presses his lips to my temple in a soft kiss then murmurs, "Just relax. She could make you look like Chucky and I'd still love you."

His words rock me to the core. He'd still love me? We haven't said those words to each other in years. I blink a bajillion times, trying to keep my tears at bay. "Okay," I whisper then shift my focus to my wine. "I'm going to need more wine to get through this ..."

"I got you covered, babe." Lee chuckles, presses one more delicate kiss to the top of my head, then returns to the kitchen.

An hour later, Sailor waltzes into the lounge as Astrid and I sing along to "Fixer Upper" at the top of our lungs, and screams. I turn to him, my eyes wide and searching for what's upset him when it becomes clear he's staring at me. His little face is pale, his brows are scrunched right up, and he's shaking his head.

"What's wrong?" I ask at the same time that Lee comes skidding around the corner, Ari on his hip.

Sailor turns angry eyes at Astrid then stomps over to the coffee table where she has splayed out all her makeup. He snatches it up, stuffs it all back in her little beauty case, then takes off running. We all follow, entering the kitchen just as he shoves it in the bin.

"Sailor," I say gently. "What are you doing, honey?"

He turns around, hands on hips, and declares, "Astrid turned you into a monster!"

Well, I knew I wouldn't be winning any beauty competitions, but I didn't think it would warrant a reaction like this.

"I did not!" Astrid yells back, running over to the bin.

Sailor steps in front of her. "No! You don't deserve makeups anymore."

Astrid shoves Sailor, and he teeters before launching at her. Their little bodies hit the floor, and they roll around, kicking and hitting each other.

My eyes widen. What in the hell has gotten into my children? Before I can intervene, Lee hands Ari to me and steps in, pulling them apart.

"Whoa there, big guy," Lee says, wrapping an arm around Sailor's middle as he attempts to throw himself at Astrid again when she gives him a smug little smirk. "Hitting girls is never okay. You hear me, Sailor? Never," he states firmly.

Sailor's eyes remain hard on Astrid. "She started it."

"I did not!" she screeches back and tries to shove him again.

Lee places a hand on her shoulder, keeping her at arm's length from Sailor. "Astrid, princess, just like it is never okay for a boy to hit a girl, it is also never okay for a girl to hit a boy. It's nasty and mean. Are you a nasty little girl or a princess?"

Her brows dip and her nose scrunches. "I'm a princess."

"I know, sweets, and princesses use their words to fight their battles, not their fists," Lee explains. "And they do it with grace and dignity. They don't yell or stomp their feet. They present their argument calmly, with nice words to win people over with kindness."

My eyes travel from Astrid to Lee and back again—he's getting through to her. I can't believe it. She's actually listening to him.

Finally, Astrid nods. "Okay, Just Lee. I'll fight with my words."

He smiles at her, gives her shoulder a little squeeze, then turns back to Sailor. "Alright, big guy, I think we need to have a chat. But dinner is ready, so how do you feel about helping me set the table while Mummy goes and washes her face? We'll eat, then you and me will go out the back and talk, man to man."

At the mention of sending me to wash my face, Sailor's shoulders relax. "Okay," he agrees. "You can get the plates 'cause I can't reach. I'll get the knives and forks."

"Solid plan, bud," Lee says before releasing him then standing to his full height and looking at me. "Babe, I know I said I'd still love you even if you looked like Chucky ... but at the time, I didn't realise how much of a possibility that would be." He stares at me for a minute. His pearly white teeth sink into his bottom lip, and he shakes his head.

I hand Ari back to him then make a beeline for the bathroom. And that's when Sailor's reaction makes perfect sense. If he hadn't thrown out Astrid's makeup, I would have.

Chapter Ten

Tilly

CURT HAS THE KIDS, AND IT'S LEE'S AND MY FIRST NIGHT alone since the heavenly kisses started. I'm hoping like crazy that tonight is the night we take things to the next level. So, I took Charlotte's advice and *shortened the shrubs* while in the shower.

I've dried off, and I'm standing completely naked in my bathroom, facing my reflection. My body has changed so much since Lee last saw it. I run my hand over the faint stretch marks that mar my boobs and stomach. Then, my eyes widen in horror.

What the ever-loving-crap-cakes is that?!

I poke at the offending cluster of hair positioned right above my slit.

Oh, Lord. Oh, shit. This cannot be happening ...

Trimming was a bad idea—a really bad idea. Damn Charlotte and her 'modern women lady-scape' speech.

If I didn't trim the hedges, I'd never have seen the

offensive little thatch of silver curls. But now it's all I can see. It's all Lee will see if we do cross that line.

After snatching my phone from the bathroom counter, I call Char. She answers on the third ring, and I launch my verbal assault before she has a chance to speak. "This is all your fault. You bullied me into 'tidying the landscape,' and now there's an eyesore smack in the middle of downtown Tillyville."

"What exactly are we talking about here?" my now former friend asks.

"We're talking about my silver-laced snatch thatch!" I screech.

Silence, then deafening laughter fills the line.

"Charlotte, this is serious! Lee will be here in less than an hour. What the hell am I supposed to do?" My heartbeat skyrockets as I imagine his reaction to seeing my lady-garden after six years and three children. Oh God. What was I thinking, getting into this with him again? I'm not the girl he fell in love with when we were teenagers. I'm a woman with a silver bush, for goodness' sake.

Charlotte clears her throat, her tone all business when she says, "Calm your tits, Till. This is the perfect opportunity to test out the Clitter capsules I got you."

I blink, then blink again. "I'm sorry, what?"

"I wrote an article about them on the blog a few weeks ago. Then, when Lee came back into your life, I thought it would be the perfect opportunity for you to test them out. I put some in the top drawer of your bedside table. You're welcome."

She's lost her damn mind. "You think adding glitter to this situation is going to help this? Are you insane?" Panic thrums in my veins. Calling her was a bad idea. I should never have taken her advice in the first place. She got me into this mess—I was foolish for thinking she could get me out of it.

"Are you listening to me?" she snaps.

"No," I snap back. "No, I'm not."

Char's dramatic sigh filters through the line.

I grit my teeth. "Don't you sigh at me! I'm the one going through a crisis."

"You're overreacting. He's not going to care if the carpets don't match the drapes, babe. All he's going to be worried about is getting in there. I promise."

I'm going to need another shower. I'm sweating like a two-dollar hooker at rush hour. "Charlotte," I whine. "What am I going to do?"

The sound of her strumming her nails against something in the background echoes through the line—a sign she's thinking. Then, she says, "I have an idea. It's a little crazy, but it'll do in a pinch. Do you have any permanent markers?"

At this point, I'm willing to try anything. So, I listen intently as she spells out her idea—it is crazy, but I'm that desperate. I do it.

Luckily, I spent half the day agonising over what to wear tonight, and I've already got my outfit laid out on my bedspread. I chose a cute beige-coloured mini cargo skirt with big gold buckles on the pockets and a matching gold silk cami that I tuck in.

Since we're eating in, I forgo shoes. The bruises on my knees have only just faded. I do not want a repeat of our first *date.*

I'm just putting the finishing touches on my hair, sliding a chunk in a clip to keep it away from my face, when Lee knocks twice at the front door then lets himself in. "I'll be out in a second," I call.

"No worries, babe," he calls back.

I spritz a little Woman, by Ralph Lauren, over my neck then skip out of my room.

Butterflies go crazy in my belly the moment my eyes land on him sitting in the middle of my couch, his sculpted arms on display spread across the back cushions. He's wearing his ball cap backwards as usual. His legs are extended out in front of him, ankles crossed. His feet, like mine, are bare. There's something extremely sexy about that.

His eyes roam over my body in a slow perusal, then his lips curve, and he summons me forward with a crooked finger.

He doesn't need to tell me twice. I close the space between us instantly. He spreads his legs, and I step into the area, fixing my gaze on his beautiful face. "Hey," I whisper.

"Hey," he murmurs back.

The butterflies in my belly swarm faster, and I place a hand over it to calm them. Lee sits forward, bringing his hands to my hips and tugging me down. My knees hit the couch on either side of his thighs, and his palms skirt around to cup my arse. His hands on me send chills through my entire body. My head falls forward when his fingers dig into my cheeks, kneading the flesh.

He takes full control, urging me to sit in his lap, which causes my already short skirt to bunch right under my butt cheeks and expose my thighs. His hands glide up and down my spine before they wrap around my shoulders from behind, holding me in place as his hips surge up.

"Oh, God," I moan. Lee's hard—like, super freaking hard. I grind down on the length with every one of his upward thrusts.

His head comes to rest between my breasts. "Till, babe, I need to be inside you. Please tell me you're ready."

"I'm ready," I answer, immediately pushing onto my knees to hike my skirt up higher.

"Fuck," he breathes, watching me.

When my skirt is out of the way, I tuck my fingers in his belt and tug it free, then move to the button and fly of his jeans. He digs in his pocket and holds a condom up between us, then rips it open with his teeth as I free his rigid cock.

He slides it on, rolling it down his shaft with a practiced ease he never used to possess. I don't even have time to think on that fact as he tugs my black lace panties aside and positions himself at my entrance. All I can focus on is him, us, finally coming together again.

I lower onto him slowly, allowing my body to get used to his size, inch by glorious inch. My hands curl around his shoulders, steadying myself. Lee's gifted in the cock department, and I relish the slight burn as my muscles stretch to allow him inside.

Once I'm fully seated, I pause, staring into the eyes of my soulmate. I lift a trembling hand to trace my fingertips over his perfect lips. My breath hitches when he sucks a finger into his mouth. Our eyes never stray from one another.

His big hand wraps around my wrist and removes my fingers from his face, relocating them to the back of his neck. Then, he moves closer, brushing his lips against mine as he speaks. "I'm moving back. I never want to spend a day without you again, Tilly. You're my world, my light, my life. Being with you, inside you, is where I was always meant to be."

I blink back tears and nod emphatically. "I want that so much." I sniff.

"You've got it, babe. I'm not going anywhere. We were never over. It just wasn't our time. But it is now, and I'm not wasting another second of it," he states then pushes to his feet, still inside me, and strides along the hall to my bedroom.

LEE

Keeping my arms wrapped tight around Till, I lower us to the bed, never breaking our connection. "I'm going to fuck you now, babe, but I swear I'll take it slow next time," I warn her.

Her eyes shine with lust, and she nods. "Please and thank you," she mumbles, wriggling her hips beneath me.

I smirk and drop my mouth to hers, taking her lips and tongue in a deep, forceful kiss, then draw my hips back, leaving her with only my tip before slamming back in. She moans into my mouth, and I lose it, pounding into her with everything I have. Over and over, my cock slides in and out in a punishing rhythm.

She throws her head back and groans. "I'm close. Lee, so close. Don't. Stop."

"Never," I swear, and I mean it.

Her legs wrap around my lower back, digging her heels into my arse. Fuck, it feels good. I grind my hips against her clit then pull all the way out, making her whimper, then surge forward again. My hand slides into her hair, locking into a fist as I pound harder, faster, deeper until she cries out in ecstasy, and I follow right after.

Chapter Eleven

Tilly

We lie there, panting, on my bed, still almost fully clothed. And that's when I lose it, a giggle erupting from deep in my belly.

Lee rolls to my side, coming to rest on an elbow. "What's so funny?"

I draw in a deep breath, attempting to calm myself, but it doesn't work. I wave a hand, fanning my face. "I was—so worried about—you seeing me—naked." I take another breath, this one doing the trick and slowing my laughter. I start over. "I was so worried about you seeing me naked, but it was all for nothing." I gesture down my body, still mostly covered by my clothes.

He frowns, sits up, and tugs his cap off his head before tossing it across the room. Then, he reaches behind, hooks his fingers in the collar of his shirt and yanks it off too—it follows the cap. He glances around the room, sees whatever he's looking for, then removes the spent condom, ties it in a knot, and drops it in the small bin beside my bed.

My gaze stays locked on him as he flattens to his back, lifts his hips, dips his thumbs in the waistband of his jeans, turns his head to look me in the eye, then shoves them down his hips and kicks them off.

I swallow. Holy fudge-nuggets. Lee is D.E.F.I.N.E.D. Defined. Those abs are definitely new. And I like them —a lot.

"Your turn," he says.

My eyes widen. *Umm, what?* "Lee, I—"

He shakes his head, props back up on his elbow, and rolls into my side. "Babe, I love you. I love your kids. And I'm going to love whatever you're worried I'll find under your clothes too."

Goddamn. Why does he have to be so sweet? I bite my bottom lip, but he tugs it free.

"Do you want me to help you?" he asks, brushing a soft, sensuous kiss against my throat. I shiver.

"Okay," I breathe. "But, Lee, I have stretch marks, and I'm just, I'm—"

He silences me with a kiss, sliding his tongue into my mouth as he rolls to his back, taking me with him. He continues kissing me as his hands trail along my sides. He tugs lightly at my cami, drawing it up my body. When it reaches my shoulders, he pauses. "Lift your arms."

I do as he says, lifting one arm at a time while he tugs my top free, then over my head, and it joins his clothes on the floor. He doesn't even look before he's kissing me again. His fingers tangle in my hair, and I sigh contentedly.

After a few minutes, his touch skates down my neck, tracing my spine until he encounters my skirt. His nimble fingers make short work of the zipper then help the fabric over my hips where I wiggle to assist in its removal. I kick it off when it reaches my knees.

Lee never once stops kissing me during all this. My mind is so hazy with lust I don't even care that I'm virtually naked right now. His hands and mouth have me in a trance. I'm so blissed out on an amazing orgasm and his touch, I could live in this moment forever.

He rolls us again, settling himself between my thighs as his lips move from mine to my jaw then along my throat. I shudder beneath his warm, hard body, curling my hands in his hair when he reaches my breasts, sucking and nibbling them through my strapless lace bra.

I arch my back for him, his hand swiftly taking the invitation to unclasp it and toss it away. Then, his hot, wet mouth sucks my nipple between his lips, and I moan, my fingers locking tight in his hair. "Oh, God, yes," I whimper.

But then, he's moving lower, his tongue traveling between my breasts to my belly button where he stops and places gentle kisses on my stretch marks. His eyes lift. "Beautiful. Abso-fucking-lutely beautiful," he whispers, then, keeping his gaze locked with mine, he journeys farther down my body.

At my hips, he presses his lips to the edge of my panties. He dips his fingers inside and drags them down my legs, leaving me completely exposed.

He sits back on his haunches between my thighs, and I have to fight the urge to cover myself. My hands ball into fists at my sides. He notices and takes them with his, lacing our fingers together and leaning over me. "You're perfect, Myrtle."

I cringe at his use of my given name. He smirks, knowing how much I hate it.

"I love everything about you. Even your godawful name," he says, not an ounce of humour in his tone.

"I love you too," I admit. "Always have, always will."

LEE

HER WORDS MOVE THROUGH ME LIKE A TIDAL WAVE: ALL-consuming and devastating.

I've ached for her to say it for so long, and hearing it decimates the doubts I had. I'd worried we were moving too fast, but no more.

I lower to her, careful not to crush her with my weight, and graze my lips over hers in a soft, sweet kiss, letting her know how much I cherish the gift of her love. Moments pass and our kiss deepens, our tongues tangle and teeth nip as I roll my hips into her. She responds immediately, arching her pelvis and grinding against me.

Fuck, I love it. I love her.

I want inside her again. Desperately. But ... "Babe, I

don't have another condom," I tell her. "Do you have some?"

Rolling her lips between her teeth, she shakes her head. "No. Shit. I haven't needed them, and I didn't even think to buy any."

Fuck.

I have no problem going bareback. The idea of making a baby with her makes me ridiculously happy. But she's made it pretty clear she doesn't want that.

I have to think fast because she's squirming with need, and I am not leaving my girl hanging. I drop a quick peck to her lips and whisper, "I've got you, babe." Then, I crawl down her body.

My tongue glides between her folds, and Till's hands lock in my hair again. I sink my fingers into her thighs and force them farther apart as I delve into her sweet pussy. I could eat her all day long; she tastes so fucking good.

I circle her clit with the tip of my tongue, over and over again, then move to her entrance before licking up her juices. Her legs quake, and I repeat my movements. Circle her clit, lap at her entrance. She's a shaking, quivering mess by the time I slide two fingers inside and suck hard on her clit.

She explodes. Wetness coats my fingers, and I remove them so I can drink it in.

When I'm done, I sit up, wipe my mouth with the back of my hand, and catch a glimpse of a black smear on my skin as I bring my hand away from my face. I stare at it for a second, then Till yelps. My gaze shoots to her. "What's wrong?"

She shakes her head and squeezes her eyes closed, mumbling, “Goddamnit, Charlotte.”

My brows shoot up. That is not what I was expecting her to say after I just ate her out. “Babe?”

She squints one eye open then covers her face with her hands.

“Till, babe, talk to me,” I urge, terrified I’ve fucked this up somehow and having no idea why she’d mention her girlfriend right now.

Eventually, she licks her lips and scissors her fingers open just enough to peek through. “You should go have a shower and scrub your face. But whatever you do, don’t look in the mirror.” Then, in a flash, she’s sitting in front of me, her hands curled around my wrists, demanding, “Promise me you’ll not look in the mirror, Lee.”

I start laughing at her ludicrous behaviour.

“This is serious,” she says, her expression flat. “Promise me!”

Chuckling, I shake my head and agree. “Okay, babe. I promise. But you have to tell me why.”

Her eyes widen. “Ah, I think it’s best if we just pretend this part of the evening never happened.”

“No can do, babe. You’re acting like a crazy person.”

“I’m not the crazy one—it’s Charlotte. She’s nuts, and she led me down the path to Crazy Town with her,” she says.

“Umm, okay. I don’t understand a thing that’s happening right now, so I’m going to go have a shower, without looking in the mirror, and then we’re going to talk about this.”

Her face crumples. "Do we have to?"

I drop a kiss to the top of her thoroughly fucked hairdo and take her hands in mine. "Oh, yeah. You're not getting out of this. Now, come shower with me."

"Okay," she mumbles, crawling off the bed and following me to the bathroom where I do *not* look in the mirror.

Chapter Twelve

Tilly

"It was the most embarrassing moment of my life!" I tell Charlotte and Reagan the next day over coffee at my kitchen table.

Lee is off at a fitting with his future stepfather for their wedding suits, making this the perfect time to get it all off my chest.

Charlotte bursts out laughing, holding her middle then gasping for air. "Don't make me laugh when I'm surfing the crimson wave!"

Reagan stands, going to retrieve Char's heat pack from the microwave, and returns with a smile on her face as she hot-potatoes the heat pack from one hand to the other. "Whose idea was that? Permanent marker on your pubes." She chuckles. "That's totally something I would do."

Char arranges the pack and settles back in her seat, propping her feet on another of my dining chairs. "It was a solid idea. How was I to know it wouldn't maintain its integrity when mixed with bodily fluids?"

"It was all over his chin, Charlotte. I had to fully scrub it with a loofa to get it all off. I swear, I died inside. Everything had been perfect, right up until he sat up with a beard that wasn't there before he ventured downtown," I exclaim. "Then, I had to tell him why there was permanent marker on his pretty face. I have never known such bone-deep humiliation."

"I told you to use the Clitter capsules." Char shrugs and sips her coffee. "Glitter makes everything better."

I glare at her.

Reagan's eyes light with interest. "What are we talking about? You know I love glitter."

"They're little capsules you insert inside your vagina that melt and release a flow of non-toxic glitter into your nether regions, making it all shiny and pretty," Char explains.

"Ohh, I want some of those!" Reagan says, clapping her hands like an excited child. "Rhett would love it."

I throw my hands in the air. "Am I the only one who has an aversion to glitter-ising the promised land? It's weird. You guys know that, right? It's unnatural."

They both look at me like I'm the weird one here.

Then, Charlotte's lips twitch with a playful grin. "Says the woman banging her stepbrother."

My eyes widen, and my jaw drops. "You did not!"

She arches a brow. "I did. So, tell us, does that little hint of taboo make the sex hotter?"

"Oh, yes!" Reagan chimes in. "I've heard step-sex is off the charts."

Char nods her agreement then turns her gaze on me, a pleased smile on her face. "See? So, spill. I want details."

I roll my neck, loosening my tight muscles, close my eyes, take a deep breath, then give her what she wants. "It was freaking amazing. But not because of the step-sibling thing, you kinky mole. To tell you the truth, the thought never even entered my mind. All I was focused on was him and me—nothing else mattered."

"That is the most beautiful thing I've ever heard," Reagan says, wiping a tear from the corner of her eye. "Ugh, look at me getting all emotional. I must be getting hormonal."

"No," Char says. "It is beautiful. I'm so happy for you, Tilly. You deserve this."

I blink back tears of my own. "Oh, you guys." I sniffle. "You're going to make me cry."

"Okay, okay, time for a subject change!" Reagan says, fanning her face.

We spend the next hour chatting about the sex talk with Sailor and how Lee has a way of getting through to Astrid like nobody else has ever been able to.

ONE WEEK LATER ...

"Mummy," Sailor says as he pokes his pointy little finger into my forehead repeatedly. "Mummy, we need to talk."

I pry one eye open, glance at the clock on my bedside table, then close it again. "Sweet pea, it's too early. We can talk later when the sun is up, yeah?"

"Nope," he says and resumes his poking.

Heaving a sigh, I open my eyes and look at my son. He's smiling a knowing smile. I arch a brow and go to sit, only for a big, muscular arm to tighten over my stomach. *Holy fudge-nugget*. Lee is still here. In. My. Bed ...

My mind races as the smile on my son's little face grows. "You had the sex with Lee," Sailor declares.

"Oh, God," I mumble, more to myself, but Sailor hears it.

"You said that last night too. Why were you talking to God? You don't even believe in him."

"Sailor, honey, how about we take this little chat to the lounge room so we don't wake up Lee?" I suggest.

He shrugs. "Okay."

But just as he turns to leave my room, Mr. Pickles dashes in, jumps onto the blanket box at the end of my bed, and lands on the mattress. He squeals happily and trots over to me before flopping on his back for a tummy rub, right on Lee's head.

Lee swats at Pickles, trying to shove the little pig off. I quickly scoop him up and cuddle him to my chest. Lee props himself on an elbow and stares at me. "Why is there a pig in the bed?"

Sailor giggles uncontrollably from the other side of the room. Lee's eyes widen, and he rolls over to look at him. "Oh, hey, big guy. I didn't see you there."

The giggles just keep coming as Sailor climbs onto the

bed with us, causing Pickles to wiggle out of my arms to run to him. He jumps in Sailor's lap, puts his tiny front legs on Sailor's chest, and proceeds to nuzzle him into a laughing fit.

That's when the girls come in.

"What's going on?" Astrid asks, rubbing her eyes.

Ari just wanders over to the side of the bed and puts her arms up. Lee and I shuffle to sitting against the headboard. *Thank God I'm still wearing my nighty.* Lee is shirtless, but the kids don't seem to mind. In fact, they don't seem to be reacting to the fact that he's in my bed at all.

This is weird.

Lee scoops Ari up and settles her in the curve of his arm where she snuggles in and promptly goes back to sleep. My heart is a big pile of mush in my chest.

"Come here, sweetheart," I call to Astrid, who's still lingering by the door.

She blinks sleepily then crawls onto the end of the bed and over to me. I wrap my arms around her, running my fingers through her silky hair.

A warm hand curls around the back of my neck, and I roll my head to face Lee. His smile is everything as he gazes at me, then my kids, and back to me. "*I love you,*" he mouths.

"I love you too," I whisper. My heart may be mush, but it's also full. So ridiculously full it just might burst.

Then, Sailor announces, "We're going to have a cousin-brother!"

THE KIDS AND I ARE BELTING OUT "WALKING ON SUNSHINE" in the lounge room before Curt comes to pick them up for the weekend. It has become my theme song since Lee came back into my life.

Every day is perfect and beautiful with him in it.

He's basically moved in since the kids found him in my bed last week. And I'm still wrapping my head around them having no reaction to his presence in said bed.

Except, of course, for Sailor being obsessed with acquiring a new *cousin-brother*, which resulted in a very awkward and uncomfortable conversation about pregnancy prevention.

A knock at the door lets me know Curt has arrived, and I open it for him. "Hey, come in. I'll just grab the kids' bags."

"Thanks," he says, stepping inside right before the kids swarm him. He lifts Ari and Sailor and spins them around. They squeal and laugh, wrapping their arms around his neck. I love how good he is with them.

Ducking into the hallway, I grab the kids' backpacks and return to the living room to find the atmosphere has changed dramatically. Lee is standing in the open doorway, his jaw tight as he stares at Curt.

Well, shit.

I knew the first time they saw each other again was going to be intense, but I had hoped they'd have outgrown their issues with each other.

"Hey, you," I say, approaching Lee and pressing a light kiss on his tense jaw.

His eyes immediately drop to mine, warming instantly. "Hey, babe," he murmurs, tucking a strand of loose hair behind my ear.

Curt clears his throat. We turn to face him, and he raises a brow. "I was wondering how long it would take you two to pick things back up again," he says, a warm smile slowly spreading across his face.

My heart stutters. He's happy for me. *Genuinely happy*. I rush him, wrapping my arms around his middle. "Thank you," I whisper.

His arms curl around my waist, and he gives me a gentle squeeze. Then, he pulls away slightly to look at me. "You deserve to be happy, Till. That's all I've ever wanted for you. If he's what gives you that, then so be it."

A lump forms in my throat. I have to swallow hard to get my next words out. "I want that for you too, Curt. What I have with Lee ... I want that for you."

He shrugs. "I'll find it one day. But for now, I've got everything I need. Happy kids and a happy baby-mumma." He brushes a kiss to the top of my head, winks and releases me, and turns his attention to Lee. Then, he extends a hand to him, asking, "We good?"

Lee nods, his body loosening as he steps in and accepts Curt's offered hand. "Yeah, we're good, man."

I thought my heart was full before, but this, my whole family in one room with zero tension ... I couldn't be happier.

Chapter Thirteen

Tilly

TWO WEEKS LATER …

Staring at the calendar app on my phone, I mentally tick off days. *This can't be right.* I go over it again, but the results are the same.

I'm late.

Panic rolls through me so hard and fast my head spins. *No, no, no!*

"You okay, babe?" Lee asks, approaching from behind and resting a hand at the back of my neck.

I swallow and shake my head. "No," I whisper, dropping my face into my hands.

Lee's hand on my neck tenses, and he crouches at my side. "What's wrong? You're freaking me out a little."

Keeping my palms pressed to my hot cheeks, I twist my head to look at him. "I need a pregnancy test."

His eyes widen, and his jaw drops. "Wh—" he stutters. "I don't understand. I've never not used a condom …"

"I know, but I'm late."

He nods a few times, then determination fills his gaze. "Okay. I'm on it. I'll go pick one up right now." He moves in as close to my face as he can get without actually touching me. "Either way, we got this. I promise." Then, he brushes his lips over mine in a sweet kiss before pushing to his feet and striding away.

LEE

SOMEHOW, I MANAGE TO HIDE MY SMILE UNTIL I'M OUTSIDE in my car.

Holy freaking shit. Tilly might be pregnant. With. My. Baby.

Hope blossoms in my chest. I can't deny that I would be over the damn moon if it turns out she is knocked up. I'll go above and beyond to be there for her in every single way possible. But I'm getting ahead of myself.

I haven't been inside her without a condom once. Not even just the tip. I know how she feels about the issue, and I love and respect her too much to deliberately put her in a position she wouldn't be happy with.

There are plenty of parking spots available at this time of the evening, so I pull into one right outside the front door to the pharmacy. Pocketing my keys, I stride in with single-minded focus, going straight for the condom aisle.

Where there are condoms, there are usually pregnancy tests.

I'm confronted with a huge variety of tests, and I haven't got the first clue which one to buy. I pick up a random box and read the packaging. Seems simple enough: pee on the stick. Easy. I scan the shelf again, spot a multi-pack, and figure it couldn't hurt to get that one instead, for reassurance purposes.

Fifteen minutes later, I pull back into Tilly's driveway to find her sitting on the front stoop, chewing her bottom lip. I don't say anything as I sit beside her before wrapping an arm around her shoulders, tugging her into my side and pressing my lips to the top of her head.

She releases a huge sigh and tips her head back to look up at me. I trace my fingertips over her cheek with a feather-light touch then press my forehead to hers. "No matter what this little stick says, we got this. I'm here for you, babe. You're not in this alone."

Tears pool in her eyes, but she nods. "Okay," she breathes. "Let's do this."

Tilly

"Mother. Trucker," I mumble as Lee and I stare at not one, not two, but three positive pregnancy tests lined up on the bathroom vanity.

Lee stands behind me, his arms curled tight around

my waist, holding me against his warm body. "Wow," he murmurs.

I turn in his arms, my hands coming to rest on his chest. "What are we going to do?"

His eyes bore into mine, then he asks, "Do you love me?"

My frown is instant. "Of course I do."

"Then there's nothing to do except make an appointment with a doctor and get you on some vitamins or somethin'." He smiles so big it reaches his beautiful eyes. "I guess Sailor's going to get his little cousin-brother after all." He chuckles.

I burst out laughing, drop my head to his chest, and just let it take me. Euphoria I never expected to feel overwhelms me.

I'm having Lee's baby.

His big hands slide into my hair and tug my face up, a mischievous grin lifting his lips. "You know what this means, don't you?"

I shake my head, confused.

He waggles his brows. "No more condoms," he says with a wink.

My lips twitch. "Is that so?"

"Hell yes, it is," he says then presses a quick kiss to my lips. "And on that note, I'm taking you to bed." His hands move to my waist once more, and he hoists me over his shoulder in a fireman hold.

I squeal, "Lee!"

"Hush. You'll alert the neighbours to our nefarious deeds." He chuckles then flips me back over and onto the bed. Hovering above me, his eyes darken with lust and desire. "I cannot wait to be inside you with no barriers between us, Till. It's all I've ever wanted."

His tone is husky and so damn hot heat pools low in my belly.

He rubs a hand over his already hard length through his cargo shorts, and I arch up to unfasten his pants. His eyes never leave me as I free his cock and wrap my hand around the base, stroking once, twice, before enveloping the tip with my lips.

"Fuuuck," Lee breathes, his fingers digging into my hair.

I draw him in as far as I'm able and bob my head back and forth, sucking as hard as I can.

His breaths become ragged, his hips thrusting into my mouth as his thighs tense.

I lift a hand and dip it under his T-shirt and run my fingertips over his sculpted chest, trailing my nails down the ridges of his hot-as-shit abs.

A moment later, his hand curls around my chin, and my eyes dart to his.

"You have to stop, babe. I need to be inside your perfect pussy."

Oh, hell yes. I release his cock with a pop then push his shorts and underwear all the way down his thighs until he kicks them off. He grabs the neckline at the back of his shirt and tugs it over his head then drops it and reaches for my hands. He pulls me to standing and bunches the hem of my dress with his fingers, then yanks it up and off.

I make quick work of my bra while he sees to

removing my panties. He smiles his brutally beautiful smile at me, dimples and all, and crushes his mouth to mine.

We stumble onto the bed, Lee lifting me to drag me higher up the mattress and settling between my parted thighs. Taking hold of my left leg, he lifts it to his shoulder, opening me wider. He strokes two fingers through my wetness.

"So wet for me. Always so wet," he murmurs and sucks his fingers into his mouth, licking them clean.

I shudder beneath him. I've had enough teasing. I reach out and curl my fingers around his shaft and position it at my entrance. "Now, baby, fuck me now," I beg.

Liquid heat swirls in his gaze, and his hips surge forward, burying his cock to the hilt in one hard stroke. He closes his eyes. His jaw tenses, and he moans, "Fuck, yes."

I've never felt closer to him than in this moment—nothing between us and his baby growing in my belly. I blink back tears, but one escapes.

Lee catches it with his thumb. "Why you cryin'?"

"I never knew I could be this happy." I sniffle. "*You* make me happier than I've ever been in my life. And it just keeps getting better and better."

His smile is breathtaking. "Only you, babe. It's only ever been you."

He draws his hips back and drives forward again, grinding when pelvis meets pelvis. My clit throbs. He circles his hips once again before pounding into me relentlessly. I meet every thrust, my nails digging into his shoulder blades.

His head tilts to the side. "I need you to get there, Till—I won't come without you."

"Close, so close," I pant.

Then, he drops his head and kisses me with so much love and passion I detonate around him moments before he comes inside of me.

Chapter Fourteen

Tilly

On Monday morning, I'm just finishing up my latest blog post on Charlotte's Closet about the importance of pockets. I'm very passionate about pockets in my clothing. In fact, I don't own an outfit that doesn't have at least two.

Gia knocks on the door before letting herself in. Ari runs in first, Pickles on her heels. I put my laptop away and stand to greet them. "Good morning, ladies. How was your weekend?" I ask, swooping Ari into my arms for a quick snuggle.

"We had a lovely weekend. Didn't we, Arabella?" Gia says, making her way into the kitchen.

I follow behind her, asking Ari, "Did you do anything special?"

She nods. "I helped Granma make pantakes for bwekfast." She beams.

Gia chuckles as she pulls two coffee mugs out of the

cupboard. "What she means is she helped Grandma make a big mess."

I laugh. I never have been fond of cooking with the kids. I can't handle the mess. It does my head in.

Ari squirms in my arms. "I wanna play with my dollies," she says, continuing to wriggle.

"Okay, okay. Just give me one more big squeeze first."

She grins at me and throws her little arms around my neck, squeezing as tight as she can. I place her on her feet, and she takes off to her toy box in the lounge, calling out, "Tum on, Pickles!"

I smile after her, my mind drifting to the tiny human growing inside my belly. *I guess Ari won't be the baby of the family anymore.*

Gia goes about making our coffees while I pull out a container of choc-chip cookies I made yesterday and place them on the table. I take a seat before propping my feet on the chair across from me under the table.

"You wouldn't believe who I had a phone call from this morning," Gia says, placing a steaming mug in front of me then sitting at the end of the table.

I raise a brow and shrug. "I have no idea."

She grins, that familiar sparkle in her eye that tells me she knows something juicy. "Why, it was Mrs. Wintergreen. I swear that woman knows everything that goes on in this town. She has grandchildren working all over the place, gathering information for her."

My brows knit. *God, I hope this isn't going where I think it's going ...*

"And, wouldn't you know, one of her granddaughters

works at the pharmacy on Main Street," she says, a blinding smile curving her lips.

Yep, it's totally going there ... *Fudge-nuggets.*

I say nothing. Not a single word. We stare at each other, me blank-faced, Gia grinning like the cat who got the cream.

Finally, she throws her hands up in the air. "Put me out of my misery already! Are you ..." She lowers her voice to a whisper. "... pregnant?"

My lips roll between my teeth, and reluctantly, I nod.

Gia jumps out of her seat, rushes me, and wraps me in a huge hug. "I'm so happy for you, sweetheart!"

I pat her back. "Need to breathe, Gia," I wheeze.

"Oh, sorry." She loosens her grip around my neck and eases back, squeezing my shoulders. "I'm getting another grandbaby." Her eyes glaze over.

"Umm, Gia, you get that this baby isn't Curt's, right? So, it's not your grandchild."

She drops onto the seat beside me, shakes her head, then smiles softly, reaching for my hand. "You are still a part of our family, Tilly. Any children you have, be they my son's or Lee's, as long as they're yours? They will still be *my* grandbaby."

"Oh," I murmur, once again blinking back tears as I fight to control my emotions. This baby is really doing a number on my hormones. I've been so weepy it's not funny.

Gia smiles brightly. "So, when should we be expecting this new little one?"

"I don't know. Seven and a half months' time? I'm

seeing my doctor early next week, so we'll see what he says."

"Okay, well, you just let me know if you need anything, sweetheart. Do you need someone to watch Miss Arabella when you go to your appointment?" she asks, picking her coffee back up and taking a sip.

I smile. "That would be great. Thank you, G."

THE FOLLOWING WEEK, LEE SITS BESIDE ME IN THE WAITING room at my doctor's surgery, his knee bouncing. I glance at him from the corner of my eye. "You okay?"

"Yep, all good over here," he says.

I nudge him with my elbow. "You sure? You look awfully nervous ..."

He chuckles and shakes his head before his gaze comes to rest on mine. "I'm the furthest thing from nervous, Till. I'm excited."

My words get stuck in my throat. *He's excited?* A smile stretches across my face. I rest a hand on his scruffy cheek and lean in, pressing my lips to his, right there in the middle of the waiting room.

"What was that for?" he asks when I sit back.

I shrug and murmur, "I just love you."

His lips curve. "I love you too, babe."

A few minutes later, we're called up. Lee squeezes my hand as we take our seats across from Dr. McLellan, who eyes us then smiles.

"How are we today, Tilly?" he asks the cursory question.

I lick my lips then grin. "It would appear I'm pregnant again."

He nods and laces his fingers. "Last cycle?"

"Seven weeks, almost eight ..." I tell him.

He nods again and pulls a little circular chart from his desk drawer, and swivels the top layer around a bit, then announces, "So we're looking at a due date late in September."

Lee squeezes my hand again, his knee back to bouncing.

"Should we do a quick ultrasound today? Or would you prefer to wait?" he asks.

"We can see it today?" Lee asks, his eyes wide.

I didn't tell him that my doctor has an ultrasound machine here. I wanted it to be a surprise, and clearly, it is.

Dr. McLellan smiles at Lee and inclines his head to an unassuming room off the back of his office. "I'll take that as a yes." He stands and leads the way through to the small exam room. "You know what to do," he says to me then excuses himself, drawing a curtain around us.

Kicking off my shoes, I undo the button and zipper of my shorts then climb on the table, tugging my shirt up under my boobs. "Ready," I call out.

Moments later, we're staring at a black-and-white screen. I squint because I can't truly be seeing what I think I'm seeing.

My doctor adjusts the probe on my stomach then

glances at us. "Congratulations, you most certainly are pregnant. In fact, you got a two-fer. And judging by their measurements, you're about seven weeks along. We might need to bring that expected due date forward a little due to it being a twin pregnancy, but we'll see how you go."

I blink, then blink again, this time keeping my eyes closed a second longer. But when I open them, nothing has changed. There're still two little blobs on the monitor. Not one, but *two*.

My head swings to Lee. I can't keep the accusation from my tone when I declare, "You have super sperm! Not only did you knock me up while wearing a condom, but... but—" My eyes flick between Lee and the ultrasound screen in disbelief.

Lee's eyes are just as wide as mine. Then, a slow, satisfied grin curves his lips. "Heck yeah, I do. Twins. Holy shit, Till. We're having twins."

Holy shit is right.

I was done at three. How the hell am I going to manage with five?

THREE WEEKS LATER ...

Morning sickness has hit in full force. I've been feeling so shitty I didn't even make it to Lee's mum's wedding. Joy was too over-the-moon that I was carrying her first grandbabies to even care that I had to bail on her big day.

I'm lying on the couch while the kids play and nursing some hellish nausea when there's a knock at the front door. I push to sitting and swing my legs over the side to stand when Lee's firm hand presses on my shoulder.

"I've got it, babe. Lay back down."

I don't even try to argue, lifting my feet up again.

Lee swings open the door to Gia, my mother, and his. He smiles at them and quirks a brow. "Ladies, what brings you all here?"

Joy slaps his shoulder and pushes past him. "What a way to greet your mothers," she huffs with an eye-roll.

He turns to her, jaw slack, as Gia and my mum follow Joy into the lounge room.

"We have presents!" Gia announces, gaining the kids' attention.

They swarm their grandmothers and the bags they're toting. They hand each child a wrapped gift, then oddly, Joy sends them to their rooms to open them, saying, "Stay in your rooms until we come get you, okay?"

When we're alone, they usher Lee over to sit by my legs as they proceed to take a seat on the edge of the coffee table in front of us. Their eyes sparkle with undiluted delight as my mother presents me with a sparkly silver bag.

I look at it then back to her. "What's this?"

Gia rolls her eyes, snatches the bag away from me, and opens it herself. She holds up two teeny, tiny white bodysuits—the first says *Buy One*, the second says, *Get One Free*. Then, Joy pulls out another set. These ones are navy blue with gold writing. The first: *We Solemnly Swear.* The next: *We Are Up To No Good*. And finally, my mum digs in the bag before revealing a third set that both say *Womb Mates.*

That's when it dawns on me why they sent the kids to their rooms. We haven't said anything to them yet, agreeing we wanted to make it through the first trimester before we told them.

"We couldn't help ourselves," says Joy. "The moment we found out it was twins we went on a little online shopping spree."

I'm crying—again. "I love them," I sob, my hand coming to rest over the little bump protruding from my abdomen. I wasn't even showing at this stage with my others.

One of Lee's hands entwines with mine as he takes the outfits with his other. "These are great, guys. You're spoiling them already, and they're not even here yet."

Gia shrugs. "We're grandmothers. It's what we do."

"If you think we're going to spoil them, just you wait until the kids and Dixie find out," my mum says, chuckling.

Oh, Lordy. I can only imagine how the kids are going to take the news ...

Chapter Fifteen

LEE

ONE MONTH LATER …

Till and I are sitting in my car outside the house after having just had another ultrasound. The grandmothers are inside with the kids, eagerly awaiting the sex of the babies. Apparently, unisex twin outfits just aren't good enough.

I couldn't care less about the sex. As long as they're happy and healthy in there, it's all good with me. And I told Tilly as much, but she, too, wanted to find out their sex so she could be better prepared.

Lifting our joined hands to my mouth, I press a kiss to the back of Till's and murmur, "I love you."

"I love you too."

Her smile is the most beautiful thing in the world to me. And her steadily expanding belly is a close second. "You ready?" I ask.

"As I'll ever be." She chuckles.

Today is also the day when we tell the kids they're about to be getting a couple of new siblings.

We walk in the front door. Astrid is there, waiting for us, her arms crossed over her chest, her hip cocked to the side, and her little foot tapping against the tiles. "We need to talk," she says.

"Okay, but can it wait a couple of minutes, sweetheart?" Tilly asks. "We just need to have a quick chat with your grandmas, then we're all yours."

Astrid nods, turns on her plastic princess heels, and walks away.

Sailor is in the child-sized armchair I bought him a couple of weeks ago, busy reading a book on human anatomy. And Ari is having a tea party with Mr. Pickles and her dollies.

"So?" my mother asks as we enter the kitchen.

I grin and cast my eyes to Till. She gives me the go-ahead with a short nod, and I tell them, "Both boys."

"I told you," Trudie says to Gia, who digs in her pocket and hands over a ten-dollar note.

Tilly scoffs, "You bet on the sex of your grandbabies? What kind of grandmothers are you?"

"The very best kind, darling, the very best." Gia winks.

Till shakes her head, and we laugh at their antics. Our kids are so lucky to have these strong, beautiful women in their lives.

"Okay, we'll go now and let you deliver the big news to the others," Mum says, motioning towards the front door to Trudie and Gia.

"Alright, we're going, we're going," Trudie says, rolling

her eyes at my mother before she gives Till a quick squeeze and a kiss on the cheek.

When they've filed out, we call Astrid into the lounge where Sailor and Ari are already playing. She glides down the hall and into the room dressed in a new princess gown. "Are you ready for our talk?" she asks.

I smother a smile and nod. "We sure are, princess. What's up?"

"Mummy's getting fat, and Sailor says it's because she's going to give us a cousin-brother. I don't know what that is, but I told him she ate a watermelon seed and now it's growing in her belly," she states.

We sit on the couch, staring at her. Damn, I had no idea how perceptive they were.

Sailor lays his book flat in his lap and shakes his head at his big sister. "That doesn't really happen, Astrid," he says, holding a hand across his forehead like he's embarrassed his sister actually believes her watermelon theory.

Seemingly anticipating an argument about to break out between Astrid and Sailor, Tilly says, "Okay, well, Lee and I actually wanted to talk to you guys about that."

Astrid gives Sailor a cocky look then sits on the couch beside Till.

"Ari, pretty girl, come here for a sec," I call to her. She's lost in her own little world, pouring tea for Mr. Pickles. Her blonde head pops up, and she gives me a gut-clenchingly beautiful smile before she puts her teapot down and skips over to me.

Once I have her on my lap, Tilly begins, "Lee and I

love each other, and we love you guys so, so much." She pauses, taking a second to look at each of her children in turn. "And we thought, you are such good kids and so loving and kind that maybe you would like a new baby to shower with all that goodness."

Astrid gives her a sceptical eyebrow raise, Ari frowns, and Sailor jumps out of his armchair, hurling a fist into the air. "I knew it! I'm getting a cousin-brother!"

"Not quite, big man," I interject. He comes to a stop mid-booty shake. "You're getting two," I tell him.

His jaw goes slack, and he blinks at us. "Two?"

Tilly and I nod, then Sailor takes off, running around the lounge, pumping his fists in the air, woo-wooing. Mr. Pickles picks up on his excitement and chases after him until they get tangled up, and they both hit the ground. Sailor rolls around with his piglet, laughing and crying out, "Two cousin-brothers!"

"YOU GUYS, THIS IS TOO MUCH," I TELL CHARLOTTE AND Reagan when they walk into my house loaded down with gift bags.

Reagan smiles at me and shakes her head. "Are you kidding me? We're just getting started. I found this adorable boutique a couple of blocks from my place that has the cutest little baby shoes I've ever seen. I had no idea everything was cuter when it was miniaturised."

"I know, right?" Char agrees with her.

I grin and shake my head. "I love you guys."

"We know," they say in unison then burst out laughing. Charlotte grabs a cushion off the couch, sits on the floor, and starts upending bags while Reagan sets about making us coffees.

"What are you doing?" I ask Char.

She turns her eyes to me and shrugs. "You'll take too long to open them all individually. I'm cutting out the middle man."

"Right," I mutter.

"You sit, and I'll hold everything up for you to see. Anything you don't like we can return."

I doubt I'll be letting them return anything—these girls have good taste.

A moment later, Reags strides back into the lounge room with a tray holding three steaming-hot mugs. Unfortunately, Mr. Pickles has developed a bit of a crush on our Reagan and dashes straight for her, tripping her up. The coffees go flying, and Reagan goes down, tray still in hand.

"I'm okay!" she yells, her head popping up on the other side of the coffee table.

Charlotte and I throw back our heads, laughing.

"I can't take you anywhere," Char says, chuckling.

"It wasn't even my fault," Reagan huffs. "It was this disgustingly cute little piggy's fault. I wonder if Rhett would let me get a miniature pig? He can't say no if I just bring one home, right?"

"Only one way to find out," I tell her as she rights herself then goes about cleaning up the spilt liquid and retrieving the mugs that luckily landed on the rug and didn't smash.

"Hey, you know how you said the babies are going to be identical? Well, I've been doing some research—"

"Oh, here we go," Char teases, poking her tongue out at Reagan who pokes hers right back then flips her off.

I chuckle. They're as bad as my children.

"Anyway, did you know that, even though they're identical, they won't have the same fingerprint? How cool is that?" Reagan says, eyes filled with wonder.

I tilt my head, not understanding. "But isn't that the definition of identical? They'll have the same DNA?"

She nods then goes into what I call 'Reagan mode.' "So, at first it will be the same. But between six and thirteen weeks, they start moving around in there and touching the amniotic sack. That's what creates unique little ridges and lines on their teensy-tiny little fingers."

"That's actually pretty cool," I tell her. "You'll have to let Sailor know. He's been looking for as many twin facts as he can get his hands on."

Reagan beams. "I love that kid."

I chuckle. "Me too."

Later that afternoon, I'm woken from an impromptu nap on the couch by music coming from the kitchen. I roll to my side, heave myself up, and poke my head around the corner. Lee is dancing with the kids while he cooks them dinner in nothing but a backwards baseball cap and a pair of low-slung jeans.

My mouth waters—and not from the heavenly aroma of whatever he's cooking, but the sight before me. He is, by far, the hottest thing I have ever seen. Throw in the fact that he's including the kids, and my ovaries are jumping for joy. I'm having his babies. *His.*

I'm the luckiest woman in the whole goddamn world.

Epilogue

LEE

FIVE MONTHS LATER ...

Dear God. I'd rather have my balls dipped in honey and be staked to an ant farm than let Tilly go through this *ever* again. She's been in labour for six hours, and it's been the longest fucking six hours of my life.

I'm propped behind her on the delivery bed, supporting her as best I can while another powerful contraction rips through her. The second it's over, she sags against my chest, and I brush my lips against her damp temple. "You're doing so good, babe, so good. We're almost there," I assure her.

She swallows then tilts her sweaty head back and looks into my eyes. "I love you," she mumbles. "But if you even think about doing this to me again, I'll—" Her threat is cut off by another contraction sweeping over her. She grits her teeth and bares down, pushing so hard I think she just broke my finger.

"That's it, Tilly. We have hair!" the midwife calls from between Till's parted thighs.

"Fucking finally," I mutter as Tilly lets out a low guttural groan that I feel in my bones. "You got this, babe. One more push and you'll be holding him."

She nods, determination filling her gaze. Her hands flex over mine where I'm holding her knees, and she takes the next thirty seconds to catch her breath. Then, it's go-time again. Her nails dig into the back of my hand, breaking the skin as she gives an almighty heave, then a piercing cry fills the air.

The midwife extends a tiny pink squirming baby to Till from between her legs, and my arms curve around hers as she holds our son to her bare chest. He blinks slowly then makes a little snuffling noise as he begins shaking his little head. Tears fill my eyes when he latches onto a nipple all by himself.

That's my boy. Ain't nobody gotta show him how to find the boobies.

"You did it, babe," I tell Till, holding her against my chest, my chin resting on her shoulder. "You're a freaking superstar."

She sniffles, her eyes meeting mine, and our foreheads touch. She closes her eyes and relaxes into me, but our moment doesn't last nearly long enough. Minutes later, her body stiffens, and she gasps.

Baby number two is on his way.

An hour later, I'm embracing Tilly in the shower off the birthing suite—hot water sluicing over our naked bodies—and I have never been prouder of the incredible woman in my arms. Her cheek rests against my chest as I gently run the loofa over her skin.

I rinse her off, towel her dry, then dress her. Her eyes can barely stay open, but she refused to sleep without cleaning up. The nursing staff cleaned off the bed while we were showering, and I carry her to it before placing her down with all the care in the world. She snuggles into the pillow as I tug the blankets over her, and she promptly falls asleep.

Both extremely healthy, our boys are sleeping soundly in a little plastic bassinet. I roll it to the corner by a big comfy armchair where I pick them up, careful not to wake them, then lower myself into the chair. My chest is bare, and the boys are wearing the tiniest nappies I've ever seen.

After snatching up a super-soft blanket from the arm of the chair, I tuck it in around Theo then Tyler and settle back into the cushions.

When I lost Tilly all those years ago, I lost my heart, my soul, and my happiness.

But she's given it all back to me tenfold.

Tilly

ONE WEEK LATER ...

Walking into my house with my brand-new babies in my arms and Lee at my side feels surreal.

A year ago, if you had said to me that I'd be with Lee and we'd have a baby together, I'd have been torn between laughing in your face at the preposterousness and punching you in the throat for even suggesting I would be giving birth again.

Yet, here I am, with my other half and not one, but two babies.

I swallow past the lump in my throat as my kids rush me before wrapping their arms around whatever part of me they can reach.

Sailor is the first to release me. He runs to his little armchair, shuffles back, and opens his arms. "I'm ready to hold my babies," he says.

Astrid stomps her foot and speaks over him. "No, I'm the oldest—I'm first!"

"No, me! I want to hold babies!" Ari throws in.

"One at a time," Lee speaks over their ruckus. "But not right now. Your brothers are hungry, and none of you have the required equipment to get that particular job done. So, who's going to switch the kettle on for me while I give Mummy a hand getting Theo and Tyler latched on?"

"Me!" they each call out, shoving one another as they all try to be the first to the kitchen.

I take a deep breath and smile. As crazy as it is, this is my life now, and I wouldn't have it any other way. Even if I did spot a few more silver streaks in my bush this morning...

The End

Also by JB Heller

ROM COMS

AWKWARD GIRLS

Pink Bits

Blue Beaver

Silver Bush

UNEXPECTED LOVERS

The Starfish Method

The Covert Cam Girl

The Unexpected Manny

The Ballbuster's Dilemma

Falling For His Fake Fiancé

Wooing His Accidental Wife

SHILOH SPRINGS WORLD

HUNTERS & CO.

Catastrophe Magnet

Hacker Heart

Red Hot Rebel

Poker Face

STANDALONE

What If It's Right?

BROKEN BOYS / MOMENTS

Broken Boys Break Hearts

Broken Boys Fight Harder

Broken Boys Despise Deceit

Broken Boys Crave Chaos

The Parlor (Standalone coming 2023)

ROMANTIC SUSPENSE

ATTRACTION SERIES

Complete Series

Undeniable Attraction

Pure Attraction

Fierce Attraction

ALPHA ONE PROTECTION

(Attraction Series Spin Off)

Worth The Risk

Worth The Wait

JB Heller is an average Aussie housewife and Momma in her mid 30's with a wicked sexy imagination.

These days she writes mostly contemporary romance and romantic comedies, drawing inspiration from her everyday life.

Monday to Friday you can find JB glued to her laptop weaving words or trolling Pinterest for her next potential muse. Come the weekend, it's family time. (And of course lots of reading and Netflix binges.)

Want to know more?

Monthly Newsletter Sign Up:
https://bit.ly/3FtVhyd
Facebook Reader Group:
Heller's Bookwhorders

www.ingramcontent.com/pod-product-compliance
Lightning Source LLC
Chambersburg PA
CBHW070612310726
48982CB00001B/54

* 9 7 8 0 6 4 5 5 4 6 5 5 2 *